PRAISE FOR DYLAN NEWTON

How Sweet It Is

"Newton's debut romance is laugh-out-loud funny, with enough antics, fast pacing, and chemistry to keep readers as engrossed as any of her hero's bestselling horror novels would. A hilarious rom-com romp that delivers on both sweet and heat."

—*Kirkus*, starred review

"Brimming with witty banter, sweet characters and sizzling charm." —*Woman's World*

"The funny moments had me laughing out loud. The end of this book was super romantic and very fitting! *How Sweet It Is* exceeded my expectations."

—Nerd Daily

How Sweet It Is

ALSO BY DYLAN NEWTON

All Fired Up

How Sweet It Is

DYLAN NEWTON

FOREVER
New York Boston

Copyright © 2021 by Dylan Newton
Excerpt from *All Fired Up* copyright © 2022 by Dylan Newton

Cover design by Daniela Medina. Cover images by © Shutterstock. Cover copyright © 2022 by Hachette Book Group, Inc.

Forever
Hachette Book Group
1290 Avenue of the Americas, New York, NY 10104
read-forever.com
twitter.com/readforeverpub

Originally published in trade paperback and ebook by Grand Central Publishing in July 2021

First mass market edition: May 2022

Forever is an imprint of Grand Central Publishing. The Forever name and logo are trademarks of Hachette Book Group, Inc.

The publisher is not responsible for websites (or their content) that are not owned by the publisher.

ISBNs: 978-1-5387-0877-4 (mass market), 978-1-5387-5441-2 (ebook)

Printed in the United States of America

OPM

10 9 8 7 6 5 4 3 2 1

To my mom, who introduced me to the delicious thrill of a Stephen King novel.

And to Mike, who is my proof that happily ever afters do exist.

How Sweet It Is

CHAPTER 1

Kate Sweet touched her earpiece, activating the microphone. "Carl? You and the pumpkin are in position?"

"Roger that, Kate."

"Perfect! The newlyweds are coming. Cue the bubbles."

Kate shivered in the September air. It was the first day of fall, and if this weather presaged the winter to come, she figured she'd better break out the wool outfits now. The upside of the colder-than-average temps was the stunning fall foliage—a priceless backdrop to today's afternoon wedding. Luckily, the outside portion of the reception was almost over. Just one more special touch.

An errant lock slipped out of her chignon, and she tucked it behind her ear as she fast-walked around the hillside estate in her stilettos—shoes that were made for anything except fast-walking around rocky, grassy grounds. Or fast-walking in general. But a full suit, complete with killer heels, was her trademark uniform as the owner of Sweet Events. She'd patterned the style, as well as much of her fledgling business, after an internship with her mentor, the late Maya Evert herself.

"Take it from me, people don't respect a five-foot-one woman in flats," Maya had said in her blunt way. "You want to be the boss? Dress like one. Use fashion to your advantage."

Maya wasn't wrong. It made a difference when you didn't have to crane your neck during every conversation. Kate had eventually grown accustomed to working in tall heels and now considered them, along with her project plan spreadsheets, essential armor against chaos and one of the keys to her success.

Her personal phone buzzed, and she tugged it out. Fumbling with cold fingers to activate the readout, she skimmed a text message from her mom.

Mom: Was hoping to chat with you about the Sweet Surgery Center's grand opening. Both your dad and I are in surgery now, but can we talk later? After your party?

"It's not a party, it's an event," Kate muttered to herself, her breath fogging the air as she groaned and dropped her cell back into her pocket. She wouldn't bother texting back. No emoji in the world was going to facilitate the message that she still wasn't interested in joining the family medical legacy. Never had been. But the famous Sweet surgeons were nothing if not persistent. Kate shook her head, willing the thoughts of her family's infinite disappointment in her career out of her head.

She had a happily-ever-after moment to deliver.

"Bubbles are on," came her assistant's voice in her ear. Kate rounded the corner to the flagstone patio of the ritzy Connecticut estate where the couple had chosen to have their special day, miles from New York City's hustle. The bubble machines hidden in the bushes hummed to life as the couple and their well-wishers spilled out through the bank of French doors to the gorgeous autumnal vista.

"Oh!" the bride gasped, finally noticing that the air sparkled with a million tiny bubbles floating in the cool breeze. Everyone laughed, playfully swatting at the bubbles as the bride and groom posed for pictures amid the cascade, giggling and holding their arms outstretched, the chilly weather momentarily forgotten.

It didn't matter how old you were, bubbles made everything fun.

"And now…for the 'Aww!' moment," Kate murmured to herself, smiling in anticipation. This was her favorite part of the wedding—the tiny but impactful detail that turned the event from wonderful to blissful. She'd originally dubbed it the "Happily-Ever-After Moment" in her promotional materials, but her clients had described it as the "Aww!" moment, and that's what stuck.

Right on time, the carriage pulled around the bend, making its grand entrance. The driver, dressed in white livery, had the reins of two gorgeous white horses in hand. The animals pranced up the lane, as if they knew this was their big moment. Guests lined up on the manicured lawn, cheering at the sight.

Kate grinned as the couple spotted the pumpkin-shaped carriage she'd rented. The bride squealed, pointing at the white wrought-iron frame, painstakingly

wrapped in fall foliage and glimmering with thousands
of twinkle lights. The woman gazed adoringly at her
husband. Kate was too far away to read their lips,
but it looked like she'd asked if he'd planned this. The
groom nodded, and Kate saw his face turn red with
embarrassed pleasure as his wife flung herself at him,
hugging him fiercely around the neck.

"Bingo," Kate whispered to herself.

The groom located Kate in the crowd and gave her a
delighted thumbs-up. He'd been the one to secretly ask
for a grand exit, wanting to surprise his wife. He'd left
the details to Kate, though, knowing her fame for that
"Aww!" moment.

Kate flashed a thumbs-up in return, and then the
couple dashed over and closed themselves inside the
intricate vehicle. Nothing said a Cinderella wedding
like a nod to the classic fairy-tale carriage.

It wasn't until the couple left the grounds, waving
madly to the crowd, that Kate let out a huge sigh. She
switched on her com.

"And…they are off the grounds and heading to
the honeymoon suite. All set, Carl. We can start the
tear-down of the outdoor chapel. Send the caterer and
DJ my way for the checks. Great work!" Kate listened
to her assistant's congratulations, checking off the last
of the events in the day's agenda and closing up her
Sweet Events planner with a satisfying snap. Just as
the prancing horses carried the newlyweds toward their
honeymoon cabin, her phone buzzed with an incoming call.

"They're relentless," Kate muttered, grabbing her
phone. Her grimace relaxed into a smile as she read the
phone's readout, and she clicked to accept the call.

"Congratulations on another postcard-perfect wedding," her best friend singsonged, not waiting for a greeting.

"Imani!" Kate laughed, picking her way around the last of the guests to enter the warmth of the estate house. She snuck to the back of the reception hall to snag a piece of wedding cake and a seat at an empty table next to an older couple. Pushing aside the table confetti—Shakespearean quotes about love printed on the back of paper designed to look like fall leaves—she dug into what would have to be her late lunch. "How'd you know it was perfect? Better yet, how'd you know I was done? You weren't even here."

"The itinerary you sent me said the couple would be leaving at three p.m., and it's 3:02. Everyone knows that you always run on time and on budget. I'm really sorry I couldn't be there to be an extra set of hands for you, Katie," Imani said, using the nickname only she was allowed to get away with, having been best friends with Kate since grade school. "I know those massive weddings leave you running ragged, and I love any excuse to watch the Queen of Happily Ever Afters in action."

"Carl and I managed just fine. The real reason I wanted you up here was to get you out of the city for a hot minute. I miss my old roomie and our girl talks. You know, the wild ones where you'd decorate my planner with inspirational quotes while I built a spreadsheet for your next career goal?"

"I'm still pissed you abandoned me. I mean, what's a brand-new apartment complex on Long Island's Gold Coast have compared to my tiny lofted box in Queens?

You had the world's lumpiest pull-out couch all to yourself, as well as my collection of gel pens, arranged for you in Roy G Biv order, and you up and left." Imani paused her teasing, her voice wistful. "I miss Margarita Mondays."

"Me too. My planner pages are deadly dull without you," Kate said, dragging the tines of her fork through the cake's icing, making a basket-weave pattern of eternal tic-tac-toe game boards.

"It figures. The one weekend you have a free Saturday night, I'm at an author event in LA."

Kate quit mauling the cake and took a bite, closing her eyes to savor it. "Mmm. You're missing out. The bride chose your favorite—a ginger spice cake."

"No! Damn. Does it have buttercream frosting?" Imani groaned at the sound of Kate's muffled assent. "Unfortunately, when you're dealing with writers who have egos as big as their book contracts, there's almost always a crisis on the weekend...which is sort of why I'm calling. I—I need some help."

Although her best friend was thousands of miles away in California, Kate heard the hesitant dip in Imani's voice. The last time Kate recalled her friend asking for help in that tone was six years ago when she'd had appendicitis and had to go to the ER for emergency surgery. The time before that was way back in high school when Imani had asked Kate if she could stay with her after Imani had lost her house—and her mother—in a tragic fire. Her best friend wasn't a casual "ask a favor" type of gal.

Kate frowned, putting down her fork. She gripped the phone with one hand while flipping open her planner and readying to write with the other hand, her heart galloping with a sudden nervous shot of adrenaline. "Of course. Anything. Are you okay?"

"Oh, it's not an emergency with me. Promise," Imani said. "It's work related."

"You scared the crap out of me," Kate hissed, releasing the breath she'd been holding. "Okay. What's going on at work?"

"You know how you mentioned last week that a cancellation had freed up a huge chunk of time on your calendar? You're clear until when, exactly?"

"Until mid-November. After months of planning and thousands prepaid in deposits, the Montagues decided to call off the wedding."

"Yes!" Imani's exclamation was so jubilant, Kate could imagine her fist-pumping on the other end of the line.

"Wow. You get promoted to top publicist working mostly with romance authors, and you're suddenly jaded about love and marriage. What happened to my romantic BFF?"

"Who has time to be romantic anymore? Last time I checked, you barely had time to go speed dating with me."

"What?" Kate snagged another bite of cake, laughing. "I stayed the whole time. Participated, just like I promised."

"I call bullshit on that. You asked each guy exactly one question, and when he couldn't give you the answer you wanted, you tuned out until it was time to switch."

"Why waste time? I asked each of them if they could handle a woman with a rising career who wouldn't be available most weekends or holidays for the foreseeable

future. None of them had a good answer." Kate grimaced at the memory. She'd been in a mood that night,
and while drowning her anger in tequila had seemed
like a good coping mechanism at the time, spending the
next day cuddled up to Imani's toilet bowl had not been
fun. Shaking her head to clear the thoughts of her non-
existent love life, Kate refocused on the conversation.
"Why is my lack of a client a good thing, and how
does it relate to your work emergency? You don't have
a writer who needs a quickie wedding planned, do you?
Because even I'd struggle to create a happily-ever-after
moment in only a few weeks."

"It's not a wedding. It's a book launch," Imani
said, and Kate's eyebrows rose. She put down the fork
to listen more carefully as her best friend continued.
"Okay, hear me out. It's a once-in-a-lifetime book
launch, but our marketing point person for this had
a family emergency and had to pull out. We're crazy
busy, and we need someone to step in and coordinate
the event for us, like a contractor. Naturally, I thought
of you!"

"A book launch?" Kate tilted her head, watching
the reception crowd gather their coats and purses as
she considered the idea. Romance authors wrote books
that would draw fans—and potential clients—who'd
appreciate a happily-ever-after sort of event. "Maybe
that could work."

Imani's voice raced with enthusiasm. "You've been
saying how you'll need to branch out to win that event
planning award—what's it called?"

"The EVPLEX," Kate supplied, intrigued. "But I
don't think a book launch will attract the attention of
Evan Everstone and his committee any more than my

weddings. Last year's overall EVPLEX winner was the Met Gala."

"That's just it, it won't be *just* a book launch! We've got carte blanche from our marketing partner to pull out all the stops with this event, because it'll be in conjunction with the movie studio that recently optioned the author's project. I mean, it's a jaw-dropping, huge-budget, Evan Everstone and his EVPLEX–type book launch. I just need a person to take the baton the rest of the way to the finish line."

"When?" Kate's eyes narrowed in suspicion. This was sounding too good to be true, which, in her experience, usually meant that it was.

"Um, well, it's on Halloween."

"Halloween? That's only five weeks away!"

"Which is why we need *you* to step in. You *are* the Queen of Happily Ever Afters." Imani's tone was saccharine as she added, "If you can't make this writer's launch magical, nobody can."

Kate had the feeling she was being oversold. But ideas of various love-in-autumn-themed launch events had already started filling her head. Given her experience, it would be a slam dunk, not to mention the fact that working during this unexpected lull in her planner would pay more bills than spending the time networking and passing out business cards at the area country clubs. If the launch tied in a movie deal based on the novel . . . this could only mean great exposure for her business. If she was ever going to expand beyond Carl and herself, she needed more clients and a broader portfolio of high-profile events.

Plus, Imani wouldn't throw her under a bus. She was her best friend—one who never asked a favor lightly.

Thoughts of that gorgeous gold EVPLEX award on her shelf and gleaming forever on her website's home page danced in her mind like the leftover bubbles on the breeze outside.

"You've got yourself an event planner."

"Thank God!" Imani squealed. "You won't regret it, especially after I tell you who you'll be working with. Take a guess!"

Kate pondered, spearing one last bite of the dessert as she went through her mental bookshelf of the romance authors Imani represented. "Is it Leann Bellamy? I love her books."

"No, better. It's Drake Matthews!"

"Drake Matthews?" Kate sputtered cake onto the table, her tone loud enough to draw looks from the older couple still sitting at the adjacent table. She stood, dropping her cake plate onto the nearest server's tray, and moved to an empty corner to hiss into the phone. "You're putting me—the Queen of Happily Ever Afters—in charge of a book launch for the Knight of Nightmares himself? Are you nuts? Doesn't he eat his meat raw and sleep in a coffin?"

"Oh, please. That's all garbage that the press likes to trot out to sell stories. Drake is a regular-ish guy."

"Regular-ish?" Kate asked. "What's the 'ish' part?"

"You know—he's got quirks, but he isn't a creeper or anything. Besides, he's hot."

Imani was right about that. Drake Matthews's handsome face had been plastered all over every tabloid and news show in existence a few years ago over some scandal that Kate couldn't recall. She doubted whether anyone actually read the gossip about him. Most women were too distracted by the man's mesmerizing amber eyes to care about any scandals.

"His looks aren't the point," she said. "There are no bubbles, pumpkin carriages, or a single happily-ever-after ending in any of his books. I'm not sure Sweet Events is the right fit for this job."

"Quit stressing! You can totally handle this. Our previous point person did most of the heavy lifting already, pulling permits to renovate an old barn in the author's hometown into a haunted house for his tenth book, a soon-to-be bestseller called *Halloween Hacker*. All you've got to do is make it epic! Instead of an 'Aww' factor, just make it an 'AAAAAHH' factor!"

Kate laughed at her best friend's theatric shriek. "Fine. I'll figure out something to do with this haunted house. I've never read his books, but I don't live under a rock. Even the commercial for the movie adaptation of his *Dark Dolls* novel gave me nightmares. I know he's got quite a cult following out there. How many are we expecting at this launch?"

"Two hundred-ish."

Kate scowled. "There's that half-word again. 'Ish' isn't going to cut it. I need exact numbers if I'm going to pull off feeding and entertaining this crowd on Halloween."

The garbled sound of a loudspeaker came through in the background of the call.

"My flight's leaving. I almost forgot to tell you the other cool thing—the launch is in Western New York in the village of Wellsville, the same small town my grandma Gigi lives in, so we'll have a local contact. I'll email the address and our flight details to you in a second so you can start working on securing your travel plans to Buffalo. We'll need to pitch it to him on Monday, which I know doesn't give you a ton of time."

"Today's Saturday! That's exactly no time, Imani!"

"I'm sure whatever you come up with will be...spook-tacular! And don't worry—I'll be there with you on Monday when we make the pitch to Drake in person." Imani paused, and the phone cut out, as if there was another call coming in. "I've got to go. Um, just to let you know, we're meeting him at his house."

"At that creepy Victorian?" Kate shuddered, recalling the pictures online of the house Drake Matthews lived in—an old red Victorian mansion surrounded by a wrought-iron fence fashioned to look like an intricate spiderweb connected by bats at the entrance gates. "Shall I carry a wooden stake, or do you think wearing a necklace of garlic should be enough?"

"You'll be fine," Imani said, her phone cutting in and out as she spoke, giving her voice an eerie quality. "Oh, I forgot to tell you...be careful...terrifying! Watch out for—"

The call went fuzzy with static.

"Watch out for what?" Kate yelled. "What's terrifying?"

But the call had disconnected.

With an exasperated sigh, Kate ripped the earpiece from her ear and stowed it in her coat pocket. Whatever her best friend had tried to warn her about would be a mystery until she saw her tomorrow at the airport.

She shrugged her shoulders. Imani was right. After working with overwrought mothers, fainting grooms, and jittery Bridezillas, how bad could one writer be?

*   *   *

It was almost midnight when Kate finally returned to her Long Island studio apartment. Since she'd taken over the wedding portfolio of Maya Evert's company five years ago just before her mentor succumbed to cancer, Kate's life had become almost nomadic. She often stayed on-site during pre-wedding events, and this summer's wedding season had been like a full-on sprint. And fall wasn't looking to slow down much. She'd barely been home since April, and the place smelled stale and lifeless.

Her eyes immediately went to the only living thing she owned, and she gasped.

Her succulent was dead.

Imani had gotten it for her as an apartment-warming gift when Kate moved out of Imani's pad in Queens to Oyster Bay, presumably to make it easier for Kate to meet with her clients, who were mostly located in Nassau, Suffolk, and Westchester counties. Yet while the commute to various vendors and brides-to-be was a little shorter, the trade-off was a studio that seemed to take the new, gray-toned "it" color to a whole other level.

The apartment had a charcoal-gray couch that turned into a full-size bed, a teeny, lighter gray bar, and two gleaming steel barstools that sat on the end of the triangular-shaped, gray-and-white efficiency kitchen. While the locale, nudged up to Long Island's Gold Coast, was perfect for her business, if Kate was being honest, she preferred Imani's overstuffed place with its mishmash of styles and comfy chairs and colorful throw blankets folded on every available surface.

Imani's place felt like living inside a hug.

This place felt like living inside a gynecologist's office.

"Oh, no. You can't die," Kate groaned, dumping the rest of her water bottle into the drooping, sad plant. The liquid disappeared into the parched dirt so fast, you could hear the water bubble as it settled into the planter. "Imani said this plant would help me grow roots...now that's all that's left."

She stared at the dead succulent as she emptied her travel suitcase. It was a fitting metaphor for this apartment. After almost three years here, she hadn't hung a single picture—the only "art" was a wall-size, two-years-at-a-glance calendar, filled with events written in color-coded dry-erase markers. It was to this calendar that she went, opening the windows flanking it to let in the brisk September night, erasing the Montague wedding and writing in careful print "Drake Matthews's Book Launch." She bit her lip as she circled the day of the event, wincing at how little time she had to prepare.

Kate powered up her laptop and had barely begun researching haunted houses when her cell phone buzzed. Hoping it was Imani calling back about the terrifying warning, she hit the button to answer before registering that the readout read *Mom and Dad.*

"Honey, I'm so glad I caught you," her mom began. "We need to talk about the Sweet Surgery Center's grand opening. Oh, and your father just heard from the dean at Cornell's med school, and she said you lack only four classes and an MCAT score to be considered for admission. That's twelve credits, including labs. Isn't that great?"

"Mom, we've had this discussion," Kate said, massaging the bridge of her nose. "I don't want to be a doctor. Or a physician assistant, a surgery tech, or the receptionist of your future office. I majored in hospitality, got an internship after college with the hottest event planner on the East Coast, and inherited much of her massive client base because I'm good at what I do. I love my job, Mom."

"I know you do." Her mother's voice had that patient tone Kate had come to hate since sophomore year when she'd renounced medicine as a career. "But I hate to see you throwing away your talent, honey. You have what it takes to make such a difference in this world! You completed your bio electives before you changed your major, so all you'd have to take is your organic chemistry courses. I'm sure you could fit four classes in between your...parties. Then, you could study for the—"

"I'm sorry, Mom." Kate cut her off, her teeth gritted in a losing bid to keep her temper. "I just got in and I've got a big client meeting to prepare for on Monday. I've got to go."

"I thought with the Montagues canceling their wedding, you'd have some time to at least enroll in one class over winter break," her mother said, undeterred by her daughter's deteriorating tone. "Besides, your father and I want to meet with you about the Sweet Surgery Center."

Kate rolled her eyes at how fast the news traveled in her parents' exclusive Lloyd Harbor social circle about the wedding plans of Nicholas Montague and his former fiancée crashing and burning.

"Actually, thanks to Imani, I filled the Montague spot—"

"Oh, how's she doing? I haven't seen that girl in ages!" Her mom interrupted with the most enthusiasm she'd mustered since the conversation started. "I'm so thrilled she got into Cerulean Books—it's quite a coup, how fast she's climbing the ladder. I know she's not my own, but she did live with us for over a year, so I feel...invested."

Kate stared at the ceiling, wondering if her mother heard the same irony Kate did in the investment she'd mentally made in Kate's best friend, but not her own daughter.

Probably not. Irony wasn't one of the things tested on MCAT exams.

"Imani's great. Busy. And lucky for me, she just hooked me up with one of her—"

This time, Kate interrupted herself. If she told her mom it was an author, she'd insist on knowing who it was, and Kate would never hear the end of it. As it was, her parents still told their colleagues that while their youngest daughter was in medical school, their oldest was taking some "gap years" before committing to medicine. Better to keep the fact she'd be working with the Knight of Nightmares to herself—at least until she won the EVPLEX for it. Then she'd tell everyone.

"—one of her friends, and I'm doing an event for him," she amended smoothly. "It's only a few weeks away, and I'm meeting with the client on Monday, so I really have to run. Kiss Dad for me, and tell Kiersten that just because she's in med school now doesn't mean she's too fancy to return my texts. I love you guys, and I'll see you in a couple of months for Thanksgiving. I'm bringing the pumpkin pie, right?"

"Well, yes, but we wanted to—"

"Oops—got a call coming in. I've got to let you go. Kisses to you all!" Kate quickly disconnected before her mom could finish her sentence. Maybe by the time Thanksgiving came around, she'd have gotten enough kudos to announce that she'd be a contender for the biggest prize in her business? And maybe that would allay her family's constant need to try to bail her out of this job?

Kate snorted. Not likely. But it was worth a shot.

She shook her head and pulled up a promotional YouTube video of the elusive Drake Matthews. He had what Kate thought of as a quintessential writer's look—short, wavy brown hair, a strong jawline, and behind a pair of dark glasses, golden eyes that peered out at the world in an I'm-a-serious-writer sort of way. The video advertised *Halloween Hacker*, and after a few seconds of listening to the plot about a computer hacker who is slowly driven insane, Kate shuddered, clicking on the next video.

Immediately, she knew this was no promotional piece. The jerky camera movements hinted it was being captured by an amateur with a cell phone. The footage began with a man—she assumed it was Drake Matthews—signing a book, in front of a crowd of people, his back to the camera. Kate noticed the wrought-iron spiderweb gates behind him, and there was a blur of a brick-red house in the background—she guessed the video was taken right outside the Victorian mansion he owned.

Drake finished signing and turned toward the person shooting the video.

Kate caught her breath as she took in the black tuxedo the writer wore so effortlessly. The man could have easily had a second career as a formal-wear model.

"Sorry, we've got dinner reservations. No more

autographs," he said, his hair perfectly askew, his amber eyes startled as they darted to the guy with the camera phone and the dozens of begging fans all around, jabbing pens at his face as if they were trying to skewer him.

An off-camera male voice asked, "Can you sign this book for my brother, Mr. Matthews? He's in the Navy aboard the *USS Lincoln* right now, and I think it'll cheer him up."

Drake hesitated. He turned to his left, offering someone an apologetic smile, then faced the owner of the camera phone, looking a little harried.

"Just this last one, then, for your brother. I've got two of my own who served overseas." Drake took the proffered Sharpie to sign.

The video image jiggled as the guy switched his cell phone to the other hand, offering a view of the sky, the ground, and then a brunette in a black formal dress standing off to the side.

"Drake, we're never going to make it to Ambrose's in time," came the high-pitched voice of the twenty-something woman whose beautiful gown plunged so low on her curvy figure, only a fraction of a centimeter— and probably some heavy-duty body tape—kept it from being a complete nipple reveal. She rolled her eyes, pulling out her phone. She gazed at it for a minute, then heaved a sigh as she popped it back into a matching clutch. "It's always about you and your books. I'm so tired of always coming in second."

The impromptu videographer managed to get the phone transferred to the other hand, and the camera faced Drake once more.

Kate winced at the writer's wounded expression,

which he quickly covered with a grim smile, handing over the signed book to his fan. "Okay, Rachel's right. The show's over. We've got to get to our car."

Although the camera wasn't angled to catch the woman's expression, Kate heard her—Rachel—snort in derision when it was clear the fans were not dispersing. The horror writer was cornered, pens jabbing at him from every angle.

Suddenly, Drake spun back to the fence, put his fingers to his lips, and gave a piercing whistle.

A massive, barrel-chested Doberman sprang at the fence. Paws as big as a man's fist bashed, chest-high, against the spiderwebbed iron barrier, as the beast lunged forward barking and snapping at the people just outside of his reach. Everyone except the person with the camera phone scattered like rabbits.

"Good boy," Drake said, reaching one arm through the barrier to ruffle the dog's head. Then, as if sensing he was still on camera, the writer turned, his expression annoyed. He threw his arms out in a "What now?" gesture. His move excited the Doberman, whose deep-throated, vicious-sounding snarls picked up tempo. "Listen, man, the freak show's over—"

Abruptly, the video ended. Scanning the comments underneath, Kate wasn't surprised to see his fans argue that with the books he wrote, Drake Matthews didn't need a rabid Doberman to guard his house. Living in that spooky Victorian, penning terror all day—the Knight of Nightmares was a deterrent, all by himself.

Kate shuddered. More videos of book trailers popped up, but she'd seen enough. She was just about to close out of her search when she spotted a photograph of the writer on a beach. She clicked on it, gasped, and enlarged the screen to fill her laptop. The image was of Drake in a pair of turquoise board shorts…and nothing else.

"Wow. Who'd have thought the guy would be so buff?" Kate wondered aloud, her eyes moving over every play of light and shadow. If his tanned chest and muscular arms weren't enough, his abs appeared to have been sculpted in bronze.

After staring at him for a minute, Kate clicked off, giving herself a shake.

"The only six-packs writers have come from a convenience store," she muttered, banishing thoughts of his tanned, chiseled form from her mind. "It must be Photoshopped."

Pulling up her project plan, she went to work.

She was about to give Drake Matthews the best book launch of his nightmarish dreams.

CHAPTER 2

Monday morning, Kate stood waiting for a cab under the awning of the only downtown hotel in a bitty little village called Wellsville, New York, trying not to break a tooth as her jaw chattered, shaking with the cold. She'd flown to Buffalo yesterday, and the plan had been to meet Imani at the airport and rent a car together to take them the two hours to Drake Matthews's hometown. But when she'd landed, Kate discovered a brief text from her best friend.

Imani: Flight had to change. Mtg w/a client. Meet u @ Drake's at 10. ☺

And with that, her best friend had gone dark, which was why Kate was waiting for a ride to meet the Knight of Nightmares . . . alone.

The wind gusted, spattering her with a little of the sleety rain coming down outside the overhang. Kate shivered, wishing she'd chosen another outfit. She brushed the droplets off her slightly tight black pencil skirt, curling her lip at the suit she'd picked out specifically for the meeting. She'd read online how Drake loved to wear black—her least favorite color. While everyone in her business—hell, everyone in New York City—considered it a staple, Kate wasn't one of them. Most redheads took on an ethereal, otherworldly glow in a black suit, but Kate usually spent the day reassuring people she wasn't sick. She'd bought this outfit back before she became best friends with navy blue, chocolate brown, and almost every shade of green. Back when she was about ten pounds lighter and a cup size smaller.

Now, here she was, dressed in a suit that squished her in too many places to name, made her look anemic, and whose skirt sported a walking slit that felt as though it was cut a bit too high up the back, especially for this weather. Every gust of wind flapped it open, and she was constantly smoothing the fabric down, worried she'd accidentally flash someone.

Kate sniffed, wishing she'd thought to bring tissues. Was her nose running, or was it just numb? She fumbled in her pocket for her phone and reversed the angle on her cell's camera to check herself out one last time as the cab pulled up to the small hotel lobby's covered entrance.

No snot running down her face, but that was the best she could say about the ghostly reflection gazing back. Her green eyes were wider than normal, despite the heavy black liner and smoky shadow she'd chosen in an effort to reflect her newest client's gothic vibe and downplay the dark bags under her eyes. At first, she'd put her auburn hair up in the same chignon she always wore when working, then changed her mind, letting it tumble long and wild down her shoulders, figuring that was as close to edgy as she'd get. Now, with her hair askew from the wind, her face pasty-pale, and her nose bright red from the cold, she sensed she'd missed the mark. Instead of "edgy," she looked more "on edge."

Maybe even teetering *over* the edge.

Finally, her taxi pulled around. Pocketing her phone, she made her way toward a red sedan with "Jimmy's Car Service" printed on a magnet affixed to the passenger door. Her silver-tipped black stiletto heels—a throwback to her Maya Evert internship days—clicked on the pavement, as sharp as an ice pick.

A middle-aged man in Timberland boots and a tan Carhartt jacket got out of the car.

"You the one who called for a ride?"

At Kate's nod, the man introduced himself as Jimmy, and after adjusting his blue knit Buffalo Sabres hat so it covered his ears, he came around to open the back passenger door.

The car's wipers were going full blast but were barely able to keep the windshield clear of the sheets of cold rain pummeling down as the driver wove through the streets of the sleepy little town. Jimmy's taxi wasn't anything like the screaming fast yellow ones of New York City, which was to its benefit. The inside of Jimmy's cab was clean, had no Plexiglas separating the front and back, and even had a faint new-car smell.

She hadn't, of course, told the driver she was meeting with Drake, but as soon as she'd given him the address, Jimmy nodded, flashing a knowing look at her in the rearview mirror.

"Going to the Matthews mansion? You a fan? We get a lot of folks want to stand outside and take pictures.

See if they can see the ghost in the attic window, or whatever."

"No, I'm not a fan. I'm working with him on his up-coming book launch," Kate said, feeling compelled to explain she wasn't some random stalker going to lurk around the writer's house. "He's expecting me."

The driver did a double take in the mirror, his expression morphing from interest to incredulous. "You're not meeting him *there*, are you?"

At her confused nod, the man went on.

"You do know his house is haunted, right? I've only been here a year, and I've met four people who've seen things in or around that house. Faces in the window when nobody's home. Shadows around the old well where that little girl supposedly drowned. Lights flickering in the attic. Stuff like that."

"Well," Kate said, smiling, "I don't scare easily."

Jimmy slowed for a stop sign, the wipers whining a staccato beat as he turned in his seat to look at her. His eyes beneath the knit cap were serious, and his voice dropped to a confidential tone. "But when Drake Matthews is in residence? They say the house practically comes alive...not in a good way! Some of what the media says about him is foolishness. But you gotta wonder. The guy rarely ever leaves the place, and when he does, he skulks around in that leather coat and those glasses. You know horror writers—they all turn out to have something...off...about them."

Kate gave a nervous laugh. "Oh, I'm sure that's all just to cultivate their image. You know, branding. If they act eccentric, people will buy more of their books. That sort of thing."

The driver turned around and, after checking the

four-way stop, proceeded slowly down the road. Several shops were open for business on what passed for Main Street, but they looked mostly deserted. A few people braved the weather, hustling down the sidewalk, heads bent under dark umbrellas. Jimmy flipped his wipers to low, the sleet turning to fat, wet plops hitting the windshield.

"I'm not so sure. Edgar Allan Poe was a creeper who married his thirteen-year-old cousin. The woman who wrote that spooky *The Haunting of Hill House* story—what was her name?"

"Shirley Jackson," Kate dutifully replied.

"Yeah, her. She suffered from such agoraphobia she couldn't even leave the house some days. Horror writers are, by trade, a strange breed. Just be careful, is all I'm saying." Jimmy put on the blinkers, and the cab splashed through a gulley of water, then halted.

Kate took in the foreboding spiderweb gates protecting the dark red Victorian towering over the town on top of a small hill.

"This is it?" Kate said, her voice sounding high and reedy to her own ears. She cleared her throat. "I mean, this is where Mr. Matthews lives?"

Jimmy nodded, turning to take her cab fare. "Wish I could bring you closer, but he keeps the gates locked to the driveway. Only way to the front door is through there." He gestured to the gates set at the base of the sidewalk, framing a brick path to the black double-hung doors of the mansion. "He keeps 'em locked, but if he's expecting you, he's probably got a way to buzz you in."

The gloomy day made the whole scene look just like a backdrop from one of those slasher movies she'd always been too afraid to watch. The wind whistled in a low, lonely tone outside the car, and Kate shivered.

"Miss? You okay?"

She took a deep breath, halting mid-inhale as the fabric of her suit coat stretched uncomfortably tight. "Yes. Thanks again for the ride, Jimmy."

"Here." Jimmy shifted, fetching something from his glove box. "You take my card. Call if you need to be picked up, and I'll be here in ten minutes, tops!"

Kate thanked him and pocketed the card. Gathering her briefcase and her courage, she stepped onto the wet sidewalk. She blinked against the icy wind, fought with her umbrella, and finally got the tiny thing up and over her head just as Jimmy pulled away with a final dire look at the house.

Angling the umbrella to take the brunt of the wet gusts, Kate approached the gates. She squinted against the wind to peer at the sides for any buzzer or call button. Nothing. Teeth chattering, she knocked against the gates, feeling like an idiot, and when that got no response, she reached out to jiggle the latch at the intersection of the batwings, and was surprised to find it swung open at her touch. She'd half expected the gates to screech, but they moved as if on well-oiled hinges, silently opening and then closing behind her with a faint click.

Figuring Drake must have somehow buzzed her in, she picked her way carefully up the slick, uneven brick path to the house, watching the ground so her stilettos didn't get caught between the pavers. She'd made it about halfway when a huge gust of wind caught her umbrella and blew it from her hands. It tumbled end over end to the edge of the lawn, half burying itself in the leafy shrubs lining the fence.

"Damn," she whispered under her breath, pushing damp strands of hair out of her eyes. Using her briefcase to shield her face and what was left of her perfectly curled hair, she stepped off the brick-lined walkway and onto the lawn surrounding the house. The sharp points of her heels immediately sank into the rain-soaked earth, so she adjusted her gait, tiptoeing through the grass.

Reaching the edge of the yard, she grabbed for the open fabric of her umbrella...and then something from the bushes tugged it back. She snatched her hand away as the bushes erupted in a low, steady growl.

She froze. Imani's words came rushing back to her, and Kate's mind filled in the blanks.

Oh, I forgot to tell you, her best friend had said. *Be careful... terrifying! Watch out for—*

It had to be this. The dog. The same rabid-looking Doberman from the video! Panicked, Kate's gaze shot to the road beyond the wrought-iron fence. Jimmy's taxi was long gone, and what she could see of the street and sidewalk beyond the Matthews property was deserted. She calculated the distance to the gates and all the rolling green lawn between and quickly determined the big red Victorian behind her was her best bet.

Still holding her briefcase above her head, Kate took a teensy step backward, hoping the lack of sudden movement would keep the dog from charging. The bushes rustled. Something was making its way through the underbrush. Clearly, the Doberman was onto her scheme—there was no choice now. She had to run for it.

Forgetting all decorum, Kate whirled, sprinting on her toes. Her body was pointed in the direction of the safety of the mansion's front porch, but her head was swiveled toward the bush, dreading the sight of the beast about to erupt from its leafy depths. The foliage moved as if barely restraining some massive creature, and Kate let out a panicked scream. She picked up the pace, hurtling toward the house.

She'd turned her head to gauge the distance to the porch, and her eyes had just enough time to register the dark figure. A man.

Kate shrieked in horror before her body slammed into him. Her scream cut off abruptly, the air ejected from her lungs in a massive whoosh.

"Oof," the man grunted, staggering back a step before recovering himself.

Kate was not as fortunate.

The collision was like sprinting headlong into a wall, and the impact turned her into a human pinball. Her body ricocheted off the dark figure, her arms pinwheeling in an effort to remain upright. She lost her grip on her briefcase, and the black bag went sailing as she struggled for balance. Both her stiletto heels stuck in the ground when she'd stopped and now acted as tent stakes, making the physics of adjusting her weight impossible. Kate felt herself losing the battle with gravity. She was going to fall backward—right into the path of the attacking dog!

Suddenly, strong arms grabbed her by the waist, reversing her fall.

"Whoa," the man said, his voice low and rumbly in his chest. "I've got you."

Kate clutched at him, trying to yank herself upright.

Her hands fisted into his shirt so hard, the fabric tore. She looked up, her gaze locking on to the man's eyes as he lifted her out of her stuck-in-the-mud heels, picking her up until her head was even with his. Startling golden eyes blinked at her from behind dark-framed glasses.

Drake Matthews.

Her client.

She should have been embarrassed by her lack of professionalism, but the only feeling registering in her brain was awe. This was the bookish guy she was working with—this man with the arresting eyes and the startling strength? He was holding her up, by the waist, as if she weighed no more than a bouquet of flowers. Her hands, still clutching his shirt, felt nothing but solid, well-muscled flesh beneath the fabric, and she said the first thing that came into her mind.

"You're *not* Photoshopped!"

Drake's eyebrows went up, and he opened his mouth to say something, but just then, Kate felt something wet and cold bump up against her calf.

The Doberman!

Another scream burst from her mouth, and she scrambled up him until her arms wound around his neck. She yanked her feet up out of harm's way, shimmying up him like he was a fireman's pole, inching skyward with every fiber of her body until her thighs gripped his waist. She heard the sound of more fabric tearing, and some distant part of her mind was telling her that this wasn't an appropriate way to act with a client—especially *this* client—but then she heard a small bark, and all thoughts of professional behavior were swept from her mind with the cold wind of fear.

"Your dog! Your dog—call off your dog!" she yelled

in Drake's ear, while still wildly looking over her shoulder to find the beast.

"Mmph," came Drake's muffled response, and Kate realized she was mashing his face into her chest as she clutched his head. She released some of the grip around his neck, and he turned his head enough to blurt, "It's just Sasha. She won't hurt—"

The dog gave another muffled growling noise, and Kate yelped, tightening her knees around Drake's waist. Suddenly, the man began to shake. Was he okay? Did the dog bite something...important down there?

Kate peeked at Drake's face to find he was staring at her, grinning. Laughter vibrated through his chest, and his body rose and fell with the effort to contain his amusement.

"I've never heard of an attack shih tzu before, but I guess there's a first for everything." He chuckled, shaking his head. "Don't worry—the most this little mutt will do is love you to death. And, apparently, steal your umbrella. Isn't that right, Sasha?"

Drake nodded his head to the left, and warily, Kate looked down. On the ground was not a slobbering Doberman, eager for a bite of her leg. Instead, romping back and forth on the wet green lawn beneath them was a tiny brown-and-white furball, dragging at the fabric of the open umbrella, alternately growling and shaking his head to toss the thing around only to pounce on it once more. The dog stopped playing long enough to gaze up at Kate and bark, his tail wagging so hard, his whole body swayed from side to side.

"Th-that's your dog?" Kate gasped in disbelief, wondering where the vicious Doberman from the YouTube video was. "He sounded so much more...menacing than he looks."

"She. And Sasha *is* a menace. When you're on deadline and trying to get some writing done. Other than that, the most trouble she causes is trying to get out of the gates to visit the neighbors. Which reminds me," Drake said, clearing his throat. "I think it might be best if you got down now? And, erm, adjusted your skirt? Old Mr. Penny is about to have a stroke."

Her head swiveled to look through the front gates. Fifty yards away stood an older man in a raincoat holding a black umbrella whose wingspan was large enough to shelter him and his big retriever. Both man and dog peered across the street, and it took a moment of staring back at them until the meaning of Drake's words sank in. In a rush, her senses returned, and she realized she was wrapped around Drake Matthews—*the* Drake Matthews—like a spider monkey. Her black skirt was rucked up to the tops of her thighs, and rain drizzled onto the wispy fabric of her thong...which meant her skirt, with its walking slit, had been transformed into an outfit now suitable for some deep lunges or high karate kicks.

She yelped, disengaging both her arms and legs from Drake at once, plopping down onto the wet grass. Hard. Hastily, she sat up and shoved the fabric of her skirt down, casting a look over her shoulder at the old man across the street. The neighbor just shook his head and resumed walking, his umbrella angled to the sprinkling rain. The retriever gave one bark, as if in disgust, and followed his owner.

Kate's cheeks heated, and she turned to face Drake

Matthews, who'd bent down next to her as soon as she'd fallen from his arms.

"Are you okay?" he asked, one arm reaching out hesitantly. His golden eyes glowed with wary concern behind his rain-spattered glasses, and Kate could tell he thought she was some kind of lunatic. "I'm expected in a meeting in a few minutes, but I can drive you down to the clinic if you're hurt? Or can I call someone for you?"

Just then, the shih tzu wagged her wet tail, wriggling closer, her paws stamping muddy prints over Kate's black skirt as she climbed on Kate's lap, licking and panting gusts of warm puppy breath in her face.

"No," Kate said, sighing and petting the dog. Sasha wriggled with pleasure, giving her two more dog kisses before Drake reeled in the tiny furball. "You don't have to call anyone. And you won't be late for your meeting."

"I don't understand," he said, his eyebrows drawing together.

"I *am* your meeting." Kate stood on shaky legs, her feet squishing into the rain-soaked grass as she thrust out a hand toward her client. "Mr. Matthews, I'm Kate Sweet. Your new event planner."

CHAPTER 3

Oh. Uh, hi?" Drake Matthews winced as his introduction came out as a question. He reached out and shook the small, grass-flecked hand of the event planner—Kate Sweet, she'd said her name was—as he pinned a smile on his face. "I mean, welcome, Ms. Sweet."

She beamed at him, and even with her wet hair and smudged makeup, Drake felt his mouth go dry. She was stunning.

"Call me Kate. I know you were expecting Imani Lewis, but her flight was delayed," Kate said, and he tried to act normal as he watched her tuck a damp auburn lock behind her ear before she continued speaking. "So, for now, you've got me. I'm really excited about your launch and can't wait to show you my ideas."

He struggled with what to say next. When writing a book, he could imagine every situation, but in real life his mind felt mired in molasses. He hadn't dated in months, unless he counted those awkward setups by well-meaning friends, and the last time his hands had been on another woman's thighs was back before Rachel had decided writing a tell-all book about her time with him was better than actually spending time with him.

Drake knew he needed to shift gears. Be professional. But his body was taking longer to adjust. Because forty-five seconds ago, this beautiful woman had been in his arms, her thighs locked around his waist, his face buried deep into the cleavage of her chest, his hands cupping her bottom.

And now he was standing here, shaking her hand. Getting ready to talk business. Plan book launches and make arrangements. What did one say in this situation? Joke about it? Channel Groucho Marx and waggle his eyebrows and say something like, *If that's your introduction, I can't wait to get to know you better.*

No. Who'd even know a Groucho Marx impression anymore? She'd probably have no idea, and he'd come across as a creeper. Maybe he should apologize for what had happened—it was on his property, after all. Something like, *I'm sorry my nine-pound dog scared you and made you run in those god-awful heels?* No. That sounded disingenuous and snarky, even if it was true.

If it had been a scene he was writing, he'd have had an afternoon to craft the perfect response. But in real time...he had nothing.

Sasha barked, finally bringing him back to reality. Drake saw the woman shiver, and all at once, noticed the cold and the rain around them. He winced at his terrible manners—he really needed to get out more.

"Um, Kate? Would you like to come inside? Get dried off and cleaned up?" Drake turned to lead the way into his home and had taken four of the five wooden porch steps before he realized the event planner wasn't with him. He turned, Sasha wriggling like mad in his arms, and saw the planner scurrying around his yard. It took a moment before he realized she was retrieving her heels, umbrella, and briefcase—and before he could move to help her, she was sprinting toward him, her bare feet leaving tiny prints on the dry wood of the porch as she caught up to him by the front door.

"Sorry about that. I've got all my things now. I'm ready to meet," she panted, her smile pained with obvious embarrassment. "Plus, now I've got my cardio done for the day!"

Drake wanted to say something. Smile. Make her feel comfortable. But all he did was nod and hold open the door for her. Cursing himself for his ineptitude, Drake followed her into the foyer. He hit the switch to turn on the crystal chandelier and grabbed a small towel off the metal coat hook to vigorously rub the mud off Sasha's paws before setting her down. The dog made a beeline for the event planner, dancing in circles around the woman's dirt-speckled feet, clearly aiming for some attention and petting.

Kate, however, stood awkwardly on the small burgundy Oriental rug covering the hardwood floor in the entryway, her shoes in one hand and her briefcase clutched to her chest. Her green eyes, made more vivid in color by the dark smear of rain-smudged makeup, scanned the entrance hall with something like...fear? Surely, she didn't believe all the garbage people said about his house being haunted? Or was she looking for the coffin he supposedly slept in?

Drake's expression hardened. She must be one of those people who assumed he was some sort of deviant just because he wrote creepy stories. Whatever. He was just going to have to put up with it. Cerulean Books was determined to make the launch of his tenth book—in conjunction with the announcement of its having been optioned already for a movie—a freaking circus, and since he'd already agreed to the marketing plan, he didn't have much of a choice.

He forced his lips into a smile. "We can meet in here. By the fire." He gestured to the pale-yellow room his grandmother had called the front parlor, where he'd been inspired to write this morning, and hastily went to clean off the coffee table. He gathered up the boxes of World War II–era letters he'd hauled out of the attic months ago and shoved them into a corner, jamming a thick manila folder he'd aptly labeled "Forbidden" on top to disguise the mess. He couldn't run the risk that she'd see what he'd been writing... or more important, what he *hadn't* been writing.

"Have a seat," he said after the clutter was cleared. He gestured to a plump leather couch—some piece his grandmother had collected—and was startled to see that the woman in his foyer hadn't moved, except to transfer her briefcase and shoes to one hand so she could bend at the knees to pet Sasha with the other hand. Although he'd waved her into his house, gesturing for her to take the seat by the fire, she stood, awkwardly holding her things, a smile pasted to her lips.

Was she so wary of him that she wouldn't move too far from the door, just in case?

Even though he wanted to roll his eyes at her reaction, Drake kept his face neutral as she began to speak.

"First off, let me just say how excited I am to be working with you and Cerulean Books on this launch," she said, beaming. "Imani informed me your previous point person, Jeremy Rodriguez, had to step down, and I want to take this opportunity to assure you that my reputation as an event planner is impeccable. Your tenth book launch will be spook-tacular, and I've been working around the clock to ensure the plans begun with Jeremy will continue seamlessly. I've even included a few details to make it truly memorable for both you and your fans. I'd wanted to wait for Imani, but since she's running late..."

Drake watched the woman turn her head, peering at the door behind her with a pained expression, as if willing it to open and for the publicist, or anyone, to enter.

Holy shit. Was this woman so terrified that she was going to pitch the entire thing from his foyer rug?

This realization, combined with too many sleepless nights toiling over a blank screen on his next horror novel, snapped his last frayed nerve. He strode back to the foyer, scooped up Sasha, gave her a pat, and deposited her in the dog crate at the entrance to the parlor, tossing in one of her favorite rawhide treats to calm her down. Straightening, he turned to the woman-statue in his foyer, willing his voice to be civil but not surprised when it came out curt and aggressive.

"If we're going to work together, you've got to stop with the damsel-in-distress thing. I'm not a vampire, and I don't drink blood. I sleep in a regular bed. My attic is not haunted by a dead girl, at least to my knowledge, and we've never uncovered any bodies in the walls, under the floorboards, or buried in the old well." Drake crossed his arms over his chest, meeting Kate's wide-eyed gaze with a challenge. "If you are too afraid to meet here, you should have told Imani to set up something downtown—that way, we wouldn't waste your time. Or mine."

If it weren't for the fact the lights were ablaze in the foyer, he'd have missed the pink color that rose like a summer's sunrise from her chest, to her neck, and finally to her face, tinting both cheeks with the cherry glow of embarrassment. To her credit, her voice was steady when she replied.

"I don't scare easily, and I make it a point not to listen to gossip," Kate said, taking a step toward him. She pointed at his chest with the hand holding her muddy heels. "But I *am* afraid of something, Mr. Matthews."

"Is it my attack dog?" Drake asked, raising a sardonic eyebrow and jerking his thumb toward Sasha, who chewed merrily on her rawhide a few feet away.

"No!" Kate burst out, her voice losing some of its courteous professionalism. "I don't want to drip all over your fancy rugs and furniture. It's like an antique museum vomited all over in here. If I sit on that chesterfield sofa or walk on that vintage Turkish rug, I'll ruin it, because if you haven't yet noticed, I'm a complete and utter mess!"

At the last word, Kate threw out her arms, full of a briefcase and heels, as if to showcase her point. As she did, the top two buttons of her tight, black suit coat popped off, tumbling to the entryway rug. One rolled off and onto the hardwood floors, tumbling the remaining distance to him, until wobbling to a stop at his shoe.

Drake reached down to fetch the button at the same time as Kate.

Suddenly, white-hot fire lanced up his arm.

In her effort to grab the button, she'd thrust out her right hand—the same one holding her shoes. The steely heel of one of Kate's stilettos stabbed into his forearm, and raked its way up, gouging him like a carrot peeler. Fast as a blink, she'd excavated a shallow, six-inch trench in his left arm. Blood immediately welled up in the gash, and Drake grimaced at the sting of pain and the sight of it.

"Oh-no-oh-no-oh-no!" Kate moaned, mashing the syllables into one long word of dread. "Did I cut you? I cut you, didn't I?"

"Mmm," Drake hummed agreement, gritting his teeth against the bile rising from his stomach. "I'm fine. It's nothing."

Before he could react, she snatched his arm from his chest. He whipped his head to the opposite side so that he was staring at the coat hooks on the wall and not his arm. Or the blood.

"Well, it's not 'nothing,' but we need to get it cleaned up and get some antibiotic cream on there," Kate said. "I am *so* very sorry, Drake. I was trying to grab my button before it rolled under something and forgot I was still holding my heels."

"Those shoes are deadly." Drake gently disengaged his arm from her grip. His arm burned like it had been doused with acid, but when he saw the pale oval of her face transform into a cocktail of anxiety and guilt, mixed with a liberal shot of fear, he pushed the pain away, trying for a reassuring smile. "I'll have to remember that for the next imperiled heroine I write—no woman is unarmed if dressed in heels like that."

"Maybe I should call an ambulance?" she asked, swooping in toward his arm. "It's bleeding pretty bad."

Drake shook his head, sidestepping her reach.

"It's just superficial. I'll wash it off and be right back to get you some dry clothes."

Without waiting for her response, Drake pivoted, heading for the tiny powder room at the end of the hall next to the swinging door that led to the kitchen. He had a first-aid kit in the cabinet there, which had not only bandages and ointment, but also smelling salts. The latter might be needed before the former, much to his eternal embarrassment. While he'd served six years as a reservist in the Marine Corps, it was a little-known fact he couldn't stand the sight of his own blood. Ironically, this was the only secret he'd managed to keep from Rachel—the only real phobia that he had—and he wasn't about to let this total stranger in on it.

He heard the sound of something thumping down on the floor behind him. Suddenly, Kate was at his side, her briefcase and wickedly sharp heels abandoned. The woman's green eyes were wide as she peered up at him, but her voice was low and calm when she spoke.

"We should really wash it well so it doesn't get infected. The tips of my shoes are metal, and they're pretty dirty after walking through your yard." She touched his uninjured arm as she looked down the entrance hall. "Is there a bathroom on this floor? Let's get something on that arm, and we'll get the bleeding stopped in no time."

Drake resisted the urge to look down, gesturing with his head to the door at the end of the hall.

"Bathroom's right there, but I'm fine," he repeated more to himself than to her. Only three more steps to the bathroom. "Just a scratch. I've had worse in my life, trust me. I've got some first-aid stuff in the bathroom cabinet. Head on back to the parlor—you really don't have to worry about the furniture there. If it can withstand my childhood, it can withstand anything."

"It's no worry at all. Getting you bandaged up is the least I can do."

Drake gritted his teeth, willing his stomach to keep his breakfast where it belonged. Clearly, the woman was not taking the hint to give him some privacy. Instead, she opened the powder room door and pulled him inside behind her, her bare feet making damp prints on the old black-and-white penny tiles. Thankfully, she threw open the mirrored medicine cabinet doors before he caught his reflection.

"Okay, here's some gauze...some bandages...oh! Here's the antibiotic cream. We've got everything we need."

Drake ignored the boxes she pulled out, maneuvering around her to get to the tiny antique sink. Twisting the nozzle for cold water, he waited until it was icy before turning his head aside, closing his eyes, and thrusting his left arm under the faucet.

The water stung like acid in the gash on his arm. "Seriously, why are there metal tips on those shoes?" he muttered. "Good thing I'm up-to-date on all my shots."

He felt her gaze on him and opened his eyes, careful to look only at her oval face, animated with worry. She'd wiped most of the smeared mascara off her cheeks and looked younger and more vulnerable without the dark around her eyes.

"I really am sorry," she said solemnly. "This is

not how I'd intended our first meeting to go. Imani entrusted me with presenting the book launch ideas, and we've worked so hard to give you an epic event as *Halloween Hacker* is released to the world. I was excited to show you a mock-up of the haunted house we've got planned for your fans."

"A . . . haunted house?" Drake squinted an eye, trying to recall when he'd ever agreed to anything like that. He shook his head. "I don't remember that being part of the launch."

The woman smiled, mistaking his horror at the idea for mere confusion.

"That's because the previous planner had just confirmed the rental of a site before he left for his family emergency—Imani said he'd emailed the plans to her, but they wanted to wait to surprise you with it only after we'd pulled the proper permits," Kate gushed. "But we've got it now. It's outside of town in an old barn that's just dilapidated enough to be creepy, but not unsafe, and it'll hold all two hundred of your guests with room to spare."

"Two hundred guests?" Drake gaped at her. "We have that many coming?"

Kate nodded, giving him a smile so brimming with enthusiasm, he felt his own lips curving in something like a reflex, despite his dawning horror. Her eyes danced as she continued. "And . . . I was going to wait to tell you this until we sat down and I showed you all of the drawings, but we've already had a structural engineer out there, and we're good to go on most anything we wanted to hang from the rafters."

"Like what?" he finally mustered.

Kate leaned forward in a conspiratorial tone. "Like

a coffin! I called the local funeral home, and they've agreed to rent us a coffin for the event, and we're going to have it hung so that you'd be standing upright inside of it when it opens for the big reveal when you pop out to greet your fans at the end of the haunted house."

"You have me popping out of a coffin?" Drake momentarily forgot about his bleeding arm under the cold water. This was insane. Did his publisher think he'd agree to something so cliché and ludicrous? Drake was speechless. His mouth opened and closed, but words wouldn't come.

"I know. Isn't it perfect?" Kate raised her fists like she was shaking tiny, imaginary pom-poms by her head. "And I thought we could rig up some fog machines so that it looks like you're floating when you step out of the coffin with a copy of the book in your hands, and we'll have you all mic'd up so you can start reading from chapter one in *Halloween Hacker*. Your fans are going to go ballistic!"

"Ballistic. Yeah. Someone's going to go ballistic," he muttered, thinking of the conversation he would have with his publicist when she arrived. There was no way in hell he'd be a part of any circus like this. His contract stated he agreed to participate in a book launch and reading event for his tenth book and the subsequent movie adaptation announcement. Nowhere in the fine print did he remember reading he'd be in a coffin dangling from the rafters of a barn-turned-haunted-house. No way. He'd rather be in breach of contract than go through with this nightmare. He and Imani were going to have a serious sit-down about this launch, but in the meantime, he needed to figure out how to nicely dismiss Kate Sweet and her nightmarish plans.

Before he could speak, Kate shut off the water tap and plucked a clean white hand towel from a neat pile in a cupboard over the toilet and pressed it to his forearm.

"You're still bleeding. We need to apply pressure so it'll stop."

"No, it's fine—"

"Don't worry," Kate interrupted, tugging his arm back to her as he tried to pull it away. "I won't touch the bloody area, so I don't need gloves. I'm actually CPR and first-aid certified. You wouldn't believe how many times I've had to bandage up a groom who fainted. I've even had to start CPR on a mother of the bride once before the emergency responders arrived."

"Chest compressions? Who knew a party planner's work would be so fraught with danger?"

Drake meant for it to be a joke—something to distract him from his irritation over the launch event, as well as the blood still oozing from his arm. Yet even though Kate was smiling, he could tell by the hurt in her eyes that he'd said something wrong.

"*Party* planner? If that's all I did, I could pin up streamers, roll out a few kegs, make sure nobody pukes on your furniture, and I'd be done," Kate said with a short laugh.

"Right." Drake nodded. Then, because he couldn't help himself, he asked, "But isn't that what you do, on a larger—and less vomit-filled—scale?"

The woman's grip on his arm got tighter as she spoke, and Drake worked to keep from wincing. "Throwing parties is like blowing a soap bubble—fun, but quickly over and forgotten. But event planning is like crafting a sphere out of iridescent glass and gifting it to someone forever. Events are momentous. Some of my clients have dreamed of their special day—be it a wedding, a quinceañera, or a bar mitzvah—their whole lives. I'm expected to succeed. To do that, I coordinate with vendors, and obtain permits. I work with caterers, decorators, stylists, DJs, and even janitors to ensure success. If I screw up—don't triple-check every minuscule detail—I've shattered that delicate sphere. Yet, if I do my job right, it creates a magical memory my clients will treasure forever. Event planning is a high-stakes job. Contrary to popular opinion, it's anything but parties and flitzing around."

Wow.

Drake blinked, taking in all that she said, guessing only some of that monologue had been directed at him. He supposed she was used to having her career consistently misjudged and maligned.

He could relate to that.

"While I'm not quite sure of the exact definition of the word 'flitzing,' from the context, it sounds very frivolous," Drake said in a mock-serious tone, trying to cajole that smile to her face again. "Although we've just met, even I can see that you don't...flitz...casually."

Her face lost some of its rigidity, and a wry smile turned up the corners of her pink lips.

"You've got that right."

Then Kate lifted the edge of the towel, focusing on his arm.

"It's still pretty bloody, and we'll need to snip the skin that's hanging here. But I think we can bandage it up now."

Drake jerked his gaze up to avoid peeking at the wound and caught sight of his reflection in the mirrored

doors of the medicine cabinet. His face was pasty, he
had beads of sweat at his temple, and the pupils of
his eyes were tiny black pinpricks suspended in pools
of amber.

He looked like a guy an inch from fainting.

Drake took a deep breath, drawing on his Marine
training at Parris Island. *Focus. Clear your mind. Think
of something else besides a ribbon of skin dangling from
your arm.*

Every reader, reporter, and friend would invariably
ask Drake what the hardest part about being a writer
was, and everyone was surprised at his answer. The
hardest part of his job was the fact that his imagination
never took a break. Ever. His mind was always in high
gear, presenting all sorts of mental pictures of fake
scenarios that were usually more drama than reality.
Like now. He could see the wound in his mind as clearly
as if he were staring at it. The deep gouge, the bright
red blood running down his arm to spatter against the
floor, turning the white tiles a garish rust color...

"Damn," Drake groaned. The pictures were surging
through his mind, like a faucet on full blast, and no
amount of mental focus was going to shut off the
torrent. He staggered out of the bathroom. He had one
mission: make it to the front room and its sofa before
he embarrassed himself.

Kate said something, but Drake couldn't hear it over
the ringing in his ears. He registered the horror on her
face before gray clouded his vision. His body tilted, like
the mast of a ship suddenly overtaken by a tidal wave,
and he reached out for the wall.

"I'm going down," he said.

And the darkness swallowed him whole.

CHAPTER 4

Kate recalled a band practice in middle school when she'd seen a girl slump over, right in the middle of doing scales. Her name was Jennifer, and she'd played the oboe and sat two seats over from Kate's clarinet section. When the director had asked the girl to play the C scale, Jennifer had gotten a glazed look in her eyes—like they'd been miraculously switched from living flesh to marbles—and then she'd collapsed with a boneless grace, as if a puppeteer dropped the sticks controlling her strings. Jennifer plummeted to the floor, smacking her forehead into the music stand on the way down, splitting open a gash above her right eyebrow.

It was this oboe player's sightless gaze that flashed through Kate's mind when Drake Matthews had turned to her, his face pale and slightly shiny with sweat.

I'm going down.

If Drake—with his six-foot, muscular frame—took a header onto these hardwood floors, she'd have a dead client. And nobody wanted a dead client.

So she did the only thing she could think of to

prevent her client from injury: she used her own body as a cushion to break his fall.

"I've got you!" Kate dashed around the man as he lurched down the entrance hall. She positioned herself in front of him just as his knees softened, shoving her shoulder under his armpit with such force, she accidentally knocked off his glasses, and they went clattering to the floor somewhere behind them. Kate winced, but had no time to see if she'd broken them because Drake's head fell forward, bashing into her shoulder, and the rest of his body suddenly followed suit.

"Oh no!" she yelped as she realized she couldn't take all his weight. She'd planned to guide Drake slowly to the leather couch she'd seen in the parlor, but no amount of her CrossFit training would enable her to lift his 180-plus pounds of dead weight that distance. All she could hope to do was slow his descent and protect his head.

She crumpled with him to the floor, keeping her arms and legs beneath him in the hope of cushioning his fall. They crashed onto the hardwood floor with a thump that shook the tiny table in the entryway, making the Tiffany lamp on top teeter precariously.

She had just enough time to duck her head against Drake, shielding both their faces as the multicolored glass shade smashed into pieces just a foot away.

When she was sure the worst was over, Kate opened her eyes. Her left leg was underneath her at an uncomfortable angle, but it wasn't broken, and while the rest of her body felt bruised and squished, she was okay. Glass shards lay on the floor about three feet away, catching enough rays of dim light from the window in the door to glitter dully. Sasha gave one startled bark, then was quiet.

Drake lay on top of her, his big body entangled with hers, his weight pressing her into the floorboards in a very unromantic way. His head had mercifully landed against her shoulder, and they were pressed so close together, she felt the reassuring beat of his heart against her chest, and his breath tickled the hair at her neck. Her client was breathing. He was alive.

"Thank God," she whispered. "I didn't kill Drake Matthews."

She lay there, thinking about how she was going to revive her client without smelling salts, when a knock came at the door behind her.

Sasha's bark sounded excitedly from the parlor, and Kate could hear the dog's little collar tags jingling as if she were jumping against the bars of the crate.

"Hello?" A chirpy woman's voice came from behind the old wood door. "It's Imani!"

Kate held Drake's head to her as she craned her neck around to see the front door. Her friend's silhouette showed through the door's frosted glass panel.

"Mr. Matthews? Drake? Are you okay?" Kate asked, first jostling the writer with her hand, then shaking him by twitching her whole body in an attempt to revive him. But he didn't move.

With effort, she straightened out her leg, leaving her still trapped but now spread-eagled under the world's most infamous horror writer. While the position was a bit more comfortable, it could have been the picture above a caption reading *Super Awkward*.

Luckily, Imani wouldn't judge.

"Dra-aake? Kaaa-te?" Imani pounded on the door

again. "Sorry I'm late, but I brought along a bii-iiig surprise."

"C'mon in, Imani," Kate called. "We've got a...bit of a surprise for you too."

The door opened, and Imani breezed in, impeccably dressed in a white tunic-style top paired with black palazzo pants, matching heels, and an ornate, geometric belt under her burnt-orange trench coat. Her signature red lipstick looked freshly applied, and her long chestnut hair had the perfectly coifed look Kate's had lacked in this weather. As always, she was armed with her massive black Mary Poppins bag, and she looked prepared for anything.

"I'm so glad you're here." Kate arched her neck to give her friend a relieved smile...and then she froze.

Her best friend wasn't alone.

Next to Imani stood an older white man in his mid-fifties, carrying a cane and wearing a black overcoat. The man's thinning salt-and-pepper hair was barely mussed from the rainstorm outside, and his signature handlebar mustache was perfectly waxed, the ends turned up like a smile above his lips. With the cane he always carried, he looked like a trim, updated version of the guy on the Monopoly board.

Evan Everstone.

Kate had never wished for the earth to open up beneath her more fervently than she did right now. Standing two feet from her was the "it" Hollywood producer, known primarily for his special effects and blockbuster films. He also happened to be the star judge for the annual EVPLEX awards—the award she'd been striving for since starting her business five years ago.

And here she was, trapped under the Knight of Nightmares.

Evan's eyes widened as his gaze traveled from Drake's prostrate form, her spread legs under him, and finally the blush burning up Kate's cheeks.

"Oh, my," he said, turning to Imani. His fingers twisted the ends of his mustache in a rapid gesture that looked more like a tic than like grooming. "Should we, perhaps, come back at a better time?"

Imani opened her mouth, but all that came out was a warbled, distressed noise, like a cat whose tail had been half stepped upon.

Realizing that the ground wasn't going to swallow her and she had no other way to escape, Kate offered a weak smile to the two standing in the doorway.

"Surprise!" She grinned like a maniac at her best friend and the judge who could single-handedly give her an EVPLEX on a gilded platter. "Apparently, my book launch idea was so amazing, it knocked him out. Literally."

Sasha chose that time to renew her barking, the sound of her paws jangling the door of her metal cage illustrating her eagerness to be part of whatever fun was happening in the entryway. At the dog's barking, Imani recovered, hurrying to close the door behind them and turning the bolt for good measure. She rushed to Kate, shushing the dog on the way, and dropped to her knees, smelling of rain and rose-scented perfume. Imani's hands hovered over her client's body, as if to yank him up.

"Be careful. He's bleeding," Kate said, and Imani froze, her chocolate eyes wide. "Don't worry, though. He's not dead. He just looks that way."

"What in the world happened here?" Imani asked. "Did he hurt you?"

"No, nothing like that. It was an accident, but I'm fine. Just squished. I don't dare move him in case he whacked his head on the wall before I caught him. Or tried to catch him," Kate said, a little breathless from explaining the inexplicable under the watchful gaze of the world's most famous movie producer. "See, he fainted. Sort of unexpectedly."

"Should we call for some, erm, help?" Evan asked, spinning slightly around as if hoping help would arrive from either the parlor or the front door. Hanging his cane on his wrist, he reached into his overcoat, pulling out a cell phone. "Maybe a doctor?"

Just then, Drake's breathing changed tempo and he sighed, mumbling incoherently.

"No, I think he's coming to," Kate said. She reached around the writer's broad shoulders, shaking him slightly. "Drake? Mr. Matthews?"

The writer groaned, shifting his weight on top of her. Lifting his bleeding arm, he rubbed his face but didn't sit up. "Mmph. Wh-what happened? Where's . . . glasses?"

"I think they fell off, but we'll find them," Kate said, then shifted her attention to Imani. "He's got a pretty nasty cut on his arm, but I don't think he'll need an ambulance. Let's let him come to and get him cleaned up. There are some first-aid supplies in the bathroom down the hall."

Imani sprang into action, her long legs easily side-stepping the debris. "Of course. And I'll get a broom to clean up this mess so nobody cuts themselves."

"Watch your step," Evan said, grabbing Imani before

she could crush the black-framed glasses on the floor next to the wall. Using his cane to brush shards from the Tiffany lamp out of the way, he stepped over Kate's and Drake's bodies to scoop up the specs, peering at them in the dim light. "The bow is broken at the hinge. I'll go check the kitchen to see if our Mr. Matthews has any tool sets lying around, and we'll see if we can salvage these. Unless you need me here?"

Drake moved on top of Kate, his arms and legs beginning to take some of his own weight, allowing her to take the first full breath she'd had since falling to the floor.

"No. We're fine. He's coming to."

Without waiting for any other assurances, Evan beat a hasty retreat down the entrance hall, disappearing through the swinging door behind her best friend just as Drake lifted his head from her neck. His face had a sleepy quality to it, and his striking amber eyes blinked as they focused on her. In this close proximity, without the glasses hiding them, she could see the little flecks of black and green in their bronze depth, and his pupils—both the same size, she was glad to note—dilated as he gazed down at her. Although he'd lifted most of his weight onto his forearms, Kate's breath caught as he used his uninjured hand to brush an errant lock of hair from her forehead, smoothing it back, his touch deliberate and slow. Kate's heart picked up tempo as those amber eyes followed the movement of his hand in her hair. Then he cupped the side of her cheek, his thumb brushing something gently from under her eye.

"Are you okay?"

"Am I okay?" Kate asked, her voice barely above a whisper. His gentle touch had unnerved her, reminding her how long it had been since anyone had caressed her like that. Too long, judging by her body's immediate and eager response. Kate stumbled to put things back on their appropriate, and professional, track. "Th-that's my line. Are *you* okay?"

Drake's eyebrows drew together in confusion, and she felt his words vibrating from his chest as he spoke, deep and low.

"I...don't want you to take this the wrong way," he began, looking at their bodies, then squinting at the glass and the toppled lamp base around them. Meeting her eyes, he smiled crookedly, finishing his sentence. "But I can't seem to remember how I ended up...here. Not that I'm complaining."

Kate wasn't sure what to do with her hands. Oh, she knew what she *wanted* to do with them. She wanted to wrap them around his broad shoulders, yank him down to her, and see if those soft, sensual lips tasted as good as they looked. But she was supposed to be working *for* him, not *under* him, so she patted him awkwardly on the back again, ignoring the crazy signals her body was throwing out there.

"Well, um, you sort of passed out. On me. And I tried to catch you to make sure you didn't...die...and we ended up like this." Kate gestured to their bodies.

Drake winced. Slowly, he took his weight to his knees and sat up, holding his arm against his chest. Kate moved to sit up as soon as he did, and was surprised by how strange it felt to have his weight lifted from her. Strange...and sort of bereft, like she'd gotten used to his warmth and the woodsy smell of him, and with it taken away, she'd just now noticed the chill of her rain-damp body. She adjusted her disheveled skirt, but since he was still sitting, she made no move to stand amidst the glass.

"Okay," Drake said, "it's all coming back now. I leaned over to pick the button up off the floor, and you stabbed me with your shoes—"

"Accidentally," Kate put in.

"—accidentally," Drake amended, but raised an eyebrow as if he doubted her words. "And when I went to clean off my arm—"

"You saw the blood and you passed out," Kate finished. "I tried to get you to a couch, but we didn't make it. After stabbing you, the least I could do was save you from cracking your head open."

A hint of a smile replaced the grimace on his face.

"Fine. You saved me. After you filleted me open with those killer heels, you saved me, and since I saved you from an attack of the deadly shih tzu, I guess that makes us even. We are true heroes."

An unexpected laugh burst from Kate's mouth.

"Yeah. And we both seem to have a knack for drawing a crowd at the least opportune time." Her face reddened at the memory. "Your neighbor saw more of me than I intended, and with your unexpected visitor—"

Drake's gaze sharpened. "What do you mean?"

Just then, Evan burst through the swinging door, brandishing his cane in one hand and a pair of black-framed glasses in the other.

"Well, my dear Mr. Matthews, we have fixed your glasses at last!"

Drake turned to her with a wounded, almost betrayed expression, reminding her of how he'd looked on that YouTube video when his date—that Rachel woman—had told him she was tired of always coming in second to his books.

Before Kate could say anything to reassure Drake that she'd had nothing to do with any visitors, he stood, swaying only slightly, and put a hand out to help her up, using his boots to swish away the glass next to her bare feet. He avoided her gaze and dropped her hand once she was steady.

Kate brushed herself off, feeling awkward in the movie producer's hawk-eyed scrutiny, and was relieved when Evan's attention focused on the writer once more.

"I'm afraid there are some scratches on your lens, but we were able to get the bow straightened around," Evan said, holding the glasses up to the light of the chandelier to inspect his work. "Lucky for you, Imani had a tool kit in her purse. Can you imagine that? Ms. Lewis is a woman to have at your side if there ever really is a zombie apocalypse."

As if on cue, Imani flew through the swinging door into the hallway with a towel and a broom. Her innate grace, honed by decades of taking and then teaching dance classes, made her maneuvers around the glass-strewn hallway appear like an elaborate bit of choreography.

Drake took the clean towel she offered him and wound it around his left arm, nodding his thanks. From Kate's vantage point, the gash seemed to have stopped bleeding, and inwardly, she breathed a sigh of relief.

Imani cleared her throat. "Maybe I should find you some gauze, or bandages, or something?"

"No, I'm good." Drake finished wrapping the wound and dipped his head toward his publicist with a ghost of a smile. "Nice to see you again, Imani. I'd offer to shake your hand, but..."

When Drake turned toward Evan, Kate noticed the writer's expression had transformed to more of a teeth-baring gesture.

"Evan," Drake said with a curt nod. He accepted the pair of black-framed glasses from the older man and slipped them up the bridge of his nose, one-handed. Once his glasses were on, it was like Drake donned a suit of armor. His earlier smiling banter with Kate was miles away. "To what do I owe the...pleasure...of your company this morning?"

"I ran into the amazing Imani in LA," Evan said. "She was updating me on your publisher's new book launch–movie adaptation announcement plans, and since I had some open time on my schedule, I thought I'd fly in and hear them for myself from your new point person."

Kate pinned a smile to her face when the movie producer glanced her way, but he apparently didn't expect a verbal response, as he continued with barely a breath of a pause.

"With what your publisher's marketing team has planned, the lead-up to this event will be like chumming the waters. We can gin up your fan base about the movie adaptation, and really take advantage of all this free press."

"That's what you and your people do best—take advantage." Drake scowled first at Evan, then Imani, and then—to Kate's horror—he scowled at her, as if she were in on this group visit.

Evan gave a full-bellied laugh, as if Drake had cracked a joke, but Kate sensed it was just a cover.

Clapping the writer on the back, the older man steered Drake around the glass shards in the hallway and into the parlor.

"Let's get you by the fire. With all that's going on, your nerves must be frazzled. You got anything to drink in here?"

Drake mumbled a response, and their voices faded as Imani quickly swept the glass into the corner and propped the broom against the doorway to the parlor. She grabbed Kate's arm, marching her in the opposite direction.

"What. In the hell. Happened?" Imani's hand tightened incrementally with each word until her grip felt like a tourniquet.

"Everything terrible! That's what happened!" Kate hissed, allowing herself to be dragged into Drake's tiny powder room, where she pulled free as Imani closed the door behind them. "I was like a living embodiment of Murphy's law from the moment I stepped inside the gates."

At the sight of Kate's distress, her best friend's face softened.

"It's not all bad, I'm sure." Imani snagged the last clean towel from the cabinet and dampened the edge with hot water from the faucet. She positioned Kate in front of the mirror, dabbed at her face, then put the towel down. "Tell me about it while we get you cleaned up."

Kate caught sight of her reflection in the mirror and groaned. Her makeup looked like she'd slept in it. For a month. And her hair! She frantically tried to collect the snarled mess in both hands and then realized she didn't even have a rubber band to pull it all back.

"Oh my God, I am a walking nightmare. You should fire me. Right now before something worse happens." Kate turned from her reflection to snatch at the doorknob, but Imani blocked her escape, stepping neatly in the way while unbuttoning her trench coat and reaching into an inside pocket.

"I think you might be exaggerating." Imani pulled out a black hair tie with two fingers, and Kate reluctantly took it and began wrestling her hair into submission.

"I can't believe I blew it. You seriously won't hurt my feelings if you take me off the launch. I'll go in and apologize and then help you find someone else."

Imani rolled her eyes. "Don't be weird. It can't have been that bad—you've only been here, what? A half hour? Forty minutes, tops. I'm sure we can salvage this...just as soon as we clean you up. Here. Let's trade—your skirt is ripped so far up the back, I can almost determine when you had your last Brazilian."

Kate released a stream of profanities under her breath, her hand automatically clutching the skirt closed, even though they were still in the bathroom. She allowed Imani to help her out of her wet, dog-stamped, buttonless jacket and into her friend's burnt-orange trench, cinching it tight to cover her exposed bits.

Imani folded the bad-luck jacket, setting it on the closed toilet lid. Her red lips curved into a smile. "There. Now you look like the Kate Sweet we all know and love. The best event planner in the business. The gal who puts the pro in professional. The Queen of Happily Ever Afters!"

"Not today." Kate shooed away the pep talk. "Look at me! I wore the only black suit I owned because I read online that he prefers black. This suit was too tight, so my buttons popped off, and then I accidentally stabbed him with my heels—"

"Wait. You stabbed him with your heels?" Imani's face was taut with concern. "Were you defending yourself? Drake has always been a perfect gentleman. I've never even heard of him being disrespectful of anyone, but if he touched you, I'll make sure he never—"

"No! He didn't touch me!" Kate soothed, patting the air between them with both hands in a calm-down gesture. "Well, except when he had his hand on my bottom in his yard when I was trying to get away from his dog. He wasn't being unprofessional, though—it was the only place he could hold on when I climbed him."

Imani squinted, shaking her head. "I can't figure out what you're telling me, Katie. You...climbed Drake Matthews? Because of Sasha?"

She nodded, miserable. "Saturday afternoon when we were on the phone, the connection cut out as you were trying to warn me about something terrifying. When I heard Sasha bark at me from the bushes, I thought you meant his Doberman—the one from the YouTube video. So, I panicked. I scaled him like a freaking koala on a eucalyptus tree!"

"Wow. That was disturbingly specific." Imani chuckled. "I'm sorry—I didn't realize you hadn't heard me. All I said was watch out for the fans who gather around his house—they're like stalkers and can be terrifying in their zeal to get an autograph. His Doberman, Cade, passed away a few years ago. Look, I'm sure if we go back and talk with him, we can—"

Suddenly, there was a knock at the powder room

door. Kate's heart leaped in her throat. Had Drake heard her whole whining fit? Had he been witness to even this embarrassing moment?

"Ladies?"

Worse than Drake. It was Evan. The man who held her future EVPLEX in his proverbial hand had likely just eavesdropped on her meltdown.

Kate wanted to die.

Imani put a hand on Kate's arm. "Sorry, Evan. Give us one more second here, and we'll be out to join you both."

"No rush. No rush at all, because I'm afraid to say that he's left. And, erm…" Evan cleared his throat again, and Kate could envision him giving a nervous twirl to the ends of his mustache. "…he fired us."

"He fired us?" Imani spluttered, throwing open the powder room door. "*All* of us?"

One of Hollywood's most famous film producers stared back at them—his face and shirt wet, and his mustache drooping, stuck to the sides of his face. He looked like he'd been out in the rain, but only the front of him was wet, and he smelled like whiskey.

He fingered his damp mustache, and then dropped his hand, nodding with a sigh.

"His exact words were, 'There will be no next book, no movie, and no book launch. I'm done with all of you. Let yourselves out, and don't come back.'"

CHAPTER 5

All right, I don't know about you, but after that debacle, I'm in dire need of a coffee and something decadent." Imani tugged Kate out of the hotel where, after depositing Evan in his suite, Kate had changed out of her bad-luck suit and into a Tiffany-blue sweater and a pair of jeans. Imani had called the office to talk to her boss—Trisha Cabot, the head of sales and marketing—so she could explain what happened. But she learned that Trisha had to go in for an emergency root canal and would be out all day.

Kate had never been so thankful for tooth decay in her whole life.

"You're one of the most clever, resourceful people I know," she had reassured Imani. "And I'm sure we can come up with something to fix this."

Imani gnawed at the inside of her lip. "You're right. If we can figure this out before Trisha is back in the office tomorrow, then my update will be simple: we had a crisis. It's managed. And if we can't fix it..."

"Then, I'll call Trisha myself and explain it was all

my fault. I'll step down, get you someone else, and still help you in the wings. For free. No way am I letting my best friend be fired." Kate hugged Imani to her, planting a loud kiss on her cheek.

Now, three hours later, if Kate hadn't been so jacked up with adrenaline from their brainstorming session, she might've done like Drake Matthews and fainted from nerves as she trailed Imani out of the hotel. How did she screw things up so royally? She was the responsible one. The one who created detailed plans to avoid failure at any cost, and here she'd blown it so spectacularly, she might have cost her best friend her job!

"What kind of arctic wormhole did we enter?" Kate asked, shivering as they trotted down the uneven sidewalk, headed away from their hotel and toward the four blocks that composed the entire "downtown" area. "It's only the first week of October, and this place might be shoveling snow by tomorrow? It's ridiculous."

Suddenly, Imani's phone trilled. When she checked the readout, she halted so abruptly, Kate faltered on the icy sidewalk, almost falling for the second time that day.

"What is it?" Kate asked, gripping her friend's arm to steady herself as she peered over her shoulder.

Imani used her teeth to pry the glove off her hand to activate her phone readout. "Drake replied to my apology email."

Kate's heart thudded in her chest. "What does he say?"

Imani's brown eyes darted back and forth as she read, her cherry red lips moving silently. When she finished, she exhaled, tipping her head to the sky, letting the snow melt on her face.

"It says he's sorry he kicked us out, and he didn't mean to say I was fired. He said there's a past with Everstone I couldn't have known about, and he's willing to listen to my ideas for a launch but will no longer promise to commit. And…there's some other stuff. But the point is, he's willing to discuss things with me. Isn't that great?"

"Oh, thank goodness." Kate hugged her friend so tightly she squealed. "What time will we meet him tomorrow, then? I want to have several ideas, so in case he kills the haunted house, we'll have a few solid backup plans."

Imani pulled away, fidgeting with her impressively messy-yet-every-hair-in-place bun.

"Well, here's the thing…Drake didn't exactly say he wanted to…um, I mean he sort of alluded to…"

"To what?" Kate asked, moving out of the way as a woman carrying a huge pink bakery box passed them on the sidewalk. The smell of vanilla and baked goods wafted out, but Kate was too focused on her best friend's face to care.

"He said *I'm* not fired. He didn't say anything about Evan. Or you."

Kate blinked in astonishment. "What? Are you saying that he reconsidered firing you, but he doesn't mean to un-fire me?"

Imani's face took on a queasy expression—the look she always got when put in a position where there might be conflict.

"Well, I think he might need some time, Katie, before we bring you back on the project. Thing is…" Imani winced as if expecting a blow, and Kate braced herself. "Drake is still 'undecided' about having a launch at all, after hearing your ideas. He's...well, he's going to call his agent to see if he can get out of the launch part of the contract altogether."

"Oh." Kate's heart sank to her toes. Although it stung her ego to be fired from the project, it gutted her to think her best friend's job working with Cerulean's top clients might be in serious jeopardy. All because of her.

Noticing Kate's expression, Imani tugged her hand, steering them both down the town's tiny Main Street toward a promising sign that read *PattyCakes and Coffee*.

"Don't freak out. I'm sure Drake will come around. Give me a couple of days with him. Maybe a week. Then he'll be back on board with the best event professional in the business."

Her best friend grinned with confidence, but Kate saw a glimmer of doubt behind her expression.

"I'm so sorry I've put you in this position," Kate repeated for the millionth time since leaving Drake's Victorian. "I'll do whatever it takes. He doesn't have to know I'm helping you."

Imani pushed open the door to PattyCakes and Coffee, releasing an aroma of baked goods so heavenly, both women paused to inhale deeply, saying "Mmmm" in unison.

"It'll be fine, Katie, I promise. Let's treat ourselves to something sweet enough to put us both in a sugar coma for the rest of the day. What do you say?"

Kate gave a wan smile, swallowing the bile in her throat as they approached the front counter. The café wasn't as small as she'd expected from the street, extending far enough to allow for several tables. The bakery had a cute 1950s décor, with black and white tiles done on the floor in a diagonal, as well as vintage-inspired red Formica tables and chairs. It looked like something from that old sitcom *Happy Days*. Lining the walls were vintage photographs of various people and buildings—presumably things from Wellsville's past.

They headed to the back to order, and Kate's mouth watered at the selection of treats in the curved, glass-encased counter. The smell of cinnamon, vanilla, and sugary goodness made Kate's stomach rumble, reminding her she hadn't eaten in hours.

"Welcome to PattyCakes," said a woman with snapping blue eyes and salt-and-pepper hair done in a straight, chin-length bob. She stood in a frilly pink apron behind the counter, giving them a sparkling smile. "I'm Patty, and this is my place. Are you two from out of town? Would you like me to go over my specials for fall?"

Imani nodded, and after listening to the myriad of options, they both decided on chai tea lattes and a pumpkin-and-ginger–spiced cupcake called the "Pumpkin Maniac." They took a table at the side of the mostly empty café to wait for their order, and just as they'd wrestled out of their coats and sat down, Imani's cell phone dinged.

"It's Evan," Imani said, standing up. "He bought a flight out of Buffalo to LA tonight and needs a ride to the airport. I'm summoned to come and pick him up. Now."

Kate groaned. "But we need to finish brainstorming a few more ideas for this launch. Isn't that a bigger priority? Can't Mr. Everstone rent his own car and drive himself?"

Imani barked a laugh. "First, Evan is my boss's VIP, and if I screw up that relationship too, I might as well resign. Second, the guy is constantly on his phone, working. He'd never willingly give up two hours of productivity to do something as mundane as driving. Besides, I can use the time to smooth things over with him and Drake before either of them quit on the movie adaptation of *Halloween Hacker*. We can't lose Evan Everstone—his name is like Hollywood gold, as you very well know, my EVPLEX-seeking friend."

Kate blew out a breath, sagging into her seat. "Fine. But I'm eating your cupcake."

Imani laughed, sliding on her leather gloves.

"It'll be late by the time I get him on his flight, so I think I'll crash in Buffalo and drive back early tomorrow. I'll call you once I'm checked in, and we'll button up our approach options, and I'll send them in an email to Drake tonight. Then, if we haven't heard from him by morning, I can swing over to his place on my way back into town and..."

"Offer me as a willing sacrifice?" Kate gave a grimace-smile.

"Drake is a reasonable guy, so I'm sure he'll come around about the launch and about you." Imani rolled her coffee-colored eyes at Kate's skeptical expression. "Trust me. I've known him for a while and I can tell: he's one of the good ones."

Kate waved Imani off with a smile. "Don't worry about me. Focus on saving yourself from the mess I got you into. Drive safely, and I'll talk to you later."

With Imani gone, the whole weight of her idiocy crashed in on Kate, and she stared at the tiny boomerang shapes on the vintage, chrome-lined table, racking her brain for ways to fix this debacle.

"Did your friend have an emergency and have to leave?" asked a woman's voice at her side.

Kate jumped as Patty deposited two steaming cups of fragrant tea and two cupcakes, each on a beautiful chintz plate, in front of Kate. "I can put the tea in a to-go cup and box up that extra cupcake, if you'd like?"

"Oh, thanks, but she'll be gone for the night." Kate sat up straighter and blinked away the tears she hadn't realized were right there. "Wow. These smell delicious! What a great name too. Who doesn't want a 'Pumpkin Maniac' cupcake in their life?"

A smile wreathed the woman's pink-cheeked face.

"They are Drake Matthews's favorite cupcakes, after all, so we figured they ought to be aptly named. Next to snickerdoodles, it's the only other baked good he eats. He always says it's the salty snacks that are his downfall, not the sweet ones."

Kate pasted a smile on her face, although the mention of the author's name brought with it a wave of anger and despair, in equal measure. "Is he in here often, then?"

The woman tilted her head, considering. "Hardly ever. But his picture is everywhere, so it feels like he's here more often than he actually is, I guess."

The woman's gaze had drifted to a framed photo on the wall a few feet above Kate's head. Looking up, Kate was surprised to see she'd been sitting underneath a photo of Drake, smiling and posed next to a full book-shelf. Summoning a pleasant expression, Kate cleared her throat.

"Must be a pretty fantastic cupcake to pass muster with Drake Matthews. He seemed very particular about what he'd give his approval to when I met him. I assume you know him, then, being that he lives a few miles away?"

The woman smiled, her right eyebrow raising a fraction. "Of course. Everyone here knows Drake. Or at least, they think they do. You met him recently?"

Kate nodded, unable to keep the grimace off her mouth.

"I sort of made an idiot of myself earlier today while in his presence. Accidentally, of course, but it doesn't matter anymore. Anyway, I'm sure the cupcake is going to be a bomb dessert if he's approved it. Thanks so much!"

Kate meant the last to be a subtle dismissal of the shop's owner. But instead of taking the hint, she sat in Imani's seat, cupping her chin in her hands with the manner of someone settling down to hear a good story.

"I can't leave until you have some," she finally said. "I hardly ever get anyone new in here, and I like to know I haven't lost my touch. Besides, nothing in this world is so bad that a good cupcake can't fix it, if only for a while. Go on, try it!"

When it became clear the woman with her frilly pink apron wouldn't leave until she'd witnessed a bite, Kate peeled away the wrapper and nibbled at the mountain of white frosting. Her mouth flooded with the decadent taste of thick cream cheese—not the buttercream she'd expected—and Kate moaned, opening wider for the second bite.

"Mmm!" Kate closed her eyes to savor the flavors

of pumpkin and spices on her tongue. The cake was the perfect consistency—not too dense or too moist—and the smooth frosting provided enough cream cheese goodness to cut the sweetness. "This is outstanding!"

Patty clapped her hands in pleasure.

"All right, I'll leave you to finish in peace. Did you want me to box this up for your friend, then?"

"Nah. Leave it," Kate managed around another mouthful of pumpkin cupcake. "I'm going to finish hers too. This is literally the best thing that's happened to me. All. Day. Long."

The truth of the statement hit her hard then, and even with a lump of delicious dessert in her mouth, her chin began to wobble. The day's stress chose that time to unload its baggage, and first one tear fell from her eye, then another, and before Kate realized what was happening, she was bawling right in the middle of the café, all over her dessert.

"I'm so s-s-s-sorry," Kate stuttered through her tears, finally swallowing down the mouthful of cupcake before she choked, as the mass of it battled the lump in her throat. "I don't know what's gotten into m-me. I don't mean to cause a scene!"

She snatched napkins from the table's dispenser, burying her face in them so the woman wouldn't see her cry. Other girls could pull off crying and still look lovely.

Kate knew she wasn't one of those women.

Albeit infrequently, when the tears came, so did the blotchy red skin on her neck and cheeks—the bane of every redhead on Earth—and her eyes would be as red-rimmed and bloodshot as one of those African tree frogs for the rest of the night.

"Oh, my dear," came the woman's voice at the same time as a gentle pat on Kate's arm. "Please don't worry about it. It's just you and me left. Everyone knows I close at four p.m. Let me lock the front door, and you can take as long as you'd like to collect yourself. Nobody will be the wiser."

Kate picked her head up enough to confirm the café was, indeed, empty. At some point while she'd been moping, all up in her own feelings, the rest of the customers had left. Kate wiped her eyes and nose on a few more of the napkins and fanned her face, blinking fiercely as she took deep breaths to get hold of her emotions. By the time Patty flipped the sign to *Closed* and twisted the shades shut on the big plate-glass windows, Kate's breath had stopped that stupid cry-hitching thing it did whenever she broke down.

"Now," the woman said, bustling back to retake her seat across the table, "this place may look like a cupcake shop, but I can tell you it doubles as a counselor's office, think-tank, and an all-purpose battle station, when necessary. You look like you need someone to talk to, and I'm always looking for a reason to delay doing the dishes. So why don't you say we help each other out, and you finish your cupcake while you tell me what's got you so worked up?"

Ordinarily, Kate would never have talked to a complete stranger about anything more than the random comments about the weather she might make to people on the subway. But here, in this tiny town, in this quaint, homey shop, with this sweet, well-meaning woman, Kate found herself wanting to unburden herself of the weight of today's rotten start. Patty reminded her of

her late mentor, Maya. Minus the apron, of course—
Maya was like Kate with her lack of culinary skills.
It was more in Patty's demeanor: calm, collected, and
filled with a genuine concern for others' happiness—
that drew her to the café owner.

Pointing with her fork to the picture of Drake,
she began.

"It all started with this guy, and I can't give you the
details, but my job involved planning an event—"

"His book launch." Patty filled in the blank, smiling. "We all know about the upcoming release. It's on
Halloween, his favorite holiday."

"Right." Kate nodded miserably. "And to make
a long story short, I did my research online and
believed... well, a bunch of stuff I shouldn't have."

"Such as?" Patty's right eyebrow raised in that subtly
challenging gesture.

Kate ducked her head.

"He wasn't anything I'd prepared for. I thought he'd
be this... angsty, darkly mysterious guy who... I don't
know, dressed in steampunk garb, complete with some
Gothic cape. I prepared this whole over-the-top scary
launch for a writer I'd pictured as the brooding Heath-
cliff character from—"

"*Wuthering Heights*," Patty finished, a side of her
mouth quirking up at the corner. "But then, you met
him, and..."

The woman clearly expected her to fill in the gap.
Why not tell her the whole tale? It's not like it probably
wouldn't be all over this small town soon, anyway—
how she'd practically accosted the man, then gotten
tossed from his house.

"He's not like that at all. So, I made a total ass of

myself and blew a great opportunity. That I can handle. But I might have gotten my best friend, his publicist, in some hot water, and her career may take a hit unless I can convince him to be on board with some much more laid-back version of a book launch. But after what happened this morning at his house, he'd sic the rest of his dogs on me if I were to come back and beg for Imani's job. I wouldn't blame him after I accidentally gouged his arm with my dumb shoes and the sight of his own blood made him woozy."

The woman's eyes bugged out. "Oh, my."

Kate sensed more tears threatening, and she put down her fork to fan her face again, nodding.

"Yeah. 'Oh, my' just about sums it up. He's okay, I think. I caught him when he fainted and made sure he didn't hit his head or anything going down. But when he was passed out on me, he was seen by..." Kate caught herself before revealing the movie producer's name, shaking her head. "...someone important in that compromising position, and I guess it must have embarrassed him, because soon after that while I was cleaning up in the bathroom, he got really angry and fired us all. I didn't prepare for this event proposal, like I should have, and I have only my stupidity to blame for my failure."

"I don't think you're stupid, Miss—um, what did you say your name was?"

Kate hadn't said, but she shrugged. What difference did her name make at this point?

"It's Kate," she said. "Kate Sweet, and I own Sweet Events—the company that was previously handling the launch."

"Well, Kate." Patty slid her chair up closer and

tucked one side of her salt-and-pepper hair behind her ear. "I happen to know the Matthews family. Very well. And I know that while they aren't perfect, not by a long shot, they are decent people. I don't think it's a lost cause for either your friend or for you."

"You're so kind," Kate said, giving the woman a watery smile. "Thanks for listening, and I'm sorry about all the waterworks. I'm not normally like this. In fact, I'm not *ever* like this. It's been such a day. Such a horrible, nightmarish day."

"If there's one thing I know, it's nightmares and how to cure them," Patty said, untying her apron strings and setting the pink material on the table, gazing thoughtfully around the café. After a moment, she got up and skirted behind a nearby table, plucking three framed pictures from the wall and bringing them back to Kate, where she slid them next to the crumb-covered plates. "I think this might be the answer to you and your nightmare."

Frowning in confusion, Kate stared at the pictures. One was a grainy, black-and-white photo of two men in camouflage, and the other two were in color, one more recent than the other. She examined the most recent photo. It was Drake, complete with his black glasses, standing in between two taller men, all of them in Marine dress blues. Drake's arms were thrown around both of their shoulders. She didn't recognize the tall, blond guys with him, but they all looked impossibly young to be serving their country. Kate noticed the date inscribed at the bottom was from ten years earlier.

"I didn't know Drake Matthews served in the

Marines," Kate said, peering at his young face. Having met the man, she noticed the years had added only a few lines by his eyes—he basically looked the same.

"It's in his DNA. He and his brothers followed in their father's footsteps, and their grandfather's before them." Patty nodded and then pointed to the older, black-and-white picture. "This is Drake's great-grandfather, Hawthorne Matthews, the man who built the house that's still owned by the family. Standing next to him is Drake's grandfather, Hawthorne Matthews Jr. Funny story: these two presented themselves at the recruiter's office together, four days after Junior's eighteenth birthday, to sign up for the war together in 1941."

"Wow," Kate said, then looked at the third picture. It was color, but faded with age, of a middle-aged man dressed in a Marine uniform, sitting ramrod straight. He held a baby on his lap and his chair was flanked by two small boys. "Is this...Drake's father, then?"

Patty nodded, cocking her head at the picture and pointing to the older-looking boy with the dark hair and serious eyes. "Yes, and that's Drake right there. You may not know this from your internet research, but Drake sponsors several county-wide veterans' shelters and other groups that aid our veteran population. I think the answer to your problem might be to change Drake's mind through where he feels it most—his heart, and through the things he loves."

Kate's eyes lit up. "So, if I can figure out a way his launch might benefit veterans, you think he'll change his mind?"

Patty smiled, using her apron to wipe the finger smudges from the pictures before hanging them carefully on the wall again. "I can't promise anything, but I believe this boy has a good heart, and he's always looking for ways to raise awareness for wounded veterans."

Inspiration struck, and Kate pulled out her phone.

"Excuse me for one second, Patty. I'm about to call in some favors."

CHAPTER 6

Drake slumped against the leather couch in the front room. He stared at the fire, focusing on Sasha's puppy snore as she lay zonked out on her favorite plaid blanket next to him. He envied her ability to sleep through all sorts of shouting matches—like the one his brothers were now waging. Over him. Or rather, over what he should have done to Evan Everstone instead of throwing a drink at him.

"You drink the alcohol first, *then* throw the glass," Zander said, shaking his shaggy surfer locks in disappointment as he poured three glasses of whiskey at the makeshift bar on top of Nana's old tea cart. Although technically the baby of the Matthews boys, Zander towered over them all at six foot five. "Haven't I taught you anything?"

"Someone should kick that cane out from under Everstone and make him stand on his own perfectly good feet for once in his life," Ryker said as he accepted the drink from Zander and plopped down on the couch next to the dog, giving her a pat when she snorted awake.

Ryker, the middle Matthews boy, with his younger brother's blond, blue-eyed looks and his older brother's drive and ambition, was a perfect combination. The only one of the boys to do more than one tour as a Marine, Ryker was following in the footsteps of their late father and grandfather before him, becoming an officer, and had planned to serve until retirement.

Until one hot day in Afghanistan when he'd been the loser in a showdown with an IED.

The medics saved his life.

But they couldn't save his leg. Or his career.

Ryker had been medically discharged, destroying his lifelong ambition and leaving in its place a nagging phantom itch for a career so brutally ripped from his grasp.

"You had the perfect chance to settle the score with the dude who convinced your ex-snake Rachel to publish that trash about you, and you blew it!" Zander made a fist in frustration, splashing whiskey on Ryker in the process.

Ryker cursed, glaring thunderously at Zander as he wiped off his shirt. Then he hefted the heel of his metal, spring-like, titanium prosthesis onto Nana's antique table, crossing his legs. "Zan's right. Throwing a drink is a rookie move. Next time, give him a good, solid punch, right between the running lights, and knock some sense into that lying, lady-thieving loser."

"Alliteration—pretty impressive," Drake said.

Zander whistled. "Watch it, or you're going to blow your rep as the Grease Monkey to the Car Gods," he said, alluding to Ryker's day job as a classic car restoration and customization mechanic. "Now get your Terminator leg off Nana's antique table, or else—"

"Or else what?" Ryker challenged, a gleam in his blue eyes. "You've been spending too much time breathing in the paint fumes in your art studio, and too little time in the gym to be chest-thumping with me. I'll put you on your ass."

Ryker's go-to tease for his younger brother's über-successful ceramics art chain struck a nerve, and just like that, it turned into a scrum. The two youngest Matthews brothers jockeyed for position on the couch, shoving and wrestling good-naturedly, like two bear cubs.

Sasha jumped down from the couch to avoid being crushed, shaking her coat and barking at the ruckus, while Drake leaned out of the way, protecting his drink and chuckling.

Despite his crap morning, Drake's mood lifted, as it always did around his brothers—the two people in the world he trusted most. They'd arrived in Zander's tiny Prius—what their mom termed the "Clown Car" for how the large men piled out of it, like performers in a circus—only ten minutes after Drake had left the walk-in medical clinic. Their timely arrival led Drake to assume someone in town had seen him and called to tattle. His brothers were ostensibly here for a social visit, but Drake knew they wanted the skinny on why their typically rattle-proof brother tossed two women and a billionaire out of his house and ended up with a gouge on his arm that required a trip to the clinic to close.

As if reading his mind, his younger brothers finally settled down onto the leather sofa, their drinks remarkably intact. Then, using some sort of bro-lepathy, they fixed their blue eyes on Drake, asking questions in rapid fire.

"Dude, why'd you fire that gorgeous publicist of yours? Imani seemed pretty amazing." Zander brushed his shaggy hair out of his face, only slightly out of breath from the couch wrestling match. He gave a wicked grin. "You should introduce her to me. I am the best Matthews boy—took Mom and Dad two times before they got it just right."

"Speaking of Mom, she got a call from Mr. Penny today about a…let me see, how did he phrase it? A lewd sex act in your front yard with some hot red-head?" Ryker asked, his silvery blond brows rising in question.

Drake groaned. "Mr. Penny called *Mom*?"

Ryker straightened, his eyes alight. "Damn! You did the nasty with a ginger in the front yard? I feel like we're in one of your novels where a demon double possesses the clueless, dorky writer and ushers in Armageddon."

"*Demon Double*. That'd be a good title for your next book," Zander said, standing to put his empty glass on the antique tea cart. He wandered over to the front window, peeking out of the lace blinds. "Well, bro, I hope you used protection. Casual sex with a fan might sound like heaven, but there's nothing holy about chlamydia."

Drake sputtered on his drink. "I thought you said you were here to cheer me up?"

While Drake appreciated his brothers' company, the fact his actions were already the talk of the town—as well as his mother and who knew how many reporters— made his stomach clench in anger.

"You know how Mom is about people who talk trash about you. She told Mr. Penny if he didn't shut his flapping gums, she'd ban him from the café," Ryker said. "Care to let us in on the whole story?"

Drake sighed. "There isn't much to tell. My publisher hired an event planner for the book launch. She came here...and it got a little crazy."

"Define 'crazy'?" Zander crossed his fingers, holding them up dramatically. "Please, *please* tell me it's *Girls Gone Wild* crazy!"

Tipping his drink back until the ice cubes clinked against his teeth, Drake drained his whiskey and handed the empty to Ryker, who leaned over the leather couch to snag the bottle, giving him another three fingers' worth. Drake gave his brothers a quick, *CliffsNotes* version of the story.

"So, in summary," Ryker said, his face serious, "a hot girl scratches you with her shoes and you conk out. Then you fire her, and your publicist, because you're pissed Everstone was here? I mean, that was your best move? He is producing your next book-to-movie adaptation, so logically, you'll have to work with him sometime. I think you're misdirecting your anger, Drake—and while that's a topic I could write volumes on, you're supposed to be the level-headed one of the bunch."

Drake touched his bandaged arm, remembering the stunning woman with her killer heels and terrible launch ideas.

Shit.

His brother was right. What a jerk he'd been to her, and Imani too. The only one who'd deserved his ire today was Evan, but like the IED that had gone off under his brother's tank, his anger erupted like an all-directional grenade. He'd been curt to Imani, but atrocious to the poor event planner. While misguided, she'd only been doing her best.

Kate.

His mind still whirred with the electric zing of their first encounter. His fingers itched to be on the keyboard, capturing the details while they were still fresh and visceral. He remembered the smooth heat of her upper thighs, the floral scent of her hair, the way her eyes gazed up at him like he was some sort of superhero, when all he'd done was pick her up out of the mucky grass so she wouldn't break an ankle. He recalled his sense of awe when he'd come around after passing out and found himself on top of her. The feel of her silky auburn hair in his hands, the sprinkle of freckles across her nose, the way she looked up at him, her green eyes wide—all of it had goosed his muse into overdrive. He wanted to start typing. He knew exactly what to do now with his hero when he first meets the woman he's to marry. He'd write about how they literally ran into each other, the plot device allowing for forced intimacy, bringing his characters together faster...

"Hey," Zander asked, interrupting his thoughts. Drake looked up and saw his youngest brother crouching down next to a box by the parlor window. "Why do you have all of Grandpa Matthews's letters to Nana down here? Are you finally pitching some of the stuff in this house and making it your own? I mean, it was cool of you to buy the old place when Nana had to move to assisted living, but she doesn't expect you to keep it like a shrine. Nobody does. And what's in here that's so 'Forbidden' it needs its own folder?"

As soon as his brother made the air quotes around the title to his clandestine project, Drake shot up from the couch. He vaulted over Ryker's legs and snatched the manila folder from Zander, thrusting the whiskey glass into his hands instead.

"That's just something I'm working on. Backstory for *Twisted Twin*." Drake piled the boxes carefully onto each other again, and this time shoved them in the corner behind the pink needlepoint-covered ladies' chair nobody sat in.

Zander squinted one eye at him. "I thought that was set in the present? These are letters from the Second World War. I read through some of them that time when you two locked me in the attic and told Nana I'd joined the circus. They're less about history, and more about hanky-panky. Grandpa Matthews really had it bad for Nana. Did you know he wanted to marry her before heading off to war? But Nana was only sixteen, so her parents wouldn't give their permission."

Drake nodded. "He was persistent. Their whole four-year courtship was largely epistle-based. Pretty romantic, really."

After a beat, Zander looked at Ryker.

"'Epistle' means 'letter,'" Zander said, enunciating every word.

"I know what it means, asshole," Ryker shot back.

But instead of being drawn into another scrum, Zander—always the more intuitive of them—turned back to Drake and said, "Sounds like you're evolving into another genre?"

Should he tell them?

Sure, his brothers might razz Drake about writing romance, but they'd still support him. He could confess about his writer's block and how sick he was of mining nightmares for a living. He could admit how trapped he felt, the literal author of his own misfortune.

But other than garnering their sympathy, what was the point?

It was better to forget this stupid historical romance novel and remember what paid the bills on this house, the local veterans' shelter, and where the funds had come from for both of his brothers' start-up businesses: his horror books. That's what he needed to figure out— how to get rid of this writer's block for *Twisted Twin* and get the thing done already, cash the check, and move on to the next one, and the next one.

Lather, rinse, repeat. Until he was dead.

Drake cleared his throat and changed the subject.

"I was thinking of getting rid of some of Nana and Grampa's old stuff," he lied. "I started cleaning out the attic and happened on those boxes and then got side-tracked reading them, but I wanted to check with Nana to see if she wanted anything before I pitched them. I haven't been over to visit her this week. You guys seen her lately?"

"I visited yesterday. Still as spry as ever. She says she works out in their gym four times a week," Ryker said, then speared Drake with an accusatory look. "Speaking of, how many times are you going to blow off our workouts? Or have you joined some bougie gym and can't be seen slumming it in my garage?"

The landline rang, sparing Drake from having to fabricate some excuse as to why he'd dropped his workouts, along with every other thing in his life, lately. He trotted into the kitchen to grab the cordless phone, groaning when he noticed the receiver's readout: *Patty-Cakes.* This just wasn't his day. He answered.

"Hi, Mom."

"Drake, in about five minutes, there's going to be a knock at your door," his mom said, her voice as no-nonsense as any drill instructor's. "And you're going to answer like a gentleman, and I do not need to remind you that a gentleman honors his commitments. He also apologizes when he's acted like a jackass and made a grown woman cry."

"Mom, I didn't—"

His mother spoke over him, not missing a beat.

"I would never dream of telling you what to do, but I thought you should know I spent the last hour and a half with Kate Sweet, and while she does *not* know I'm your mother, she *does* know a good cupcake when she eats one, and she's ordered three hundred of them for your book launch."

Drake closed his eyes. "I'm not sure if that's appropriate, Mom. It probably violates some sort of ethics or accounting rule—"

"Just hear her out," his mom said, her voice growing softer. "That's all I'm asking, honey. Your father, God rest his soul, was a stubborn old mule, and I'm afraid you've inherited that Matthews trait in spades."

The gate buzzer rang then, and Sasha started barking. A moment later, Drake heard one of his brothers call out to him.

"Drake! There's a woman at the front gates. I think it's the redhead who stabbed you earlier. Should I let her in?"

"Oh, that must be her," his mom said, not missing a thing. "I'll see you Saturday at the Harvest Festival. Don't forget, you promised to be the emcee for the pumpkin-carving competition."

The call disconnected, and he shoved past his brothers to the front door.

Ryker asked in a mock whisper, his tone ringing with incredulity, "She's the one you kicked out earlier?"

His youngest brother shook his shaggy mane, managing to vocalize his disappointment in one long syllable.

"Duuuuuudddde."

Shooing them back into the parlor, Drake flung open the door. Stepping into the bright light on his front porch was Kate. She looked totally different in a pair of slim-fitting jeans tucked into black boots, with a navy parka thrown over the top of it all, the faux fur–lined hood obscuring all but the perfect oval of her pale face.

Her parka was speckled with snowflakes, and the imprints of her footsteps were outlined by the light dusting of flakes lazily drifting down. He thought about what he'd learned from his mother—how Kate had been crying in her shop, and how she'd given his mom a huge chunk of business for the launch—and much as he wanted to believe she was innocent of any nefarious planning with Everstone, he'd learned the hard way it was never a good idea to give a pretty woman his blind trust. Rachel taught him that, if nothing else.

"Hello again." Kate appeared poised except for her hands, which kept fiddling with the handles of the soft-sided black briefcase she'd carried—then thrown—earlier. "I'm not asking for you to invite me in, but I hope you'd be willing to hear my apology."

"You're in a different outfit" was the brilliant greeting that popped out of his mouth.

Drake heard his brothers groan from the parlor

behind him, and he flipped them the bird, his hand hidden from view behind the door.

Kate's face flushed, the pink color reminding Drake of the delicate inside of a tiny conch shell he'd collected from the beach one summer.

"And I didn't wear dangerous heels." She held up a booted foot as proof. "I see you've changed as well. Um, I'm sorry about ripping your shirt."

Drake glanced down, having forgotten he'd had to toss his earlier shirt—ruined from his encounter this morning—in exchange for a black button-down that was neither ripped nor bloodstained. He stood in the open doorway, torn between wanting to be polite and invite her in and wanting to stand outside for this discussion, avoiding his brothers' snickers and loud whispers. Before he'd decided his best course of action, Kate spoke, her voice low and urgent.

"Please hear me out. I know I gave a bad first impression—"

"No, you left your impression quite clearly," Drake said, holding up his arm, allowing the black, unbuttoned sleeve to fall away. A rectangular gauze bandage covered the skin from the inside of his wrist to just shy of the crook of his arm. "Almost twelve stitches' worth of a first impression. Oh, and a tetanus booster. Turns out, my shots weren't up-to-date."

"Tw-twelve stitches? And a shot? I can't believe—I didn't mean to . . . " Kate sputtered, her throat working reflexively as she swallowed. She took a deep breath, held it for a moment, and then continued speaking in a more measured tone. "I'm here to see what I can do to fix the mess I've made. I'm not asking you to rehire me as your event planner. I recognize after this morning, there's little chance of that. But before I leave town, I have been working on your launch with Imani, and she's gotten an agreement from Cerulean Books and the movie studio to send a fifty-thousand-dollar donation to your favorite veterans' shelter. You name the charity, and Imani is set to get the paperwork going on her end to make it a reality by the end of the day."

Drake's mouth fell open. His mother hadn't told him that. How could he turn down business to his mom's shop, plus a hefty donation to veterans in need?

His brothers poked their heads out of the parlor door, waved to Kate, and hissed at him.

"Stop being a douche."

"Say she's rehired!"

"All right, I'm not having a discussion with you two cretins standing behind me." Drake snagged a set of car keys from the hook on the wall and dashed out before his brothers could say anything more. Once on the wintry porch with the door closed, he immediately regretted not grabbing his jacket. Stuffing his hands in his jean pockets, he gestured with his chin toward the sidewalk. "Do you mind if we continue this outside? I'm sorry to be rude and not invite you in, but..." He trailed off, shrugging. "Brothers. You know."

Kate fell into step beside him as they walked off the porch toward the splash of streetlight on the blessedly empty sidewalk outside his front gates. "I don't know. Not exactly, anyway. I have one sister, but I'm the oldest as well, so I get it. Look, I wanted to apologize to you. Sincerely apologize. You'll have to take my word for it that I'm known as a professional—"

"You're the Queen of Happily Ever Afters. Supremely

popular in the tri-state area for planning show-stopping weddings, you've been featured in national magazines, and one of your fairy-tale–themed events was even in a *Say Yes to the Dress* episode." Drake's interruption was rewarded with a sharp look of surprise. He chuckled a little at her wide-eyed expression. "What? After this morning, I looked you up."

They left his front yard, the gates clicking closed behind them. He turned to punch in the code, locking it again—something he'd forgotten to do this morning, which led to Kate in his yard, unannounced, and the whole thing had gone downhill from there.

"Yes," she said, "although I don't seem to be the queen of much of anything today, except maybe—"

"Chaos?" Drake supplied, then softened his words with a smile.

Kate paused, narrowing her eyes, but allowing a half grin to touch her lips. "Touché. But for the record, I saved you when you passed out."

"And then you neglected to tell me we had guests. You let them see me in that state." Drake's lips thinned, and he looked away from Kate briefly, reining in his anger. She had nothing to do with Everstone's visit, nor did she likely know about his past with the Hollywood producer and how the man had conspired with Rachel to ruin his life.

She bit her lip. "I thought it was just Imani coming in. Trust me, the last person in the whole world I would've let through the door to see us like that was Evan Everstone."

Drake whipped his gaze back to her. "Really? Why?"

Kate hesitated, giving him an appraising look. Finally, she seemed to come to some sort of decision and spoke matter-of-factly. "Because he holds the key to what I want most in this world."

Drake's eyebrows drew together in a scowl. "Are you some aspiring actress or looking to write a tell-all book, or something? What on earth could Everstone have that you want so badly?"

"An EVPLEX." The words came from Kate's mouth as quietly as a church confession. If he hadn't been holding his breath, he wouldn't have heard it.

"A what?"

"It's an award that stands for Event Planning Extravaganza." She sighed, stopping to face him. She tucked a stray strand of auburn hair back into her hood as the wind whipped around them. "Evan sits on the EVPLEX award committee, and everyone knows his vote is the one to get if you want to ever be anything in this business. But he never awards weddings— says they're innately selfish and unworthy. So, when Imani offered me this job, I jumped at the chance to do something he might consider worthy."

"Ah," he said, the pieces clicking together. "Hence the barn and the coffin dangling from the ceiling beams. I get it. I used to think the only thing I wanted in this world was to hit the *New York Times* bestseller list. Like having that would somehow..."

"Legitimize what you're doing. Validate your choices in life," Kate finished, surprising Drake by nailing his thoughts exactly. She wrinkled her nose, giving a short laugh. "Yeah, that's how I feel about the EVPLEX for a lot of reasons, but mostly it's like a checkmark in life's report card, you know? Imani said you absolutely *despised* the idea of coming out of a hanging coffin. I went overboard in my pitch to you—I realize that now."

They'd arrived at the sidewalk corner, and when Kate made as if to cross, Drake put a hand to her back, stopping her progress. "I don't see a car. Did you walk here?"

She nodded. "I was eating at a café downtown, and the owner there—a really nice woman named Patty— said she knew you."

Drake nodded, raising one eyebrow. Did Kate really not know she was his mom?

"Well, she said Jimmy's cab was hard to hail at dinnertime, and she said it wasn't a bad walk, and that all I had to do was go behind the shop, cross the train tracks, and I'd be on Maple Avenue, only a couple blocks from you." Her teeth chattered slightly when she admitted, "It was lighter outside then, so I didn't mind the walk, but I wasn't expecting it to be this cold. And you didn't bring a coat, so I should probably let you get back inside with your family."

Drake shook his head. "They're not going anywhere. I have the keys to their car." He dangled them in the air. "And Zan parked right behind my truck so I can't take that. As long as you don't mind riding home in what my mom calls Zander's clown car, I'll get you safely back to your hotel."

"You'll drive me home?" Kate snorted a laugh as they rounded the Victorian and the small driveway and carriage house came into view. "No offense, but by the, erm, smell of your breath, you shouldn't be driving anywhere."

Drake halted by the gates, feeling himself swerve. Damn. She was right. He'd downed three Zander-size glasses of whiskey. He wasn't safe behind the wheel.

He shrugged off the problem, his alcohol-greased brain coming up with a solution.

"Okay. You drive, then." He tossed her the keys and was surprised when she plucked them out of the air like an outfielder.

"Okayyyy." Kate Sweet dragged the word out, squinting with one eye. "But, um, if I drive us back to the hotel, then you'll be at my hotel without a way to get home. So, why don't I call Jimmy's Cab? He's probably done with dinner, by now."

"Nah. I'll walk from the hotel. Or I'll call Jimmy. If I know my brothers, they're going to order pizza, have another drink, and overstay their welcome until tomorrow, so they won't need the car tonight." Drake brushed away her concerns, entering his code into the security gates for the second time, focusing on each number, until the thing beeped a happy set of tones, and the gates purred open. "I have to lock everything—honestly, the front gates should've been locked this morning, but I'd forgotten to do it after taking Sasha for her walk."

"Why do you—"

Kate was interrupted as a young man came sprinting from a beat-up, two-door Camry that had been idling with its headlights off across the street.

"Excuse me, Mr. Matthews," said a kid dressed in ripped black jeans, a long, black overcoat, and black boots with chains and buckles that jangled as he ran. He held a book out to Drake—one of his old bestsellers, *Dark Dolls*—and his kohl-lined eyes were pleading as he asked, "Can I get your autograph? I'm a huge fan! Been reading you since I was ten years old, and this is the first hardcover book I ever bought myself. All the rest of yours I have on my Kindle."

He was about to give the kid his standard I-don't-do-signings-outside-of-events-put-on-by-my-publisher excuse when he caught Kate's expectant smile. She looked almost thrilled to see him accosted by a fan who'd obviously been sitting outside of his house, stalking him, waiting for his chance to pounce for an autograph. He knew it was a testosterone-fed ego thing, but the glimmer in her eager expression made Drake want to impress her.

While he inwardly rolled his eyes at his caveman-like behavior, he nodded to the teen, whose face broke into an excited grin.

"Oh, great! Could you make it out to Trent?" the guy asked, bouncing on his toes as he handed Drake the book. Belatedly, both he and the fan realized neither of them had a pen.

"Here," Kate said, digging into the black briefcase she held. "I've got one."

Drake accepted the proffered pen, the barrel of which was crusted in what must have been thousands of rhinestones encased in glass so it could be held without slicing your fingers. The streetlamps caught the gems, casting little glittery reflections all over the book as he double-checked the spelling of Trent's name, and wrote out his usual inscription for *Dark Dolls*, borrowing a line from the book.

For Trent,
   Best wishes. Never leave the dolls out while you sleep.

Underneath this, he scrawled his autograph and today's date on the inner title page with a final flourish and presented it back to him. The kid took the book back, reverently touching the signature. Then, he snapped the cover closed, whooping as he held the book over his head and jogged back across the street. His car revved away, horn tooting, moments later.

Drake handed the pen back to Kate. "Well, that was a first."

"Getting asked for an autograph next to your house?" she asked, following him to Zander's Prius.

"No. That happens almost every day," he said. "I meant signing with a rhinestone pen. I fully expected the ink to be pink and glittery."

"They're Swarovski crystals, not rhinestones," she said, "and the pen was a gift from the first bride I worked with when I started my business six years ago. It's my lucky pen."

He blipped the hybrid car's alarm off and opened the driver's door for Kate and then hopped into the passenger seat.

"You sure you want me to drive your brother's car?" Kate asked. "I'm happy to call Jimmy's, if that's easier."

"Maybe I want to talk with you for a few more minutes," Drake mumbled, not meeting her gaze.

Out of the corner of his eye, he saw Kate shrug, and then she used the levers to pull her seat forward, clicked on her seat belt, adjusted the mirror, and started the car. Drake cranked the heat and flipped the radio off as she carefully backed out of the driveway and onto Maple Avenue. Something of a plan formed in his head, but it all depended on this woman—the one he'd put in the driver's seat, literally and figuratively.

"So, why are you here, and not Imani, talking to me about the launch?" he asked.

"I wanted to deliver the news about the veterans' shelter donation in person, so maybe...you'd not back out of the launch?" Kate took her eyes off the road, glancing over at him with a pained expression. "Otherwise, my best friend is going to be in some very hot water at work."

Drake's eyebrows rose. "Imani Lewis is your best friend? I figured you worked with Cerulean Books."

"No, they hired me as a contractor," Kate said, then elaborated. "Imani and I grew up together. Her dad worked with my parents as a surgery tech at the hospital, and they recruited him when they opened their first practice, so we're close. We took dance classes together as kids, and she even lived with us for a year after her mother died when she was in high school."

Drake's eyebrows shot up. He thought he'd known his publicist—they'd certainly worked together long enough—yet he'd had no idea that they both had a parent pass away at a young age.

Following Drake's direction to take the next left by the Methodist Church to stay on Maple, Kate continued.

"Actually, Imani's the one who got me my first break—an internship with Evert Events after college. I owe her so much, which is why I wanted to come out and explain to you that Imani did nothing wrong. And she doesn't know I'm here, by the way. I'd, um, appreciate it if you didn't tell her when she contacts you when she gets back. She was pretty specific that she wanted to handle all conversations with you in the future. I can't say I blame her."

"When she gets back? Where did she go?"

"To the airport. To drop off Evan."

"Him." Drake curled his lip. He directed her to take the next right onto State Street, then a left onto Main Street where the sign of the hotel glowed blue at the end of the block.

She pulled into the entrance, and as she parked in a spot at the front of the lot, he had a sudden epiphany. Without significant legal intervention, Drake couldn't oust Everstone as the producer bringing *Halloween Hacker* to the big screen. He was just the author, after all. Those decisions were made at a higher pay grade. Same with the launch—he'd signed the contract and had to do it. But, if he were to get Kate on his side, the launch might be a hell of a lot less painful. Look at what she'd done already with getting his publisher to do the unprecedented—making a donation to his charity. Wouldn't it be nice if someone benefited from all this madness?

Plus, if he were being truly honest, the writer's side of his brain—the one buzzing in overdrive since he'd seen her this morning—recognized inspiration in the chaos-inducing event planner. Maybe if he were to flat-out write only the historical romance for the next few weeks and finish it up, it would be out of his system? He could return to churning out horror with the same zeal he used to have, back before this romance idea gummed up his synapses.

"I won't fire Imani, and I'm not firing you, either." Drake held up a finger to cut off Kate's effusive thanks. "I'll agree to your launch ideas—let you have whatever circus you need for your EVPLEX—on three conditions: First, you have to ditch the haunted house nonsense at the barn, including me climbing in or out of any coffin. It's never happening."

Kate grinned, and Drake noticed she had a small dimple at the bottom of her left laugh line, like an upside-down semicolon. The discovery made him pause so long, Kate filled in the silence.

"You want me to tone the launch down, right? That's fine. We'll plan something less cliché. We'll work together to figure out a better way to meet your expectations, while still maintaining the timeline for an engaging Halloween reader event," Kate said, practically vibrating with enthusiasm.

"Second, I need your help for my next book." Drake evaded her brilliant, green-eyed gaze as he filled in his fib. "In your spare hours, I need someone to assist with my . . . research. You game?"

"You've got a deal." Kate stuck out her hand over the gear shift, shaking his vigorously. "Now, should I call you a cab? I have a Jimmy's Car Service card in my pocket."

"You didn't hear my third condition," Drake said, releasing her soft hand.

"Oh. Right. You said three. What is it?" Kate's smile dimmed, and the upside-down semicolon vanished.

Drake resisted the urge to make her laugh so that it would reappear. Instead, he focused on something he'd been wondering about since this morning.

"Earlier in my front yard, when we first met and you jumped into my arms, you said something I've been curious about ever since."

"I didn't jump *into* your arms. I jumped *away* from

what I thought was your Doberman," Kate corrected. "I was trying to avoid being mauled."

Somewhere in his brain, he wondered how she knew about his old dog, Cade, but right now, another thought crowded forward. "What I've wondered is this: when you plowed into me, you said, 'You're not Photoshopped.' What did you mean?"

Although they were in a dark parking lot, lit only by a few lampposts scattered around the perimeter of the hotel, he could see her face well enough to notice her cheeks flushing.

Her mouth opened, then snapped shut, as if she were rethinking her answer.

Finally, she spoke.

"When I researched you online for this morning's launch meeting, I stumbled across some old pictures of you. In a bathing suit. On a beach."

Drake blinked, taking a moment to process, and then it came to him. "My trip to Barbados when I researched the Animal Flower Cave, the setting of *Alien Abyss.* A photographer there recognized me and slapped the picture on the internet." Drake paused, connecting the dots. "Wait. Which part of the picture did you think was Photoshopped?"

Kate's hand came up to rub at her throat. "Um, the abs? I'd thought maybe a fan or someone Photoshopped that part. You know. Gave you a six-pack. But, um, I was wrong."

Drake tipped his head back and laughed—something she'd made him do twice in one night. "Okay, glad you cleared that up for me, and I hope I can continue to surprise you as we work together this month."

He waved off her apologies and protests as he clambered out of his brother's car.

"No, don't say you're sorry for being honest. Thanks for telling me the truth. And for being real. I don't get that much in my life anymore."

Drake reached out his hand, shaking hers one last time.

"I'll call you in the next couple of days, and we can discuss your new plan. Here's to us both getting what we want from this launch."

CHAPTER 7

Excuse me?" Kate lifted her cell off her ear, sure that she must have misheard because of a bad connection, but she had full bars. She returned her phone to her ear. "You want me to meet you...where?"

"I'm at the Sacred Heart Cemetery at the end of South Main Street," Drake said, his voice muffled, as if the phone were being shifted around. "I'm about to be shut into a mausoleum as part of my book research, and this is the only open time I have to talk to you today about the launch. And we did have a bargain—help me with my research, and I'll sign off on all your ghoulish plans. But you've got to get here in the next ten minutes."

"O-okay. See you soon." Before Kate could say anything else, the call disconnected. She stared at the phone for a moment in disbelief. It wasn't the craziest thing a client had ever said to her...but it was close. Then again, Drake had a definite knack for throwing her off-kilter.

"Was that Drake?" asked Trisha Cabot, Imani's

boss and the head of sales and marketing at Cerulean Books, her voice sounding tinny from Imani's cell phone's speaker.

Thankfully, Trisha's root canal had gone well, and she'd understood when Imani admitted their almost-failure with Drake. Yet she'd insisted on a full update via conference call from both Imani and Kate this morning, and Kate read in Trisha's tone that while her unfortunate first meeting with Drake hadn't totally tanked Imani's career aspirations, it had definitely dented them. Imani assured her boss that Kate would provide them both with daily text updates—hourly, if necessary—and if anything even smelled remotely off with his demeanor or enthusiasm for the plan, she was to notify all parties. Immediately.

"Yes, that was Mr. Matthews," Kate said, shooting her best friend an "it's okay" glance. She was determined to do whatever it took to be absolutely, one-hundred-percent perfect in the future.

"Does he need me to call him? Has he changed his mind about having the launch?" Trisha asked. "I need Imani on this next call with Leann Bellamy, but if she needs to come with you, I can—"

"No, he's still on board, and I've got it." Kate gathered her papers from the small, round table she and Imani used as their workspace in the hotel room, stacking the project plan together and neatly paper-clipping it at the top. "In fact, he called to ask if I'd meet with him, in person, on the new launch plans we emailed him. He's...eager to get started."

"I think that's because of Kate's idea to donate the launch event proceeds to his charity." Imani offered Kate a supportive smile, handing her the keys to the car she'd rented. "His fans will see his altruistic side. And I've already worked it into a promotion scheduled for Veteran's Day, giving us an after-launch boost."

"I have to run," Kate interjected, "but I'll text, call, and email you both later." Gathering her tablet and purse, she pumped her fist in a "woo-hoo" gesture to Imani, who mouthed a "call me later."

Kate pulled up the GPS on her phone as she hopped in Imani's rental car. She glanced over at the empty spot at the front of the parking lot where she'd parked Drake's brother's car and was happy to see someone had picked it up.

Drake had seemed so different last night—more introspective and...vulnerable. Maybe it was because he'd been drinking, but she'd felt almost protective of him. She'd loitered by the snack bar, watching to make sure he'd be okay until Jimmy's Car Service arrived. He'd had his hands in his armpits as he'd jumped and stomped intermittently, trying to keep warm. She hadn't been able to breathe easy until she'd seen him leaving with Jimmy out of the parking lot and back home, where his brothers were likely waiting to razz him.

It was refreshing to see that no matter how much you made in life, and how successful you were, family was still family. Recalling her mother's insistence she come back into the Sweet family surgeon fold, Kate shuddered, putting it out of her mind. She'd call them in a few days when this book launch found more stable footing.

Her GPS led her to the cemetery's entrance. She'd been hoping for some sort of office to meet in—maybe an old brick building at the edge of the graveyard where bereaved families picked out plots or conducted whatever business one might conduct at a cemetery. But as she pulled through the arched, wrought-iron gates beneath a sign proclaiming *Sacred Heart Cemetery*, she saw no such brick building. No buildings at all, in fact. Only grave markers dotted an expansive park-like space. After rounding a few bends, she saw a silver SUV and an old truck, next to what looked like the edge of a forest. She swung her rental car down the single paved path in that direction, slowing to a crawl to avoid the tree roots and potholes as the paved portion ended and a gravel-lined path began. Soon, she'd arrived where the cars were parked, and she pulled up behind a black Chevy truck, admiring the matte paint job. Someone had really spent some time and money on this overhaul. She didn't know trucks, but from the bulbous nose of it and retro lines, she'd have guessed it was originally manufactured sometime in the 1950s.

"Cool ride," she said to herself, putting the sad little economy rental car in park. "Wonder if that's the Knight of Nightmare's wheels?"

Peering out the passenger window, she noticed a small group of people huddled next to an old stone structure. She gathered her bag and laptop—then looked outside at the group who'd all turned as soon as she'd parked—and changed her mind. She dumped her laptop back onto the passenger seat, taking only her purse. She had her phone in there, and a small notepad and pen, as well as a printout of the new project plan— the one she'd been up almost all night figuring out once Drake had said she was hired once more.

She slammed the door shut behind her and beeped the car's nasal-sounding alarm, then began the trek downhill toward two men and a woman. As she strode deeper into the forested recesses of the old cemetery, Kate cursed her wardrobe choices. Again. This morning, guessing she'd be meeting with Drake at some point, she'd pulled out what she thought of as her most stylish, chic outfit—one that conveyed that Monday's too-tight black suit was an aberration. This outfit, she hoped, would show Drake he'd done the right thing to keep her on board with his launch party. She'd worn her favorite, a forest-green Givenchy skirt with a matching, three-quarter-length–sleeved top, nude suede heels, and a sand-colored wool-blend coat thrown over the top.

Her late mentor, Maya, would have approved. It was a perfect power meeting outfit.

Unless said power meeting was held among a collection of wet tombstones.

Now, as she carefully picked her way through the partially damp brown, red, and yellow leaves in her pumps, she regretted every wardrobe choice, including the burgundy structured Strathberry tote she'd spent an entire wedding fee on last year. If she had to set it down, her choices were a dirty headstone or the cold, damp ground. She debated on returning to Imani's rental car and ditching the bag, but that meant retracing her steps. In this wet grass and soft ground, a return trip in heels might tempt the goddess of chaos to notice her once again.

Thankfully, the dusting of snow had melted, and today's temperature hovered in the low fifties. She gazed around with interest at the old tombstones. Some were tall, marble obelisks with the family name etched in bold, blocky typeface, but most of what dotted the landscape were the more traditional rectangular gravestones standing upright or canted slightly to the side due to decades of undergrowth. She saw several "Giopolus" markers, "Ingalls" stones, and "Barnett" tombs as she walked, each family clustered together as if seeking warmth in the afterlife.

There wasn't anything, however, that looked mildly interesting for a horror novel. In fact, with the old oak and maple trees stretched overhead, most with a riot of tinted leaves that acted as a sound buffer, the whole place had a peaceful, if somewhat neglected, park-like feel. While she'd always heard about the area's beauty, especially in the fall, she'd never spent any time in Western New York before. Kate now saw she'd been missing out. Although her time here was relatively short, she made a mental note to return. When it wasn't threatening to snow, this place was a little slice of heaven!

Suddenly, a question popped into her head, distracting her from the serenity. What type of research was Drake planning to do here today?

Then she spotted a yellow backhoe in the distance. Her steps faltered. A backhoe? There weren't many things you did with a backhoe in a graveyard, except maybe use it to bury a corpse.

Or dig a corpse back up.

She swallowed. The thought of witnessing an exhumation slowed her steps to a creep.

She spotted Drake standing to the side of the stone structure, his pen flying across the pages of a yellow legal pad. He wore a pair of faded jeans and a chestnut-brown leather jacket with a navy-blue shirt underneath. On his feet was a pair of rugged hiking boots—as if he might be ready to jump down into a hole with a shovel himself.

Next to Drake lurked a tall, thin man dressed in

denim overalls and a thick, flannel-lined plaid shirt. He held a crowbar in one hand and a pair of long, wickedly sharp bolt cutters in the other.

At the sight of the man's tools, Kate's palms grew slick.

To his left stood an older woman dressed in a red parka, her blond-gray hair in a helmet-like bob brushing her shoulders. She appeared to be speaking, gesturing with her hands to the old building, pointing out things as Drake scribbled on his legal pad, scowling as he wrote.

Kate's mind whirled with various excuses she could use, if the plan was to dig up bodies today. She could say...what? That she had a weak stomach? Admit she was so scared of zombie movies that when she'd seen an episode of *The Walking Dead*, she hadn't been able to sleep for a month without the lights on and a baseball bat in her bed?

No way. The person in charge of a book launch for Drake Matthews could *not* show fear.

Mustering up her courage, Kate approached the trio, catching the end of the woman's speech.

"...the building stands about sixteen feet high and is made to look like a small church. The filigreed iron grates at the outside of the stained-glass windows are original, as is the elaborate ironwork cross at the top. The stone is quite old, and it still bears the original name of the family who built this mausoleum after the town was established, around 1898."

The woman gestured to the name, GOODRICH, carved in block capital letters into the stone at the top of the mausoleum. While the lettering was still crisp, moss grew in the hollows of the rounded letters and in the crevices of the "H." Mostly brown and frost-burnt English ivy clung to the sides of the stone structure, trailing vines up to the roof and encroaching on the front, as if determined to swallow the Goodrich family, returning them all to the forest floor.

"Good morning," Kate said, approaching the group with a wave and her bravest smile. "Sorry I'm late."

Drake smiled. "Not at all. You're here just in time. Kate Sweet, may I introduce you to Wendy Scanlon and Curtis Clark. He's the cemetery's head caretaker, while Wendy is the head of the Wellsville Historical Society. They were about to lock me into the mausoleum to see what I could hear and see if I were, say, interred alive with no way out. I always do my research firsthand, whenever possible. They've agreed to break the lock to allow me in while they do their annual check on the integrity of the mausoleum's roof. It's been repaired in the past, is that right?"

Mr. Clark nodded his long, thin head in a slow, deliberate way. "The Goodrich family has no living descendants. The line died out, so we do maintenance only if it's falling apart."

"Isn't it, um, disrespectful to go into a mausoleum?" Kate asked, thoughts of partially rotted bodies with exposed bones rampaging through her head. She cleared her throat, willing her voice not to crack. "You know, disturbing the dead and all?"

Mr. Clark banged the crowbar against the bolt cutters in three loud, sharp cracks, making Kate jump. Then, he put a hand to his ear, pantomiming that he was listening.

"They don' appear to be easily disturbed," he said. "Are we openin' this crypt or not? I got a grave to dig over yonder. The ground's gonna freeze if I don't get it done today."

"I think I'll wait for you out here." Kate scrambled for an excuse, looking down. "I'm...I'm not really dressed for, uh, crypt...things."

Drake looked to be hiding a grin. "What? I thought you didn't scare easily. Are you superstitious, Kate?"

"I don't scare easily, and I'm not *super*stitious—just a *little*-stitious," Kate said, giving a wan smile as they laughed at her joke. "All the same, I think I'll wait out here until you're done. Give you the time you need in there, and then we can talk when you've finished."

Drake shrugged. "Suit yourself. I'll likely be around an hour. That time frame's still good?"

Kate's mouth dropped open. *An hour?* She'd be standing out here—in heels and a skirt—for an hour while he explored a tomb? Before she could process this, the older woman grinned, bobbing her head.

"Absolutely," Mrs. Scanlon said. "I've cleared my calendar for the next two hours to help in your research. I'm a big fan—we're all big fans of yours."

Drake smiled. "I appreciate it. A writer is nothing without readers."

Mrs. Scanlon used a key to open the barred door that acted as an additional deterrent to trespassers over the crypt's original white marble doors. Then the tall Mr. Clark used his bolt cutters on a rusty padlock as long as Kate's hand.

"Lost the key to this one five years ago when old Yancey was mowing, so we gotta put a new lock on 'er when you're done."

The lock broke open with a loud snap, and the rusty chains looped around the door handles clattered down onto the stone pavers at the mausoleum's threshold. Now, all that was between them and the dead was a pair of white marble doors, their brass handles tarnished to a dark brown-black.

Mr. Clark raised the crowbar, and Kate gasped.

"You're not using the crowbar on those marble doors, are you?" She knew it was none of her business, but she couldn't stop the protest. "That's probably Tuckahoe marble, quarried right here in New York State."

Everyone gave her a blank stare.

"Tuckahoe marble," she said, enunciating it. "The same one they used to build St. Patrick's Cathedral in Manhattan and the Washington Monument. It became very popular in the late 1800s—they even built Sing Sing prison next to the quarry to get free labor to pull the stone from the ground. I know all this because I've married two couples at St. Patrick's, and I had the task of matching the linens to that marble. It's a big deal, since it's all white with no veining and few blemishes. You can't use a crowbar on it! If you crack it, you'll never get a piece to replace it. The quarry closed sometime in the 1930s."

"Great detail for the book." Drake chuckled, scribbling on his legal pad. "Tuckahoe marble. Quarried by prisoners. Who knew?"

"No, the doors will open jus' fine," Mr. Clark said, looking down his sharp nose. He hefted the crowbar. "This is for the rats."

"Rats?" Kate squeaked, taking a giant step backward.

The cemetery groundskeeper took hold of the handle for the door on the right side and pulled. Iron hinges squealed in protest, but the doors opened.

Kate held her breath, ready to sprint back up the hill, suede heels or not, if she saw even a whisker. But nothing came out of the tomb except a swirl of leaves from the gust of wind created by the door's opening.

Craning her neck, Kate saw a dirty floor covered in some sort of decorative tile. No skeletons lay by the doorway, and no zombies staggered out. The morning was alive with the sounds of birds chirping and squirrels chittering and scolding each other as they sped between the memorials of the dead.

Her heart stopped its frantic attempt to escape her chest, and Kate released her breath in a whoosh of relief.

Drake laughed. "Did you think because I was here, something supernatural would happen?"

The other two laughed, joining Drake, and Kate gave a weak smile.

"Well, I'm not a zombie hunter by trade. It's not every day I break into a mausoleum."

"There's no vandalism here. It's an authorized visit." The groundskeeper gestured for Drake to go inside. "There's the empty crypt by the far wall. Always been there—nothin' in the record it was ever occupied."

"Yes, it's very authentic and undisturbed. We don't let just anyone into our crypts!" Mrs. Scanlon said, looking very pious. "You're welcome to poke around—whatever you need for your book. I brought along a lantern and a flashlight for you. And I have a whistle too."

The woman retrieved a brown paper bag from the side of the building and handed it to Drake. When it became clear nobody was going to ask, Kate couldn't stand the suspense.

"A whistle? What's that for?"

"Cell phones don't work in the old section of the cemetery," Mr. Clark said, gathering his bolt cutters and crowbar in one hand. "You want to be let out before the hour's up, you're gonna want to blow that so Wendy here can let you out. I'm heading to the west side, if you need help. Jus' don't break anything, and let the dead sleep undisturbed."

Drake clipped his pen to the top of the yellow legal pad. He glanced at Kate.

"You coming in to help me research?" he asked. "I can take notes and discuss launch plans at the same time—that was our deal, wasn't it?"

Kate sighed. Her choices were stand out here for an hour in the cold, shouting her ideas through the marble doors at him like some sort of lunatic, or be an adult and go inside, endure the graveyard vibe, and get her spreadsheet plan approved. What option did she have, when she was the one who'd agreed to help with his research, after all?

"Coming." Clutching her Strathberry tote to her chest, Kate climbed the two stone steps, her heels clicking on the marble.

"After you," Drake said, gallantly sweeping his hand for her to precede him into the tomb.

Taking a deep breath, she squared her shoulders.

"I don't scare easily," she muttered to herself, and led one of the world's most infamous horror writers into a crypt.

CHAPTER 8

Drake stifled a laugh as Kate came to a dead halt just inside the mausoleum's marble doors. Clearly, the day had taken a turn she wasn't expecting. He, on the other hand, was thankful he'd downed a whole pot of coffee this morning, because now he was raring to go with his plan: use Kate's muse-goosing powers to write the hell out of this romance. Exorcise the damn book from his mind—and his heart—so he could return to what paid the bills. His first run-in with her had produced an exhilarating almost-all-nighter at the keyboard. Who knew what spending another hour together would bring? His hands itched to write. But first, he had to convince her to stay with him in the old building.

"C'mon, Kate. This is nothing." Drake gestured with his chin at her purse. "You've got your sparkly crystal pen in there, don't you?"

Kate nodded, looking confused. "Yes. My pen is still in here. Why?"

"Whew. Then we're safe! It is your lucky pen, after all."

Kate made a noise of amused annoyance so subtle, he wouldn't have heard it unless he hadn't been hyper-aware of her reactions. It was like his subconscious had absorbed their random physical closeness two days ago and decided it all meant something. Now, his every internal antenna was tuned in to Sweet Radio, like a satellite orbiting Earth.

He smelled the scent of her light floral perfume as she swept by him into the mausoleum.

"See you in an hour," Wendy Scanlon said as she shut the marble doors behind him, grinning so wide, the skin at the corners of her mouth wrinkled and dramatically folded in on itself, like a shar-pei's. They were plunged in a sea of inky black, and Drake heard the metallic clang as the outer metal doors were also secured, locking them inside. Before his eyes adjusted to the darkness, a piercing blue-white light shot up like a laser in the old crypt.

Kate had activated the flashlight app on her cell phone.

"You look like the Statue of Liberty." His voice echoed in the small space, and she jumped, whirling to shine the light at him, blinding him momentarily.

"I feel like a girl in a B-level horror film," she said, her voice a little breathier than her typical tone. "The girl who when she appears, everyone in the theater yells at the movie screen, trying to warn her she's made some dumb decision that's about to get her eaten by zombies."

"Nah. Those girls are usually in bikinis or lacy paja-mas. They're never dressed in professional suits with heels and designer bags, so you're safe from typecast-ing." Drake fiddled inside the brown paper bag Wendy had given them, pulling out the lantern and switching it on. He pitched the bag with the other supplies by the door and moved into the center of the space, taking it all in. "You're more like a superhero in disguise—the one the audience doesn't realize has superpowers until danger threatens. You're the one they cheer for when she comes on the movie screen."

Kate paused in her quest to illuminate every corner of the mausoleum to gape at him. "Wow, that's a really nice compliment. Thank you. So, if I'm the superhero in disguise... does that make you the one in distress?"

"Hmm. Maybe." Drake didn't know what else to say. He wished life came with a pause button to give him time to come up with a cool, snappy rejoinder. Instead, he focused on what he did best: writing. He hung the lantern on his wrist and flipped open his legal pad, ready to take notes and capture the atmosphere. Kate cleared her throat and disabled her cell phone's flashlight to peer around the space.

"So, what research points are you hoping to nail down in here?" she asked.

He'd scheduled this mausoleum visit with the historical society and the caretaker a few weeks earlier, hoping it would help jump-start his overdue horror novel. But he didn't dare confess that to Kate.

"I'm not sure," he finally admitted. "I wanted to see what it might be like to be... interred. Or trapped. Inside a mausoleum. It's more of an inspiration activity versus actual book research."

Kate nodded, as if that bunch of BS made sense. "I do that when I'm scoping out new wedding venues."

Feeling as though he needed to say something, do something, to justify his visit—to Kate, if nobody else—

Drake examined the white marble walls of the crypts and the names of the deceased inscribed upon them. He did a 360-degree turn with the lantern, illuminating the names as he spoke to fill what was becoming, for him at least, an awkward silence.

"Bigger in here than I thought. There are five interments on this side. Let's see, we have Ada Victoria Goodrich, who died first in 1898 at the ripe old age of thirty-two, and then we have Charles Goodrich, and Cora B. Goodrich, and finally..." Drake squinted to the uppermost stones. "...there's Joseph and Jennie Wray Goodrich, who both died on the same day in 1937. Huh. Wonder what took them."

Kate took a breath, wrinkling her nose from the stale air. "Hopefully not suffocation from being closed in a tomb."

"Hmm. Not likely," Drake said, noticing only after Kate's reaction that the crypt did smell...funky. He set the lamp on the floor, squinting at his legal pad as he described the scent for a future horror book. It smelled like leaf mold mixed with a faint trace of ammonia. "There's plenty of oxygen. See that?"

Kate followed his gaze to the back side of the mausoleum where a tiny, iron filigreed window sat, cozied next to the roof. "Is that...a vent? That seems odd."

"Death was a messy business, especially before modern embalming. The vent was built for the dead and their escaping...odors."

"Eww!" Kate gaped at him. "And you know this how?"

Drake shrugged. "Book research. When I was writing *Scared Stiff*, I shadowed a mortician for a few days. People think I'm the Knight of Nightmares, but all they have to do is talk to their local crematory owner to see how my fiction pales in comparison to their daily jobs. Speaking of jobs, how'd you become an event planner?"

He'd been careful to use "event" and not "party" this time. He'd learned that lesson already.

"I've been obsessed by weddings, and big events in general, ever since I was little and was asked to be the flower girl at my aunt's ceremony. They had this elaborate affair in a grand old church, with a stretch limousine that whisked us away to a reception with glittering chandeliers over every table."

"Sounds magical," Drake murmured as she paused. His footsteps echoed hollowly as he drew near a rectangular dais with a stone sarcophagus on top. He lifted the lantern to peer in, but the space appeared to be empty, except for some dust.

"It was. At least for me," Kate said, joining him to peek into the crypt. When she saw nothing inside, she sighed like she'd been holding her breath, and continued her story. "My aunt ended up divorcing the guy six months later. But I remember that day. I wore a pale-pink ball gown and satin shoes with rhinestones on the top. I thought to myself: I want to feel like this every day when I grow up—like I'm living in a fairy tale. So, I became an event planner."

Drake grinned, taken with her storytelling. "I'll bet you were an adorable flower girl."

"I was a terror. My parents spent the whole day chasing me around the reception. I barged in on every couple's waltz, making the man twirl me around instead." She laughed at the memory, shaking her head. "After that, I was hooked. And with my parents being surgeons, either one or the other would typically be called in for an emergency on the weekends, so I got to stand in a lot as the plus-one on the invite."

"I did my share of that, growing up." At her incredulous expression, he elaborated. "My dad was career military and away a lot. Many times without notice. If my mom had already RSVP'd to an event with two meals, she thought it was rude not to go to the wedding, and since I was the oldest, she usually took me in lieu of my father. I became quite the connoisseur of wedding cakes. Or, at least, wedding cake frosting."

"Really?" Kate laughed, and her smile lit up her face, making that tiny dimple appear. "Who knew the Knight of Nightmares was a frosting fanatic? Now I have to know—do you prefer buttercream or fondant?"

Drake shuddered. "Who in their right mind actually enjoys *eating* fondant? It's pretty, but it tastes..."

"Like sugary cardboard," Kate finished, wrinkling her nose.

"Exactly."

Kate paused, seeming to collect herself. "As long as we have a second of peace and quiet, can I ask you about the plans for the revised launch? We had an idea—"

Drake put up a hand, nodding his head. "In a minute. Let me finish up and then we can talk. I'm getting inspiration for the next novel."

"Oh. It's such a...quiet process." Kate's voice sounded almost, but not quite, annoyed. His previous event planner had fawned embarrassingly over him, calling him "sir" so often, Drake wondered if the guy thought he'd been truly knighted, and not just jokingly called the Knight of Nightmares.

He found Kate's annoyance refreshing and hid a smile as she struggled to come up with a follow-up question.

"Do you, um, have an outline or a title yet?"

He instantly thought of the file folder holding his notes for the romance novel he was calling *Forbidden*. It was a crappy title for such a beautiful love story, he realized, and he'd have to come up with something better...just as soon as he figured out the rest of his plot. But he couldn't tell her anything about what he was *really* writing, so he used the name of the book he was *supposed* to be writing.

"I'm calling it *Twisted Twin* right now, but my publisher will likely change it. They always remind me it's my job to write the books, and theirs to sell them, and titles sell books." Drake fell silent, his pen motionless above the yellow paper. He'd hoped the magic of just being with Kate would ignite his muse, just like it had after meeting her on Monday.

But nothing was coming.

He felt a tingle of apprehension at the base of his spine. What if he was blocked on *all* writing now? What would he do then? He had three mortgages. One was on his grandparents' home, which he'd bought above market value, so his nana could afford to live in a single room in the assisted-living facility. The other two were the office buildings he'd bought for his brothers—a garage for Ryker and a ceramics studio for Zander. He had investments, sure, and he wasn't strapped for cash, what with every new novel reinvigorating sales for his previous books. But still, no new words meant no new books. No new books meant no new cash flow coming in—a situation he hadn't been in since graduating from college and finishing up his Marine reserve commitment, ten years ago.

Suddenly, Kate cleared her throat. "Why aren't you writing anything?"

Drake snorted. It was as if she'd read his mind. Why *wasn't* he writing anything? The million-dollar question. Literally.

"I suppose it's because I'm not inspired. Yet. Tell me, what do you see when you look around you?"

"Um...an old mausoleum?" Kate shrugged.

"Besides that," Drake said, desperately glaring at his legal pad. "Pretend for a second you have a client who...I don't know, wants to have an event here."

"A wedding? In a crypt? That'd be bizarre." Kate seemed to check herself when she saw his serious expression, and she cast her gaze around the room, sizing it up. "I'm not good with words. I'm no writer. I mostly plan weddings and I've never done one in a graveyard. But I have to say, the acoustics in here are...interesting. It's sort of like a church, echoing yet muffled at the same time. Close-sounding. Might be fun to have a small quartet in here, by the entrance. Guests would walk in and be treated to an orchestral-like sound in a micro-environment."

Drake looked up sharply at her, and then a grin spread across his face.

"That is an excellent observation. And you say you're not good with details. Go on. What else would you notice for your client if you were, say, planning something in this burial vault for them?"

Apparently, he'd said her magic word: planning. Kate's hands lost their death grip on her purse and the lines of her body grew less rigid. He sensed she was moving into a space he used to know really well—the creative space.

She pointed up to the window at the front.

"The stained glass. It's beautiful."

Drake came to stand shoulder-to-shoulder with her, directly in front of the window, facing the front of the mausoleum. Realizing the lantern prevented them from seeing the pattern from the sun's light streaming through, he clicked it off, standing next to her in the semi-darkness.

He stared at the dust-filmed stained glass and cocked his head, still seeing nothing but colored glass held together by black leading.

"How so?"

"Check out how the shapes work together," she said. Her hand pointed to the interwoven pieces of variously tinted yellow glass, mostly curves and wavy shapes, leading to the window's center, where four curls of yellow-orange framed an oblong piece of cobalt-blue glass, shaped like a shield. "That blue part, and the way it's being cradled there, in the center with all of those paisley sort of shapes, looks faintly nautical, and yet medieval at the same time. The yellow and orange fanning out from it is like a sunrise. Coupled with the intricate leading and ironwork on the outside, it all feels like a portal returning us to the age of knights and princesses in beautiful castles. It's exquisite. Maybe it could be a medieval-court wedding?"

"Hmm. I like it. A portal back to courtly times," Drake muttered each phrase, his pen flying across the page, barely able to see his scribbling in the dim light. "What else?"

"You know what would be really fun? I'd work with

the groom-to-be to design a surprise gift for his bride, and we'd have a jeweler create a necklace pendant inspired by the stained glass." Kate smiled, her gaze going soft as if she were envisioning the moment the groom gave it to his bride. "My 'Aww!' moment."

"Your...what moment?" Drake asked, captivated by the way her mind worked.

She elaborated.

"Well, I am known as the Queen of Happily Ever Afters, partly because of my fairy-tale weddings. But the details are what set my events apart. I usually don't tell my clients—or at least, I don't tell the bride—but there's always one little detail I plan to surprise them with. It's something I like to call the 'Aww!' factor. I think it's that, more than the weddings as a whole, which gets me referrals, if you want to know the truth."

Drake was intrigued. He wondered if Kate had an "Aww!" moment planned for his book launch but decided not to ask. It was best to keep her off that topic until he was ready to accede to the details of the upcoming launch circus. Although he'd only known her for a short while, he guessed Kate was a woman who, once given the reins, would keep galloping until she got to the finish line. He'd give her the project and set her free, but his muse needed more time with her before she became all about business.

An idea flashed in his mind about a piece of jewelry his hero would give the heroine before he went off to war in his historical romance work-in-progress.

"Can you draw what the pendant looks like, in your mind?"

Nodding, Kate took his legal pad and drew a quick sketch, then handed it back to him.

"I'm no artist, but that's how I'd envision it. The groom would give it to the bride right here. Under the window. Maybe as a part of his vows? That would be romantic—should be enough to elicit some tears from the bride, creating an 'Aww!' moment for them and their well-wishers."

He switched the lantern back on and inspected the paper. Her drawing was quite good—she had a definite artistic streak and a flair for description. He pictured the scene she described, the bride's face illuminated by the soft candlelight in the room, and the groom tenderly fastening the pendant around her neck, his fingertips brushing auburn hair from her soft, pale skin. Suddenly, he was immersed in the hero's point of view so firmly, he imagined wiping the tear from his bride's face, the wonder he'd feel gazing down at the woman he was lucky enough to spend eternity with—

"Why are you grinning? I know it sounds sappy, but in real life, I think it would be sweet."

When Kate spoke, Drake jolted, as if being woken from a nap. He fixed his expression, embarrassed to have been caught daydreaming about a scene for his *romance* novel. He cleared his throat, feeling the heat climbing his neck, and looked around for a diversion.

He spotted the empty crypt behind him. "Your description is outstanding. I may borrow it for a book someday. I'm wondering—" He paused, considering whether he really wanted to push her willingness to help him this far. But then, he recalled he'd likely need this detail for the bread-and-butter books he'd have to return to once he got this romance out of his system, and he hardened his heart. Might as well use her fantastic descriptive genius while he could. He plowed on with his request.

"Maybe you'd be willing to help me out? The coffin is too small for me—my shoulders won't fit inside. Could you climb inside and tell me what it feels like and looks like, just as you did with the stained-glass window?"

"Are you serious? No way." Kate shook her head. "I didn't wear appropriate clothes for lying down in a tomb. I don't even know what the appropriate attire *is* for lying down in a tomb."

"I get it," Drake said, a little disappointed. He'd had an idea to have his heroine hide from the bad guys—he hadn't really defined the villain yet—in a cemetery that was preparing for a funeral. But he was a writer, after all, and could invent what he didn't know about lying in a cold, stone coffin. "I shouldn't have asked you. I realize you're my event planner and only my research assistant to get your friend out of hot water. Time to get Wendy's attention and head up for a tour of the grave Curtis is digging. Would you like to try your hand at a backhoe?"

Kate put a hand on her hip. "I feel like this whole day today has been some sort of elaborate punishment. I thought you'd accepted my apology and were ready to move on?"

"Oh, I have. And I am. But I know whatever you're going to ask me to do is going to be..." Drake searched for the right words. He didn't want to hurt her feelings, but he did want to be honest with her—it somehow seemed important. "Well, it'll be like a circus sideshow."

She made a sound of offended incredulity. "Let me assure you, I don't run *anything* like a circus or a sideshow. I have spreadsheets in my bag here that'll show you my events are no free-for-all, buy-an-armband-and-ride-all-night affairs."

"I know you won't *mean* for it to be a sideshow, but really, what else can you do?" He shrugged his shoulders. "It's all about selling me and my freak-show books."

Kate paused, as if his last sentence totally derailed her prepared response.

"You don't write freak-show books, Drake," she said, to his surprise. Her eyes gleamed in the lamplight, and he noticed tiny flecks of hazel in their green depths. "Yes, they are scary. Yet they all have the hero or hero-ine triumphing in the end. They showcase a person's extraordinary ability to survive—even thrive—in spite of the ugliness that happened to them. That's more motivational, and reflective of real life, than other genres. Drake, I think the world *needs* your books, just to remind us that we're stronger and braver than we know."

Drake didn't know what to say.

His chest was alight with emotion, but he managed to string together a halted response.

"Have you ever actually *read* one of my books?"

Kate hesitated, licking her lips. "I, um...no."

Drake burst out laughing, and after a moment, Kate joined in.

"But I did skim the advance reader copy Imani gave me for *Halloween Hacker* as research for the launch. Your characters are so human, so flawed, yet when they face terror, they show such innate fortitude," she said, shaking her head as if unable to articulate her feelings. "You don't write freak-show books, and while I admit

I believed some of the rumors about you I read on the internet before I got here, now I know you're exactly what Imani said you were."

"Which is?"

Instead of answering, she removed her coat and thrust her handbag at him. "Hold these. The inside of this thing is filthy and God only knows what's crawled through here in a hundred years."

"Wait. What are you doing?"

"You're going to get the whole experience in this crypt so your next book has that ring of authenticity. And when I'm done, we'll talk plans. Deal?"

"D-deal." Then, before Drake could trip over any more words, she'd climbed the two steps of the dais, sat on the edge of the sarcophagus, and swung her legs inside. In one smooth motion, she sank into the black interior with no more hesitation than if she were entering a warm bath.

He whistled. "Damn. You're fearless."

A wicked laugh rose from the darkness.

"No. I'm dedicated."

Drake was going to set her coat on the edge of the stone, but recalling the amount of filth on the floors, and the light color of her jacket, he thought better of it. Stripping off his leather coat, he laid that on a diagonal over the corner of the crypt and balanced Kate's coat and bag on top where they wouldn't get dirty. Then he snatched up his legal pad and pen, marveling that this woman—basically a stranger—was willing to crawl into a tomb because she believed his books were...good for the world? He knew she was also doing it for her own ends, but still, those words seemed heartfelt. That giddy, too-large-for-his-chest feeling was still there, and he was a little worried he might recognize it.

It felt an awful lot like...a crush.

But that wasn't quite right. Too sophomoric for what he was feeling. His mind riffled through a mental thesaurus.

Affection? Attraction? Infatuation?

"Drake?" came Kate's voice from the darkness, jolting him. "Should I start describing it now?"

He cleared his throat, shoving the synonyms out of his mind to deal with later.

"I'm ready. You talk, and I'll transcribe."

Haltingly at first, she reported how it felt to lie in the empty sarcophagus, her voice floating, disembodied, out of the dark interior. She noted the chill of the stone, the texture of the rock to the pads of her fingers, and even the disturbing sensation of looking up and seeing only a faint, gray-lit rectangle of the world above her.

Drake's pen flew across the page. While he might be on a hiatus from horror, he'd be an idiot not to take down her observations. If he decided not to use it in the romance, he could always employ it for the next horror book, or the one after that, or the one after that. Eventually, her transcribed experience would be sucked into the churning gears of the publishing world, chewed up and regurgitated to scare the bejesus out of every possible person on earth.

After a few minutes, Kate paused. Drake heard curiosity mingled with hesitation in her voice.

"Although I know it's probably my own heartbeat, it's almost like I can hear something in here. There's maybe...a whisper of a breeze from the vent up there. It keeps blowing on my hair, almost imperceptibly, moving tiny strands of it," she said, her disembodied voice sounding puzzled. "Unless...Drake! Knock it off! I can totally tell it's you trying to scare me."

At her yell, he swept up the lantern and peered into the crypt. "I'm not doing any—" Drake's protest froze in his throat.

Kate wasn't alone.

"What?" she asked, her green eyes wide.

"Kate, don't move. There's a bat in your hair."

CHAPTER 9

Kate, don't move. There's a bat in your hair.

When Drake said those words, it was like she truly had become a superhero.

She'd have sworn on a stack of Bibles that she'd levitated out of that crypt, because before she'd made any conscious decision to do so, she was out of the stone box and halfway to the door, shrieking like a banshee. She slapped at her hair, both desperate to find, yet terrified to touch, the bat that had apparently been hiding in the dark corner of that tomb.

"Kate!" Drake yelled, grabbing her hands, holding her wrists in a vise-like grip. "Don't smack at your head—you'll scare it or hurt it, and it'll bite you. Just come here and let me see if he's still there. I think he flew away when you stood up, but you knocked the lantern over, so I'm not sure."

The lantern was rolling on the floor, casting crazy, moving shadows all over the marble crypts and walls.

"Can you see anything?" she gasped. "Is there anything in my hair?"

"Come closer. Let me look." He tugged her to his chest and told her to look left and then right. "I don't see anything. But let me take your hair down and I'll look. Just stay still—can you do that?"

She shuddered.

"It's okay. I've got you." His voice was soothing, like he was willing her calm with his words. "I'm just going to grab the lantern."

In two heartbeats, he'd snagged it and was back at her side handing her the light.

"Hold this shoulder height. I'm going to make sure nothing's in your hair."

Drake worked with careful delicacy, removing each bobby pin with deft fingers, then gently unwound her chignon. His touch felt intimate, and suddenly a whole different kind of shiver went through her body. A strand of hair and his warm breath tickled her neck.

He ran his fingers through her mass of hair.

"Anything?" she asked, her voice practically a squeak.

"No," he replied, his tone suddenly gravelly.

She turned toward him to find his eyes slightly glazed and his hand still reaching for a curl on her shoulder. He looked . . . mesmerized.

She felt a rush of heat to her cheeks. Somehow she, Kate Sweet, currently had the Knight of Nightmares silent and spellbound.

In a tomb.

That last realization sobered her, as did the fact the guy happened to be her best friend's client—one she'd almost lost for Imani due to her lack of situational control.

It wasn't going to happen again.

"All set?" she asked, her voice bright as she forced herself to pull away from his touch.

"You are officially bat-free," he said, flashing Kate a reassuring smile. "Here. These are yours."

Drake took the light from her hands, replacing it with a handful of pins and the elastic that held up her chignon. He stepped back. Suddenly, his smile grew tight, and Drake swung the light higher.

Kate peered fearfully over at the crypt, following Drake's gaze.

"What are you looking at? Is it still over there, or did it fly out?"

"There's...a few of them. I think our rapid movements and your...screaming stirred them up." Drake cast the lantern toward the vent near the ceiling, revealing inky black shadows.

Some of them were moving.

Kate's stomach clenched, and like a reflex, she crowded close to Drake and the weak, flickering lantern he held.

"Let's give them some room," he said in a low voice.

Slowly, like a strange waltz, they backed away from the center of the vaulted ceiling together, toward the structure's only doors.

"You think loud noises, like the whistle to call Mrs. Scanlon, will stir them up even more?" At his nod, Kate hugged her arms to herself and ducked her chin to her chest, attempting to be as small a human target as possible. She hissed her words. "So, what? We're just going to chill in here with the bats for the rest of the hour? How much longer do we have?"

Drake looked at his watch, and then winced.

"Twenty-eight minutes."

"Uh-uh," Kate said, "No way are we staying in here that long with a bunch of vermin. I hear you on the whistle, but maybe we can use our cell phones? Mine sometimes works in elevators, so—"

But Drake was shaking his head.

"Mine is in my jacket pocket—which I laid under your coat so it wouldn't get grimy from the sarcophagus. And I'm assuming yours is in your purse?" At Kate's reluctant nod, he grimaced. "Then we have no choice but to stay put. I wouldn't want to risk either one of us grabbing our stuff."

Kate closed the remaining distance between them, crowding so close she could feel the heat radiating through his sweater.

"Oh my God, why did I agree to come in here? Who in their right mind agrees to being locked in a crypt?" Kate tried to focus on the faint, woodsy scent of Drake's cologne. "I thought yesterday was the worst day in my life. But here I am today, courting rabies and giving myself guaranteed bad dreams about zombies for years to come."

"You agreed because you're being a good sport. The last thing I'd hoped to achieve today was to give you everlasting nightmares. But that seems to be my superpower," Drake said, his lips a thin line in the semi-darkness. "I pressured you into this, and I'm sorry, Kate."

Although she inwardly agreed that she'd felt pressured to come, she had to admit that the initial thrill had been exciting.

Up until the bats arrived, anyway.

"It's okay. You didn't know it would be infested," Kate said, shivering. Then she snorted. "At least you're going to have some killer material for your book. A bat-infested crypt, wading through bat poop—surely that'll appear somewhere in *Twisted Twin*? It's horror gold!"

Kate was surprised when Drake didn't readily agree. In fact, he shifted on his feet, and just as he'd opened his mouth to reply, the lantern in his hand flickered, and then went out.

Kate gasped, closing the last foot between them, her heels accidentally tromping on the tops of his boots.

"Ow, okay," he said, his hands coming to her shoulders to steady and reposition her so she was standing on her own feet again. "The lantern's batteries just died. Don't worry—she will be here to let us out soon. The bats won't bother us if we don't bother them."

"Ha. Says the horror writer who should know better," she said, gripping one of his biceps, ready to dodge behind him or duck under his arm at the slightest sensation of air movement around her. "Can we talk about something else? Anything else?"

"Why don't you tell me your launch plans now? We seem to have time to kill."

Finally! Kate's heart lifted . . . and then sank when she recalled her spreadsheets were in her purse, right next to the bat-infested sarcophagus. Licking her lips, she racked her brain for the broad strokes of the plan.

"Okay, well, we've nixed the barn and haunted house idea, of course," she began. "In its place, one idea we had was to have both a general fan event, as well as a different, more exclusive VIP version. We want to commandeer your entire block—"

Just as she threw her arms out on the word "entire," she saw a bat swoop down from the center of the room, its trajectory illuminated in the dim light cast from the stained-glass windows.

It was coming straight toward them.

Drake must have seen it at the same time, because just as Kate ducked, screaming, he grabbed her. One arm wound around her waist, dragging her to him, and his other arm cupped around the top of her head. He spun her until her back was pressed against the door, and his back faced the threat. His body bowed around hers, as if he'd become a human shield, and his voice was calm and controlled when he spoke in a low voice directly in her ear.

"Don't scream, Kate. And no more hand movements." His voice had a hint of irony when he continued. "Damn, these things are crazy aggressive. It's as if they know who I am, and they're showing off."

It took every ounce of Kate's resistance not to bury her face into his chest, wrap herself into a small bundle, and cower there until the threat was over. Instead, she took a deep breath, and then another, reminding herself that not all bats were rabid, and logically, they must be much more afraid of her than she was of them. Although right now, she wouldn't have bet on it.

"This is the most scared I've ever been in my life," she whispered. "You?"

His arms tightened a fraction around her. "Not even close," he whispered back. "But it ranks right up there with most embarrassing."

Wait. What? Kate wanted to pull back and look at his face to read his expression.

"I know. We do seem to be making a habit of extreme awkwardness," Kate replied. She remembered the way his hands had been all over her thighs at their first meeting. And now with his arms wrapped so tightly around her...

Damn.

Kate promised herself that she'd reactivate her Tinder account after this gig. Clearly, her body was ready for something—if not a relationship, then at least a good time. She sank into Drake, mortified but too scared to care as he clarified.

"That's not what I meant. I'm embarrassed I put you in this situation. Where in the hell is Wendy?" Drake breathed in her ear, and Kate assumed it was a rhetorical question, because he was the one with the watch, not her. "We can't have more than five minutes. Tell me the rest of your launch plan. Let's just cap off this afternoon with at least that check in your spreadsheet."

Kate's neck got that yummy-shivery feeling with him whispering in her ear, but she squeezed her eyes shut, picturing the spreadsheet and what she and Imani had determined to be the most audacious plan Drake might accept—one that would wow his fans, bring in those paid VIP tickets for charity, plus satisfy the movie production company's desire for an event worthy of the adaptation announcement. While it wasn't as conspicuous as the haunted barn and dangling coffin idea, as Kate spoke, she cursed their close quarters that hid his expression.

She couldn't tell if he loved or hated the pitch.

He jolted a little when she'd mentioned the giant mechanical spider they'd purchased to scramble up his house from the porch to the turreted attic and back all during the night, yet he hadn't shot the idea down. When she described how the fans would be treated to a haunted maze that started on Maple Avenue and wound around his grounds, ending at his house, he shifted a little on his feet, and when she said how the VIPs who'd paid the most for their ticket would get to see his writing office, he exhaled slowly, as if deflating.

She hurried to reassure him.

"It won't be a circus, Drake. I promise it will be fun, and the maze will pay homage to each of your books in a spooky but tasteful way. We'll place guards in costume all around your house, and we'll block off rooms where the public is not allowed." Kate mentally ran through the objections she'd anticipated and gave him her contingency plans for each. "Your house will be redone so that it's infused with enough gothic-style horror to wow your fans, while absolutely not making you look like—"

Drake supplied the words on the tip of her tongue.

"Like a sideshow freak?"

"Drake." Kate lifted her hand to touch his face, but then quickly detoured to his shoulder. More professional. She needed to be more professional. "I give you my word that it'll be appropriate. I'll keep you in the loop—daily updates, in person—so you can veto anything that strikes you wrong, no matter how big or small, and we'll pivot to something else. What do you think?"

He was silent for a breath.

"Daily updates from you. In person?" he asked, his voice low. At her nod, he sighed, his breath stirring her hair, warming her neck. "After what I've put you through today, how can I say no? Let's...let's win you that EVPLEX."

Kate gasped and pulled her head off his chest,

peering up at his face in the dim lighting, taking her chance with the bats to grin up at him in disbelief.

"Drake, that's—that's so…" She lost her train of thought. His face was so close. He smelled so good. His gaze drifted down to her lips, and Kate felt the scene tipping, as if gravity had reversed, forcing her face to tilt up toward his…

Just then, a pounding came on the door, and she heard the light tinkling of keys rattling in the lock. Suddenly, the vault door opened. Sunlight spilled into the dusty mausoleum, and she backed away from Drake, blinking owlishly and looking—she knew—guilty as hell.

As her eyes adjusted, she spotted the bewildered faces of Mr. Clark and Mrs. Scanlon peering in.

"Are you two…done?" Mr. Clark said, putting his hands on his overalls and cocking his head. "Or do you need a few more minutes?"

Kate bolted for the doors, almost knocking over Mrs. Scanlon in her desire to move as far as possible.

Whether it was to escape from the almost-kiss-tastrophe or from the bats, she wasn't sure.

It wasn't until Drake emerged a minute later, carrying his notepad, her purse, and both their coats that she realized she'd left them behind. He shook out her jacket and his, then he gave her purse a once-over before returning her belongings.

"Vermin free. I've got a few more things to research while I'm here, but I think…" Drake's neck and ears were flushed, yet he smiled—really smiled—at her when he continued after a pause. "…you've done your part for the day. You can put me down as a 'yes' to all your plans. I suppose you'll need to get into the house soon to measure, or whatnot?"

"Do you have time tomorrow?" she asked. "The sooner I can get measurements and pictures, the sooner I can lay out a plan for the designers. What fits your schedule best?"

"Morning. Around ten o'clock. I'm more of a late starter with my writing, so if we can wrap it up before noon, that will be best."

"You got it," Kate said. She'd have to work fast to get the permits for the road closures and mechanical spider in to the appropriate official today to provide adequate notice. "And, Drake, I promise I won't embarrass you or make you regret it. It's going to be the best book launch you've ever had!"

Drake looked unimpressed. He shrugged. "It'll all be worth it if Everstone has to give you an EVPLEX for a night honoring me."

Ten minutes later, Kate keyed herself into her hotel room, kicked off her heels, and rubbed her sore feet. She toggled into her cell phone's favorites menu and clicked on her best friend's picture.

Imani answered on the first ring, sounding out of breath and laughing. "Hi, Katie! Are you back so soon?"

"I'm back. What's got you in such a good mood?" Kate couldn't help smiling along too.

"I thought you'd be working longer, so I went to visit my grandmother. You remember Gigi?"

"Of course I do."

"I'm going to eat dinner with her tonight, so we can have some time together, and then I'll walk back to the hotel. I've been waiting for you to call. Do you have good news?"

"Apparently, the key to Drake's cooperation is willingness to do crazy stuff with him," Kate reported, unzipping her skirt. She wrestled out of her clothes, stuffing them in the hotel's dry-cleaning bag. She fervently hoped they had some magical detergent that removed ground-in tomb dirt and bat poop.

"Ooh, really?" Imani's voice cooed on the other end. "Should I go out to the porch to hear the details, or can I leave you on speakerphone?"

Kate shook her head, laughing as she peeled off her pantyhose—full of runs and rubbed-on stains—and stuffed them into the trash can. "Not like that. I mean crazy stuff like hang out in a mausoleum with him. Which I did, for an hour."

"Your version of crazy and mine are vastly different." Imani sounded unimpressed.

Kate snagged the white hotel robe from the closet and slid it on. "Well, have you ever lain down in an empty mausoleum tomb to describe the experience to a writer? Because I had to. Drake was too big to fit. That's how much I love you, Imani. I'm willing to risk rabies from the bat that crawled on my hair as I lay in a freaking stone sarcophagus. In a suit. And heels. Just to give you a client who'll say 'yes' to our new ideas. But I did it, and Drake agreed to have the launch in his yard and his house. We have a green light to begin."

Kate purposely left out the bat-forced, stand-up-snuggling that happened. And she definitely left out the almost-kiss-tastrophe. No way was she confessing to anyone, including her best friend, that she'd been so close to blowing it all. Again.

At the news of Drake's capitulation, Imani's jubilant

shout echoed in the hotel room. "Woo hoo! What was it like?"

"Um, well, he was really nice, like you said. I'd been so worried after our initial meeting, but you're right. Once you get to know him, he's really funny. A real gentleman. And he listens, you know? A writer thing, I'm sure, but—"

"No, I meant what was it like inside the coffin. With the bats? I know Drake's a good guy. I work with him, remember?"

"Oh," Kate said, embarrassed. "Right."

She filled her friend in, giving her the bare bones of it, and leaving out what she felt sure now was flirtation on his part...with the eager return of the same from her. It had been the result of being scared—like when you grab your date during a spooky movie, or on a roller coaster. It didn't mean anything, and telling Imani would only serve to worry...and disappoint her. It was the latter reaction Kate couldn't stand. It was one thing to disappoint her family. She'd come to grips with that. But she wouldn't put Imani through hell to scratch an itch.

"Good work," Imani enthused when Kate finished. "I'm not surprised. If anyone could wring an agreement out of someone, it's you, Katie. Oh, did you get Drake to agree to dress up like a vampire too?"

"What? No!" Kate's voice rose an octave. "He'd never agree to that. Since when was that in the plans?"

Imani gave a wicked laugh. "Just checking to see how much you had my superstar writer wrapped around your manicured finger. I've got to tell you, I'm surprised he caved. After the original pitch, he was pretty set on keeping it low-key. He hates the camera and limelight more than any other writer I've represented, and that's saying something. Most writers are so private, they're almost reclusive. And"—Imani's voice lowered—"between you and me, I heard he's not having a good time with his work-in-progress."

"Really? He—he didn't say anything about that. What's going on?"

Imani's voice dropped to a whisper. "Writer's block. His editor told me about it yesterday. First time he's extended a deadline. Ever. I'm a little worried about him. He's...not quite himself lately. I can't put my finger on why, and when I ask him about it, he shuts down." Imani spoke again at a normal volume. "Gotta run—Gigi and I are making anatomically correct zombie cookies. I'll bring some back with me. See you in a few!"

As Kate hung up, she sat in the massive hotel robe, feeling oddly dejected. She should be elated over this big win, but after hearing about Drake's writer's block...his capitulation to the new launch plans felt all wrong.

But he'd said yes, and time was slipping through her fingers. With only a few weeks until launch, plans had to be put into motion, or the man wouldn't have an event at all.

It was too late to change course now.

CHAPTER 10

Drake sat at his kitchen table as he reread the first chapter he'd created for *Memory's Lane*—the novel previously known as *Forbidden*—on his laptop. Sasha nuzzled against his leg, annoyed that her morning walk was delayed, and he picked her up. Tucking her down into his lap, he stroked her soft fur, scanning his work-in-progress to see if it looked the same on paper as he'd imagined it.

Sam strode down a dark stretch of one of Picadilly's mist-soaked cobbled streets toward his commanding officer's hideout, the thick fog clinging to his boots and legs like a wispy shroud. His mood was as bleak as the English weather, a never-ending cold drizzle. As he brought the ragged ends of his Da's old peacoat around him to hide his tuxedo, he had no idea that the empty, dank misery of his

life was about to change; along with
a sweeping, all-consuming passion,
the universe was about to deliver a
gut-punch.

Perhaps sensing the mechanisms that
fate had set in motion, Sam shivered
as the wet wind found its way through
the thin fibers of his coat. He peered
into the distance, wishing for more
visibility than the flickering yellow
glow of the intermittent gaslights.
He reassured himself that the British police couldn't have discovered
him already—not when he'd taken so
many precautions. But his heart ham-
mered in his chest as he picked up
the noise of soft footsteps—someone
creeping up behind him.

With his leg wound, he'd never outrun
a pursuit, so he hid in the shadows.
The streetlamp revealed the vague outline of his follower as the stranger
approached, jogging fast, almost at a
run. Sam pulled out his pocketknife,
flicking the sharp blade open in his
palm. If he was going down, it wouldn't
be without a fight.

He waited until the footsteps were
right up to him before throwing his
body into the path of his pursuer,
the impact of their collision driving
the air from his lungs and tossing
him back a step.

Sam recovered, and in a heartbeat, he had his knife jammed against the short guy's ribs. Just then, a few things became very clear: the man he'd intercepted was tiny and thin and soft in all the wrong places. Small hands gripped his peacoat so hard, the old fabric tore, and then a voice—a woman's voice—exclaimed under her breath.

"Please! You've got to help me—they'll kill me if they find me!"

The clouds parted briefly, allowing the moon to illuminate the woman gripping him. The hood on her black coat was up, but bits of auburn hair peeped out as she gazed up at him with a heart-shaped face and eyes as green as a summer's field. She looked so terrified, Sam's arms automatically wove around her, and she buried her face into his chest, quiet sobs racking her body.

"Please, I beg you."

Sam felt a lurch, as if the Earth had grown unstable beneath his feet, and suddenly, right then and there, he knew nothing in his life would ever be the same.

"Shhh. It's okay," he said, after a moment. He scanned the darkness as he guided her off the cobbled street toward the old fishmonger's stall,

```
his  arm  around  her  thin  shoulders.
"I've got you. Follow me."
   She nodded, and they both started as
a shrill whistle split the night—
```

Drake stopped mid-sentence, petting Sasha as he examined the scene where his hero meets his heroine. It was okay—cliché at parts, and he'd definitely have to go back and fix that "going down without a fight" bit and find a way to show his heroine was stronger than to just dissolve into tears, but he thought the unexpected sweetness of the scene was there. He'd been struggling with how to have his American spy hero and his British secretary heroine meet, and then Kate slammed, quite literally, into his life, and he had the inspiration he'd needed.

He felt a little guilty at using her to achieve his goal for the romance novel, but then he rationalized that she was using him to achieve her EVPLEX.

"Besides," Drake said, ruffling Sasha's fur, "that's what we writers do best. We take inspiration from our own lives to craft our stories."

What he'd never admit to was how real the last part of that scene was.

Like a guilty tell, his eyes went to the box of his grandparents' World War II love letters he'd hauled to the kitchen this morning. He'd pored over those letters for months, captivated by their sweeping love story.

What must it be like to be carried away, just like Nana and Grandpa Matthews had been? For months, he'd yearned to write such a love story, even if he'd never lived one, but other than research…the well was dry.

Yet ever since he'd taken Kate Sweet in his arms, his world had shifted, altered, and would take a while to set right again. He suddenly understood a little better those early letters from his grandparents—their wondrous, tentative excitement. Having Kate in his arms the day before had felt so good, even if she'd only stayed tucked up against him for fear of rabies. It didn't mean she liked him.

But then there had been that moment at the end. A heartbeat of time when he thought she might kiss him. And that tiny hope fueled him through five thousand words this morning. He'd been more energized at his writing desk than he had for years.

He checked the time in the corner of the screen, noting that he had around five minutes before Kate was due to arrive, so he clicked *Save* on *Memory's Lane* and put his laptop to sleep. He'd left the scene mid-sentence as he always did—a trick he'd picked up from other writers as a way to stave off the dreaded writer's block. If you always knew at least that much of a scene— enough to finish a sentence—you had enough to start the day writing as you waited for your muse to clock in and fill those blank pages with words. Although the trick hadn't worked for him in months... until now.

As he cleaned the kitchen table of the letters, Drake dreaded Kate's plans for his house and this launch. He reminded himself he was allowing fans inside for a hefty donation to veterans in need, but the thought of his private sanctum being invaded, people judging and gawking at his ancestral home, made him cringe.

Suddenly, his gate chime sounded, and he raced Sasha to the security panel. She beat him to it, her tiny paws pattering on the door as she barked excitedly, her

tag wagging wildly as he punched in the code, buzzing
Kate inside. He picked the dog up, letting the fluffball
plant kisses on his chin and neck.

"Who's here, huh?" he asked, ruffling the fur on her
head, chuckling at how the gate chime and doorbell
made her go berserk.

He still thought it was odd the way she'd come into
his life. Two years ago, he'd gone out to get his morning
paper and discovered a small puppy shivering in a crate
that had been lowered over his gates with a makeshift
rope-pulley. There was no note, just a paper showing
her shot records with the vet's header and logo trimmed
off. "Sasha" had been written in a child's scrawl on a
piece of masking tape adhered to the top of the crate.
It was the strangest fan gift he'd ever received.

He opened his door as Kate ascended the porch
steps, professionally dressed in a tailored navy pantsuit.
Her hair was up in what he now knew was a chignon,
crafted by folding those luscious auburn curls over and
over themselves, and then fastening them with four
strategically placed bobby pins. He'd already written it
all in his notes—how it had felt to take her hair down,
as if he were somehow undressing her—and he looked
forward to what he might be able to steal from their
encounter today.

His smile of greeting changed as he noticed what
was behind her. Clinging to the bars of the iron fenc-
ing stood his fans, waving and cheering at him amid
flashes from cell phone cameras. When it was a sunny
day, no matter the temperature, you could count on a
crowd outside for hours snapping pictures and sometimes shouting to the house, begging for him to come
out and sign books. It was only thanks to the rain

and miserable weather that Kate hadn't encountered the throng previously. Drake's scowl deepened as he motioned her inside.

"Good...morning?" she said, turning the greeting into a question.

He fixed his face. "Sorry, the mob out there sets my teeth on edge. It's creepy the way they stand there, like zombies, and—never mind," he interrupted himself, wondering why he was always reduced to a stuttering teenager around this woman. "Come on in. And don't worry. I've got Sasha. She won't attack you."

"Ha-ha," Kate said, stepping inside and bending her head down to the level of the dog in his arms. She ruffled the shih tzu's hair, crooning as Sasha wriggled madly. "We have an understanding, now, don't we? I don't sneak up on you in the bushes, and you won't chase me using your big dog voice, right?"

Sasha barked, and Drake set her down. She danced around them for a couple of seconds before racing away to her crate to drag out her favorite toy. Drake hung up Kate's coat and, despite his protests, Kate removed her shoes before following him toward the back of the house as he attempted to be a good sport about his end of the bargain.

Kate would have her circus-like event, and he'd reap the benefits of her presence in the interim, resulting in the culmination of this romance novel.

It would be worth it. It would.

"Do you want a cup of coffee? I thought we'd meet back here," he said, leading her through the swinging door into the kitchen. "It's more private."

"Yeah, some of your fans had professional cameras, like they were trying to get a picture of you through the lace blinds. And I'd love a cup of coffee. Just black, no sugar." Kate set her leather satchel on a chair, gazing around the kitchen with interest. "Is this where your chef prepares all your meals? I expected something...more industrial and modern."

Drake raised an eyebrow at her. "Why would you think I had a chef? Is that one of the rumors out there—that I've got some poor bastard trapped back here, carving raw meat off a cow carcass for me, freshly dipping it in warm, bloody au jus?"

Kate's face did that captivating transformation from creamy white to peachy pink in the time it took for her to reply.

"Well, not the fresh au jus part. But don't worry—I won't tell."

Drake laughed. God, he loved how she surprised him into humor!

"No chef. Just me," Drake said, searching through the mugs with stupid sayings that Ryker had given him for an appropriate one. No way was he handing Kate a mug that said *Coffee Makes Me Poop*. He finally located one of the tall blue-and-green glazed mugs handcrafted in Zander's ceramics studio. He poured her a cup and got another for himself, all the while watching Kate's gaze take in every nook and cranny. His empty stomach churned as he wondered what her event planner's mind made of the space. He didn't have to wait long to find out.

"Drake, this kitchen is amazing!" Kate grinned at him when he turned from the coffeemaker. "If I didn't know any better, I'd say you spied on my Pinterest boards. I have a table with four red, vinyl-backed chairs just like this set on my board, and that cherry-red

Elmira Stove Works gas range is literally my kitchen goal. You've got a great eye for decorating—I love the nostalgic 1950s aesthetic you've got going on and the fact that it's juxtaposed with modern appliances and that drool-worthy white farmhouse sink…" Kate paused in her admiration, looking at him with embarrassment as he sat down opposite her at the table. She finished lamely, "Well, I just really like it."

Drake slid her mug to her, admiring the beautiful flush of red in her cheeks as he leaned back in his chair. "I can't take any credit. My mother knew the kitchen needed an upgrade, so she designed it and had it renovated after Nana moved out and before I moved in. Mom's sort of a vintage-design nut—I'm sure you noticed it when you were in the bakery."

"The bakery?"

"PattyCakes," Drake said, his eyebrow raising at her in disbelief. "The bakery where you placed an order for three hundred cupcakes for the launch? Did you really not know that was my mother—with those pictures of me all over her walls?"

Kate's eyes grew round.

"That was your mom? I—I didn't know, actually. I just thought you were all over the walls because you're a local celebrity. She never said anything, even after I told her…"

"Told her what?" Drake asked.

"Well, I sort of broke down," Kate admitted, ducking her head to gaze at her coffee. "I'm not a crier, but with everything that happened that day, I was so worried about Imani's job, and your mom was so kind to me, it hit me all at once. We were alone, and she was so easy to talk to…I sort of told her everything.

Flashing your neighbor, the accidental stabbing, you passing out on top of me, Evan Everstone—"

"She knows about Everstone being here?" Drake's fingers tightened around his mug. The fact that cretin had seen him unconscious and weak made his blood boil. You never showed your enemies your weakness.

"Sort of." Kate met his eyes, wincing. "Are—are you going to kick me out again?"

Drake chuckled, letting out a breath and his anger. While he wasn't sure of much in life, he knew this much: Kate was no Machiavelli. She was almost transparent, she was so easy to read, and her expression held no guile or cunning. True, she probably shouldn't have told his mother all of that, but then again, he knew his mom—she could force the pope to confess his sins, with her lethal combination of piercing eyes and coma-inducing desserts. He had to trust Kate if this bargain was going to work.

"Nope. I'm not tossing you out on your ear. We've got a deal, remember?"

Kate gave him a tentative smile. "How could I forget? I'm doing insane things like climbing into caskets for you to help you research this new novel, and in return—"

"I'm going to do insane things so Everstone has no choice but to give you that award you've been coveting." Drake nodded, standing up. "Let's get started with that tour of the house you requested."

"Great!" Kate stood, and her stomach growled so loudly even Drake heard it.

He changed direction, heading for the fridge. "Right after breakfast. How's an omelet sound?"

She laughed with a self-conscious grimace, putting a

hand to her stomach. "Apparently, it sounds amazing. How can I help?"

Drake's first instinct was to tell her that she didn't have to do anything. He was raised that a guest was to be treated like royalty, and his mother would stroke to hear what he was about to say. But as soon as the idea popped into his head, he knew he had to take advantage of this situation for his book.

They were going to cook together.

His mind was already whirring with where he'd place this scene in *Memory's Lane*—right after his hero rescues Ingrid from her pursuers in the silent movie, they take alleyways and back streets to his flat, where he cooks breakfast. He can tell she hasn't eaten for days and is dirty and waif-thin. But his leg injury makes him clumsy in the kitchen, so he needs her help and—

"Drake?" Kate's voice startled him back to the present. She peered with him into the fridge, cold air blasting them both as they stared at his shelves of food. "Everything okay? You seemed to be...lost for a second."

He grabbed the eggs, butter, and the green peppers from the crisper. He feigned a limp as he walked toward the nearest counter.

"I pulled a muscle. From my run this morning," he fibbed, turning away from her. He was a rotten liar— his brothers caught him out on every single one he tried to float by them—but he reasoned that the lie was innocent enough. Plus, it sounded a hell of a lot better than telling her he was playacting the scene in his head to see how his heroine—or Kate, for now—might respond in this situation. Heat crept up his neck as he furthered the lie. "I might need you to give me a hand?"

"Of course!" Kate bustled over, taking the items from his arms and laying them all on the countertop. "I don't have a huge kitchen repertoire, but I can cook an omelet. I think. Or at least an egg scramble with a bunch of ingredients, which is pretty much the same thing. Right?"

"Right. Thanks so much." Drake smiled, his fingers itching for a pen and paper. Instead, he folded his arms, leaning a hip against the countertop, drinking in every gesture and facial expression as Kate buzzed self-consciously around his kitchen, opening random drawers and cupboards. She was like a whirlwind of chattering determination, and what she lacked in efficiency she made up for in brimming self-confidence. She really was like a pint-size superhero in her stocking feet and with wisps of auburn hair escaping the tight chignon as she worked.

He had no idea how real-life Kate would achieve her goal of winning that award, but he knew one thing: having her work with him on his romance novel, albeit clandestinely, had been a stroke of brilliance.

CHAPTER 11

W ell, that didn't go as planned," Kate muttered, as she picked bits of eggshell from the mixing bowl with the spatula. She'd been a little overaggressive breaking the last egg and now shells littered the bottom of the bowl beneath the raw eggs. She tried a different tool, dipping in with a metal spoon, but instead of scooping them out, all she seemed to be doing was chasing the shell pieces around the bowl.

"Seems to be your theme song," Drake said, and when she glanced up sharply, he wasn't leaning against the far counter. Instead, he stood behind her, watching her fishing expedition with those golden eyes that seemed to miss nothing.

"That's not a compliment." Kate bristled, nudging a stray hair out of her face by using her shoulder to avoid getting raw egg in her hair. "I'm a person who lives by a spreadsheet of detailed line items. Things *always* go according to my plans. Normally."

Drake shrugged, and out of the corner of her eye, she caught a smile blooming on his lightly whiskered face. "If you say so. From what I've seen chaos seems to follow you around like a lapdog."

Kate resisted the urge to be goaded. It felt like he was looking to provoke a reaction from her for some reason. He reminded her of a tiger she'd seen at the Bronx Zoo once who just lay there and seemed to be content, but all the while studying the people pressed against the fence, his tail thumping idly against the ground. Unseen by the crowd, his lethal claws extended and retracted, as if waiting for his prey to step closer so he could pounce.

Kate noticed Drake had that same idle intensity, and it was as distracting as it was...thrilling. If she were being honest, maybe a small part of her enjoyed being the object of his interest. What might it be like to have that intensity focused on her for an hour? Or a night?

Kate shook her head, clearing the crazy thoughts. None of that today. She'd promised herself, for Imani's sake, she'd ignore Drake's rock-hard abs and wouldn't be lured in by his rumbling, infectious laugh. She would focus on the task at hand. First—make this stupid omelet. Next, tour the house, and last, come up with a decorating scheme and get Drake to sign off on it. That was the plan. Those were the steps.

Kate glared at the bits of eggshell littering the bottom of the bowl, going after them from the top instead of the side. Maybe that was the trick?

"Can I give you a tip?" Drake's voice sounded right behind her, his warm breath fanning her ear. Heat rose up her neck, and she knew she was blushing. Why did that always happen around this guy? "Crack your egg on the counter next time—the flat surface is better than the edge of the bowl, and you won't get shells in the mixture that way."

Kate set the spoon down, giving him a sour look to hide how flustered she'd become at his proximity. "Thank you, Gordon Ramsay. But lucky for you and your upcoming book launch, you can rest assured that when chaos strikes, I can adapt. Like now. Where's your colander? I'm about to alter my plan, and it's still going to be incredible."

Drake limped to the other side of the kitchen, and Kate swore he was favoring the other leg this time. He bent down, retrieved a plastic strainer from a cupboard, and handed it to her. Then, saying nothing, he watched as she chopped veggies, then turned on the stove.

Kate grinned with delight as the gorgeous red stove ticked several times and whooshed to life, a blue-white flame dancing merrily above the burner. She put the chopped green pepper in first with the butter, and then she turned to Drake.

"Are you okay if this is more carnivorous? I mean, you're not vegetarian, are you?"

"Nope, I like it all," he said, his full lips tilted up at the edges in an expression of amusement that made her want to swat him. Or kiss him.

No. Focus. Think of the plan.

Kate stalked to his refrigerator, throwing open the door to grab some precooked turkey sausage and shredded cheese she'd spotted when she peeked over Drake's shoulder as he'd seemed confounded by his earlier foray to the fridge. She quickly sliced the sausage links into thin discs, then tossed them in with the peppers. Next, she poured the whisked raw eggs into the pan through the strainer, hoping the holes would catch all those pesky shells, and gradually coaxed the eggs into a scramble, breathing in the delicious scent of sweet sausage and fried green peppers in anticipation. Just as it firmed, she topped it with cheddar cheese.

"There! Chaos managed." Kate blew a stray hair off her forehead, turning off the burner. She'd felt him staring at her the entire time she was cooking, and it had made her nervous and self-conscious, but oddly, she wasn't weirded out by his silent observance. It didn't feel stalker-ish—more like she was being seen, really seen by a man. And Lord knew it had been a hot minute since that had happened.

Drake reached behind him and pulled out two plates and silverware, handing one set to her. "I stand corrected. You are the master of chaos—it dare not master you."

He poured a top-off to their coffee, and they sat at the red-trimmed enamel table.

Kate dove into the egg scramble...and stopped chewing as her first bite crunched.

Damn. An eggshell.

But Drake was shoveling the food into his mouth, so she assured herself it was the only bit of shell that'd gotten into the pan. She swallowed it all down with hot coffee, trying not to gag. Then, she heard Drake crunch on his bite, as if he'd put a Dorito in his mouth instead of eggs, fully cooked peppers, sausage, and cheese.

Kate's eyes widened, and she held her breath.

Yet his expression never changed. He swallowed the bite, and took another, never breaking stride. He must not have wanted to hurt her feelings.

"Um, sorry about the shells. Thought I got them all."

"Doesn't bother me." Drake shrugged. "Bit of extra

calcium, is all. The best thing about Marine boot camp, followed by my weekends of reserve training, is the absolute disregard you have thereafter for the taste, texture, or temperature of the food entering your body. I've literally eaten dog food, so I'm not bothered by crunchy scrambled eggs."

"Well. My breakfast is better than Alpo. Good to know." Kate wrinkled her nose, picking around the egg to spear the safer, less shell-riddled sausage with her fork.

"What I should have said first was, 'Thank you for breakfast,'" Drake amended, reaching across the table to tap against the hand she'd cupped around her mug. "Although I think I'm the one who owed you a meal after yesterday's adventure in the cemetery. I hope it didn't scar you for life?"

Kate ignored the tiny whirl in her stomach as he pulled his hand away from hers. "I don't scare easily. Besides, what a great story I'll have to tell my kids one day—I was once trapped in a mausoleum with the Knight of Nightmares himself!"

Drake grimaced. "I hate that name."

"Well, you can't let one label define you. I mean, the Queen of Happily Ever Afters isn't all I do. I'm about to create a horror launch so epic, they'll be calling me the Mistress of Maleficence soon."

"And you'd like that?" Drake laughed, popping another egg bite into his mouth, and chewing another crunchy bite.

Kate made a face as he plowed through the egg shrapnel, but she answered his question. "People like to label others. It makes them feel as if they know you, or at least, they know in which box you belong. Some people put me in a career box, some put me in a box that's about my surgeon family, or a box about people who grew up on Long Island. All those boxes are a part of me, but none of them define me. I've tried to be true to what's inside. I'm sure you didn't set out to be the Knight of Nightmares at the beginning, did you?"

Drake took his time to answer, chewing the last of his breakfast.

"No. At the beginning, I was writing things just for myself. I'd fill those black-and-white-speckled composition notebooks with stories. Short ones, usually with a twisted sort of moral at their core that reflected my worries and fears. I even dabbled with longer, more literary tales. Things that told a larger story. But then, I was taking a writing class during my last year in the Marines and the professor gave us a Halloween assignment. Scaring people was easy to me. That's what I used to do when I was little—scare the pants off my younger brothers by telling ghost stories before they went to bed."

Kate shook her head at him. "Poor things! I bet they didn't sleep a wink."

"This one time, Zan got so terrified, he leaped off the top bunk and sprinted to Mom and Dad's room, but he forgot the door was closed. He face-planted into it. Broke his nose." Drake chuckled, looking into his cup of coffee as if gazing into the past. "That's when I first knew I had a talent for scaring people. That horror assignment spooked my professor so much, he insisted I send it in to a contest. That's how I earned my first two hundred dollars in this business, and I became hooked. Now, manufacturing nightmares is my full-time job. Typically."

That last word reminded Kate what Imani had told her about his writer's block. She put her fork down.

"You know, I'm glad you asked me to help with your, um, research while we prepare for your book launch," she said, nodding at him across the table as he gave her a dubious look. "I was thinking last night about how many phobias I conquered in just an hour with you. Being buried alive, attacked by bats, claustrophobia…"

"What about zombies?" he asked. "You talked about them three different times yesterday in the mausoleum."

Kate's mouth fell open. She wasn't sure what surprised her the most: that he'd remembered she was afraid of zombies? Or that he'd counted how many times she'd talked about them?

"I know zombies aren't real," she countered, raising her chin. "But, yes. When I entertain the thought of dead people crawling out of graves, I get the shivers. Michael Jackson's *Thriller* video makes my palms sweat."

Drake laughed. "You're an easy mark. I see now why you don't read my books."

"Everyone is afraid of something. I'll bet even the Knight of Nightmares has a fear. Come on—now that you know my aversion for the undead, what's your phobia?"

He gave her an easy smile, but Kate saw something flit across his features as he answered. "I exorcised all my dark dreams long ago by writing them. It's like immersion therapy—when you put your imagination in scary places daily, you become immune to terror."

"But what about real fears?" Kate persisted. "Not

the irrational ones, like zombies. But real ones. Want to make a deal? You tell me yours, and I'll tell you mine."

Drake picked up his plate and silverware, scooping up hers with them, and headed to the sink. Kate figured she'd scared him off, and he wasn't going to answer, but then he turned around.

Leaning against the counter, he said, "Deal. Mine's a fear of rejection."

Kate blinked. "Still? I mean, you've been publishing books since you were, what? Twenty-four? A book a year for the past ten years, all bestsellers. How many people are rejecting the notorious Drake Matthews?"

"Nope. That's not the way it works. I told you my fear, and now you've got to tell me yours." Drake smiled as if he knew how annoying she found it when people did not fully explain things.

Kate crossed her arms across her chest. "Fine. My biggest fear is letting people down. Being somehow responsible for ruining an event. That's what terrifies me. That's what keeps me up at night checking and double-checking my plans."

"You want to be the hero," Drake said, nodding. "I get it. Makes sense when you have parents who are surgeons."

"Parents and a younger sister, once she's done with med school," Kate corrected. "Everyone in my life works to save people. Their work means something. I want my work to mean something to people, and while I know my mistake probably won't result in someone dying, I can't imagine anything more horrible than ruining a wedding or some other happy occasion."

"Has that ever actually happened to you?"

Kate shuddered. "No. Because I plan, I double-check my plan, and I have a great assistant who helps me ensure that we never, ever ruin someone's special day. And on that note..."

"The tour. Right. I guess there's no putting it off. Follow me." Drake sighed, pushing off from the counter, only limping slightly now.

Kate followed Drake around his house in her stockinged feet, using her smartphone to take pictures and jot notes about ideas for various rooms. As the tour progressed, she experienced a wave of envy...quickly followed by one of despair.

The envy part was easy—the Queen Anne Victorian was gorgeous. Thick Turkish carpets covered hardwood floors that sometimes squeaked in the way old wood floors did over time. Hand-carved, gleaming wood trim framed every doorway, and the parlors downstairs were all interconnected with beautiful pocket doors that silently slid open and closed at Drake's touch. The fire was stoked in the fireplace, the flames reflecting off the original burgundy-and-green tiles, and old, hand-painted glass globe lamps lit up each corner like an advertisement for some historic home museum. Upstairs was more of the same, with antique furniture and moody wallpaper offset by banks of windows that made every bedroom cheery and cozy. Even the smell of the place was old and rich, with lemon polish mingling with the scent of woodfire and a hint of Drake's warm, spicy cologne.

It was beautiful.

And all wrong.

While Kate oohed and aahed at every antique, some

of her dread must have shown in her expression, as Drake finally stopped the tour by the upstairs staircase, facing her.

"So, I may not be an event planner, but as a writer, I'm pretty good at reading faces. Are you going to tell me what's wrong? Or ... are you still afraid of me?"

Kate had opened her mouth to respond to his first question, and then snapped it closed at his second question, pursing her lips as she considered how to tell him something he'd likely take as an insult.

Drake gave that half smile, as if sensing her dilemma.

"It's okay. You can run back to the hotel tonight and tell Imani what's really wrong. Then, she'll draft a stellar email about it, couched in all the best flattering and politically correct language she can muster. I'll attempt to decipher it, make assumptions, likely misinterpret something, and then we can have that awkward conversation a few days from now instead." Drake shrugged. "Or, you can just tell me now and save us both the hassle."

Kate's lips quivered as she fought off a smile and lost. She tilted her head, shaking it at him in a mixture of annoyance and resignation.

"Well, I guess once you've been stabbed by a girl, saved her from a shih tzu attack, and then had to search for bats in her hair, it's hard to see how a truth bomb is going to sour that relationship."

"You're right." Drake nodded, that half smile growing. "Give it to me straight. What's the truth bomb you're trying not to lob my way?"

"It's just ... " Kate hesitated, then threw her hands in a wide arc, encompassing the open door to his bedroom with the Victorian carved headboard and the antique brass chandelier. "It's just so dowager-grandmother-next-door! Lavish and museum-like! Even your office has an antique desk in it, and it's all neat—no clutter, no drawings of werewolves on the walls. I mean, it's gorgeous, don't get me wrong, but converting your house for a spooky VIP meet and greet isn't just *Mission: Impossible*. It's Mansion Impossible!"

To her surprise, Drake threw his head back in laughter.

"Dowager-grandmother-next-door! That's...that's so accurate. I literally moved here with only my clothes. Sold my house in California when I...well, when I ended things there, and came with two suitcases. This was my grandparents' house, and it was their parents' house before them, so it's been in the Matthews line for generations." Drake pointed to the sumptuous, king-size bed covered with a deep burgundy damask comforter. "This is my bedroom, but before that, it was my grandparents', and their parents' before them. That mattress, box spring, and bed coverings are the only brand-new things in the room. Besides the kitchen appliances, every single thing in this house is exactly the way it's been for decades."

"It's all beautiful," Kate said with honest urgency. She'd purposely turned to face him, putting her back to that huge, masculine bed in the master bedroom. As soon as he'd said that was his bedroom, her mind had immediately pictured a fire in that fireplace, casting flickering shadows on his skin as he lay next to her... She shook herself out of the vision, finishing her thought. "I lived in modern, sterile houses my whole life, and trust me, this is so, so much better. There's wonderful history here."

Drake nodded.

"Every room in this house has a past. I guess I've resisted changing anything because...it's like a cup of hot cocoa. Soothing and filled with only warm, happy times." He pointed to the tiny, baby-blue room that adjoined the master bedroom. "That room was where I slept when we spent the night, which was a lot when dad was a drill instructor. My brothers shared the green room by the back staircase. Can you see what's on the very bottom of this?"

Kate knelt down next to Drake, examining the bottom of the newel post of the second floor's banister railing. She peered at the very bottom of the dark, intricately carved, rectangular newel post to a barely noticeable carving.

"Are those...initials?"

"Yep. Mine. I did that with the jackknife Dad bought me in middle school, a couple years before he died. Got grounded for a month, which I felt was a little excessive. After I filled it in with magic marker, you could barely see it." Drake looked at her, shoving his glasses onto his nose with an embarrassed smile. "I know it's bizarre to live in this place like a—what did you say that first day? Like an antique museum had vomited all over in here. But it's the one place I can just...be me. Everywhere else, I'm pretending. Being someone else. But here, I'm the fourth generation of Matthews men. And I fit in." He straightened, and she stood with him.

"I didn't mean any offense." The words hurried out of Kate's mouth. "I love your house, and I think it's an amazing legacy they've left you, and it's awesome how you've kept it so authentic."

Drake's eyebrow rose.

"But?"

"I'm just saying it's hard to envision that a horror writer lives here. Like, really, really, *really* hard." Kate winced as she gestured to his boyhood bedroom he'd now converted to an office with a daybed in the far corner. "There isn't a single skull or dead thing in the entire place. Nothing in this house is going to ... satisfy your horror readers."

Drake paused. "Well, there's one room you haven't seen that is a little creepy. It's where I got my idea for *Dark Dolls*, actually. And ... if I'm not mistaken, there's a skull up there and something that's been dead for at least a few decades."

Kate's heart lifted with hope. Maybe this could be saved, after all?

"Can I see it? Where is it?"

"The attic. I can take you up there, but it's not insulated or heated, so you need to get some shoes on your feet. Plus, it still has the old knob-and-tube wiring, so promise me you won't grab the wires. I don't want you to electrocute yourself. With your penchant for chaos, I'm a little worried to take you up there."

Kate rolled her eyes. "I'll go grab my shoes, and I promise not to touch anything."

"One more thing," Drake said, his eyes glittering as he led her to a door at the end of the hallway that she'd assumed was a closet. "The attic is supposedly haunted."

CHAPTER 12

While nothing accosted them from the dusty confines of his attic, Drake was thrilled that at least one thing had been accomplished: he'd taken that frown off Kate's face.

"This!" Kate said, spinning in the dim space, her hair catching the light so that it looked like glowing copper as she flitted first to the big turret window and then to the boxes stacked hither and yon. "This is the perfect spot! Have you ever done it up here?"

Done it? In the attic? Then, he dragged his mind from the gutter, and realized she was talking about writing.

"No," he said, gesturing to the dark, rough-hewn boards on the ceiling and walls. "It's not even insulated. I'd get frostbite nine months out of the year if I tried to write up here."

Kate frowned, ignoring his raised brow of disbelief. Then her expression smoothed.

"I know! We'll drag your laptop up here for a little while, and you can write a few sentences. Then, when we give a tour and say you write up here, it won't be a lie. Will you let me unpack some of these boxes? That old doll and carriage are truly terrifying. We can arrange a small writing desk in here, and the belongings you already have can be artfully arranged. Where did you say the skull and the dead thing were?"

Drake started. He'd been busy watching Kate light up with the spark of creativity that comes when your muse is flaming hot, enjoying the way her cheeks flushed in exhilaration despite the chilly air. He mentally rewound her words and pointed at the attic's only oddities.

"The skull is over there leaning against that old Marine footlocker. It's from a steer my grandfather found in the desert when he was out in Arizona. And the dead thing is right there—a taxidermy squirrel, complete with probably a century of dust."

Kate bustled over to the skull and the squirrel, her heels leaving tiny, triangular prints on the dusty floorboards. She surveyed both and turned to give him a thumbs-up.

"This is perfect! Would you mind if we bring in some more creepy stuff for extra ambiance? Nothing too over-the-top, but I'm thinking a rusty machete nailed to the attic wall, just there, and maybe some other antique dolls grouped together with this one. I'll see if I can't find a few tarnished candelabras and maybe a rusted bird cage...I'll have to read the backs of your books to get a better idea, but we'll put enough goodies in here that the fans will love it!"

Drake noticed she'd not committed to actually *reading* one of his books—just the back covers—and was reminded once again of the stark difference between Kate and all the people who fawned over his fame and his books. If he didn't have his horror talent going for him, what did he have?

He thought again of his notes, stacked on the inspiration box of his grandparents' letters downstairs. Maybe, like Kate said, he could rise above his label—be more than the Knight of Nightmares? But, then, when this romance was finished, what was the point if he was the only one who knew he was about more than terrorizing people?

"We don't want to disappoint the fans," he finally supplied, filling the silence.

Kate reached out, and for a second—a really nice, long second—he thought she was going to hold his hand. Instead, she brushed her fingertips against the sleeve of his shirt by his elbow.

"You're worried that we're going to destroy something, aren't you?" Kate's brows drew together in what she'd probably thought was empathy for his privacy. "Don't worry. We'll put your vintage and antique furniture in storage so nothing is even touched by a fan. I'll get your approval every day, like I promised, on everything from the outside changes to the downstairs decorations, all the way up to this attic. What we add or change, we remove immediately after the launch. The beautiful Matthews family Victorian will be exactly the same when I'm done. This launch will be done in the very best taste, giving your readers horror, with class. I promise."

Drake had his doubts. "Taste" and "class" were two words rarely used in conjunction with the occasions associated with "Drake Matthews." But he didn't have the heart to tell her all this work would still result in the same thing: a circus with him on the main stage.

"I'm okay with whatever you want to do. We have a deal, remember?"

Over the next few weeks, he had seen Kate almost every day, as promised, including weekends. He'd given her a gate code and found himself as eager as Sasha to get to the front door when the security panel did the double-beep, alerting him someone had stepped onto his front lawn. Granted, some of those days, all she'd had time for was to pop her head in and check measurements of a room, or ask him if it would be okay to have a caterers' meeting on his back porch and allow them a tour of his kitchen, where the staff would warm the food and perform the last-minute preparations before it was set outside.

But his favorite days were the pages full of empty checkboxes on her spreadsheet.

On those days, he could convince her to eat lunch with him in the kitchen. He'd determined, early on, what her favorites were, and stocked his virtual cart with those grocery items, having them delivered fresh a couple times a week. He used his writing breaks to prep and chop her favorite lunch staple: Cobb salad. He'd even called his mom, asking for a good home-made dressing recipe for it, and while his mother was suspicious, she gave it to him without forcing him into an awkward confession.

Those lunches—where she oohed and aahed her appreciation for his limited culinary skills—were made even more gratifying in that they'd usually have almost a half hour privately together to talk about nothing, and everything.

Drake discovered, to his delight, Kate loved to be

asked questions. It didn't matter the topic—she'd give her opinion on everything from the proper way to put on a toilet paper roll (with the paper coming over the top toward you) to what could be done to encourage more girls to enter STEM careers (a multi-pronged approach involving teacher funding, a revamp of toy development and marketing, and big corporation involvement and investment in education). What's more, he found Kate was widely read, her mind a sparkling treasure chest of details and facts she'd accumulated. He loved playing archeologist in her mental wealth.

Of course, he didn't squander that alone time, either. He couldn't afford to. His historical romance was churning out of him at an unprecedented rate, and he anticipated being done with *Memory's Lane* by mid-November. Yet he was ever-conscious of his dwindling access to Kate as his muse, and he often peppered her with questions directly related to his heroine's circumstance, scribbling her answers in his longhand scrawl as she rattled off various thoughts.

Sometimes, he'd have her act out snippets of scenes— never telling her that when he'd asked her to scream, "Noo!" and fall to her knees in his living room, it wasn't for a gruesome dead body scene in *Twisted Twin*, but so he could capture the moment Ingrid discovered Sam's amnesia. Kate was always a good sport, often volunteering to do a scene a few different ways, as if she were enjoying the playacting as much as he was enjoying the kick to his creativity. His time with her always left him emotionally breathless; unable to do anything else, he channeled all of his feelings into his manuscript, rushing before the Kate-sparkle wore off.

But time with Kate came with a downside.

Most days, his house was filled with vendors and various workers measuring, taking pictures, or building support structures for various spooky displays. The constant hubbub of people talking, and saws, drills, and paint-sprayers operating had been a difficult change from his home's typical, tomb-like quiet. Kate attempted to keep the distraction to a minimum, giving vendors wireless headsets to communicate with her, as she bustled around, giving direction and taking charge in her classy suits and upswept hair. But no heels. On the first day of her plan, she'd come in with a black pair of ballet slippers, keeping them by the door so she could change out of her heels and proceed, cat-quiet, with her inside duties. He secretly loved that she had a conniption if anyone came in the house who dared keep their shoes on. He'd have been able to fund a dozen other veterans' charities if he had a dime every time he heard her yell: "Shoes off! These floors are over one hundred and thirty years old, and we will *not* be the ones responsible for ruining them!"

Drake wasn't the only one who'd had to adjust to daily life in an extrovert's world.

Poor Sasha had given up greeting everyone at the front door. The parade of people was just too exhausting for the tiny shih tzu, who gave a valiant effort every morning until around lunch, when she curled up on the floor underneath whatever table, desk, or boards on sawhorses had been set aside for Drake to use as a writer's desk that day.

The latter had actually happened this morning, when Kate made good on her word to stick him in the attic to write.

"First off, we'll all feel better giving **VIP** tours of

your attic writing space if you've actually written there. Second, today is the perfect day for it, because we'll be in the kitchen, parlors, and in and out of the front and back doors today moving your furniture to the storage unit so nothing gets damaged or ruined. It's best for you and Sasha to be up here for a little while," Kate said, wrinkling her nose in anticipation of his reaction to being relegated to the attic. "But don't worry. I've got a plan."

Ten minutes later, dressed in a thick coat and fingerless gloves and with Sasha positioned in his lap both for her warmth and his, Drake was left to pound out words. At the beginning, armed with only one cup of coffee, he'd glowered around him, truly resenting the intrusion for the first time since Kate had worked her magic on him and his creativity. Here he was, a big-deal bestseller, and he was writing on a few boards balancing on a pair of sawhorses in an attic that had to be, at best, forty degrees Fahrenheit? Where was the justice?

But then his fingers had hit the keyboard, and he'd been transported.

For five hours straight.

A quick glance at the word count, and his eyes bulged. Sparked by this change of scenery, he'd just written five thousand words in his historical romance, right up through the climax and black moment where his hero's memory is finally restored, and Sam realizes the woman he's just arrested is Ingrid—his true love. His hero's worst fear is realized, and now he must decide between his love for his country and his love for this woman.

Of course, Drake knew that for this to be a romance, his hero must choose the woman, but he still hadn't figured out the dire consequences resulting from that choice. The scene he'd written was set next to a frozen lake in the dead of winter—the whole thing concocted by his own cold and discomfort. The last time he remembered typing a sentence was when he'd typed the opening for the scene.

> Cold nipped at him from every angle as he sat motionless in the fork of the tree. Unyielding wood pressed into his backside and legs, morphing from uncomfortable to torturous as minutes turned into hours, but he dared not move anything other than his eyes. Sam scanned the lake's surface, which winter had transformed into a dune-swept tundra, looking for any sign of the enemy.

Just like that, Drake was transported. He'd no longer heard the workers hammering outside or Kate's directions as she buzzed around his house. The entire world vanished, and he'd been fully immersed in the misery of Samuel Shelton as his main character waited to see who it was—man or woman—who had betrayed him and his country.

If it weren't for the knock at the attic door and the smell of coffee, Drake would have likely stayed on that frozen lakebed, feeling Sam's heartache and desperation.

"Drake?" Kate's face appeared around the doorframe, and she bustled toward him in a forest-green pantsuit, an elegant silk scarf protecting the exposed part of her neck from the house's chill. She set the steaming mug of relief on the makeshift desk. "I thought I'd bring you some coffee. Brr! It's colder in here than I thought. You must be an ice cube! We're done in the backyard area, so your kitchen is safe from distraction if you want to move there."

Drake cupped the ceramic mug, a gift from Ryker a few Christmases ago, and he was careful to use his hand to block the words that Kate had likely already noticed. It was hard to miss the figure of a man, dropping it low, next to the bright red letters reading *Whistle While You Twerk* emblazoned on the front. He was so grateful for warmth, though, that he barely registered the embarrassment.

Sipping, he sighed into the cup. "This is perfect. Thank you. I'll grab my stuff and move down there— I hadn't realized I was cold until now. I hit the word-count jackpot, thanks to this change of scenery."

"Really? Let's see." Kate grinned, and moved to look over his shoulder.

Drake would normally have blocked her view. He hated anyone reading his manuscripts in first draft, always sticking to his rule that nobody laid eyes on the book until he'd done at least one round of edits, but she'd moved so unexpectedly, he didn't have time. If he were being honest, he didn't mind her reading his rough draft, even *this* rough draft, which wasn't the one he was supposed to be working on for his publisher. He was astonished by the realization he actually *wanted* her to read the pages. It was as if crafting the real Kate into his fictional heroine, he knew her better somehow. Knew that she wouldn't judge his book. It was absurd to jump to such an illogical conclusion, after only knowing the woman for less than a month. Yet it seemed after casting Kate as his book's heroine, he had found it impossible to see her as anything else in real life.

He held his breath as she scanned the page, her mouth moving slightly as she read. Drake was struck by how adorable she looked, leaning over him, her face rapt in concentration with her lips caressing his words. His hands twitched—not to write that description down, but to cup her face in his hands and tug her to him, tasting those lips, basking in her sweetness...

"Looks like you captured the frigid temperatures really well." She touched his arm, and Drake froze, afraid to move, lest she take it away. "I'm so sorry to have stuck you here for so long. I'd only wanted you here for a half hour or so, just so that we weren't lying to your fans that you wrote in your attic, and I lost track of time. Your fingers...they're not frostbitten or anything?"

Drake reached up, squeezing her hand. He told himself it was just to prove that he was fine, but he held her small, warm hand in his for a beat too long before he forced himself to be the one who backed away.

She was working, here.

A professional.

Not his heroine, or his...whatever his mind had been fantasizing about. The real Kate wasn't in distress. She didn't need Drake to save her or romance her. All the real Kate needed was his approval of her ideas to win her award, and all he needed was to keep his distance from the living version of Kate, while still hijacking scene ideas from every encounter to get this damn romance book out of his head.

He manufactured a smile, pinning the corners of his mouth up as if he weren't really dying inside.

"Don't worry. My fingers and toes are fine. Nothing will have to be amputated today. At least not here. In my book—well, that's another story. Actually, that's a good idea."

His previous discomfiture momentarily forgotten, Drake turned to his laptop. Setting down his coffee, he positioned his fingers above the keys to type a note to himself in the manuscript, and then remembered he wasn't alone in the room. He winced, removing his hands from the keyboard.

"Sorry. I get so caught up sometimes wanting to write down a detail, or a bit of conversation, or a metaphor, I forget where I am and check out of reality to scribble it down before I forget. An old girlfriend used to accuse me of being obsessed about my writing. She said I cared more for my characters than real people. It's not that, though. At least I don't think so. It's just that experience has taught me it's freshest if I get it down right when it comes to me. If I wait until later—"

"You might forget those little nuances." Kate laughed, nodding her head. "Happens to me all the time. If I don't write down details, I will forget. It's not a question of 'if' but of 'when.' So, jot it down. I'll wait."

To Drake's surprise, she stopped talking, her smile patient, as he pecked out two sentences on his laptop. For her benefit, he read them as he typed.

```
Might be a nice bit of added drama
to have my hero, or my poor heroine,
lose a finger or toe from the cold, or
```

at least be in danger of frostbite.
If not, having Samuel check Ingrid
for black spots on her fingers/toes
might provide a nice transition to
the next scene.

Drake finished typing and put his laptop to sleep,
closing it up. "Thanks—it's nice to have someone
who—"

"—gets how crazy it is when your mind moves faster
than your fingers can type?" Kate nodded. "You've
seen my spreadsheets. They contain that level of detail
so I can fall asleep at night. If I don't write everything down that needs to be done—and I mean every
little, teensy thing—I will obsess about it and lose
sleep. Speaking of which..." Kate paused, lifting up
her printed spreadsheet. "I need to move a few things
around in here to amplify the creepy factor."

Drake looked around the attic's dusty boxes, trunks,
and stacks of original moldings and baseboards that
had been saved when his grandfather had repapered the
walls. The only thing creepy was the broken-down baby
carriage with its dingy-haired doll and the cobwebbed
figure of the gray squirrel that hung in the corner.
Apparently, one of his ancestors had either bought or
stuffed the creature himself, decades ago, and the squirrel was perpetually frozen on a branch in the corner
of the attic, staring down at the floor below as if he'd
just spotted a cobra lying in wait next to the old box
containing the entire set of the *Encyclopedia Britannica*
from 1970. Unless you had a phobia of stuffed squirrels or outdated information, it didn't look particularly
menacing to him.

"What are you going to do? Looks like an average attic to me. Only the exposed knob and tube wiring gives me the heebie-jeebies. The electrician said they weren't live, but I make my living off asking questions that begin with 'What if,' so I know how the best-laid plans are set aflame."

"They aren't live. The wires have long since been disconnected," Kate said, reaching above her head to grab an exposed wire with a bare hand and shaking it twice for emphasis while she scrolled through her phone. Drake winced, but she didn't get shocked and seemed oblivious to any sort of danger, never glancing up from her device. "Nothing to worry about there— that one was checked off last week. What I'm hoping you'll give me permission to do is go through some of those trunks, maybe push them around and set things up in a more...helter-skelter manner?"

Drake rolled his eyes. "What happened to not making me a sideshow freak again?"

"Not like that," Kate said, holding her phone up to him. She'd screenshot a picture of an old attic with dolls set up on trunks facing the camera, things mysteriously draped in white sheets, and random debris set up in a haphazard, almost demented, manner. "I want it to seem as if you gaze around this space when you're looking for inspiration. I want your fans to picture you here, writing, and for that picture to align with how they believe a horror writer seeks inspiration. We'll do it classy and tasteful—just an old attic, which their imagination will transform into something way more sinister than it is in real life."

"Sort of like how they view me," he said, nodding in understanding, taking a drink of his coffee and ignoring her sound of protest. "No, I get it. That's fine. There's nothing of any real value up here—just a bunch of junk that nobody's gotten around to getting rid of yet, like the rest of the house, I suppose."

"Your house isn't filled with junk, Drake. It's filled with memories, and coming from a family who's moved a dozen times over the years, bringing along only those mementos that hang in diploma-size frames, I like the vibe you've got in this Victorian. It's anchoring. It gives off the feeling of…loving security. Belonging. Personally, I wouldn't change a thing." Kate gave him a bright smile, brushing past him as she investigated the trunks next to the window. "In fact, I could live all day long in your front parlor, curled up with my laptop in that pink needlepoint ladies' chair next to the fire. This house is synonymous with happily ever after, in my book. I'm going to miss these daily visits."

Her words hit Drake like a sucker punch.

Mentally, he calculated the day—it was October 22. In only nine more days, this woman would roll up her decorations, her bright enthusiasm, her positive attitude and badass planning…and she'd be gone. Snatched from his life, leaving him rattling around in this big house like the last penny in a big, empty piggybank.

Her light perfume wafted by his nose in the breeze of her passing, the same sweet, floral scent she always wore that made him want to lean in to smell deeper. Not for the first time, he wondered what she'd say if he were to ask her out. On a real date. Not a research date, where he'd scribble notes while she screamed, acting out scenes for his book. But a real one where he'd take her to dinner, pamper her, shower her with his undivided attention while he basked in hers.

He could ask her now…

Instead, he set Sasha on the floor and reminded himself that Kate was here in his employment. Well, technically, in his publisher's employment, but the fact was, she was working. Yes, they had an agreement that allowed him to borrow her as a prop to his writing, but he refused to put her in a position where she felt uncomfortable. He'd wait until after the launch. By then, he'd have figured out a way to do it.

He slugged his coffee and started gathering up his things to move to the kitchen and warm up. He needed to take his mind off the gorgeous woman standing before him in real life and focus more on the fictional woman in his book. The former was off-limits—the latter was, in theory, more accessible. He could write a romance. Living it? That was a completely different story.

And not one where he was a bestseller.

"Ms. Sweet?" A voice boomed up, echoing in the attic. "Can you come down here? We need to know how high you want the spider to crawl, exactly."

Kate, who'd been crouched down, unlatching a trunk, spun and stood, the trunk lid thunking closed behind her. Her mouth was set in a thin line as she sped by him in those quiet, black ballet slippers.

"I've literally told them three times where I'd like the track to be placed. Three times," she muttered and tossed him a smile as she lingered at the attic door. "I've got lunch catered in today from your mom's café, so don't be surprised if a bunch of bags appear in the kitchen from PattyCakes soon. We're bribing the workers with food to keep them here for eight full hours until we get the outside set up. Shall I bring Sasha with me? She's got to be chilled to the bone. Come here, girl! Let's get you a treat!"

Sasha's ears perked up at her name, and she completely abandoned Drake at the sound of her favorite word: "treat." She trotted away, following Kate out of the attic and down the stairs without a backward glance.

"So much for man's best friend," Drake mumbled to himself, standing to stretch his cramped muscles. Just then, he heard a mad, buzzing sound coming from behind him. He patted the phone in his pocket—not his. Turning, he spotted a pink, sparkly case on the floor next to the trunk Kate had been searching through moments before.

Kate's cell phone.

Drake set down his laptop and crossed the age-worn thick pine floors to snatch it up. The thing vibrated in his palm, buzzing in a subdued but insistent way.

"Kate!" he called, walking toward the attic entrance. He heard her downstairs, giving directions out the window to a team of men and women who were building scaffolding to gain enough height for the mechanical spider to traverse down his house and hang over his doorway. "Kate, you've got a call! No name, just a number."

"Go ahead and answer it," came her distant response. "It's probably one of the vendors. Might be from your mom's café, confirming lunch delivery. I'll be there in a sec."

Drake didn't recognize the number or the area code, but it could be one of his mother's helpers.

He swiped to answer. "Hello?" Drake said, putting the phone to his ear.

"Uh, hi?" came a woman's uncertain voice on the other end. "I think I might have dialed the wrong number—"

"Wait, this is Kate Sweet's...office," Drake supplied, a smidge late. He moved toward his laptop, gathering up his papers. "She stepped out for a minute. Uh, did you want me to take a message?"

"This is Kiersten, Kate's sister. Who the hell is this?" the woman asked, her tone becoming frostier as she continued. "Kate never leaves her phone. Ever. You'd better get my sister on this phone in thirty seconds, or else—"

"Okay, hold on. She left it in my attic while she went downstairs to see about the spider," he said, and about a nanosecond after the words left his mouth, he realized how truly bizarre he sounded. "Wait. Let me start over. I'm Drake Matthews. Her client. And she just went outside to see about the mechanical thing she's got rigged to crawl up my house as the finale for the fans coming to my Halloween book launch."

Kate's sister was silent for so long, Drake pulled the sparkly phone from his ear to be sure he hadn't accidentally hung up on her.

"There is so much to unpack in that sentence," she said finally, and Drake heard the echo of Kate's dry humor in her sister's tone. "Let me start with this—my sister is doing a book launch for *the* Drake Matthews? The guy who wrote *Alien Abyss* and *Creature Crypt*?"

At his confirmation, he was surprised to hear Kate's sister whoop on the other end of the line.

"No way! I called from a friend's phone because I thought this whole time, she was vibing on some

Florida beach somewhere, dodging my parents' incessant calls and ditching me to deal with their crazy by myself," she gushed. "And the whole time she's working on Drake Freaking Matthews's book party?"

"It's not a party. It's an event."

Drake chuckled to himself at the correction. Kate would be proud.

Wait. An idea to do something nice for Kate slammed into his head, and he switched the phone to the other ear, uncapping his pen again and flipping over a new sheet on his legal pad.

"Kiersten, I'm wondering: do you think you and your parents would like to come to the book launch? Kate assures me it's going to be a classy and . . ." Drake searched his memory bank for her exact descriptions from the past. " . . . spook-tacular Halloween night, and I can have three tickets sent to you and your folks if you'd like to attend?"

Kiersten squealed in his ear, a high-pitched noise he was sure Sasha heard downstairs.

"Yes, we'll come to Drake Matthews's book launch! We'd love to come. My parents are going to stroke—"

"Well," Drake interrupted, "I was thinking we could surprise her. She's mentioned to me that with how hard your parents work, and with you in med school, you don't get to see Kate in action. She's worked so hard here, and between you and me, this launch might even win her an award."

"Really? I mean, that's so cool! She doesn't tell us much about her job, and I've never seen her really big weddings."

Kiersten's enthusiasm was contagious, and Drake grinned at the phone, taking down the physical address that he could give to his assistant to send three invites. When he was done, he packed up his things and left the attic. Speaking in a low tone, he used the short trip downstairs to conclude the call.

"Will you call back in two minutes? I'm going to pretend that I lost the call in the attic, and then you can call and I'll find Kate for you. That way, she won't know we've been planning behind her back."

Kiersten agreed, and the phone went dead as he rounded the carved newel post and jogged down the rest of the stairs to the first level. Drake spotted Kate with a set of white bags in her hand, the PattyCakes logo emblazoned on the front, and walking in lock-step with her, also laden with PattyCakes bags, was his mother.

"We scored on this delivery, getting lunch and Patty both," Kate said, raising the bag in triumph as she flashed a smile to Patty. "I thought we could—"

The phone in Drake's hand rang, and without asking permission, he answered it.

"Good afternoon, Sweet Events. Kate Sweet's office. How can I help you?"

Kiersten's voice sounded uncertain on the other end.

"Uh, can I talk to Kate?"

"Yes, Kate's right here," Drake said, and then pretended to listen to her sister's earlier objection. "Oh, don't worry, she's okay. No, Kate is better than okay. She's amazing. Absolutely, one hundred percent *incredible*, in fact. Hold on, and I'll get her on the line."

Looking puzzled, Kate took the phone, handing Drake the PattyCakes bags.

"Hello?" She paused, and her puzzlement turned to worry and then to embarrassment. "Oh, Kier! I'm so glad you called. No, that's not my new secretary. He's...a client."

Kate moved her mouth from the phone to speak to Drake and his mom.

"If you'll excuse me—I'll join you guys in a minute."

"What in the world are you up to, Drake Hawthorne Matthews?" Patty Matthews said once they stood alone in his kitchen, unloading bags. "You may be thirty-four years old, but I know when you're up to mischief. You have the same expression on your face you had when you colored Zander's face with red and black markers to make him look like Spider-Man."

Casting a look at the door, Drake swiftly explained his plan with Kate's sister, cautioning her to silence.

"For goodness' sake," his mom said, with an affronted sniff. "Of course I can keep a secret!"

Just then, Kate entered the kitchen, tucking the phone into her front suit-coat pocket.

"What secret?" she asked, casting her look from Drake to Patty, then frowning when neither one leaped to answer. "Is it...do you both secretly hate the decorations? Are you regretting the spider? I can still change things if you tell me now—"

"No," Drake said, waving her off, although part of him wanted to ask that the spider not make an appearance on Halloween. "We were just talking about..."

Drake trailed off, cursing his hours at the keyboard where all of his creativity in dialogue and intrigue had apparently been sucked into the manuscript, leaving him adrift in a black hole of slack-jawed stupidity.

"We were just talking about the Harvest Festival this weekend," his mom said, tossing a lifesaver to him in the void. "And he was saying that he'd like to ask you to come with him."

Kate looked dubious. "Then, what's the secret part?"

"The fact that he's never brought a date with him to the festival, and he was worried about asking you," his mom said.

And just like that, the lifesaver was yanked away.

Then, as if unable to help herself, his mom furthered the lie.

"I was saying he should go for it. I knew you'd be perfect for each other as soon as I sat down next to you in my café. I said to myself, 'Here's a woman with a brain in her head and one who doesn't have frost running through her veins, to boot.' That last was the secret part."

Drake's mouth opened and closed, and he looked at Kate apologetically while giving his mom a warning glance that she shrugged off. Finally, he managed to string a sentence together.

"Which is no longer secret. But as I was getting ready to explain to my mother, I don't want to put you in a strange conflict of interest. We're working together for the book launch. And we need to be focused on that. Kate doesn't have time for..." Drake riffled through his mind for an appropriate verb and selected one Kate had created. "...flitzing around."

His mom threw Kate a wink.

"So, it won't be an *official* date. But it's okay to come as his event planner, isn't it?"

Now it was Kate's turn to flounder. Warm color flooded her neck and cheeks. "I, um, guess it's appropriate for me to promote the launch at the festival, maybe chat up some of the town council to smooth our path for the permits? I could check out the local vendors to see if they can help with food trucks too."

"Then it's settled!" Patty clapped her hands. "Festival starts at eleven, with the pumpkin-carving competition to benefit the women's shelter starting at one o'clock sharp, which my oldest son has promised to announce. Can you make sure Drake doesn't lose track of time, or that he's not squirreled away in a corner somewhere writing in that notebook of his, oblivious to everything?"

Drake watched, helpless, as his mother orchestrated his first date with his event planner, realizing it was as possible to stop her as it was to halt a blizzard. He turned to Kate to tell her it was okay to say no, but instead of the awkward look he expected, he saw Kate wasn't frowning. Instead, she had a bemused, almost gobsmacked expression.

"O-okay. I'll do my best, Patty," Kate said. Although her face was now the color of a deep pink rose, she met Drake's gaze. Her green eyes were direct as her mouth curved into a wry smile. "After today, I think we both deserve some time to flitz, and the Harvest Festival sounds perfect."

The rest of lunch flew by in a haze of disbelief as Drake realized the impossible: although presented with the world's most awkward date-ask . . .

She'd said yes.

CHAPTER 13

Kate debated on her outfit for a full ten minutes before deciding that casual was better than professional, given today's activities. Saturday morning had dawned bright and balmy, with the temperatures forecasted to be in the low sixties by the afternoon, so Kate determined layers were most sensible. She had on a pair of jeans and a trendy, long-sleeved shirt she'd bought a few days ago at a local boutique. The outfit was topped off by her black suit jacket—the unfortunate one she'd chosen for her first meeting with Drake. Today she wore it unfastened, making it less constricting and disguising the fact she still had two missing buttons. With the sleeves rolled up and pushed back, the blazer lent the ensemble a casual vibe.

Or at least as much of a casual vibe as Kate was able to muster. She just felt more comfortable in a suit than she did in jeans, but Drake had reminded her via text that she should *"Definitely leave the heels at home,"* so she'd cobbled together an outfit with boots that had more of a riding heel than a stiletto.

Kate sighed, checking her reflection in the hotel's bathroom. She'd skipped the chignon and secured all but the shortest layers into a low ponytail. She hadn't realized how long her hair had gotten, having only opted for a quick trim a couple months ago, and now it hung almost to mid-back, with the front layers not quite long enough to secure in a ponytail, but too long to really look elegant. Kate tried once more, unsuccessfully, to tuck the errant strands into the rest of her hair, and then huffed a breath, giving up.

"It is not a date," she told her reflection. "We clarified that. It's a scouting mission, focusing on food vendors for my client's launch and chatting up the town council. It's work."

The words of Drake's mother were still ringing in her ears when she'd returned to the hotel last night— empty after Imani had returned to the city two weeks ago, both she and her boss pleased with Kate's handling of the event. Kate herself was proud of what she'd accomplished in twenty-ish days; all the boxes were checked off on her spreadsheets, and the only thing overdue was obtaining the town permit for the mechanical spider and the one authorizing the blocked street for the haunted maze. She should've slept like a baby, but her mind kept replaying Patty's words.

I knew you'd be perfect for each other as soon as I sat down next to you in my café, Patty had said.

While she rationalized that the woman was likely doing what mothers across the universe seemed to do— set up their older, unwed sons—her mind had snagged against Drake's response to Kiersten on the phone when her sister had called from a friend's phone to check in on her.

Kate is better than okay. She's amazing. Absolutely, one hundred percent incredible, *in fact.*

Had Drake meant that? He'd seemed so sincere when he'd said it. Her mind turned the words, and the maybe-date today, over and over, attempting to place the checkmark in the appropriate box in her mind—was it under "definitely getting vibes from this guy," or under the category "he was just being nice"?

She wanted to ask Imani her opinion, but since she'd returned to Manhattan, she was busy with her other clients. She wasn't due back until next Thursday, before the Halloween launch on Saturday night. Also, Imani would not be thrilled that Kate was mooning over her client and possibly distracting him, especially since he was already late on his deadline. She was still under the assumption Kate and Drake were acting like professionals did when they worked together—not...whatever it was that she and Drake were doing right now. Flirting?

"It's not a real date," Kate reaffirmed, giving her reflection a stern look. "You just go, scope out the food vendors, and maybe meet someone from the town council to put in a good word about the permit. Do your job, Kate. Do your damn job."

She repeated the mantra as she caught the hotel's shuttle down to the town's Island Park, so named because it was a large wooded area surrounded by the swift-flowing Genesee River. She breathed a sigh of relief as she spotted Drake's black vintage truck parked at the front of the gravel parking lot in what must amount to the VIP section, telling herself that the fluttery sensation in her stomach was probably nerves. Or maybe she was hungry. It definitely was not giddy excitement at the thought of spending time with him today without a spreadsheet of to-do items in front of her.

She marched through the Harvest Festival's entrance, flanked by scarecrows and haybales, smiling professionally as she checked out every volunteer's nametag, repeating her mantra as she searched for the names she'd memorized for the town's council members. She was all business, moving confidently through the crowd, checking out the decorations and the huge amount of pumpkins set on tables in the center of the wooded park. She'd just caught the tantalizing whiff of a pretzel truck and was following the scent of baked goods, when a familiar voice sounded in her ear.

"Just like a superhero, you're here when I needed to be rescued," said Drake, the low rumble of his voice causing something deep in her belly to twirl and purr to life.

"Good morning to you too." Kate turned, her professional smile melting away as she took in Drake's attire.

He stood, shoulders hunched as if to blend in, which right now was pretty impossible. He wore a silver, upside-down funnel as a hat on his head, and a skin-tight, silver bodysuit that left nothing to the imagination. Thrown over it all was the leather jacket he'd worn the day of the cemetery visit; a jacket that was several layers too warm for the day, if the sweat at his brow and the scowl were any evidence.

"Um, why are you dressed as a...grumpy robot?" Kate asked.

A single bead of sweat trickled down Drake's temple, and his black glasses slid down his nose. He pushed them up impatiently.

"Mom decided on a *Wizard of Oz* theme this year, and I'm the—"

"Tin Man," Kate filled in. "I see it now."

From behind them came the sound of male laughter.

"He does look like a grumpy robot," said a man dressed in a massive, tawny-colored fur costume. His face was painted elaborately to look exactly like a lion's. "Whereas, I am the King of the Forest. Nice to see you again, Kate. Where's that stunning publicist? I've yet to officially meet Imani. Is she here today?"

Kate blinked, recognizing Zander, Drake's youngest brother.

"Hi," she said. "No, she's in New York City, but she'll be back for the launch."

"Zan, if I didn't know any better, I'd think you had a crush on Drake's publicist," came the voice of another tall man sauntering up to them. The guy wore a flannel shirt with straw sticking out at the sleeves and faded denim overalls that ended just above a gleaming metal foot on one side and a foot in a combat boot on the other side. Although he wore a tilted straw hat, Kate immediately recognized the man as Ryker, Drake's other brother.

"Shut up, dude," Zander growled.

"What? I'm just speaking truth. And, bro, you're not the king of anything. You're the Cowardly Lion," Ryker said, tugging on Zander's tail and evading the big man's swatting hand. He glanced over at Drake, his mouth curving in a wicked smile of delight. "But you, big brother, you look like a male stripper from a bad Terminator-themed porn movie. Bow-ba-da-bow, bow!"

Ryker did a hip gyration, his hand snaking around to pinch Drake's backside.

In a blur of motion, Drake snatched his brother's hand, twisting it around until Ryker's arm was behind his back.

"Mom chose the right character for you, Ryker," Drake said, as his brother tapped out, laughing good-naturedly. "You are brainless."

"Naw, she just didn't want me to be self-conscious as the Tin Man," Ryker said, flexing his shoulder. "I'm partly metal nowadays. Besides, everyone knows the Scarecrow's the one with the best moves."

Ryker did a pretty good imitation of the Scarecrow's dancing jig from the movie, and Kate stifled a giggle.

Drake blew out a frustrated breath. "Don't you two have somewhere to be? Somewhere that's not here?"

Zander nodded with a knowing look on his whiskered face. "Ah, he wants us to give him some privacy with Kate. I get it. Mom said you guys were dating. No accounting for taste, I suppose."

Kate flushed. "We're, um, not dating."

Drake nodded in agreement as he plucked the silvery fabric off his abdomen, trying in vain to stretch it out, while he glanced at the passers-by self-consciously. "It's a strictly professional relationship."

Kate glanced sideways at Drake, trying to read how much he believed in the "strictly professional" part, but he was über-focused on his costume. He released the fabric he'd attempted to stretch, and it lay against him like a sheen of metallic sweat, showing every bulge of his muscles as the writer gritted his teeth and muttered a curse.

She swallowed and looked away. "Totally professional."

"Oh yeah?" Ryker said, holding up a large shopping bag. "Then why did Mom send for this costume at the last minute so you could match us? If you were *just* his event planner, she wouldn't have bothered. Or if she felt obligated, she'd have chosen a flying monkey. If she didn't like you, maybe the Wicked Witch."

Zander nodded his shaggy head. "But she gave you Dorothy. You're definitely dating if she gave you Dorothy and wants you to be a part of her booth's activities."

Kate's eyes bulged as she took the bag being thrust at her. Blue-and-white gingham fabric with frothy white eyelet lace peeped out at her. "I—I didn't agree to dress up today. I mean, I'm not a cosplay actor. Being Dorothy Gale is not in my plan."

Drake shook his head. "You don't have to dress up. I think Mom wanted to include you. For my sake, probably."

Mollified, Kate turned to give Drake a grateful smile, but was stopped by the younger brothers, who shook their heads.

Ryker and Zander turned to their older brother, who was still scowling and plucking the silver Lycra off his crotch.

"You'd better tell her," Zander said.

Ryker nodded, lifting his cell phone from his pants' pocket. "Gotta bolt. We're needed at the photo booth."

The two ambled away, Zander's tail swishing and

swatting random people as they were swallowed up by the crowd.

Drake cursed and finally shrugged out of his coat, setting it down with a backpack on the ground between them. "Holy hell, it's hot out here."

"Tell me what? Don't change the subject—what were your brothers talking about?" Kate folded her arms across her chest, rounding on Drake.

Her client was full-on stretching the fabric down by his thighs, his forearm muscles bulging in metallic relief as he strained against the material, which sucked right back down to his skin with a snap as soon as he let go.

Kate forced her gaze up, looking at his face to avoid the distraction. "All your mom asked me to do is come to the festival and make sure you got where you needed to be. She never mentioned dressing up. What's going on?"

Drake opened his mouth to answer, but his words were cut off as a pack of older women stopped a few feet away. One of them gave a long, appreciative wolf whistle.

"Hey, there, Drake! Lookin' good!"

The women snickered, and one older lady wearing a shirt with pumpkins embroidered on the front stepped forward, leering over the tops of the bifocals held by a gold chain around her neck.

Kate glanced sideways at Drake, who had frozen in place, his hands on his hips as if he were a silver Superman.

He cleared his throat. "Kate Sweet, I'd like you to meet Mrs. Nowakowski. She was my Sunday school teacher."

Something pinged in Kate's brain at the mention of the name, but she was distracted by the drama unfolding in front of her, as Drake's old religion teacher's gaze traveled from the man's toes, up the muscles of his bunched thighs, and lingered at his crotch. As if his greeting had emboldened them, the women inched closer with a rapacious look in their eyes, like a bunch of hungry bridesmaids descending on the wedding buffet.

Mrs. Nowakowski adjusted her glasses to finally stare into Drake's eyes. "You were such a scrawny thing. Who'd have thought you'd grow into such a fine hunk of a man?"

Kate saw Drake shift uncomfortably, his hands slowly coming around to clasp in front of him, like a groom standing at the altar. Except it was clear this was more to protect his . . . assets from prying eyes than it was to appear composed.

Another one of the ladies crept to the side, angling her head to see around the writer.

"You could bounce a quarter off that butt! You must do more than just write to get a rear like that! Do you do squats?"

"No, he's a runner." One of the gray-haired ladies in the back leaned against her walker to pin Drake with a shrewd glance. "I've seen him doing laps on the high school track on the weekends."

"How do you see him, Aggie? Your eyes are so bad, you can barely read the Sunday paper," came the response from Mrs. Nowakowski.

"With my binocs," said Aggie, grinning to reveal a pearly white set of dentures. "He goes round and round and round. Sometimes he does the stadium steps, and then does a bunch of sit-ups on the infield. After he does that, he usually takes off his shirt."

The ladies gave a chorus of "ooh's," and Kate cast her gaze to her author client.

Misery radiated off him in waves, but Kate gave him credit; he never lost his polite smile.

"That's how I get all my best ideas—sweating it out with an audience of you beautiful ladies," Drake said. "Now, if you'll excuse us, we've got—"

"A date. We know. Patty told us all about her," Mrs. Nowakowski said, leveling her eyes over her bifocals at Kate. "I'm Shirley Nowakowski, and you must be the event planner. I heard about your request to our town council. I love the idea of a street maze, and I've always thought the Matthews mansion could be such a fun place at Halloween."

"I'm glad you liked the idea!" Kate beamed, jolted as the name she'd memorized earlier finally clicked in place. She shook her hand, surprised by the older woman's steel-hard grip. "It's lovely to meet you. I was hoping to introduce myself to some of your fellow council members today and answer any concerns you might have. It'll take a load of worry off my plate knowing the permit has your endorsement."

"Well, I'm not sure about everyone else, but you have my vote. Now, you'd better hurry up and get changed, missy," Mrs. Nowakowski said, giving what Kate interpreted as a nod of approval. "Patty wants you both at the Allegany County Abuse Shelter's booth before the pumpkin carving starts. Don't force us to call you out, Drake-y."

With that, she shoved her glasses back in place,

straightened her pumpkin-covered shirt, and led the ladies to another stall across the park.

Drake watched the last of the posse leave, her red-enameled walker bumping across the park grass, and then tilted his head back, glaring up at the autumn leaves above him as muscles in his jaw bunched. He looked as though he were two seconds away from howling in frustration. Finally, blowing out a breath and batting the funnel hat back to swipe at a fine mist of nervous sweat at his forehead, he gave Kate a look so wretched, she bit her lip to keep from laughing at the dichotomy of his expression with his blindingly silver costume.

"Think you can do me one massive favor this morning? For my research?" Then, Drake shook his head. "No. That's a lie. It's not for my book. It's for me. Well, maybe for my mom, but that's for me, really. She's sort of a nut about Halloween. And her women's shelter. See, my mom's sister was abused by her husband, and although she finally left the guy, my aunt never really did recover from the emotional trauma. She ended up taking her own life."

Kate gasped. "That's awful. I'm so sorry for your loss."

Drake sighed. "It was twenty years ago, but Aunt Beth was Mom's only sister and fall was her favorite season. The first anniversary of Aunt Beth's death, Mom coordinated a big festival here, with the proceeds going to the local women's shelter. She's made us boys dress up in coordinating costumes for it every year, whether we want to or not. Five years ago, I told her I couldn't make it back to the East Coast for the festival, because I was speaking at the annual Horror

Writers' Convention in Sacramento, and she made me regret that decision."

Kate's eyes widened. "What did she do?"

"She gave my cell number to every aunt, female cousin, and family friend to call me and tell their stories of how they themselves, or those they knew, had been traumatized by domestic abuse. Mrs. Nowakowski was one of the ones who kept my number on speed dial." Drake's face was grim. "Super humbling stuff. Made it into the book I was writing at the time, which is why *Attic Asylum* has such a loyal cult following. The heroine of the story gets the ultimate revenge against her abuser."

Kate glanced again into the bag and let out a resigned breath. "Fine. I'll do it. Where can I change?"

Drake's face lit up. He cupped her face in his hands, and for one, hot, glorious minute, she thought he was going to kiss her. Instead, he stared into her eyes, his gaze so intense, it was like he was memorizing her features. Then, he let go.

"I owe you. Big-time. I don't know how I'm going to repay you, but I will. That's a promise, Ms. Sweet."

"I'm holding you to that, Mr. Matthews," she grumbled, but inside she was picturing ways he might fulfill those promises.

None of them were G-rated.

Fifteen minutes later, she'd cleared her mind of Drake-inspired smut and was dressed in a Dorothy costume that fit surprisingly well, right down to the ruby slippers. She almost walked out like that, but then changed her mind. If she was going to do this, she was going all in. She rapidly finger-parted her hair in the back and wove two Dutch braids close to her head, tying them off with the costume's gingham hair ribbons high at the shoulder, leaving low ponytails, Dorothy-style, that hung down to the bibbed part of the gingham dress. Peeking into a jewelry stall owner's mirror, she nodded in satisfaction. It wasn't perfect, but it was close enough for only seven minutes' warning.

She walked out of the changing tent and found Drake half-hidden behind an oak tree.

He spotted her immediately and stepped out of hiding. He gave her a brief up and down, smiling as he gestured toward the end of the park where the Allegany Abuse Shelter booth was set up.

"They're waiting for us down there. You look great, by the way. I love the braid thingies."

"I'm resisting the urge to take your arm and skip while we sing about visiting the wizard," she said. "But at least this costume will help me break the ice with your local board members. If you see any others, point them out. They still haven't approved our permits, and although Mrs. Nowakowski loved the idea, I'd like the opportunity to speak to more of them and get that item checked off."

"Right. The checklist, which contains answers to all the mysteries of life. Or at least my event," Drake said, holding his backpack in front of him as he walked and stared straight ahead. The crowd parted for them, giving both Drake and Kate a look as they passed. "Answer me this. Why is it that you still look professional and poised in a last-minute Halloween costume? How is it my mother nails the size of a lady she's met only twice, while she stuffs me, her oldest son, into this thing?"

Drake plucked the elastic material at his groin, and Kate caught herself staring as the fabric resettled, revealing such a mouth-watering amount of him, she stumbled. Drake put a hand at her back, helping to right her again, and Kate couldn't remember the last time a guy had done that. She was so lost in her thoughts, she didn't hear the rest of Drake's conversation until the very end.

"...tag says large, but she's got me crammed into a Sh-medium. Ryker's right. I look like a damn stripper."

"Sh-medium?" Kate hefted her gaze with effort from his groin to his eyes, purposely not touching the stripper comment, and the mental images that poured into her head. "What's that?"

"A woman's medium. A Sh-medium. This doesn't begin to fit me. It's indecent."

Indecent is a good look on you, Kate thought. But instead she said, a bit too eagerly, "Do you want me to go downtown and find something else?"

"No!" Drake grasped her arm, his tone desperate as he tugged her to a narrow, secluded area behind the backdrop of the makeshift stage and a supply truck that advertised the abuse shelter. Peeking around the backdrop, she and Drake spotted a podium, microphone, and a folding table with two plastic chairs set up on the stage in front of a growing crowd. "No time. Besides, nothing's open today. Everything's shut down for the festival."

"It's not that bad," Kate said, turning back around to cast an eye over his costume. "Just maybe a smidge...tight."

"You think?"

Patty spotted them hiding behind the stage, and she

waved, coming over to the microphone stand. Taking the mic, Drake's mother tapped on the black top of it, and the amplifiers squealed in protest.

"Oopsie! Okay, thank you for coming out today to support us at the Allegany Abuse Shelter! In a couple of minutes, we're going to have our very own Drake Matthews come out to start the carving competition, so go ahead and take a seat next to your pumpkin while I tell you a little bit about our shelter and who we serve."

Patty continued to speak to the crowd about her charity, but Kate was distracted. Drake had taken her hand. Kate glanced down. How was it possible that even his fingers were muscular? But they were—strong and thick and capable, his hands gripped hers briefly, to punctuate his words as he spoke.

"Kate. You're an expert at switching gears—at dealing with a crisis, right?" Drake rolled his head around his shoulder, as if attempting to relieve tension. "I can't go up there looking like a stripper. It's. A. Crisis."

Kate bit her lip, tamping down her laughter. Instead, she nodded, switching into problem-solving mode. She could do this—act professional. All she had to do was pretend Drake was a jittery groom. Not a scorching-hot author with abs like a model on the cover of a fitness magazine. Or abs like a male stripper.

Kate kept her eyes on Drake's face as she held out her hand for his backpack.

"What do you have in there that we can use to make your costume...more appropriate?"

He handed her the backpack, and she unzipped it. Jeans. Perfect!

"Here. Just slip these on over your tights to cover,

um, your lower half," Kate finished, her face suffusing with color as she gestured at his crotch. "They'll only really see the top half over the tabletop, and I'll arrange the pumpkins so that they block your..."

"Yeah," Drake nodded, interrupting her awkward pause. "Got it. Good idea."

Except as he started to tug the jeans on over his Tin Man costume, Kate saw it wasn't going to work. The costume came with Tin Man boots that slid on over his sneakers all the way to his knees. No way could the costume fit under his jeans. At least, not without alterations...

Spotting what she needed on a nearby table, Kate gave Drake the "one second" sign with her index finger and sprinted in her sparkly red shoes to a table on the far side of the stage. Snatching what she needed off the top, she gave Drake's mom a thumbs-up when Patty's eyes caught the movement in the middle of her speech, and then Kate rushed back behind the backdrop.

Drake was panting, the waistband of his jeans only pulled to his knees where they'd stuck, the legs unable to be tugged farther over the Tin Man boots. He took in what Kate was holding, and froze, that half smile tilting up the edges of his lips.

"Hacking me up with a knife wasn't *exactly* the solution I'd had in mind, but considering my latest book release, I guess there's some poetic justice in meeting my Maker this way."

"Ha-ha," Kate said, adjusting her grip on the serrated carving knife she'd grabbed from the pumpkin table. "The only way to get these up is to cut them, at least to the knees. Take those off and I'll—"

Suddenly, Drake's mom's voice changed in that

subtle way Kate had come to recognize from the number of toasts and speeches she'd heard in the wedding business. Patty was wrapping up her comments to the large crowd gathering at the tables in the park. She had that tone Kate knew meant it was time for the main event.

"So, I guess it's time that we get to carving these pumpkins," Patty said, and the crowd obediently cheered. "And who is more appropriate to start a bunch of people hacking into helpless gourds than my oldest son? In a second, I'm going to invite him up here—"

Kate tuned out, focusing her attention on her client, struggling and staggering with his pants at his bulging thighs.

"Your mom's almost ready to introduce you. No time to take them off!" Kate gripped Drake's hips to stop him from moving, as she lowered herself to her knees in front of him. She looked up, feeling heat rising to her face as the obvious eroticism of her position flooded her mind. Her voice was not much above a whisper, as she gazed up at him, knife in hand. "Do you trust me?"

Drake hesitated for only a fraction of a second. Then, he nodded, his gaze behind his dark glasses unreadable.

"Implicitly."

His tone was imbued with such heartfelt honesty, Kate's stomach did a little flip of joy.

Steadying her hands, she gripped the knife.

And she began to slash.

CHAPTER 14

S weet Jesus," Drake whispered, holding on to a small maple behind the stage, attempting to be as steady as the tree as Kate went to work.

His body was caught somewhere between lust and terror, as the woman kneeling in front of him used a carving knife on his jeans in a really effective imitation of Edward Scissorhands. Her fingers worked rapidly in conjunction with the knife, ripping fabric six inches below his crotch, and her head was bowed such that he saw only the bridge of her freckled nose and flushed cheeks.

That part was hot as hell.

Yet the way she slashed at the denim, slicing through the fabric at his knees with the single-minded ferocity of a Samurai warrior, made his balls want to crawl up to a safer vantage point.

Like, say, his throat.

"Done!" she said, leaning back on her heels, using the back of the hand still holding the carving knife to brush away a tendril of hair that had miraculously escaped one of her Dorothy braids. "You can pull them up over those tights and button them now."

Drake did so, looking down at himself.

She'd hacked his favorite jeans into a pair of redneck booty shorts.

Yet each leg was the same length, and they still showed most of the silvery fabric on his legs, as well as the silly Tin Man boots, so his Mom couldn't accuse him of not being in full costume. He was the Tin Man, sporting a pair of jean shorts. It wasn't a traditional Tin Man costume, but at least the shorts hid his junk, and that was what mattered.

"Thank you," Drake said, extending a hand to help Kate stand. "Saving the guy in distress. Again."

Vaguely, he heard his mother say his name.

And then Kate's flushed face was turned up to his, laughing in relief.

"Whew! Just in time!"

His heart leaped at her expression. It wasn't the business-card smile she gave when she had on her professional hat—he'd said something to bring up that adorable dimple to the spot an inch above her jaw, right underneath the smile line.

"There's that upside-down semicolon," he said, grinning. "That's my favorite."

Kate's smile didn't slip, but her gaze was quizzical. "What upside-down semicolon?"

"Right here is the curve of the comma," Drake said, his index finger tracing her smile line down to where it ended, and then dotting the spot where her dimple indented her cheek. "And there's the dot. Just like the punctuation, it always gives me pause when I see it."

His mind told him touching her face was all sorts

of wrong—lawsuit wrong. Yet his fingers, caressing the silk of her cheek and then tilting her chin up, up, up to him...

When his lips met hers, it was as if they'd suddenly fallen into a portal, far, far away from the crowd and the noise, where all that existed was Kate in his arms. The soft texture of her lips, her sweet scent, the feel of her hot breath as she exhaled in a sigh, all of it was a myriad of unexpected sensation. Pure pleasure. The seconds stretched out like warm caramel as she wrapped her arms around his neck and kissed him back.

His mind spun with the thought. *She kissed him back!*

"Drake?" his mom called, peering around the stage's backdrop.

Kate snapped her head back, tottering a half step in her ruby slippers, breaking free of his embrace. Her hand came up, half-covering her lips, like she was hiding a smile. Or a scream.

Before Drake could say anything to her—apologize or make some sort of an excuse—his mother was speaking again.

And she'd forgotten she was holding the microphone.

"Drake Matthews, I've called your name three times now, for Pete's sake!" The microphone canted to the side but projected her voice as if it were held directly under her chin. She scowled at them. "You two need to quit making out back there and start this contest!"

The crowd behind her chuckled, and a few men in the back cat-called and whistled.

Kate's chest, neck, and face flushed crimson, and she ducked her head. He didn't know what he would've done if she'd been frowning or, worse, appeared horrified. Lucky for him, as she frantically waved him toward the stage, her lips lifted at both edges.

And the upside-down semicolon was still there.

Drake put a hand on the stage and leaped to the side, suddenly as light and agile as a parkour athlete.

The next five minutes were a blur. Drake remembered taking the microphone from his mom, and he recalled his first two sentences to the crowd.

"Hi, everyone! I'm Drake Matthews, and I assure you everything backstage was completely appropriate and PG—everything this costume was not, hence the addition of these shorts."

The crowd laughed appreciatively, and Drake babbled on about being happy to be there to raise money for the shelter, and then his mouth switched to autopilot. He'd done enough of these charity events to know his role: turn the spotlight from him and his books to the nonprofit organization and badger the attendees to open their hearts... and their wallets. As the expected words poured from him, he glanced to his right, watching his mom escort Kate to sit at the table on the stage, overriding what appeared to be Kate's reluctance.

He could've told Kate that, like *Star Trek*'s infamous Borg Collective, resistance to his mom was futile. Sure enough, his knife-wielding planner was soon plopped into a plastic lawn chair behind a table full of various-size pumpkins. Clad in that absurd, but adorable, gingham dress with her red heels glittering in the sun, Kate gazed out at the crowd of roughly a hundred locals and visitors, and Drake was surprised to see she was still flushed. And distinctly uncomfortable.

Although he kept saying all the right things to

the audience, his brow furrowed. Was her discomfort simply a result of suddenly becoming the centerpiece, with all eyes on her? Or was it more complex? Was she mortified that his mom had announced their kiss to the crowd, despite the fact he'd just done his best to dispel any rumors?

Probably. It was, admittedly, awkward as hell.

But what if it went deeper than that? Was she, even now, regretting that kiss? Or regretting it now that he was here, in full daylight, and she'd just realized the implications of kissing him—the Knight of Nightmares?

By the end of his speech, he'd talked himself down from his earlier high, convinced all sorts of terrible thoughts whirled around in Kate's head, like debris from a tornado. All he wanted to do was apologize...and then slink away into a corner somewhere. Not sit onstage and pretend everything was fine.

His voice, at the end, lost a bit of his earlier enthusiasm, and Drake forced a smile as he wrapped up his speech to start the pumpkin-carving competition.

"Okay, so here's a little-known fact. I'm pretty good with a carving knife. On a pumpkin," he clarified, to the laughing crowd. "So, let's see what you've got, and let's get this contest started!"

His feet seemed to be made of heavy steel as he gave his mom the microphone, ignored her curious look, and shuffled in his modified Tin Man costume across the stage to sit in the empty chair next to Kate. He glanced over, but she scowled at the pumpkin in front of her, using a Sharpie to draw out some sort of design.

Damn.

He'd been right.

She was regretting their backstage kiss, and she was angry, mortified, or both.

Pulling over a pumpkin, he grabbed a paring knife and stabbed it next to the stem, viciously carving out the top as he debated what to say. He'd ripped the jack-o'-lantern lid off and was just scooping out the guts when he heard Kate snicker.

Turning his head, he saw she was laughing. At him.

"What's so funny?" Drake heard the petulant tone in his voice, but he didn't care. "Look, I apologize about what I did back there, and I get that you're embarrassed. All I can say is I thought I was getting some signals from you, and I'm sorry."

Kate shook her head, putting her hand over her mouth.

"No. It's not that. It's—you're digging into that pumpkin like some kind of maniac, which is a little terrifying, but—"

"Oh, so now I'm terrifying too?" Drake asked, dragging out another handful of orange, sticky, seedy goop, and flicking it off his hands onto the newspaper covering the table, and plunging his hand back into the gourd's chilly innards. "You're welcome to leave anytime and I won't hold it against you."

Kate's smile morphed into a pursed, annoyed expression. Her green eyes glittered as she squinted a glare at him.

"You have never terrified me, Drake Matthews, and if you'd quit jumping to conclusions and interrupting me so I can finish a stupid sentence, you'd know I'm giggling because you're disemboweling that pumpkin with your hands, looking all badass, and you've still got my pink lipstick smeared on your lips. It's too faint for the crowd to have noticed, but I can see it glittering on your mouth," Kate said, gesturing to the places on her mouth to use as a guide map to his face. "Right there, and there."

Drake was going to swipe at his lips when he realized his hands were covered in pumpkin guts. He used his arm, instead, wiping his mouth against the silvery leotard. Sure enough, when he was done, a pink smear remained on the fabric.

"And another thing," Kate said, scowling once more at her pumpkin as she traced a perfect circle around the stem. "I regret nothing."

Drake stared at her for a moment until her words sank in.

Wait. She didn't regret the kiss?

Yet she was still frowning. It was as if what she'd meant to say was, "I regret nothing, except..." and some large barrier hung in the air between them. Did he call her out on what she wasn't saying? Or let it alone? Real women were so much harder to read than heroines in novels, and trying to act like a book hero, with all the right words spoken at just the right times, was impossible.

Drake focused on his carving, planning his next words carefully.

"I don't regret that kiss, either," he said, softly. "Except, maybe, the timing."

Kate's head snapped up from the pumpkin, relief softening her features. "Exactly! Oh my goodness, I'm glad you said that. Because the timing isn't ideal for either of us. I mean, I have a job to do for you, and you have this massive deadline looming. Let's just pretend it didn't happen, for now, at least. You write fiction—

pretending is what you do, so you can pretend we're still a strictly professional thing, right?"

Drake's mind sifted through, unpacking that sentence and decided to base his reaction on the four words that mattered most... *for now, at least*. Because those words meant a future where the timing might allow another kiss. Maybe more.

He nodded. "I can pretend we're professional. If you can."

Kate's chest flushed, and the pink color rose up her neck, but before it reached her cheeks, she pivoted back to her pumpkin.

"I am always professional. Until you distract me." Jabbing the knife in the top like a serial killer, Kate hacked, attempting to follow her perfect, Sharpied line in a circle to cut out the stem, and failing miserably. "And don't be mad at your mom. I think it's sweet she wants to be with you and wants to help your career. Not all parents take an interest in their kids' jobs."

Drake recalled what her sister, Kiersten, had said on the phone, about how none of them had ever been to one of Kate's big events this whole time, and inwardly he congratulated himself for having the foresight to have invited them to the launch. If there was one event to see Kate in action, surely it would be at his Halloween book release.

But he didn't want to blow the surprise, so he nodded, tugging up a painful parent memory of his own.

"I hear you. To say that my dad would have been disappointed by me going into the Marine reserves, versus active duty, would be a colossal understatement."

Kate looked confused. "But aren't you all Marines? Isn't it the same?"

Drake snorted. "You'll have to ask my brothers sometime. They call reservists like me 'Weekend Warriors' when they're being nice. Here on the East Coast, we all attend Parris Island boot camp, but after MCT—Marine Combat Training—I started college, while other Marines, like my brothers, transition to active duty and receive specialized training. Other than my one-weekend-a-month responsibility, I was never called up to active duty. So I did my six years, got my degree, and transitioned to civilian life. Compared with others in the Corps, it is perceived as...less than."

"But you still served your country."

Drake nodded, then shrugged. "I can't explain it. It's a different mentality if you're in the fleet, and then a completely other level when you're a career Marine, like Ryker and my dad. Anyway, I'm just saying I get it. This disappointing your parents, living up to a legacy thing you've got going on. I think it's one of the reasons I'm writing this—"

He stopped his mouth just in time. He'd been about to blurt out "this romance."

Kate was nodding. "Right. The horror novel you're writing from a World War II perspective. Makes so much sense. We exorcise our demons in our own way, right?"

"You've been spending too much time with me." He grinned. "You sound like a horror writer."

They carved in silence for a while. Drake glanced up to peer at the people clustered around tables in the park, laughing and focused on their own pumpkins, paying no attention to the two at the table on the stage. Slowly, his body relaxed, and with it, his mind.

"Can I tell you a secret?" Drake gave Kate a sidelong glance over the pumpkin he was carving into a skull.

Kate was scooping out the insides of her pumpkin with a large metal spoon, her brow furrowed in concentration.

"You just want to distract me from winning this contest."

"Distract you from winning an award? Never. That's a waste of energy, isn't it?" Drake smiled to show he was kidding. "No, a secret. Well, it's more of a confession, really."

Her eyebrows rose, and she paused her pumpkin excavation to look at him. "I'm all ears."

Drake used his paper towel to wipe up orange pumpkin juice from the skull he'd carved, not looking at her as he spoke.

"Remember when I had you cook in my kitchen and said I was hurt?" He waited until she hummed assent. "I wasn't. I was writing a scene where my protagonist had an injury and needed help cooking dinner. From the girl. Having you there gave me a great opportunity to be in the hero's shoes and watch so I might be able to use snippets of it. In my book."

"You used me as a substitute for a character in your scene?" Kate put down her spoon, using her hands to scoop out the seeds.

"It's weird, I know," Drake finished, finally looking up to give her a crooked smile. "I should've told you, and I'm sorry. You've been a good inspiration for me."

"Really? Is there anything else you've used?" Kate asked, her face unreadable.

Drake thought about how he felt like he'd grown, as

a writer, using her as inspiration. It was as if writing a romance novel had unlocked a previously hidden well of emotional depth he'd never realized existed, or maybe having Kate's sunshine-and-sparkle personality had dredged up the old Drake—the one from so long ago who'd written his heart out in those black-and-white composition notebooks. Since Kate had worked her magic, it was like he'd been given a key to a lock he'd thought had rusted shut.

He owed her some of the truth.

"Our time together has already yielded over a hundred and fifty pages in my manuscript, and it's likely some of today will appear in a book at some point too."

Kate dumped orange-gooped seeds onto the newspaper, shooting him a look. "*All* parts of today?"

Drake winced. "Maybe. Probably. The scene with the old ladies ogling my junk...well, that seems pretty ripe for a horror scene in some book, don't you think?"

To his relief, Kate scoffed in mock indignation. "So, what you're telling me is I'm not your only muse?"

"Well, you're competing for the spotlight with Mrs. Nowakowski and her crew, so there are big shoes to fill."

"Now I know my place." Kate laughed. "For a minute there, I was feeling pretty special."

Drake's heart rose at her last statement. He watched as she put the finishing touches to her octopus carving. Maybe she didn't think he was too much of a freak? She did, after all, agree to go on this quasi-date with him, and she had kissed him back. Feeling as though he was pushing the boundaries, but wanting it too much to care, he put the question out there.

"How much work do you have to do this Tuesday evening for the book launch?"

"By then, I'll just be overseeing some loose ends. We're in a holding pattern until the permits are approved Wednesday morning, and we can start setting up the maze. We've got the partition frames done, and the strobe lights and props ready with a scare for each of your books, but we won't be doing anything major until Thursday—two days before the Halloween launch." Kate wiped her hands on a paper towel, frowning slightly. "Why? Did you—you don't want to change anything now, do you?"

"No. Nothing like that. I wanted to do something to thank you for your help. For being such a good sport in my research." Drake kept his eyes on his pumpkin when she turned to gaze at him. "There's a yearly promo gig Imani books for me in Niagara Falls for the Western New York Writers' Guild—they were the first writers' group I joined back before I was published, and their classes helped me refine my craft. At their invitation, I attend their annual conference, or at least the end-of-conference dinner, and say a few words to promote their membership. I'll probably have to plug *Halloween Hacker*, but after all that, they put on a nice dinner. It's a beautiful venue, and I thought...you might want to join me? Celebrate your hard work, and give you a chance to get away before the big day? I'll pay all your expenses and get you back here by Wednesday morning so you won't miss any time."

"It's an overnight trip?"

Then he did look at her, but couldn't figure out the expression in her eyes. He nodded.

"Separate rooms. All professional. Here's the bonus:

I have it on good authority that Everstone has flown into New York and plans to attend the conference to promote his movie adaptation, as long as he's on this coast. So, you can chat with him about the EVPLEX, or at least remind him of who you are and your goal."

"Niagara Falls? I've never been there," Kate mused, picking bits of pumpkin from under her nails. "Is this really just to help me get that EVPLEX, or have you got an ulterior motive—like more research for me to help with? Tell me the truth."

"Honestly, it's one of the curses of knowing a writer. Nothing is sacred, and all of my life usually ends up somewhere in my fiction." Drake held her gaze. "But no. It's not research. You don't have to go, and I'll still do whatever you need me to do for the launch."

Kate leveled him a look. "Can I think about it for a while?"

"Of course. It's not until Tuesday, so you have a few days." Drake hid his disappointment and bobbed his head toward her pumpkin. "Better finish up your octopus. Looks like my mom is ready to call an end soon, and you'll have to put your carving on display with everyone else's."

"Octopus? It's not an octopus." Kate frowned, then tilted her head and groaned. "Oh, no. It *does* look like an octopus. It was supposed to be a princess tiara."

Ten minutes later, Drake was paraded down a line of pumpkins that had been haphazardly arranged on the edge of the stage. He paced in front of the pumpkins, pretending he was having a hard time deciding.

In truth, he'd already picked the winner.

He'd spotted a little girl, dressed in a Wonder Woman

costume, placing her carved and glittery pumpkin on the stage, and when she'd turned to wave, her grin revealed two missing teeth. How could he resist? The girl's pumpkin, which had a pretty standard carving, with triangle eyes and nose and a jagged-toothed mouth, was so glopped with glitter glue, most of it had transferred to the girl's hands, her face, her costume, the stage, and the two pumpkins sitting next to it. It was adorable.

But the real determining factor was when he saw Kate put her hands on her hips when she saw it and fake her outrage.

"Hey, no fair! Why didn't our table have any glitter? I could've used that for my pumpkin."

Drake placed the huge blue ribbon on the stage next to the gap-toothed girl's pumpkin, fastidiously avoiding getting glitter on himself—he was sparkly enough already.

His mom called the girl, whose name was Arianna, and her parents onstage to give them the big gift basket prize that went along with the blue ribbon. The crowd cheered, and his mom gave Drake the microphone for final words.

"This pumpkin is fantastic, Arianna," Drake said, handing her the ribbon to more clapping from the crowd. "Its triangle eyes look like it's staring at me—at all of us. It's perfect. And that glittery smile you carved—it's cute and creepy all at the same time. I think those sharp, sparkly teeth might give me nightmares. You're going to put me out of a job."

Arianna stepped forward with her parents, giggling along with the audience, to accept the award. Her dad grabbed the pumpkin and the three of them posed for a picture with Drake. Then everyone stepped back, allowing a reporter to snap a picture of the girl and her winning creation.

"Hold your pumpkin, honey," the dad told Arianna, and reluctantly the girl took it, looking sidelong at the glittery gourd, as if seeing it for the first time.

Then, Drake watched in horror as the girl burst out into loud, wet sobs.

"Ith lookin' at me!" the girl lisped through her tears. "Punkin' ith thcary!"

Adults of every variety and size sprang into action.

Drake backed away, wide-eyed, as the mom jumped back onto the stage.

"I'm—I'm sorry," he stammered to the woman, whose lips were pressed in a thin line as she comforted her daughter. "I—I was trying to be funny. I didn't mean to make her afraid of the pumpkin."

"It's fine, Mr. Matthews," the mom assured him, snatching up the pumpkin from her daughter. "She's just going through that night terror time. You know how it is."

The mom tried, unsuccessfully, to hide the orange monstrosity behind her back, retreating down the stairs off the stage as the girl pointed and shrieked.

"Ith tharing at me, Momma! Ith teeth are gonna bite me, like Mithter Drake thaid!"

The reporter snapped another few pictures, chuckling.

Drake winced. He envisioned tomorrow's headlines: "The Knight of Nightmares Lives Up to His Reputation."

Then Drake heard his mom's voice and turned to see Patty snatch up the nearest box of cupcakes, flip open the lid, and offer the wailing child her choice of confections.

"Oh, sweetie, don't be scared. It's okay. Have a cupcake. See that one right there? It's chocolate and it's got a special surprise inside." Patty led the girl and her dad away from the mom, who surreptitiously pitched the sparkly, terrifying pumpkin into the nearest trash can.

Like someone had come in with a giant firehose and doused the audience, everyone dispersed, most taking their pumpkins. Some were snickering, and some looked stern as they glanced at Drake and the tear-streaked child behind him, stuffing a cupcake into her mouth.

All he wanted to do was disappear. But when dressed in a silvery metallic bodysuit with an upside-down funnel hat, disappearing in a crowd was hard. He was examining escape options when a hand slipped around his waist.

"Over here, Tin Man," Kate said, steering him off the stage and toward the far edge of Island Park, onto a grassy knoll overlooking the river where they finally stood alone.

"You okay? You looked a little panicked."

Drake glared at the river, ripping the funnel hat off his head.

"I can't even have one day without creating a nightmare for someone. How did I get to this place, Kate? How did I become the guy whose pumpkin description makes a little girl cry?"

Kate took his hand, turning him to face her. She gazed up at him, her expression serious.

"You are kind and good. Kids are goofy, and in another few moments, she'll have forgotten all about it." Kate gestured behind her. "Look, already she's grinning. Your mom's box of cupcakes was the best prize she could've hoped for today. It was sweet of you to award her the ribbon. Why did you choose her, anyway? I thought you'd be looking for really good carvings, like Pumpkin Masters–challenge ones."

"She had a superhero costume." Drake shrugged. "She looked so badass with her cape and gauntlets, and glitter all over everything. Sort of reminded me of you."

Kate's eyes crinkled, and her smile grew until the upside-down semicolon appeared.

"Drake Matthews, I think I will accept your invitation to dinner in Niagara Falls."

CHAPTER 15

Early Tuesday afternoon, Kate donned the only casual outfit she had with her—the same jeans, chunky boots, and chocolate-colored long-sleeved tee she'd worn a few days ago at the festival—and she packed her overnight essentials and the evening dress Drake had suggested for tonight's dinner event, placing everything carefully in her small rolling suitcase. She met Carl in the hotel lobby, thanking him again for flying in from the city to help with the last-minute preparations. He'd be working with the local crew she'd hired to set up the maze the moment Kate got notification that the town council approved her permits.

"It'll be late tomorrow morning when we'll get the green light and you guys can start," Kate said, as Carl parked a block away from Drake's house. She tugged her small suitcase out, rolling it behind her as they walked the length of Maple Avenue to where it intersected with Pearl Street. "The maze will begin here, and it'll twist and turn through this section for *Alien Abyss*. Then they'll go to this marker..." Kate pointed to a green

stake in the ground by the sidewalk on the south side of
Maple. "...where the guests will reach the scare team
for *Soul Salvation*, followed by *Creature Crypt*..."

Carl trailed her up the street, holding a copy of the
spreadsheet, as they reviewed where all nine of Drake's
previous books were represented in the maze, ending in
front of his house.

"And here is where we'll set up the white, bloodstained sheets arranged in a zigzag pattern like this."
Kate showed Carl the picture she'd drawn of the
Halloween Hacker sheet maze. "Only VIP guests will
be allowed after this point and they will have to walk
through those to get to the front door for their souvenir
picture and inside tour."

Kate keyed in her code on the pad so cleverly hidden
in the bushes next to the bat gates in front of Drake's
house. She pushed them open, allowing Carl to enter
before locking up behind them.

"Whoa," he said, halfway up the brick-paved walk
to the house. "This is where the Knight of Nightmares
lives? It's...spooky."

Kate paused in her recitation of the plan to look up
at the cheery red Victorian with its wraparound porch
and the stained glass surrounding the front door. She
sighed, smiling.

"I think it's gorgeous."

Four hours later, after she'd finished the launch plan
walk-through with Carl, including the inside and backyard of the Matthews mansion, Kate heard Drake's
truck pull into the carriage house–style garage. Her
heart leaped in her chest. She hadn't seen him since
the festival three days ago, although he'd lived in her

dreams every lonely night. In fact, she'd spent so much time thinking about him and that kiss that this morning she'd made a decision, which forced her to make a detour in her drive to work. Kate glanced at her overnight bag, sitting innocently in the corner, and her face flushed with the knowledge of the provisions she had stashed inside that suitcase next to her evening dress and shoes.

Forcing those thoughts away, she scanned the rest of the spreadsheet.

"That's pretty much it, except for the spider attraction. We can't put up the mechanism and test it until we get the go-ahead. I'd get that crew working first, and then supervise the people putting up the Master of Monsters Maze along Maple."

"That's a lot of 'M's." Carl chuckled, squinting at the spreadsheet. "Everything's set up for the banquet already?"

Kate nodded. "That's Drake's private property, so we didn't need permits. The spider scaling the house is the exception because it falls twenty feet, so it technically qualifies as a carnival/amusement ride and is subject to different permitting and inspection rules."

Carl's bushy eyebrows rose, and he switched the toothpick that was eternally in his mouth from one side to the other. "A carnival-grade spider attraction. That's one we've never done before."

Kate checked behind her before lowering her voice. "About that. Can you avoid using the word 'carnival' or 'circus' around our client? He's a bit...sensitive about the label."

Carl shrugged. "Sure. You're the boss. By the way, where are you headed tonight?"

"A business dinner," Kate said, hearing the back door to the kitchen open, and Sasha barking, tags jingling. "It's with Drake at a writers' conference in Niagara Falls."

"Uh-huh," Carl said, the toothpick flipping to the other side of his mouth as he grinned. Next to Imani, Carl was her most loyal friend, despite their two-decade age gap. They'd worked together for seven years now—first when she was an intern with Maya Evert, and then he'd come to work with her a year after she'd started her own business—so she knew from that expression she was about to be teased. "Writers' conference. At the honeymoon capital of the world. Totally business. When are you coming back into town again?"

Kate's face flushed, and she gave him a sour look as she bustled over to her suitcase, tucking her spreadsheets inside. "Tomorrow. It's not what you think."

"It's not what who thinks?" Drake entered the front parlor, setting down Sasha, who sprinted over, jumping and greeting everyone with a bark.

Kate bent down to pet the dog, averting her overheated face as she made up an answer. "The surprise awaiting your fans in the attic. It's not what they'll think—I was just explaining to Carl Wexler, my tech guru and handyman extraordinaire—that it's just a normal attic. Nothing spooky and no scare teams up there."

"Mmm-hmm," Carl said, nodding his head at her lie, and extending his hand. "Pleasure to meet you, Drake. Fine place you got here."

Drake shook Carl's hand, scanning the parlor with a dubious expression.

"Thanks, but right now it looks like it's prepped

for a bunch of painters to work." He pointed to the crisp white sheets draped over the antique furniture in the front parlor. "What's with the tarps? You're...not painting the rooms, are you?"

"Of course not," Kate said, standing with Sasha in her arms. "We're protecting the furniture that's staying as the movers come through with items for the other rooms. We don't want to damage any of your family's antiques."

Drake appeared unconcerned. "If they survived my brothers and me, they can survive anything. Are you ready to go?"

Kate nodded, setting Sasha down to glance at her watch.

"When exactly is your dinner? You said to be here at four, and now it's four ten. It's going to take at least two hours to drive to Niagara Falls, then I'm guessing there is some sort of prep you'll want to do before you speak. Like get changed." Kate gave a pointed look to her jeans, and Drake's casual outfit of jeans and a black, long-sleeved shirt. "I mean, I don't want you to be late."

Drake grinned. "Don't worry. You're getting the VIP experience tonight. Let me grab my suit and we'll head out."

Drake took the stairs two at a time, and Carl waited until the floorboards creaked above them before whispering to Kate.

"Did you hear that? You're getting the VIP experience tonight." He waggled his bushy eyebrows, and then dodged her hand when she swatted at him.

"Knock it off. It's just business," Kate said, shaking her head. "Strictly professional."

But the whirling in her stomach said otherwise.

*   *   *

Drake held the door open to his truck, and Kate climbed inside, breathing in the smell of Drake's cologne combined with the warm black leather of the upholstery. Although it was rad and vintage on the outside, the inside had been completely redone with modern conveniences. Buckling in, Kate complimented him on the vehicle, and Drake grinned, patting the dash as he set Sasha down on the plaid blanket between them and started the truck and pulled out.

"She's a beauty. Ryker did this for me, as a 'Welcome back to Wellsville' gift when I returned from the West Coast. He does these incredible vintage restorations and remodels full-time now after he was medically discharged from the service."

"Ryker does great work," Kate said, giggling as Sasha hopped from the blanket to her lap, tail wagging and her furry face seeming to grin. Kate scratched behind her little peanut head, cooing, "Isn't that right, sweetie?"

"Yes, sweetie, it is right, and I'll let him know," Drake replied. "Oh, wait. You were talking to the dog. My bad. Speaking of which, we're heading over to drop Sasha off at my mom's. She loves to babysit this furball. Says it's the only grandchild she has, so she might as well spoil her. Plus, there's someone there I'd like you to meet."

Kate looked at him quizzically, but he didn't offer anything else. Surreptitiously, she checked her watch, doing the math. If it was a quick visit, they'd still have plenty of time to drive to Niagara Falls, barring any traffic. Mentally, she shrugged it off—she wasn't going

to worry about the time if he wasn't. After all, she wasn't
in charge of this event. For once, she was a guest.

Drake took several turns, and soon they were in a
neighborhood full of houses built in the 1950s to the
1980s—sprawling, ranch-style homes next to tidy colo-
nials and small bungalows. The yards were well used,
with backyard grills, wooden playsets, and basketball
hoops attached to the front of most garages. Bikes and
skateboards were parked, helter-skelter, in driveways,
and children dashed around in fall coats, playing some
eternal game of tag, soaking up the late-October sun.

"Is this where you grew up?"

"Yep. We moved to Wellsville when I was five."

Kate enjoyed the idea of a young, less serious
Drake Matthews, sprinting from yard to yard, his coat
unzipped and his jeans covered in dirt. Her heart
pinged in envy at the well-used lawns, fields, mature
trees, and park-like green spaces, with houses dotted
all over in an obviously close-knit neighborhood. In
contrast, her parents had moved several times, and
while the houses she'd lived in at Lloyd Harbor were
far grander, the well-manicured yards and impressive,
circular, gated driveways in the Suffolk County of her
childhood were never, ever the sight of impromptu bike
ramps or grills set up next to a swing set with an
obnoxiously yellow curvy slide. The homes they'd lived
in were all beautiful. Stunning, in fact. But they lacked
the natural wonder and the...family accessibility that
Wellsville had in abundance.

What must it be like to live in a place designed
for neighbors and their kids to interact together, as
opposed to the sheltered, schedule-a-playdate-at-the-
country-club childhood she and Kiersten had been

privileged to enjoy? If it hadn't been for the fact she'd been best friends with Imani, and spent much of her time with Imani's family at their well-loved house, she'd have never tasted life away from Lloyd Harbor's sheltered existence.

Kate thought about returning to this part of the state once this job was buttoned up. Maybe she'd purchase a vacation home here? Heck, maybe a *real* home—one she'd hang pictures in, buy some throw pillows for, and make it more than a place to wash her clothes and park her car. She'd moved away from Imani's Queens apartment thinking it would be more convenient to be closer to her Gold Coast clients, but after living in Oyster Bay for the past couple of years, she'd discovered it hadn't offered many benefits. She was lonely and had found herself mostly meeting with prospective clients via video conferencing anyway these days. Living in a place like this could still happen; she was a tiny, hour-long flight from any big-city client, vendor, or event.

"This is Riverview Heights. My brothers and I took the bus to school from that corner," Drake said, interrupting her thoughts to point out a nondescript grassy spot next to a stop sign. "And the third house on the left is where we grew up."

Drake pulled into the driveway of a light gray house with black shutters and a brilliant red front door. The garage stood open, and Patty was inside, pulling Halloween decorations out of cardboard boxes. Kate waved as the woman tucked her bobbed hair behind one ear, grinning as she met their truck.

Then Kate spotted a tiny figure, huddled in a buffalo-plaid blanket on a folding chair next to the tiny front porch. This woman appeared much older, her hair a cotton-candy puff of white around her head. Even at this distance, Kate saw the woman's hand that came up to wave was thin and slightly shaky.

"Come on in while I drop Sasha off," Drake said, grabbing the happy shih tzu, shoving his black glasses up when the pup's ecstatic wriggling nudged them out of place. "I want to introduce you to my grandmother. She's been asking to meet you."

"Oh, okay." Kate's belly whirled with sudden nerves as she followed Drake over to the garage. She hung back, letting him have a moment to greet his mom with a kiss, then hand over Sasha. The dog went nuts, licking the older woman's face as though it were covered in treats.

Then he approached the frail lady sitting in the metal folding chair, hovering over her and looking massive in comparison. He kissed the top of her head, then took her hands in his, chafing them together before wrapping the black-and-white plaid tighter around her body.

"Kate, it's so nice to see you again." Patty ambushed her with a fierce hug as she got closer to the garage and its spill of cardboard boxes on the driveway. "I'm a little late getting my decorations out this year, but I wanted to put something up. I mean, I have a rep to maintain as the mother of the nation's nightmare-giver."

Kate assured her the place looked great, noting with pleasure the skeleton Patty rigged to stand on the tiny porch. She'd somehow wired it to hold an open, plastic-wrapped copy of Drake's book *Scared Stiff*, angling the head down as if it were immersed in the book. Propped next to the skeleton's legs was a sign that read *Drake's biggest fan*.

"That was clever." Kate grinned, pointing to the

skeleton. "Do you care if I borrow that idea for the launch?" ·

Patty's cheeks lifted in a pleased smile as she set Sasha down. "Not at all. In fact, why don't I just bring him with me that afternoon when I come with the cupcakes, and you can put him wherever you want?"

Drake appeared at Kate's side. With no hesitation at all, he took her hand, leading her to the front porch.

"Nana, this is Kate Sweet," he said, his voice louder than his normal tone. "She's the fantastic event planner I was telling you about. Kate, this is Grace Matthews, my grandmother."

"Nice to meet you, Kate," his nana said. While her body was hunched with age, and her thin, white hair trembled with every breeze and movement, her voice was strong, and her eyes—the same arresting shade of golden brown as Drake's—were alight with her smile.

"It's lovely to meet you too, Mrs. Matthews," Kate said, copying Drake's louder pitch as she took the older lady's hand and gave it a gentle shake. The skin under Kate's touch was chilly and silky soft, showing every single vein traversing her hands and swollen-knuckled fingers. "I absolutely love your Victorian. Drake told me that you're the one who procured most of the antiques in the house, and your collection is lovely. The tea cart is my favorite piece—that and the pink ladies' chair in the front parlor. Exquisite!"

"Call me Grace," the woman said, beaming to reveal a sparkling pair of what were likely dentures. She tugged Kate's hand, pulling her forward, as if wanting to tell her a secret. "Come here so I can see you, sweetheart."

Kate lowered her head until she was bent at the waist,

like she was executing a deep bow to a royal. Then, Nana's hands were cupping Kate's face, smooshing her cheeks as she heaved herself off the back of the chair to lean forward and scrutinize her features.

"You're so fair. And those pretty Irish eyes, and just enough freckles." The woman nodded, as if finishing a final pronouncement, and then she released Kate's cheeks with a final pat. "Do you know, Drake, that green is the rarest eye color?"

Drake chuckled. "I think I read that once, Nana."

Turning to Kate, he explained in a lower voice, "Nana's maiden name was Carney, or as the Gaelic say it, Kearney. Her parents both emigrated from Dublin, Ireland. You and your freckles just got the ultimate stamp of approval."

Kate flushed, her finger brushing the spatter of freckles she'd had on her nose since childhood.

"Oh. Well, that's good. I'll take all of the approval I can get."

After a few minutes of light conversation, Drake kissed both his nana and his mother, and explained they had to leave. Drake reversed out of the driveway, and Kate watched through the windshield as both Patty and Nana Grace waved madly until they pulled around the corner.

Kate sighed.

While she loved her parents, she rarely saw them, and when she did, the visits were conducted between texts, calls, or visits to resolve patient issues. If meaningful conversation occurred, it was invariably littered with veiled insinuations about her career choice. Or at least that's how it seemed.

Drake's small-town life seemed so Norman Rockwellian in its simplicity and goodness. In contrast, Kate flitted from city to city, planning someone else's big day. While she loved her career, she'd never realized what she'd missed as she led her nomadic lifestyle. It might be time to reevaluate her goals and create her own life spreadsheet that had more to do with her needs, rather than a two-year, career-focused calendar filled with other people's special occasions.

Something of her pensive mood must have shown on her face, as when Drake pulled up to his old bus stop, he paused.

"You okay?"

"I am." Kate affixed a smile that became real as Drake grinned, his amber eyes lighting up in that expression she'd come to covet. "I'm excited for a night away from everything. But we'd better hurry, or we're going to miss your dinner."

"Oh, I don't think there's much chance of that." Drake winked. "You'll see."

Ten minutes later, Kate saw.

They'd pulled into a small airport situated on what appeared to be one of the biggest hills in the area. "Small" was maybe too generous of an adjective for the Wellsville Municipal Airport. There was no main terminal, nor was there a security line, baggage area, or a single screen showcasing arriving and departing flights. The airport was a collection of hangars along a wide, paved tarmac. And not much else.

Kate squinted at the wind socks blowing here and there, but she spotted no control tower. She'd barely gotten her overnight things out of the cab when Drake appeared at her side, grabbing her rolling bag and hefting it along with the two suit bags thrown over his shoulder.

"Ready to go?"

"We're flying? From here?"

At Drake's delighted nod, Kate followed him into the airport's tiny waiting area, which consisted of a few office chairs set against a wall covered from ceiling to floor by a detailed map of New York State. She'd barely glanced at it before entering the warehouse that acted as a hangar, with a few planes peeping out from under canvas covers. While she heard an engine in the distance, none of the planes here seemed likely to take off in the near future. In fact, it was so quiet inside the hangar, she heard her boots on the cement floor.

"Um, do I need to check my bag, or go through security or something?"

"Nope. But maybe I should frisk you before we board? Just in case you're carrying contraband." Drake winked, clearly enjoying her discomfiture as he led her across the warehouse-like hangar to the opposite side. He pushed through a metal double door, and the origin of the engine noise Kate had heard was apparent.

A large, sleek, red helicopter sat on a circular pad, its rotors whirring and its door standing open.

Kate gaped at Drake, who grinned back as she raised her voice to be heard over the chopper.

"I thought you were driving us to Niagara Falls?"

"If it were just me going up, I would have. But I promised you a VIP experience, and I always keep my promises. You ever been in a bird before?"

"Definitely not." Kate gulped, following Drake across the asphalt to the edge of the concrete pad where the helicopter waited in the center of a painted yellow circle, the rotors whipping up the wind with such ferocity, she wasn't even sure he'd heard her.

A man with a thick coat and a pair of bulky ear protectors approached Drake, smiling and shaking hands. Their words were lost over the roaring of the engine, but they seemed to have no trouble understanding each other as he took the bags from Drake and stowed them in the aircraft. The air buffeting her from the rotors was chilly, but the sky was cloudless and bright blue. Kate's heart thudded in her chest as she followed Drake's gesture and climbed into the aircraft while two men with clipboards and ear protection buzzed around the chopper, checking things off what she assumed was some sort of preflight list.

She buckled herself into a bench-like seat, copying Drake, and put on the headset she'd been given, immediately muting the ear-splitting whine and thud of the helicopter engine. She pushed the wayward strands of hair behind the headset, feeling like a crazy troll doll, with her hair standing up all over her head.

"This will allow us to talk to each other and to John, our pilot," Drake said, gesturing to the Black man in the thick coat outside who wore an identical set of headphones almost lost in his mass of curly hair. He finished signing some sort of paperwork on a clipboard, and then swung into the cockpit, securing the door behind him.

Introductions were made, and Kate shook John's hand, licking her dry lips in an attempt to put some moisture in her mouth.

"It's my first time in a helicopter."

"Mine too," John said, the skin next to his eyes crinkling as he grinned. Then he faced forward, hit some switches, and adjusted his mouthpiece, rattling off numbers on gauges and checks for various controls.

Kate's eyes widened, and she looked at Drake, who patted her knee.

"He's joking. John's a graduate of the Army's Flight School program at Fort Rucker, and has more medals for valor than he has a chest to pin them on. He's been a private pilot since he retired from the military, and he's done some work as a medevac pilot for some regional hospitals."

"Yep, if I'm not flying dying people, I'm flying this deadbeat in the back," John said, hooking his thumb toward Drake. "What do they call you? The Master of Morbid?"

"Something like that." Drake chuckled.

John flashed Kate a smile. "I never get to do these fun jaunts, though. Having you aboard is a real treat. Sure you don't want to ditch this guy and head to the falls with me instead?"

Kate murmured something about this being a work night for her, and John returned to his gauges and preflight, saying only, "Drake's a lucky bastard."

Kate raised an eyebrow, wondering if Drake would disabuse the pilot of the notion that this was anything other than work, but the writer just shrugged in a what-are-you-going-to-do gesture.

"We are a go for takeoff. Ms. Sweet, you be sure Tall, Dark, and Twisted keeps his hands to himself. There'll be no mile-high club inductees in my bird."

The helicopter's engine took on a lower, thumping noise, as the whine increased outside of her headset. Kate gripped the edges of her seat, as the thing lifted off the ground with barely a lurch. It felt nothing like a plane—there was no taxiing down a runway to gain speed before the physics of aerodynamics lifted the machine. It was just a sensation of being gusted up in the air by something huge and powerful.

"Look up—it's going to be a beautiful ride," Drake said, and it was only then that Kate realized she'd been staring down at her feet.

They gained altitude quickly, and Kate saw that they were not on top of the largest hill in Wellsville, but one of many tall hills surrounding the town that was tucked in the valley between, nestled in like something from an old Currier and Ives print. She thought briefly about taking out her cell phone for a picture, and then the chopper bobbed left, and she decided her hands were best gripping the seat sides.

Drake, however, was not troubled at all by the rapid rise in elevation. He reached into a cooler secured to the floor, revealing a chilled bottle of champagne, two flutes, and a covered tray of goodies—the latter of which bore the sticker logo of PattyCakes Café on the lid.

Popping open the food container, he offered her a selection of finger sandwiches, along with some bite-size cupcakes. As Kate shook her head to refuse, he gave her a faux-stern look.

"My mom made these especially for you," he chided, and pulled out his cell phone. "In fact, I have strict orders to feed you as soon as possible, given the late hour we'll be eating. And she wants proof."

Reluctantly, Kate unlatched each finger from the seat bottom, her hands shaking as she reached out for what looked like her favorite mini Cubano sandwiches. She'd no sooner gotten it close to her lips than Drake snapped a picture, nodding happily.

The helicopter did a small up-down dip, and Kate stuffed the entire sandwich into her mouth so her hands were free to grip the seat once more. He snapped another picture, chuckling as her eyes bulged at him in warning.

"I'll delete that. As soon as you let go," he said, his face more vibrant and thrillingly alive since the day at the festival. "You're the Queen of Happily Ever Afters, for God's sake, and you're acting like this copter is going up in flames at any moment. You're buckled in, you're in a top-of-the-line bird with a decorated pilot. It literally doesn't get any safer than this. Enjoy, and leave the nightmares and disaster scenarios to me—it's what I'm built for."

Glaring, she loosened her death grip on her seat, edging closer to the window. The view beneath was all rolling hills and forests, the trees bright with fall colors. It was like staring at a giant red, orange, and yellow quilt that had been laid over the Earth, stitched together by the rural roads and dotted with houses. Between the forested squares lay larger, rectangular swatches of green fields, plowed brown farmland, and lush evergreen forests. Not for the first time, she recognized what she'd missed, living so close to New York City for so many years.

She managed to finally chew and swallow the mass of sandwich. "This is so incredible. I can't believe you set this whole thing up for me."

John interjected: "He did. Lock, stock, and barrel of wine—all for you, Ms. Sweet."

Drake smiled and handed her a glass of champagne.

"You're always working on crafting amazing memories for everyone else. I thought it was high time you had one of your own." Drake raised his own glass of champagne. "Here's to...what do they call this in a romance novel? A happily-for-now moment!"

They clinked glasses, and Kate flushed. He'd done all of this...for her? She still had too much to do to pull off the launch to allow herself a distraction...but she had to admit, she'd fallen for this guy who was so full of contradictions. On the outside, he was like the hard shell of a chocolate-covered candy, but when you got to know him, cracked open his defenses, he was all warm, sinful, gooey sweetness. While she knew at least some part of him must feel the same about her—no man could kiss that well without passion hiding somewhere behind those dark glasses—she was at the place to take the next step, but wasn't sure if he was there with her. The same question she'd asked on her ill-fated speed-dating night with Imani still pestered her.

Was he the type of guy who could handle a woman whose career meant she wouldn't be available most weekends or holidays for the foreseeable future? Or would he expect her to give up her dreams for his? If so, this whole thing was only a happily for now. Could she be okay with that? Was it worth putting her heart at risk?

But now was not the time to ask those questions. Instead, as they rode, Kate helped Drake polish off the bottle of bubbly in addition to the small tray of PattyCakes goodies, and the pilot interrupted their laughter and talk to intermittently point out a landmark in the autumnal-tinted world rushing beneath them. Yet it wasn't until an hour had passed and they were passing over a particularly dense cluster of houses and neighborhoods that John made an announcement.

"This is Buffalo, and we'll be landing in Niagara Falls International Airport in about five minutes. We're awaiting clearance for a pass-over of Rainbow Falls, so get your camera ready, Ms. Sweet."

Kate fumbled in the purse she'd put at her feet, eager to obey.

"Give her the million-dollar view, John," Drake said.

"Roger that." John banked the copter, turning toward Kate's left, bringing a wide, brown river into view.

"That's the Niagara River," Drake said, indicating the flow of water winding through the city below. "The force of its water churns out millions of kilowatts in the hydroelectric plants, powering the whole region, all the way down to Wellsville and up through Canada."

"It looks so calm and lazy." Kate noted the muddy, brown water. "Why is it so filthy? Pollution?"

"Mostly it's run-off from the hills and the rain we had a few days ago that created a lot of silt in the water. The Niagara looks a little like a mud puddle right now," John said, and then nodded toward the front. "But in a second she'll look as white as snow."

Chatter came over the radio.

"Okay, we're a go to buzz the falls," John said into his mouthpiece, flashing a grin back to Kate and Drake. "Here's the best way to view one of the natural wonders of the world."

The helicopter rocketed forward, and Kate gripped her phone tight as they raced the river below, following the Niagara as if it were a road.

"We're getting awfully close to the water, aren't we?" Kate asked Drake.

Drake smiled. "You're in good hands, I promise."

Kate nodded, unconvinced.

"And there's the money shot." Drake nudged Kate toward the cockpit windshield.

It looked like they'd found the edge of the world.

The river appeared to fall off the face of the Earth, reminding Kate of those infinity pools owned by some of her parents' colleagues in the Hamptons. Kate held her breath as they sped along with the water, toward the edge. She gripped her seat belt with her free hand so hard, the canvas bit into her palms.

Suddenly, the water ended, and the helicopter seemed to also dip over the edge, eliciting a small gasping scream from Kate. Drake plucked the phone from her, and she was grateful to have both hands to clutch the seat belt as the craft lurched and dipped in the mist-filled air currents that rose above the large basin of water beneath the falls.

"Oh my God!" Her heart thudded in her chest. She turned to face Drake, who had her phone in his hands and appeared to be taking a picture of the view from her side of the helicopter. "It's the most incredible thing I have ever seen!"

Drake pointed at the boats bobbing along the white-churned waters below filled with people dressed in identical blue rain slickers. "*Maid of the Mist*," he said, and then pointed toward the back of the chopper. "Check out the Rainbow Falls from this angle."

Kate stared transfixed at the water gushing over the invisible precipice. Her mind was unable to fathom the gallons and gallons tumbling through the air to smash the massive boulders beneath it with such force, mist rose like plumes of smoke all around.

John's voice boomed into the headpiece.

"I've only ever given this follow-the-river tour to one other person, and that would be the commander-in-chief. Drake pulled out all the stops tonight—still can't believe he got clearance for this little maneuver. Turns out, he has some fans in high places."

"I promised Kate a VIP experience for everything she's done for this book launch." Drake shrugged, but was clearly pleased. "Every once in a while, making a living from freak-show novels filled with nightmares results in some nice perks."

"Don't talk that way about your books," Kate said, absently putting a hand out. She'd intended to put it on his arm in admonition, but ended up hitting Drake's hand, instead. When his fingers closed over hers, she squeezed them once and gave him a smile. "You're always looking to use your craft to bring happily ever afters to life. You just do it in a . . . unique way."

Drake leaned toward her, chuckling.

"I think this place is affecting your judgment—it is the honeymoon capital of the world, after all. Now, let's give the Queen of Happily Ever Afters a picture to blow up her social media accounts." He let go of her hand to switch her camera's view, and quickly snapped a picture of the two of them leaning together, grinning, the falls a spectacular backdrop behind them. "There. Now how many event planners have a picture like *that* in their personal feed?"

The helicopter bobbed down, and she gasped, her hand clutching Drake's arm.

"Sorry about that. A little turbulence here because of the water vapor," the pilot said, pushing on the joystick. They rocketed forward, ascending another fifty feet. "I'll swing over Horseshoe Falls, and then we're cleared to land at Niagara International."

The helicopter banked to her side again, and she touched the cool glass of her windowpane reverently.

"What an amazing place to get married! I wonder why nobody has ever booked me here? As you said, it is the honeymoon capital of the world."

"Too wet," Drake replied, pointing to the mass of people on soaking-wet wooden platforms connected by staircases that clung precariously to the sides of the cliff rocks lining the gorge walls. They were all dressed head-to-toe in identical, bright yellow rain slickers, the hoods pulled all the way up to ward off the mist roiling from the water that thundered down just feet from them.

"Well, if I ever marry, my wedding will be someplace like this that needs no decorations to be jaw-dropping," Kate said, nodding with conviction. "And after that, we'll have a huge party."

"Not an event?" Drake joked, and she snorted.

"No, for once. I'm too type-A to let someone else plan an event for me, so if I take the plunge...it'll be a fun, spreadsheet-free kind of day."

Just then, the chopper veered, sending Kate careening into Drake. He caught her hand again, and she gripped it hard as the helicopter took a minute to right itself, ascending farther and lifting completely away from the falls until they were postcard-size beneath them.

Kate sighed into the microphone, loosening her grip on Drake's hand, but not releasing it this time.

"It's perfect," she said, watching the falls until they disappeared from view. Then she turned to look at the only view that rivaled the falls. "Thank you, Drake—this has been the most magical afternoon."

Drake's mouth widened in a soft, slow smile.

"You're welcome. But it's not over yet."

Her stomach whirled again. She squeezed Drake's hand, refusing to let go until they landed.

And maybe not even then.

CHAPTER 16

Drake enjoyed watching Kate's reaction to the helicopter ride, followed by the stretch limo that picked them up. He had to admit: so far, his plans to make Kate feel special—to bring that light to her eyes and the genuine, semicolon smile to her lips—were going spectacularly.

"I'm always the one reserving these, never the one inside them," Kate said, her head on a swivel as she examined the back of the limo, flipping switches that adjusted the lights and music. It was like she was finally comfortable abandoning the armor of her professionalism and letting down her guard to have fun. But maybe that was what he wanted to think, after that kiss behind the bandstand that was still on replay in his mind.

Drake shrugged. "It's all part of the VIP tour I promised. Besides, calling a car service typically involves waiting, and as you've seen in my hometown, the more time I'm out in public, the more I'm mobbed by fans. It's even worse when I'm outside of Allegany County."

"So, what do you need to do tonight? Are you signing books or speaking, or both?" Kate asked, finally settling back with him into the limo seat.

Her hand easily fell into his, as if they'd been holding hands their entire lives, and just like Grandpa Matthews had described in his letters, Drake could feel his chest constrict, the yearning for more days like this—more days with Kate—making it hard for him to breathe. He'd wanted this kind of all-consuming passion for so long. Now he was terrified he might do something to screw up his chances with the woman who inspired it.

Somehow he managed to speak around the feeling igniting in his chest.

"This one's not a signing event, technically, but since everyone knows I promote this group's conference every year, there are usually a bunch of readers there," Drake said, wanting to prepare her for the mob scene. He did not want this to spoil their night. "I'll likely get asked for autographs at first, but typically readers leave me to eat in peace. This hotel is known for their cuisine, so you'll enjoy at least that much of the evening."

Kate's face softened. "You don't need to give excuses for doing your job, Drake. It doesn't bother me. Sign all the books you'd like. I'm...well, it occurred to me on the way here that I haven't taken time off in a hot minute. This is a welcome break."

Suddenly, the phone in Drake's pocket buzzed. He hauled it out, reading the display.

"It's a text from Imani." He groaned, read it aloud. "'Heads up. Have it on good authority that Everstone has a plus-one. Do you need me to cancel for you?'"

Kate's brows crinkled in confusion. "Why would you care that Evan brought a date?"

"Because he's dating my ex-girlfriend. Rachel Lackey. The author of a tell-all book about her relationship with me titled *Living Horror: My Terrifying Time with the Knight of Nightmares*," Drake said, keeping his voice neutral, as Kate gasped in surprise. "Her book, filled with lies and vitriol, hit the bookstores exactly two months after our breakup."

Kate was fast to put the puzzle pieces together. She jolted, grabbing his arm as the realization hit her.

"Do you mean she wrote that book while she was still *dating* you?"

Drake nodded his head. "Mmm-hmm. I found out later that she was cozying up to a famous Hollywood producer at the same time, which is how she got a fat book contract so quickly."

"Evan Everstone?"

"One and the same." Drake rubbed his forehead, suddenly exhausted. "Lucky me."

"Now I know why you were ticked when Imani brought Everstone to your house at the beginning of October." Kate shook her head, her eyes wide. "And you have to work with him for the movie adaptation?"

He nodded. "I hate like hell that he won the contract to turn *Halloween Hacker* into a movie, but the decision wasn't mine to make."

"I think I'd have tried to sue her for libel," Kate said, crossing her arms over her chest in an adorably offended expression. "That can't be legal, what she did to you."

"I briefly entertained the idea of taking legal action, but ultimately, cooler heads prevailed. As my publisher reminded me, Rachel's book, evil as it was, acted like a double-shot of adrenaline to the sales of my previous titles, so from a business perspective, it was a lucrative thing." Drake shrugged as Kate looked indignant. "I'm a big believer in karma. What goes around will come around for them both. At the same time, I'm not going to hold my breath. Everstone's untouchable."

Kate's lips pursed, as if she tasted something sour.

"That just...that just sucks! What are you going to tell Imani?"

The limo pulled up to the portico for the main entrance.

"I don't know. So much for a relaxing dinner out, huh?" Drake offered a lame laugh, cursing his luck as he got out of the vehicle before the driver opened the door. He wanted to help Kate out of the vehicle himself.

But before they'd shut the limo door, there was a commotion. A group of a few dozen people, loitering by the hotel's revolving front entrance, spotted him.

"There's Drake Matthews!" a man in a gray hoodie shouted, pointing at him with a sniper's accuracy. "Right there, behind the redhead."

Suddenly, people streamed out from inside the hotel, joining the waiting throng on the sidewalk. Soon, the small trickle of readers was more like a tidal wave.

Drake had enough time to step in front of Kate, feet in a wide stance, as he braced for the onslaught. He reached behind him, blindly, and Kate squeezed his hand, as if sensing his need to ensure she was safe.

Kate's voice sounded in his ear just before the group descended on him.

"You do your job. I'll be here when you're done."

*   *   *

He did as he was told, a bemused smile on his face as he signed book after book thrust at him from the waiting crowd. While he greeted each fan, checking the spelling of their name before signing—a lesson he'd learned the hard way, years ago—he kept an eye on Kate, who seemed to have suddenly become the coordinator for this impromptu meet-and-greet.

She'd gotten the valet to take the velvet ropes that lined the entrance of the hotel and fashion them into a queue, of sorts, for his readers to stand in without blocking the rest of the building's traffic or causing some sort of unintended hazard from the sheer crush of humanity on the threshold of the hotel. Then she went down the line, instructing each fan to open the book to the title page to expedite the signing process. Kate was a bundle of surprises, sprinkled with goodness and grace, and wrapped in a hell of a gorgeous package.

He wanted to drop everything, scoop her up, and make off with her to somewhere they could be alone. Preferably a place with a bed.

Yet for now, he was stuck giving autographs. When the hotel's manager came out, Kate intercepted her neatly, and although Drake only glanced their way between signings, he saw Kate had it all in hand. In fact, a few moments later, a concierge was taking their bags from the limo, and the manager was handing Kate sets of what appeared to be room key cards.

Drake signed book after book, until only one fan remained. Out of the corner of his eye, he saw Kate edging closer on the pretext of putting away the hotel's ropes, but his attention was focused on this last fan— the only one with empty hands.

"Mr. Matthews, I don't have any books for you to sign because I borrow all your books from the library," said the thirty-something woman standing in front of him, her face shining with earnestness. "But I came down here today to tell you that your writing matters. And I'm living proof."

"Well, thank you. That's quite a compliment." Drake noticed the woman was dressed in layers of shabby neutral clothes, and the laces on her sneakers had been knotted in several places where they'd been frayed and ripped.

"I didn't have a good home life, growing up. My parents divorced when I was five, and my older brother and I lived with my mom until she died from an overdose. My dad took in my brother, but he couldn't take me, so I got shuffled from relative to relative. Most of them couldn't afford another kid, and those who could didn't want me for long." The woman's large hazel eyes were clear and unblinking as she cracked open her mental diary of pain. "Some homes I was in, well, they weren't the best places. For little girls, I mean. And I got real low in high school. Real low. I thought maybe the world was better off without me."

The woman paused, looking like she was back in high school, reliving that dark time.

He reached out, taking her hand in his. Nothing he could say would eliminate her pain, so he helped by staying silent, letting this woman tell her truth.

"Then I found your book in the library. *Attic Asylum*. I read the foreword where you talked about losing your aunt and how her suicide impacted your mom, and it was like you were talking to me." The woman's hand gripped his, giving them a little shake for emphasis. "You said, 'Even if you don't think so, someone out there cares about you, and you need to give them the chance to tell you.' After I read that, I thought about it and realized my brother cared about me and probably my father too, although I hadn't seen them in years. I used the library internet to find my brother and connected with him on social media, and it was like someone had flipped on a light. I hadn't known how dark it was until I'd reached out to my brother, and that was all thanks to you.

"Now, I've read every one of your books, and I love how you take me away from my troubles and show me that while things may seem bad, at least I'm not battling demonic dolls or aliens." The woman smiled, making her look years younger. "And I'm alive. All thanks to your writing. I just wanted to say thank you, Mr. Matthews."

Drake blinked a couple of times and cleared his throat until he was sure his voice wouldn't crack. "What is your name?"

"It's Judy. Judy Billings."

"Judy, do you mind if I give you a hug?"

Instead of answering, Judy opened her arms, and when Drake embraced her, he felt her silent sobs against his chest.

As he held her, he spotted Kate, watching from a few feet away. Her hand was balled up into a fist in front of her mouth, pressed against her lips. When he motioned behind Judy's back for her to approach, Kate gave a big sniff and came up, stopping a discreet distance away.

"Judy, I'd like to sign something for you, just the same," Drake said, gently disengaging from the hug, but keeping his hand on Judy's arm. "Do you spell your name J-u-d-y?"

"Yes, but I—I don't have any paper, Mr. Matthews," Judy said, wiping tears from her cheeks. "I dropped everything and left the shelter when I heard you were going to be here today. Meeting you is enough."

"I've got some paper, I think." He reached into his back pocket. "Ms. Sweet, may I trouble you for your lucky pen?"

Kate nodded, fishing in her bag until she pulled out the sparkly pen.

Judy's eyes were exactly where he'd intended; by asking Kate for the lucky pen, he'd ensured Judy would miss what, exactly, he was pulling from his wallet. Working fast, he removed a one-dollar bill and a hundred-dollar bill, fingers deftly lining them up so the hundred disappeared behind the single.

"I'm going to sign this dollar bill, just for you, Judy, and I'm signing it with what my event planner assures me is the luckiest pen she owns," Drake said. "You keep this in your wallet, or in your pocket. Every time you see it, I want you to remember I'm thinking of you and that someone in this world cares."

Drake used the side of the hotel building to sign the dollar bill, careful so that the hundred beneath it didn't show as he folded it in half, then in half again before handing it to Judy. The woman took it, pressing the bill to her lips.

"Thank you, Mr. Matthews. You continue writing your stories, and I promise to read them. I'll keep this always."

The woman waved, bustling off as she clutched the money in her hand.

Drake sighed, putting away his wallet. "Thank you so much for waiting, Kate. I so appreciate what you did with that flash mob of readers I had there. Did you check in already? Looked like you'd taken care of everything."

Kate nodded, looking straight ahead at the hotel, her gaze fixed on the doors. She cleared her throat, and her voice was tight when she spoke. "All checked in. They've taken our bags up, and the manager gave me both sets of keys, so we can head to our rooms."

Drake winced.

She wasn't even looking at him.

He knew it had been rude of him to sign autographs for so long, but his fans had been waiting a long time in that cold...and she had said to do his job, hadn't she? He followed Kate inside the elevators, his shoulders slumping. Hadn't he learned from his past relationship? Women didn't like coming in second for his time, especially when it meant being waylaid by a throng of horror fans eager for a signature on his freak-show books.

Kate pressed the button for the top floor, and he waited until the doors closed and they were alone in the car before beginning his apology.

"Look, I'm so sorry. I should've warned you they'd be probably camped outside for me. My fans know I attend this conference every year, and—"

"Drake, stop!" Kate's voice was soft but emphatic. "You don't need to apologize. You were amazing out there, and it's humbling that people love you so much, they'll wait outside in forty-degree weather on the off-chance they'll see you. It's just as much part of your job to validate your readers as it is for you to write your books."

Drake shook his head in confusion.

"Then why are you angry?"

"You think I'm angry?" A strangled sound came from Kate's mouth, and she blinked furiously, glaring at the elevator ceiling. "I saw what you did for that poor woman. You heard her story, hugged her, and then you hid a hundred under that single and gave it to her!"

Drake fumbled for words. "I thought she could use it. I mean, her shoelaces were barely holding up her sneakers, and it's not like I can't afford—"

"Stop!" This time, Kate looked at him, swatting his chest with her hand. A tear raced down her face, followed by another one. "Stop t-t-talking right now."

Drake's breath stalled in his throat, horrified he'd made her cry.

She sniffed, glaring and blinking up at the ceiling again. "What you did out there was kind. And honorable. You gifted her with your words, your thoughts, and your riches, all in one gesture."

"B-but," Drake stammered, intercepting her hand as it smacked at his chest again, "then why are you upset?"

"I'm not upset. I'm overwhelmed. And I'm trying really, really hard not to cry." Kate swiped at her eyes, looking at him as the bell dinged, announcing they'd arrived at the penthouse floor. "Because now my skin is going to be all blotchy for your fancy conference dinner tonight."

Drake put his hand to the small of her back, allowing her to precede him out of the elevator and down the hallway toward the only two doors on the floor. He worked to untangle her words and actions.

"So, you're not angry I made you wait?"

Kate gave a teary laugh. "No."

"And...we're still on for dinner tonight? Even though it's likely to be awkward and miserable with Rachel and Everstone there?"

Kate handed him a set of keys and pulled out another paper pouch with her own set. Setting a card against the door sensor on the left of the hallway, she waited until the reader blipped, opening her door before responding.

"Here's what I think." She wiped the last tear from her face and jutted her chin forward, eyes sparkling. "You're going to knock at my door at seven, and we're going downstairs together, and neither Rachel nor Evan will ruin our dinner."

Then, before Drake could process that answer, Kate's lips were on him, her kiss deep and wet and so fierce with emotion, he could only blink, speechless, when she finally pulled away. She brought her finger up to Drake's mouth, carefully rubbing something off before cupping his face, drawing him down until he could see every fleck of hazel in her green eyes.

"Sometimes karma just needs a swift kick in the ass, and trust me," she said in a low voice, her mouth curving in a sexy smile that made him instantly hard, "I have the perfect set of size-seven stilettos for the job."

CHAPTER 17

At seven o'clock, a knock sounded on Kate's door.

"Are you ready?" Drake asked, his voice muffled by the door. "Everyone expects us to be fashionably late, so if you need more time—"

"I'm almost ready." Kate hauled open the door, and there stood Drake, dressed in a black suit, a crisp white shirt, undone at the top, and holding two black ties in his hands.

He looked gorgeous.

As he paused in her doorway, Kate was glad she'd thought to pack more than her typical suits. After tearing up in the elevator, then practically mauling him in the hallway, she'd taken time with her updo and makeup to ensure she'd live up to the promise she'd made him—to do her best to kick karma in the ass, and help him stand tall and enjoy this evening in spite of Rachel and Evan. She'd brought with her a light gray, washed-silk slip dress that was her go-to for when she wasn't sure of the level of formal wear required at an event—it could easily straddle uptown chic and laid-back classy, depending on her hair and accessories.

"C'mon in," she said, feeling suddenly shy.

"I, uh, didn't want to clash with you. So I brought two ties." Drake gave a lopsided grin, holding up the ties for her perusal.

Both were black and would clash with exactly... nothing.

"Hmm. Tough choice. There's this one, which has black stripes on black, or this one, with black paisleys on a black background," she said, starting out sarcastically, but then realized he might actually be serious when his eyebrows drew together and he peered at each option, then her dress, as if the two were a challenging sudoku puzzle.

"Your dress is gray, so which one would you think?"

Kate bit the inside of her cheeks, warding off a smile. She took a tie in each hand as if debating. Finally, she stood on tiptoes, slipping the paisley one around his neck. She leaned in close enough to smell that amazing cologne he wore and, under it, the warm scent that was uniquely Drake, then lowered herself back down, smiling.

"This black paisley on black is perfect with my dress. You're so thoughtful to check."

Drake smiled as he flipped his collar up and knotted the tie with quick, practiced movements.

"You look outstanding. And your toenails match your dress." Drake nodded at her bare feet as he adjusted the length of his tie. "But I'm thinking some sort of footwear might be required. You know—so that you're armed for any battle, and all."

"Okay, now it's your turn to choose." Kate dumped

out the two pairs of heels she'd brought, slipping one foot into the nude heel and the other into the black stiletto with the silver tip—the same one she'd accidentally stabbed him with a few weeks ago. She turned first to one side, then the other, and then she caught Drake's frozen expression.

He looked a little...stricken.

She kicked off the black one, laughing.

"I'm just messing with you." She slipped on the neutral shoes. "You only just got those stitches out of your arm last week from these bad boys. I brought them as a joke."

"No," Drake said thickly. "Wear the black ones with those deadly silver tips. Definitely."

"Really?" Kate looked at him in surprise.

"Please." The intensity of Drake's gaze ignited something deep in her belly.

"Okay." Her cheeks warmed, but she acted natural, slipping out of the nude heels and into the black stilettos.

Kate grabbed her clutch, then took Drake's arm. As they waited for the elevator, she smoothed her hair, giving herself a once-over in the mirrored doors. Instead of making her look washed out, the gray slip dress made her pale skin glow, and the black stilettos gave the whole ensemble a more edgy vibe. Luckily, she'd halted her almost-cry before it had done serious damage to her complexion, and there wasn't a bloodshot vein to be seen in her eyes. And Drake—he was like a formal-wear model. One she hoped to have all to herself tonight.

Kate smiled at the picture they made together in the mirror.

"Don't worry," she said as they got out of the elevator. They walked past the first ballroom, which was hosting a large wedding reception, and paused before the doors to the second ballroom with the label *WNY Writers' Guild Conference* affixed to the sign by the entrance. "I've got a good feeling about tonight."

They pushed open the ballroom doors. Drake stiffened, coming to a halt.

"Damn. Imani was right. Everstone's not alone."

Kate scanned the crowd, following her client's gaze...and then she recognized the bored woman from the online fan video. Drake's ex-girlfriend, Rachel. She wore a purple sequined dress with spaghetti straps and a plunging neckline, and was more posed next to Evan Everstone than with the man as he carried on a conversation with the huddle of people around them, oblivious to the gorgeous woman at his side.

In other circumstances, she might have felt bad for Rachel, who was so obviously being treated as just another pretty decoration. But these weren't other circumstances. Kate reminded herself that directly in front of her was the woman who had, single-handedly, given Drake a complex about his writing and his love life.

"She's...a lot," Kate murmured, and Drake laughed.

"Yeah, well, I'm glad you're here. She's a lot...less, now."

Rachel spotted them entering the ballroom, and Kate noticed her spine straighten as she noticed Drake wasn't alone.

"Excuse me, Mr. Matthews?" A man in a gray pinstriped suit approached, reaching to shake Drake's hand. "I'm Preston Ball, the new president of the Guild."

"Great to meet you. I'd heard you were voted in this year," Drake said, then gestured to Kate. "I'd like you to meet Kate Sweet, owner of Sweet Events, who is managing the launch party for *Halloween Hacker* this weekend. I wanted her to meet the group so instrumental in jump-starting my writing career and allow her to mingle with writers, readers, and fans of the genre in case there are any last-minute book launch ideas from it all."

"Excellent," Preston said, shaking Kate's hand. "So glad you both made it. I spoke on the phone with your publicist, and she's asked me to seat you two at a table toward the back, and not at our VIP table. Is that—I mean, are you aware of those arrangements?"

Drake's polite smile never faltered. "Imani knows I prefer to sit in the back when possible. More unobtrusive that way when I have to leave. Deadlines, you know."

"I'm sure you keep a grueling writing schedule." Preston bobbed his head and adjusted his red tie, tugging it away from his neck. "We're so thrilled to have you again this year at our Western New York Writers' Guild. I'll be introducing you personally as our keynote speaker. But, uh, we had a last-minute guest who requested the VIP table. We're thrilled, of course, to host the man who is, I understand, producing the adaptation of your new book?"

"Evan Everstone," Drake supplied, an expression of distaste ghosting across his features. "We've met."

"He'll be seated at the VIP table, and he's agreed to speak after your keynote speech as they begin to serve dinner." The man adjusted his tie again, fidgeting with the ends. "Are you certain you don't want to sit with us this year, as you have in years past? I mean, it's exciting to meet Mr. Everstone, but our people were so looking forward to sitting with *you*."

Drake paused, clearly unable to come up with a response that wouldn't offend the group's president, yet not give up his seat away from the VIP table, Everstone, and his ex.

Kate cleared her throat.

"I'm afraid it's my fault." She pasted on a pained expression. "We'll be leaving early tonight to resolve some last-minute issues with the launch preparations. But there may be a good compromise—how about we meet each of the VIPs before the dinner begins? Drake can take pictures, have time to chat with them, and then he'll speak and we'll slip out before anyone is the wiser. Will that work?"

Preston Ball beamed. "Absolutely. What a wonderful idea! I'll take you to them myself."

The writers' guild president led them around the ballroom, and Kate estimated Drake shook hands, took selfies, and signed books, napkins, and even a full-size poster of himself, for more than two dozen various important personages for the WNYWG. He was always gracious, humble, and cognizant of his role, never passing on an opportunity to deflect praise toward the writers' guild, his agent, his editor, his publicist, or his readers.

Kate found her way to the table that had a card with *Reserved* written in marker with a fast, shaky hand, and poured herself a glass of wine from the bottle they'd placed on the table in a chiller at the hastily arranged second VIP table. Other people helped themselves to chairs at the table, ignoring the *Reserved* sign, and soon all but a couple of places were taken by people she didn't know. She set her clutch on an empty chair for Drake, enjoying this opportunity to relax. She smiled and made small talk with strangers until the room became silent with a tapping on the microphone.

Preston stood at the podium onstage and greeted the crowd, thanked the organizers and sponsors, and finally introduced Drake, giving what Kate was coming to understand was the standard introduction—likely written by Imani for such occasions. It provided a synopsis of Drake's writing career, from his first short story sale to his upcoming Halloween release. But before he turned the microphone over to Drake, Preston added his own flair to the last of the author's bio.

"If you've had a chance to know Drake Matthews, as we have here in WNYWG, you'll know he lives his life by this simple saying: It's nice to be important, but it's more important to be nice." Preston bobbed his head at the smattering of applause, and then finished off the introduction. "Without further ado, please give a warm welcome to our very own Western New York Writers' Guild bestselling author, Drake Matthews!"

The room erupted in applause as Drake shook Preston's hand and took the floor. Kate smiled to herself as Drake gave the same wholehearted speech, with slight variations, that he'd given at his mother's charity event, interspersing personal anecdotes about the group's members here and there, to give it an unmistakable feeling of authenticity. The man may say his gift was with the written word, but Kate had seen far too many botched toasts and speeches to know a good public speaker when she saw one.

Kate lifted her wine, noticing she'd drained her glass.

Normally, when she was working, she'd limit herself to one glass of wine, just to be social. However, since her work was basically done, she wanted to celebrate. It had been an amazing day—with the helicopter trip, followed by the limo ride and being with Drake on what wasn't technically a date, but what *felt* like a fantastic date. All of that made her decide that two drinks were allowable.

She'd just poured her second when Drake wrapped up his speech. Kate set down her glass and stood to clap with the rest. Drake ducked his head, waving and grinning as he was whisked offstage.

Preston returned to introduce his next special guest, Evan Everstone, who came up and began to speak— much less eloquently—about horror on the big screen. It was about five minutes into his talk when someone snatched Kate's clutch off the seat and tossed it onto the table, knocking over Kate's wine in the process.

"Whoa, that's my purse!" Kate snatched her clutch, using her napkin to soak up the wine, wiping off the droplets that had splashed her clutch before glaring at the individual who'd plopped down in the now-empty chair.

It was Rachel Lackey.

Drake's ex.

Kate waited, assuming the woman was going to apologize, but Rachel only flipped her brown, wavy hair over her shoulder. Her perfectly shaped eyebrows drew together as she speared Kate with an icy glare.

"Who in the hell are you?"

Kate gaped at her rudeness, but she'd been raised not to make a scene and she sure wasn't about to do anything to ruin Drake's time in the spotlight. So she extended her hand in greeting.

"I don't believe we've met. I'm Kate Sweet." Kate put her professional smile on as Rachel gave her a limp, sweaty-palmed shake. "I'm Drake Matthews's event planner—"

"Among other things," said a voice at her back, and Kate recognized Drake's low voice before she turned to him.

Drake smiled, his eyes apologizing for Rachel being there even as his mouth continued to speak like he wasn't at all bothered. "She's also a passable field surgeon, a whiz with a paring knife, an organizer of impromptu book signings...and so much more it's impossible to list."

Kate gave a weak smile, hoping to convey she'd had nothing to do with initiating this conversation. "I'm sorry. I tried to save you a seat."

"Oh, he doesn't mind." Rachel waved her hand, dismissing Drake without even looking in his direction. "I'm Rachel Lackey, soon to be Mrs. Everstone, and I'm always glad to meet Drake's assistants. I mean, how could we writers function without people like you to do all the dirty work, allowing us to focus on our craft? Isn't that right, Drake?"

Only then did Rachel bother to look up at Drake, her blindingly white smile tight with what Kate interpreted as a challenge.

As if. Rachel had no idea whose date she'd just decided to troll.

Kate gathered her clutch and placed a warning hand on Drake's arm.

She'd handle this.

"You are so right, Ms. Lackey," Kate said. "In fact, my assignment tonight is to make sure Drake doesn't get caught up in awkward, meaningless conversations. I'm sure you understand. If you'll excuse us? Drake has a very tight schedule, and we have some important details to cover before his big book launch this weekend."

"I heard about that," Rachel said, swirling the swizzle stick around her fruity drink with a crafty expression. "Rumor has it, the party might even get a look from the EVPLEX committee. I mean, with the movie adaptation being announced at the same time, it's more important now than just another freak-show book release."

Kate rocketed up from her seat, the abrupt motion causing nearby attendees to glance her way before refocusing on Everstone's speech at the podium. She'd just opened her mouth to retort, intent on giving Rachel a piece of her mind, when Drake's voice sounded low in her ear.

"She's right. Let's stick around for dinner. I can handle my ex, and it'll give you the chance to chat up Everstone with your final plans for this weekend's launch. That was our plan, remember? You *deserve* that award."

Just then, as if on cue, Everstone finished his speech. The attendees clapped dutifully, the noise a fantastic cover as Kate looked down at Rachel, smiling genially as she left her with one parting thought.

"I'm so happy your book brought you together with Evan. You two are obviously made for each other, and it left Drake gloriously single. A fact I plan to take full advantage of tonight." Kate winked at Drake's startled expression, knowing he'd overheard. "You enjoy your night. I know I will."

Drake kept tight hold of her hand until they meandered through the tables, nodding at various people here and there, but not stopping for handshakes or conversations until he'd finally cleared the gauntlet of well-wishers and pushed open the doors to the hallway outside the ballroom area of the Niagara hotel.

"Well, that went well, I think," Kate said, and was relieved when Drake laughed, pulling her into a one-armed embrace as they strolled away.

"I'm sorry to tell you this, but you can likely kiss that EVPLEX goodbye this year," he said, genuine regret in his face. "And I'd planned to give you the whole VIP experience tonight and make sure you got an outstanding dinner. Maybe even...a dance. The band, I've been told, is pretty good."

Kate's eyebrows rose. A dance? She glanced at her phone, noting the time. Eight o'clock. She was going to recommend they take a cab to a nearby restaurant when suddenly Drake began to chuckle.

"Hold up. Do you hear that?"

Kate put her phone back in her purse, pausing to listen. "What? The music?"

"That's the sound of me keeping my plan intact," he said, reversing course toward the other set of ballroom doors. "Now you get to say that Rachel and Evan didn't ruin our evening. It's time to meet...Mr. and Mrs. Paul Jonas. The newlyweds."

"Wait. We're...going to crash a wedding party?"

Drake clutched his chest with mock outrage.

"Absolutely not! We're going to crash a wedding *event*."

He pushed open the doors before she could object, and Kate saw the dinner had just been cleared. The décor was subtle but effective, with scatters of faux fall leaves and tea lights in cute homemade votive holders flickering at every table. Lovely, hand-drawn chalk signs indicated table numbers and various activities around the room, like the signature album and photo booth.

Couples were already on the dance floor. The DJ was doing an outstanding job getting the crowd into the event, playing Lizzo's "Good as Hell." Kate was delighted to see that in addition to the twenty-somethings joining the bride on the dance floor, a handful of gray-haired women left their tables to join them, belting out the lyrics, tossing their hair and checking their nails with the rest.

Drake was tugging her in toward what appeared to be a cash bar, but Kate stopped him.

"Wait. Before we go in, we need to do one more thing," she said, going up on tiptoe.

She leaned against him to slip off his glasses, folding them and putting them in her clutch. Her hands trembled slightly as she reached up to adjust his hair where she'd accidentally mussed it, spending more time than was necessary in getting it perfect, enjoying that look of intense languor on his face. She was reminded again of that tiger at the Bronx Zoo, looking innocent and relaxed as he waited for his prey to come closer . . . and her voice sounded a little breathless to her own ears when she finished.

"There. Now, maybe nobody will recognize you. For a little while, you're just a regular guy about to dance with a regular girl."

Drake wrapped his arms around Kate's middle,

preventing her from going down from her tiptoes. He touched his forehead to hers.

"There's just one problem," he said, and Kate could feel the rumble of his voice in her own chest. "You've never been a regular girl to me, Kate."

Just then, the DJ announced he was going to "slow things down a little," and Kate's heart cartwheeled in her chest as Drake released her. The ladies left the dance floor, scattering to snag their guys from their table or the bar, everyone coupling off for the slow song.

She walked with him to the tiny, parquet-floored area next to the bank of windows overlooking the falls. The natural wonder was lit up, filling the sky with changing colors of water spray, taking her breath away almost as much as her dance partner. Drake enfolded her in his arms, his hand cupping the small of her back as he led to an old song Kate recognized, "Unforgettable."

Drake spun her far from the listening ears of the other dancing couples and right next to the speakers so they had to lean in close—really close—to talk. Which was exactly what Kate did, pressing against him a little more than was necessary... and miles more than what was appropriate for a client.

"I heard what you said to Rachel," he said in her ear, his voice low and giving nothing away. "Her look of shock as you walked away was worth everything."

"Well, if you ask me, Rachel had it coming to her. I know it's catty, but, God, did that feel good! I hope I didn't embarrass you. I got a little... carried away."

When he moved his mouth up to her ear to respond, she stumbled. He caught her, steadying and righting her without missing a beat. Then, as if he knew the torture his breath and the maddening touch of his whiskers were to her neck, he bent his head again, bringing her a little closer until her breasts were only a bare millimeter from his chest before he spoke.

He gave that dark laugh again—the one that made her knees weak.

"Never, Ms. Sweet. It's never too much with you."

Drake's head was bent, allowing Kate to speak into his ear, and his breath fanned her bare shoulder, making her shiver as her nerve endings came alive. Her whole body seemed to strain to be nearer to him.

"Well, now that we've both kicked karma's ass into gear tonight," she said, breathing in the warm, woodsy tones of his cologne and feeling the heat of his skin through the thin fabric of his dress shirt, "I'm pretty sure this will be an impossible VIP experience to top."

Kate knew she should be backing away from his hard body. She should be telling him that it had been a great day, that she appreciated the helicopter ride over the falls and the star treatment, and with the launch only four days away, she should be reminding him—and herself—that she needed to get back to her room. Just as she'd done before, she needed to stop things before they eclipsed the boundaries of a "working relationship."

The entire speech was on the tip of her tongue. But then, Drake leaned in, the day-old whiskers on his face tickling her cheek as he bent to speak in her ear.

"Do you want to get out of here? Maybe go back to my room and order room service . . . or something?"

"Yes," she breathed, nodding her head, her body responding before her mind vetoed things. "I approve of that plan. All of it."

Drake's golden eyes darkened at her words, and his

hand dipped slightly on her back, slightly south of the "just friends" area, but well north of creating a spectacle on the dance floor. He lowered his face until it was barely an inch above hers, his gaze glued to her lips. He seemed to be waiting for... what? Her permission?

Kate tipped her weight onto her toes, her hand curling behind Drake's head. Unlike the time at the Harvest Festival, and then again in the hotel when the kiss had been more of an impulse, this time, Kate was determined to put her all in it. Her fingers threaded themselves into his hair as she tugged him to her lips. Forgetting all about Rachel and Everstone, and the EVPLEX and her reputation, Kate kissed him, putting every bit of her pent-up emotions into the kiss, wanting to show him he was worth more than what a couple of losers thought of him. That he was kind, and good, and damned hot.

Drake had stopped dancing as soon as she'd kissed him. His hands lifted to cradle her face, and when she finally lowered herself down from her toes, breaking off the kiss, he stood there, cupping her face, his eyes closed, and a small smile on his lips. He looked as if he was... savoring her.

Then Drake Matthews opened his eyes, his gaze dark and hungry.

"Tell me there's an encore, Kate."

At his words, the last shred of Kate's self-control vanished just like the final notes of the slow song playing behind them.

"Take me to your room, and let's find out."

CHAPTER 18

It took every ounce of Drake's willpower not to tug Kate off the dance floor immediately after she'd kissed him.

All he could think of, all that he wanted to think of, was taking that dress off Kate, kissing every inch, every sweet curve revealed as he peeled the fabric from her body. If science fiction were reality, he'd have transported them immediately into his hotel room—no, immediately into his bed, naked and with every light blazing so he could watch her beautiful green eyes when he entered her.

But this wasn't science fiction. And it took a hell of a lot longer to get to his room, what with having to put his damn glasses on so he could find the wishing well to toss some money in for the newlyweds—crashers or not, Kate insisted not to gift them would bring bad wedding juju for her business. Once they'd done all that, the people in the reception began to recognize the Knight of Nightmares dancing among them.

Kate snorted. "So much for being with the regular guy."

Yet he was gracious as they made their way to the ballroom doors, taking selfies with guests, signing a couple of napkins, until finally they spilled out into the hallway, making a beeline to the elevators. But they weren't even alone in the elevator, and he felt his jaw clenching as Kate smiled and chatted with everyone and anyone, as if she weren't just as distracted.

The thought chilled his frontal lobe, and Drake gave a start. Maybe she wasn't as distracted? She'd told him this wasn't a good time for either of them to complicate things. It wasn't likely the past three days had changed her mind. Had they?

A niggle of doubt tamped some of his desire, until Kate caught his hand and tugged it around her waist, snuggling closer to him in the crowded elevator as it practically crawled up the forty floors to the penthouse suite.

He was busy watching the numbers go by with infuriating slowness, when a young blonde entered the elevator dressed in a short leather skirt and a shorter matching top that ended in a place that seemed to indicate she wasn't wearing a bra. When she turned around and saw him, she immediately shrieked, the sound reverberating in the small space, causing an older couple to duck, putting their hands up as if warding off an active shooter.

"Holy shit! You're Drake Matthews—the Knight of Nightmares, himssself!" the blonde said, her words slightly slurred. "I've read *Creature Crypt* fifteen times, I sssswear! Can I get an autograph? I'm your number one fan!"

Kate mumbled something beside him that sounded an awful lot like, "Your timing sucks," but he wasn't sure. The drunk blonde was shrieking to the other five people on the elevator, telling them who he was and badgering them for a pen. Some Samaritan produced a Sharpie, but nobody had any paper to sign.

Undeterred, the blonde handed him the marker. Then she whipped up her minuscule shirt, showing him that, indeed, she hadn't been able to fit a bra underneath the skimpy leather top.

"Sign my boobs!" the woman shrieked, and then nudged the old lady next to her, handing over her cell phone. "Take a picture of him signing my boobs!"

Drake's mouth hung open, and his ears felt like they were going to combust. He'd never wished for an elevator catastrophe so hard in his whole life. He had averted his gaze when she'd flashed him, and stood with a Sharpie in his hands, staring at Kate in astonishment, wondering what the hell he was supposed to do next.

Lucky for him, Kate knew exactly what to do. She hit the button for the next floor, although it wasn't the penthouse suite. Just as the elevator dinged and slowed for the twenty-first level, she snatched the Sharpie from Drake's hand and used it like a dagger, poking the blonde in the chest with it.

"Put your shirt down. Mr. Matthews will *not* sign your boobs. He and I are getting off on this floor, and if you exit with us, I will assume you pose a threat to his well-being, and as his bodyguard, I will use whatever force is necessary to knock your ass out. Do you understand me?" Kate glared at the blonde, who tugged her shirt down, hastily backing away.

The doors opened, revealing the twenty-first floor, and Kate glowered at the group on the elevator.

"And the same goes for the rest of you."

She glared down the length of the Sharpie as if it were a sniper's rifle, meeting the gaze of every stranger, including the older couple, all of whom looked as stunned as Drake had been a few moments earlier.

Drake followed Kate's lead out of the elevator, moving a respectful distance from her as she stood, stance as wide as a gunslinger in her spaghetti-strap dress, pointing the marker at the people in warning until the elevator doors finally closed.

Then she turned to him, dipping the tip of the Sharpie until it focused on his crotch, her beautiful lips crooked in a mischievous grin.

"Tell you what, Mr. Matthews. You'd better be worth all this trouble, that's all I can—"

Drake swooped in, kissing her mouth. She tasted like wine and sweetness, and her tongue when it met his was hungry and urgent. The marker dropped from her hands and bounced off his shoe as Kate wrapped her arms around his neck, pressing her breasts into him in a way that made him groan with need.

"I promise you, Ms. Sweet. I'll make it worth all your trouble tonight. For a really, really long time."

He backed her against the marble wall of the bank of elevators, blindly pushing the *Up* arrow, and when the doors to their right opened, revealing an empty interior, he almost shouted with joy. Instead, he guided them both inside, returning Kate's fierce kisses with his own, and fumbled with the numbers until he'd finally hit the button for the penthouse floor.

He dipped his head down, kissing her neck, breathing

in the perfume of her skin, and nibbling his way from her ear to her collarbone. When she moaned and clutched his back as he got to the hollow of her neck, he paused, focusing on the spot until her breath came fast and hot in his ear.

"Drake," she panted, pulling slightly away to look at him. "Your hand is in my bra."

Glancing down, he nodded slowly. "It's nice in there."

Kate gave a short laugh, yet when his thumb brushed over her nipple, she gasped, her face transforming into an expression of need. She pressed herself into his hand, filling his palm with her soft flesh, and then she groaned, her leg rising up his hip as she ground against him.

"Your hand feels…so good. But…" She opened her green eyes a fraction, spearing him with a sultry gaze. "It would be amazing if it were to go…lower."

Drake's erection jumped, and he was so hard he had to take a minute to think of baseball and Christmas trees and how to conjugate Latin verbs. Anything except his hand sliding down her side, and then under the dress to her silky thighs and between them where she was wet and hot and eager. And in a thong.

Drake groaned. He said a quick prayer of thanks that he hadn't known that the beautiful woman handling his ex like a boss at the table downstairs had been in this lacy thing all along. No way would he have been able to dance upright with her, had he known all there was between his hand and her was a wispy piece of fabric. But now that they were here, all alone in this elevator, he could—

Suddenly, a thought slammed into his libido like a battalion of tanks.

What if the elevator had a camera?

The last thing he wanted was for Kate to be embroiled in some leaked video where she was caught in a compromising position with the Knight of Nightmares.

What he wanted to do was back her against the wall and use his mouth and hands to worship her. He wanted to slide a finger into her, palming her mound, drinking in her gasp or groan, then finding her sweet spot, caressing the deliciously wet inside of her, learning her body, learning her rhythm. He didn't want to stop until he felt her shudder against him, the little muscles inside of her pulsing around his finger as she climaxed in his hands.

Instead, drawing on resources of endurance and willpower he hadn't tapped since Marine boot camp, he managed to slip his hand out of her thong. Gritting his teeth against Kate's moan of disappointment, he used his body to block the view of any hidden cameras as he adjusted her dress. Tipping her chin, he captured her gaze and he kissed her once, then again, barely brushing her soft lips.

"You are so beautiful," he said, drinking in the rising flush on her cheeks and chest, confusion mashing with need on her face. "But with your track record with chaos, and my crazy fans…I don't want this to be anything other than perfect for you. We've got four floors to go, and then I'd like to invite you to my suite. I want to lay you on my bed where we can slow down. Enjoy each other."

"Drake," she gasped, her green eyes squeezing shut. Her hands fisted in the fabric of his jacket, whether to hold him to her or hold herself up, he wasn't sure. "I'd like that. Very much. Tell me, did you bring…any protection?"

The elevator dinged for the fortieth floor, and he cursed.

Kate's words were like ice chips down the front of his jockey shorts.

At home, he'd bought some condoms recently...just in case. But he hadn't thought to pack any, his mind having basically dismissed anything physical until the launch was over, just as Kate had requested. Now, here he was, up against a rock and a very, very, *very* hard place.

The doors opened, revealing the short hallway to the penthouse suite, and he turned, shamefaced, to her.

"Uh, I," Drake began, his ears piping hot with embarrassment, "I didn't. I didn't want to be...presumptuous."

"Then I'm going to have to decline that invite to your suite."

Drake started to talk until Kate put her index finger on his mouth, pressing softly. He wasn't sure what he'd been about to say, but the words died in his throat as he saw Kate's sexy mouth cant up on one side in a half smile his writer's mind immediately categorized as: wicked.

"And," she continued, tugging him out of the elevator by a hand, leading him down the hallway to the suite doors on each side of the hall, "I'm going to have to ask you to come to my suite instead. You see, I presumed. A lot."

Drake stumbled in the hallway. "Wait. You brought a condom?"

Kate used her key card to unlock her door, her face flushing a crimson sunset even as she thrust her chin at him, in challenge, shaking her head.

"Nope. I brought nine."

Drake had to bow his head and grip the edge of the door to keep himself from coming, fully clothed, in the hallway of the hotel. He'd never been so aroused in all his life. When he was sure he had himself under control, he brought his head back up, chuckling in awe.

"I'm so damn glad you are a planner, Kate Sweet."

CHAPTER 19

Kate's body was as taut as the string on Cupid's drawn bow as she led Drake into her suite.

Then she caught sight of the full-length mirror on the outside of the suite's bathroom, and what she saw in the reflection made her gasp.

Her hair was falling out of its updo, and her slip dress was crooked and wrinkled as if she'd slept in it. Her bra cup had been pushed off her breast on one side—the side that Drake had claimed as his own—and her nipple poked against the silk fabric like a bullet. Her lipstick was smeared everywhere except her mouth, and one side of her face was red and abraded where Drake's whiskers had rubbed against her while she was grinding up on him in the elevator.

"Oh my God, I'm a mess," Kate whispered to herself, her hand tugging her dress strap up, and then wiping the lipstick smears. Discreetly, she shoved her breast back inside the bra cup, shaking her head in wonderment. "What in the hell am I doing?"

"You're drop-dead gorgeous. The hottest woman

I've ever seen. And right now, you're leading me to your bed, where I can ravish you properly."

Kate's traitorous body lit up, and she felt her thighs getting slicker at his words.

Ravish. *Yes, please!*

Yet her mind raced. What had she just done? How was this man supposed to respect her when she'd told him to put his hand under her dress in a freaking elevator? Who did that? Respectable people didn't do that. Professionals didn't let their clients practically finger them in a public space. Then she'd admitted she'd bought an apocalypse-worthy stockpile of Trojans for the night! She needed to stop this before she humiliated herself even more.

"Drake, I—" Kate paused as he took off his tux coat and his necktie with fingers that she knew were crazy dexterous. Thinking of those fingers, her insides pulsed to life, but she shook it off, finishing her thought. "I feel like I may be pushing the boundaries. Kissing you in public and then what I just did with you in the elevator...that's not me. At least, not normally. That was really unprofessional, and—"

She stopped speaking as Drake finished unbuttoning his shirt. He nodded at her as he worked at the buttons on his wrist.

"It was unprofessional. But so. Very. Hot." Drake finished with the buttons and then stripped the whole shirt off, revealing those abs. "Do you have any idea how many times I've dreamed about you? Any idea how many ways I've fantasized about taking you?"

He'd fantasized about her? Kate's mouth went dry even as other parts of her grew wetter. "You...you have? When? Wh-where?"

Drake's lips widened in a slow, seductive smile as he nodded, closing the distance between them, tossing his shirt aside.

"I'd say it would be cliché if I said it was from the moment we first met, but considering your legs were wrapped around my hips, my hands were on your ass, and your nipple was about an inch from my mouth, I'd have to say that was the first time—that day. On my front lawn."

Kate giggled, her stomach jittery with anticipation as her mind replayed the scene, but from his vantage point. She crept closer to him, putting her palm against those very much *not* Photoshopped abs. "When else?"

"In my kitchen that day when you made me your crunchy scrambled eggs. I thought about taking you on the counter first and then—" He paused, using one hand to work on the button and fly of his pants, while with the other, he cupped her head, tugging her closer.

Kate kissed him, his warm mouth tasting of whiskey and sin. She helped him shove his pants to the floor, followed by his briefs, and the sight of his erection made her thighs clench with anticipation. "And then what?"

Drake's hands snaked around her, those strong fingers finding the zipper in the back of her dress and easing it open.

"Then, I thought I'd carry you to that vintage kitchen table you like so much," he said, his mouth nuzzling her neck as her dress slithered off her to the floor, as if eager to obey his command. "Because, you know, it's not all about me. So, I'd strip you down, and

I'd get to know every, single, gorgeous inch of your body. Like this..."

He unhooked her strapless bra, and her skin tingled and blossomed into gooseflesh as he eased the silk off her breasts. His head dipped down, mouth covering first one breast, then the other, the whiskers of his jaw tickling her as his teeth grazed her nipple, alternately nibbling and sucking at her as his hands moved to her back, tipping her backward to gain greater access to her body. Only her black heels remained on as he guided her back to the bed, touching and kissing her until she thought she might explode from the anticipation.

"Let me just take these off," she gasped between kisses, reaching around him to tug her feet out of the black stilettos. "So I don't accidentally stab you."

"Keep them on," he growled, grinning. "My favorite fantasy involved you on my bed. Wearing only those."

Drake eased her down until she was lying beneath him, his erection a hot lead weight against her stomach. She touched him, her hand sliding along the length of his shaft, enjoying the way he hissed in a breath, growing very still over her, as she explored him with her hands.

"You've got to stop that, or I won't be able to complete my promise to ravish you," he said, levering himself onto his elbow. He removed his glasses and laid them on the table. "These are in my way." Then with a wolfish smile, he captured both her wrists in one hand and pulled them over her head.

Kate gasped as his mouth descended upon her breast, teasing and sucking on the nipple, while his free hand swept over her other breast. He proceeded to kiss and nibble down the length of her, caressing her skin until Kate's reservations were shredded by his single-minded attention, and her body strained toward him, her thighs quivering. His mouth was like liquid fire, and his tongue! The things he did with his tongue...

"Drake," she panted, wriggling out from under his ministrations. "In my suitcase...the mesh pouch on the inside of the lid..."

It was like he'd acquired his own superhero powers, so fast did he leave the bed, find the condoms, and return to kissing her body right where he'd left off, as if he'd mentally bookmarked the place. He took his mouth from her long enough to rip a foil package open with his teeth, sliding on the condom one-handed, while he kissed down her abdomen.

She wriggled under him, willing him to enter her. Yet he continued to kiss and fondle her, as if unaware of how desperate she was for release. Then a thought hit her.

"I'm on birth control," she panted, "so we're doubly protected, if that's what you're waiting for."

Drake picked his head up from where he'd been kissing and licking his way up in a path from her navel to her other breast, and he stared at her. His amber eyes, so much darker without his glasses, were trained on hers in the room's half-light, and his teeth gleamed as he grinned.

"Good to know. But what I was waiting for," he said, releasing her hands to cup the hot flesh between her legs, "was this."

His fingers sought and found how wet she was, and his touch made Kate moan. She brought her hands around to his biceps, squeezing the muscles there, and then around to trace the front of his exquisitely sculpted chest.

Something he'd said before stuck in her head, caught in her imagination like it was a dream catcher for the naughty and erotic.

"Wait," she gasped, tugging his face back up to hers to gaze in his deep, golden eyes. "You said your best fantasy was me in your bed. In these shoes. Tell me what you fantasized about."

He gave a wicked smile. "How about I narrate while I show you?"

Kate's eyes widened as he lifted himself off her.

"First, I'd kiss those beautiful lips, like this." Drake's mouth was on hers, soft at first, then demanding entry as he explored her with his tongue. He stopped long enough to continue his narration. "Then, I'd kiss my way down here."

Kate's back arched as his mouth covered first one breast, sucking on the nipple, then the other. Kate groaned. "Th-then what?"

"Then, I'd take these long, gorgeous legs like this." Drake's hands swept down her thighs, and he hooked his arms under her knees, and he spread her legs wide. "And I'd think to myself, 'I am the luckiest guy on earth right now.' And then I'd do this."

Kate moaned as he entered her, slowly, as if he had all night. Feverishly, Kate wondered if that was, indeed, his plan.

She hoped so.

At first, Drake continued to tell her the details of his fantasy as he acted it out, the whispered words tickling her neck and igniting her imagination as they found their rhythm together. But then, passion got the best of him, and Drake's mouth was too busy on her lips, her neck, her breasts, to narrate any longer.

Kate's breath came in rhythmic gasps, and she clutched his back, pulling him closer as he drove into her, her thighs tightening around him as she spiraled toward the edge.

Then, all at once, her climax overtook her, and she cried out, arcing into him.

"You're so beautiful," he breathed, riding her, wringing every last spasm from her body. Then, his rhythm became erratic and he drove into her one last time, and Kate felt each pulse of his release as he groaned.

They lay there, panting, until Drake propped himself up on one arm to gaze down at her. His eyes were almost brown in the room's soft light, and he responded to her smile with one of his own.

"There's my favorite punctuation," he said, kissing the spot to the left of her lips. "I think you'll always give me pause, Kate Sweet."

Kate opened her mouth to say something but was interrupted by her own stomach, growling loudly. She ducked her head with an embarrassed laugh.

"Apparently, the pause is for food right now," Drake said, kissing her forehead as he rolled off her. "How about we order room service?"

They ate in the room, wearing hotel bathrobes, turning off their cell phones and putting the *Do Not Disturb* sign on the door. It should've been awkward, but to Kate's surprise it was anything but—they laughed, joked, and rehashed the evening downstairs. When the laughter morphed into touching, and then to kisses, they fell into bed as if it were the easiest thing to do.

They napped on and off that night, each time waking

up in each other's arms, each time hungry for more. Kate knew she'd feel him there for days afterward, but she couldn't seem to get enough of the smell and the taste of him.

She didn't want the night to end, but eventually, she really did fall asleep. She woke to Drake kissing her head.

"You sleep," he said. "I've already brewed some coffee for you over there, and I'm going to hop in the shower."

Kate mumbled something, pushing the hair out of her eyes as she sat up, blinking away the fog.

"You're not leaving, are you?"

Drake smiled, his finger tracing her naked breast. "I have to fly to New York City to do a couple of talk shows. Imani set it all up as a three-day media blitz because she knows I hate this crap. But the car service taking you back to Wellsville won't be here until later this morning, so you rest. Soon, it's back to reality for both of us."

Drake closed the door to the bathroom.

Kate groaned, flopping back down on the bed.

"But this is so much better than reality!"

Ten minutes later, Kate was in a hotel robe, teeth brushed and a coffee cup in her hand as she leaned her forehead against the glass of the window, staring down at the majesty of the falls below.

Drake came up behind her, and Kate loved the feel of his warm body against her back. He'd already showered and dressed in a black suit, white shirt, and the black tie with its black stripes, having readied himself for the day with a speed only a man could manage.

"If I wrote this scene, I'd have the shows all canceled,

so you'd have to stay," Kate announced. "And we'd go down and ride that boat into the mist."

"And if I wrote the scene, a kraken would emerge, wrap the boat in its tentacles, and drag it down to the craggy depths," Drake said, kissing her shoulder. "I like your version better."

She sighed, tipping her head back to lie against his chest as they both gazed out at the dawn rising over the falls. The water cascading over the edge, flinging itself against the rocks below, was mesmerizing in its never-ending abandon to get the fall over with—to get to a place of calm waters and steady normalcy. How long had she been constantly rushing toward a goal, never realizing a cliff was just ahead, but sprinting toward it, nevertheless, because what else was there except her career? Maybe Drake was the guy she'd never thought was out there? Her mind snagged on the speed-dating question—the one she was sure differentiated the "right guy" from the rest.

She held her breath, wondering if she should ask Drake. What if he gave the wrong answer?

Then she saw the waters rushing, and she took the plunge, asking it all in one breath.

"Drake, I have a question: do you think you could handle dating a woman with a rising career who wouldn't be available most weekends or holidays for the foreseeable future?"

Drake laughed. "That's easy. Of course! The real question is can you handle a man who's already at the top of his career, but hates the spotlight and spends most of his days on a laptop, mumbling to himself? Whose muse doesn't care if it's weekday or weekend?"

Kate spun in his arms. "No, I'm serious. I have goals. Literal poster boards of them, and the lives of really successful event planners involve sacrifices most men aren't willing to make."

"Okay," he said, shrugging. "Assuming we're talking about you and me, here, you do realize that even though I have a fifties-era kitchen, I'm not looking for a fifties-era woman?"

Kate scoffed. "That's a good quote, but in reality, don't all guys expect a woman to...I don't know? Be around all the time, while still having a career? I just don't ever want us to be in a position where I'm spinning plates, trying to balance being wildly successful in my career, yet you're unhappy because I'm not there to—"

"Cook? Clean?" Drake shook his head, planting a kiss above her eyebrows. "If this is directed at me, let me assure you my mother didn't raise any momma's boys. She didn't have time. As a mostly single parent, she taught us that part of being a real man was to cook and clean. Do the dishes. Dust. All of it."

"But it's more than that. It's cuddling. Date nights. Helping act out your book scenes, while you make me your amazing Cobb salad. You don't understand. During wedding season, especially, I'm barely home," Kate said, knowing she was making a bigger deal of this than she needed to, considering the newness of their relationship, but she couldn't help thinking about her bleak, gray apartment. "I can barely keep my succulent alive, let alone do the little and big things you need to grow or sustain a relationship."

"Kate." Drake gripped her shoulders, his scowl fading into a slow, warm smile. "I can write anywhere, including ice-cold attics, remember? My office consists of a laptop and a few file folders. Those are immensely portable. And let's not forget, I do make a mean Cobb salad."

Her shoulders relaxed, and she let him pull her into a tight embrace, sighing in contentment. "You're right. Good answers, by the way. You get top prize."

"Mmm. I like that you're worrying about 'us' in the future tense." Drake kissed the top of her head as they both stared out of the window at the sky growing pink behind the gray-white vista of Niagara Falls. His breath stirred her hair as he spoke. "I wish I didn't have to leave for those interviews. I'd rather be heading back with you to Wellsville. Or better yet, I'd rather just be canceling the whole damn launch to stay here with you. In bed."

"It has been almost like a dream, being here with you," Kate whispered, her fingers tracing up and down Drake's arms as he embraced her from behind. "I keep worrying that I'm going to wake up soon, and it'll all have been just a figment of my imagination. You know, like they do in novels when they want to trick you into thinking the main characters actually got together? But you know that's impossible, because there are still a few chapters in the book?"

Drake didn't answer, and Kate shook her head with a snort of laughter.

"Oh, never mind. You've probably never read a single romance novel in your life, so you don't know what I mean."

Drake's silence seemed heavy, and she turned to look at him. His expression was almost pained, and immediately, she regretted telling him her innermost thoughts. But then he gave a rueful chuckle, his lips brushing against hers.

"Actually, I do know. Before I leave, I have something I want to show you."

The last thing Kate expected to hear was that Drake had written a historical romance—that, in fact, he'd wanted to write this romance for more than a decade but felt chained to his horror deadlines.

"It's only in this last month, working with you, that I've realized I can't bottle up what's inside me," Drake said, moving toward the small table in the suite, grabbing his backpack. "For years, I've had this idea for a story loosely based on the letters my grandfather sent Nana during World War II—the ones you saw in the attic—and ideas from the heroism and tragedy based on my brother Ryker's experience in combat. These past few months, writing that tale was all I wanted to do, but I couldn't figure out the sweeping, epic love story aspect of it. Until recently. Then, it came pouring out into what I think is a pretty damn good book."

Kate listened raptly as Drake gave a brief synopsis of his historical romance, which he was calling *Memory's Lane*, and found herself charmed. The hero was an injured World War II veteran with amnesia, who was searching for a girl he fell in love with during the war but couldn't remember.

"I don't want to tell you the ending, because I'm still tinkering with it, but..." Drake paused, pulling a stack of papers around an inch thick from his backpack. "I brought you this."

Kate looked down at the papers, held together with a black binder clip at the corner. On the front, printed neatly in the middle of the page, was the title, *Memory's Lane*, and *by Drake Matthews*.

She glanced up at him, in surprise. "You're letting me read this? But I thought you didn't let anyone read the first draft of your books?"

"It's just the first seven chapters. I've got more written, but I don't write in sequence, so this is all I have at the beginning. I'll never publish it—my fans don't want to read a historical romance written by the Knight of Nightmares, and writing under a pseudonym isn't a viable solution. With all of the social media presence you need as a less established name, and with the inherent in-person signings, speaking engagements, and virtual events necessary to grow an audience—orchestrating a pen name personality's promotions, in addition to maintaining my own, sounds...exhausting. But still, I'd..." Drake hesitated, pushing up his black glasses that Kate now knew were more of a shield from the world than an actual necessity. "I'd like to hear what you think about it, since this romance was largely inspired. By you."

"B-by me?" Kate touched the manuscript draft, a feeling of something like awe and surprise and sweet satisfaction sweeping through her. "That's—wow. I don't know what to say."

Drake's expression hadn't changed, but his eyes held something that looked like...worry? Was he really afraid that she wouldn't like his book?

Then Kate remembered his biggest fear: rejection. She closed the distance between them, standing on her tiptoes to reach around his neck and tug him to her lips for a kiss so deep, he dropped his backpack. He slipped his hand inside her robe, cupping a breast, kneading it and gently tweaking her nipple until Kate finally was the one to pull away, which she did with a gasp.

"You're going to be late. But I needed to show you how flattered I am to be your muse," Kate whispered, touching the edge of his newly clean-shaven jaw. "I can't wait to read it. And I think you're wrong about people not wanting to read *Memory's Lane* just because it's a different genre. Your fans love you because of your incredible writing—not solely for your ability to scare them. This book deserves to be published, especially if it has been living in your head for so long."

Drake snorted.

"Yeah. You saw all those fans lined up out there." He gestured toward the wide world outside their window. "Do you really think they want romance? From me? If I wrote a happily ever after, they'd string me up and beat me like a piñata. Instead of lining up for autographs, they'd be vying for a chance to throw rotten tomatoes at me."

"I think you're misjudging your readers." Kate shook her head. "They'll love you for showing that the Knight of Nightmares is like a Milky Way bar—hard on the outside, but sweet and ooey-gooey on the inside. Besides, writing romance gives you access to a whole new set of readers, who will all fall in love with you—"

Kate stopped speaking just in time. What had almost rolled off her tongue was *Just like I have.* She reminded herself that she'd known this man for less than a month—too soon for declarations of love. She hadn't even told her best friend about their relationship status change.

Imani. Damn. She cleared her throat, stuffing away that thought for later as she finished her sentence.

"—and your writing, and you'll have a whole new set of Drake Matthews fans!"

He captured her hand on his face, bringing it to his lips. He kissed her palm, and then cupped the back of her neck, giving her a final, lingering kiss.

"It's kind of you to say. And while it's never going to be published, it means a lot to me to get it written—to honor my grandfather's legacy and somehow pay tribute to Ryker's loss. Hopefully, after it's finished, I'll finally be able to get my head screwed on straight and get *Twisted Twin* done and to my editor." Drake checked his watch, ran a frustrated hand through his hair, and backed toward the suite's door. "The car's downstairs. I've got to go. Text me when you get back to Wellsville. Kate, I cannot wait for this launch to be over with."

Kate frowned, setting the manuscript down, and followed him to the door.

"Why is that?"

"So you can have the satisfaction of coordinating an EVPLEX-worthy event, and I can finish this historical romance, and we can both move on to a different chapter in our lives. One that's...together?"

The last came out more as a question than a statement, and when Drake leaned in for one last kiss, Kate's heart beat faster than the water rushing over the falls behind them.

She smiled. "I'd like that."

Kate showered and got ready as soon as he left, packing her things and heading downstairs to the hotel's café, her mind busy thinking about the future. For the first time, it wasn't in terms of successful events or upcoming deadlines or checked-off spreadsheets; it was a grand anticipation of her own dreams. Of being fulfilled by more than just her career.

In a haze of happiness, Kate ordered a breakfast sandwich and another coffee. Just as she'd sat down at a tiny bistro table to eat and daydream, the sound of her phone pierced Kate's musings. She fumbled for her cell phone in her purse, thinking it was Drake and he'd forgotten something, but she was surprised to see Imani's name on the readout.

When she answered the call, it was only five seconds before her smile disappeared.

"The town council rejected our permit for the mechanical spider," Imani began, and at Kate's answering groan, she continued. "And that's not the worst of it."

Kate listened in horror as Imani told her that they'd also rejected her request to close part of the street down in front of Drake's house.

"But I spoke with one of the council leaders at the fall festival," Kate said, incredulous. "Mrs. Nowakowski said we had her vote, and it wouldn't be a problem. In fact, I heard from Drake's mom that the whole launch was a boon to Wellsville's economy and that the downtown merchants were all planning a sort of sidewalk bazaar to take advantage of the readers and news crews arriving."

"According to my sources, one of the councilmen who has apparently been on the council since the dawn of time and holds a great deal of clout in town—some guy whose last name was Penny—said that the whole idea was preposterous and an embarrassment to Wellsville. He said he'd seen what sort of people ran these events, and he called us lewd and without class. They voted it down by one vote."

The man's name filtered through Kate's memory, and then she jolted upright. Councilman Penny—was that the same Mr. Penny who'd witnessed her climbing Drake like a koala on her first day on the job? The neighbor who, according to Drake, then called Patty, telling her she should be ashamed of her son's lewd behavior on his front lawn?

"Oh, no," Kate said, the Mr. Penny and Councilman Penny phrases matching too keenly to be coincidence. "No! This can't be happening. Not this close to the launch! Can't we appeal, or something?"

"Not until the next meeting, which won't be until mid-November. I don't know what to do." Imani's voice was a mix of anger and frustration. "We're going to have to scale way back. You'll need to pull out all stops to at least come up with something passable before Saturday. I'm so sorry, Kate. I guess that puts a stake in the heart of your EVPLEX plans, doesn't it?"

"I'd pretty much abandoned that last night," Kate mumbled in reply, and before Imani could ask any questions, her friend's phone beeped with an incoming call.

"I've got to go. That's my boss," Imani said. "You're getting a car back here soon, right? I know Trisha will have some ideas, and you will too, so let's touch base in an hour?"

"Don't worry," Kate said. "We still have loads of decorations we can use. I'll...think of something."

Clicking to end the call, Kate put her head in her hands, dejected. Truth was, her mind was void of any ideas of how to salvage this at all. So much of the launch plan had been riding on the fans having experienced the street maze, featuring a vignette from each of Drake's books, and then culminating in his front yard, where the mechanical spider would be dangled over each VIP guest as they took their souvenir photo in front of the Drake mansion. Now, all that planning was shot, and she was back to square one.

A blank spreadsheet. A blank page.

Staring down at her things scattered across the hotel's bistro table, she wondered at how the day's forecast could have turned so quickly from magical to miserable. Damn that Mr. Penny and his judgey ways! She'd hoped to speak with enough council people at the festival, but she'd been so caught up with helping out Drake with his costume, then carving pumpkins and having a good time, that she'd only talked to one person on the council that day. She'd let her own happiness get in the way of doing her job, and it made her want to bash her head into the nearest wall and cry. She'd have been upset if this was a normal client, but the fact that her actions had caused it to happen to the man she'd allowed both in her bed and in her heart?

Drake had trusted her with everything—allowed her every liberty to plan—and now she was going to be left with...what exactly? What epic night could she possibly plan for this man who had shown her she could love again, when she only had three days?

Kate's eyes caught the top page of Drake's manuscript. Without meaning to, she read the first paragraph.

Sam strode down a dark stretch of one of Picadilly's mist-soaked cobbled streets toward his commanding officer's hideout, the thick fog

clinging to his booted feet and legs
like a wispy shroud. His mood was
as bleak as the English weather—
that never-ending cold drizzle. As he
brought the ragged ends of his Da's
old peacoat around him to hide his
tuxedo, he had no idea that the empty,
dank misery of his life was about to
change; along with a sweeping, all-
consuming passion, the universe was
about to deliver a gut-punch.

In spite of the recent bad news, Kate's cheeks burned
pleasantly at the words "a sweeping, all-consuming
passion." Hadn't he said the book had been, in many
ways, inspired by her?

Signaling the barista for another cup of coffee, Kate
glanced at her watch, an idea of how to save Drake's
launch tugging at her mind. What if she could tie
something from his love for vintage, classic things to
his horror writing?

Kate tapped her lucky pen against her lip. Her car
wasn't due for another hour. She'd have the entire trip
from Niagara Falls back to Wellsville to figure out this
launch debacle. But right now, her gut told her the
answer might just be in Drake's romance novel. She'd
just read a few pages...

After the first chapter, she was hooked.

Her coffee grew cool, then cold, as she read
voraciously, the pages seeming to turn themselves as
she immersed herself in the love story of Sam and
Ingrid. Something in those pages—the sweet nostalgia
of black-and-white movies, vintage fashions, forgotten

manners of days gone by—triggered an idea for how to save this launch and surprise Drake in the process.

Inspired, she stood from the bistro table, grabbing her purse to pull out money for the check as she called Imani.

"I've got an idea," she said, once her best friend picked up. "Meet me at the pumpkin patch by the cemetery on South Main Street in two hours and bring a car. Or better yet, a truck. Oh, and we're going to need every can of black and white spray paint they've got in town."

She lay down a twenty on top of the breakfast bill and checked her watch. Noticing she had only minutes to get outside the hotel lobby to catch her ride, Kate grabbed her rolling suitcase and rushed out, phone to her ear chatting to Imani the entire time, excited she might be able to fix this after all.

Behind her, the server called out. "Miss! You forgot—"

"Money's on the table!" Kate shouted over her shoulder as she shoved open the doors to the portico outside, jogging toward the car she'd spotted from the bistro windows with her name on a card in the window.

Her heart thudded wildly as she threw herself into the car and began to detail to Imani her revised plan for salvaging this launch.

CHAPTER 20

Excuse me, Mr. Matthews?" The young man in charge of guests in the green room tugged at the wrinkled yellow-and-white-striped tie around his neck, loosening the knot slightly, as he peered around the studio's door to call to the author, who still sat in the makeup artist's chair. "They'll be ready for you in about five minutes."

"That's fine," Drake said, and would have nodded but for the woman applying some sort of dark cream to his face.

"We're almost done, Mr. Matthews. Just a little more powder so you don't shine...there!" The woman, dressed in a long, flowing floral dress and brown cowboy boots, complete with a cursive monogram, stepped back to survey her work. "We'll let that dry on you and then I'll remove those tissues from your collar. What do you think?"

Drake surveyed himself in the mirror lit by large, round bulbs set into either side of the vanity and tried not to grimace. The uniformity of his complexion, and the way she'd darkened and filled in his eyebrows, made him look like a marionette—a puppet whose invisible strings kept him sitting straight in the chair, and kept him from raging or, worse, breaking down. But he supposed the makeup artist knew what she was doing, and he shrugged, forcing a smile despite the pit in his stomach as his phone buzzed in his pocket for the billionth time.

"Haven't you heard? I'm not paid to think. I'm paid to write."

Four hours ago, after John landed the helicopter in New York City, Drake's phone had begun blowing up.

First, it was his brother Zander.

"Duuuude," the voice mail began, "why didn't you tell me you wrote smut? I love smut. I want the sex scenes. Pronto."

Before he'd had a chance to return Zander's call, his mother had buzzed in.

"Honey!" she had sniffed, her voice watery with tears. "I just read your secret release, and I'll put aside for a second that you shouldn't keep such things from your mother, to tell you how much I love this story! Your Grandpa Matthews would be so proud to see you writing down some of his adventures in England, but sweetheart...you do know that he didn't meet Nana Grace there, don't you? And that scene where they kiss? Well, this is fiction, right?"

It'd taken him all of five minutes to pull up the on-line news story, and subsequent chapters, released in a blog called *The Nightmare Sentinel,* a website run by an unauthorized fan club of Drake Matthews novels. The site had published the first seven chapters of *Memory's Lane.*

The same seven chapters he'd given to Kate just hours ago.

Right after he pretty much laid his heart at her feet.

Apparently, Kate had moved faster than he'd thought possible—faster, even, than Rachel, who'd at least taken a few months to publish it all—giving the public new fuel for their ridicule. It stung him in a way Rachel's complicity never had, in that he'd been so gullible with Kate. He'd believed so much in her innate goodness that he'd never considered the benefit to her in outing him to his horror fans. He'd written the romance in such a way that he'd somehow confused his fictional heroine with reality, and as much as he wanted to lash out at Kate, lash out at the world, he knew he had only himself to blame.

Once again, he'd been the author of his own misfortune.

It took seemingly nanoseconds before the major news agencies had picked up the blog and had called his publicist to confirm if Drake Matthews's event planner was indeed Kate Sweet, and if the two of them had been at the hotel in Niagara Falls. It wasn't Imani's fault she'd confirmed those facts. When the news agencies first called, Imani had thought it was in response to press releases she had sent out on the book launch. Or, at worst, they'd gotten a picture of Kate and Drake together and were planning to print some sort of gossip column about the Knight of Nightmares finding his princess.

"I never dreamed it was some lie like this!" Imani said, her voice fiery with indignation. "We'll sue the hell out of them for libel, Drake! My boss has spoken to Cerulean Books' legal team, and they're forcing the idiots who write the *Sentinel* to take down the chapters immediately. I don't know whose they are, but they obviously aren't yours—"

"They are," Drake had said, his throat tight. "And there's only one way they could've gotten hold of them."

Seven chapters of his historical romance had been leaked to the media. Kate was the only person who had them. She was the culprit. There was no other logical explanation.

By dinner that night, Drake's voice mail was full. He'd stopped answering his phone after Imani's call, and then the call from his agent, followed by his editor. After explaining to them all that the chapters were his, but he'd never meant for them to be seen by anyone, he'd put his phone on airplane mode. He hunkered down during the much-too-brief ride to midtown Manhattan for the first day of the publicity tour. He didn't bother going over the talking points Imani had previously given him for the upcoming launch of *Halloween Hacker*. Why waste his time? The hosts would spend a perfunctory five seconds on that book before grilling him on-air about the elephant in the room—the story that was way juicier than his tenth horror launch. No way would the media waste an opportunity to ridicule him in person, about how the Knight of Nightmares dared to write a love story.

He'd briefly scanned his missed call log to see that Kate had tried to reach him almost a dozen times and left about as many voice mails. He hadn't listened to any of them. What could she possibly have to say about how the chapters were leaked? Hearing her lie to him would hurt worse than seeing what damage her leak had already done.

The phone continued to buzz in his pocket, and finally, Drake pulled it out.

Kate again.

At the sight of her name, his mind unhelpfully brought back the vision of her face in the hotel bed last night. It was like physical pain as he relived how disheveled she looked, her face hazy in that after-sex way, her neck and shoulder abraded by his whiskers from his kisses there.

Spinning the chair so he didn't have to stare at the mirror as the stupid marionette talked to the woman who broke his heart, Drake finally answered the phone. He asked the only question that mattered.

"Why?" he barked as soon as he picked up the call. He'd tried for rage, but to his horror, his voice sounded hurt when he clarified, "Why did you do it, Kate?"

He'd been expecting tears. That's what Rachel had always done when she feared his anger. She'd somehow known that a woman's tears were his kryptonite, and his ex had turned them on and off like a faucet, whenever the occasion arose.

But Kate's voice wasn't tearful when she answered. Instead, she'd taken the tactic of stuttering disbelief and apology. Drake rolled his eyes, glaring at the ceiling as he listened to her stammer.

"Do you—Drake, you can't possibly think I'd have released those chapters?" Her voice was thin and reedy, and Drake had to give her props for her acting. She truly sounded taken aback when she trotted out her fiction. "Imani had called to tell me the permits for the haunted maze and the mechanical spider were both denied by the town council, and I—"

Realization dawned for him, and he finished her

sentence, gripping the phone so hard he saw his knuckles whiten.

"And you thought you'd do the best damage control possible and leak out those chapters? I get it. Now, even if you set up a folding table with punch and cookies, you're bound to still have a massive crowd of people cooing over your launch party, considering the news cycle. That was clever, Kate."

"What? No!" Kate's voice hardened on the other end, and Drake took a vicious glee in her anger at his truth bomb. "I was freaking out, and then I got distracted by your book. I started reading it, and suddenly, it all clicked into place. I knew how we could still have an epic launch for you—"

"And still win your EVPLEX," he put in, purposefully needling her. "Can't forget about that! I'm sure Everstone will be tickled to just give you the damn trophy for leaking those chapters and humiliating me on a whole new level. Honestly, you could've saved yourself some time and just slept with him, like Rachel did. Your book launch spreadsheet would've been a lot shorter."

The line went silent, and Drake pulled the phone away, sure that she'd hung up on him. But then she spoke, her voice low and colored by tones of hurt.

"I can't believe you'd say something that rotten to me," she said. "What happened is I got excited about a new idea for your launch, and I accidentally left your chapters on the table down in the hotel's café. I didn't figure it out until I was in the car, halfway to Wellsville. I called the hotel café and was going to have the driver turn around and take me back, but they said they'd found nothing on the table. That it was probably thrown out. I thought it was taken care of, until Imani called me. It was a mistake, Drake. That's all."

"That's the only true thing you've said this whole call. It was a mistake. All of it. Trusting you, having you help me research, introducing you to my family, sleeping with you, for God's sake—all of it was a mistake. *My* mistake," Drake said. "It was my mistake to trust you. I thought I'd learned that lesson after my last relationship, but clearly, it needed reinforcing. I should have known you had only your own best interests at heart."

Now Kate's voice did sound teary. "I'd never, ever betray you. Leaving the chapters out was my own stupid fault—I own that, and I am so very sorry I made that terrible mistake. Surely you know me well enough to know I'm not the type of person who'd do that purposefully?"

The door to the green room opened, and the makeup artist with the monogrammed boots breezed in, spinning his chair back around so he faced the mirror and plucking the two tissues out from either side of his collar.

"They're ready for you, Mr. Matthews," she said, gesturing to the door leading out into the hallway of the studio.

Drake nodded and held up one finger. The woman disappeared again, and Drake took a deep breath.

"I've got to go, Kate. Gotta give my fans the opportunity to skewer me. Busy night facing the wrath of my readers."

"Drake, please! You've got to believe—"

"I believe, and I understand. The publicity drummed up by this will go a long way to getting you that

EVPLEX nomination you thought you'd blown. Your plan is back on track, after all. I'll see you Saturday at the launch, and don't think about quitting, Kate." Drake looked at his reflection in the dressing room mirror, watching his mouth move up and down as he willed his heart not to break, while he told her his only lie. "If you do, I'll sue you for breach of contract, and even if I don't win, I'll tie you up in the courts for years, making it real difficult to land another client. I want you to see this through to the very end and finish what you started."

"I'm not a quitter, and I don't scare easily." The tears were gone, and Kate's voice was like cascading icicles. "I'm a professional, and I promise that I'll give you the best book launch you've ever seen."

"I know better than to fall for your promises again."

Drake disconnected, turning his phone off.

Then, he stood, gazing into the mirror at the Knight of Nightmares.

He had finally lived up to his title.

CHAPTER 21

It was Kate's biggest fear—the one she'd even admitted to Drake—and here she'd done it single-handedly.

She'd ruined Drake Matthews's book launch.

Oh, she'd picked up the pieces, like a boss, and as she looked around at the Matthews house, she could objectively say that it was her best work. Ever. The fact she'd pulled it together at the last minute, despite the permit snafu, was pretty amazing. Except, as she watched the awed guests arrive between trick-or-treaters out for Halloween night, she wished she were happier. Prouder.

The media frenzy about Drake's secret historical romance was still actively churning, and although he'd finally admitted it was his work on the *Today* show, his fans were going berserk. Much of the buzz surrounding his launch tonight wasn't at all about *Halloween Hacker* but instead about *Memory's Lane*. The fact that much of the chatter was positive, and that his fan base was supportive, was irrelevant.

Drake's horror book's launch was ruined.

And it was all her fault.

Kate stood alone in the front parlor, wiping some glitter from her white suit coat and pants. As she waited for the event to begin, she toggled her phone to the pictures, scrolling to the last one.

As selfies go, it wasn't one of her best. The earphones she wore in the helicopter engulfed much of her head and had puffed her hair in a crazy way in the back. But her smile—it was genuine. She widened the picture to zoom in on her mouth and saw what Drake had called her "upside-down semicolon," an odd dimple she'd always disliked. Dimples were cute when they were in the middle of your cheek, not when they were at the bottom of your smile line. But he'd always seemed mesmerized by it, and Kate found that tragic. She'd ruined things with a guy who'd been so sweet, he'd even loved her weird dimples.

Then she moved the screen to zoom in on Drake. His expression was one of pure joy. His eyes crinkled at the edges, his smile wide, showing his perfect, white teeth as he gave the camera a giant thumbs-up. It was her favorite picture of them as a couple.

It was the first picture of them as a couple.

And it was likely the last.

Those facts, all taken together, were devastating.

Drake probably hated her now, and that thought was on constant repeat as she checked off the day's events, her chin held high by only a measure of will. A will that wilted as the minutes ticked closer to Drake's arrival.

As if listening to the voice inside Kate's head, Imani took Kate's free hand, giving it a gentle squeeze.

"He doesn't hate you, Katie. He was taken by surprise. We all were. But now, everyone's on board, and my boss is thrilled—the turnout of the news media and non-ticketed readers alone is incredible. Nothing revs people up more than a last-minute scandal! I told you at the beginning of all this—Drake Matthews is a good guy, with a kind heart. He'll eventually get over the timing of it and realize you made a mistake. It wasn't purposeful, and you're not set to benefit from it."

Kate shrugged. She'd heard last night that Evan Everstone had declined to attend the Halloween book launch, pulling out at the last moment. Evidently, he'd realized the romance novel news would eclipse any momentum he'd generate by his personal appearance to promote the movie adaptation of *Halloween Hacker*.

"I gave up the EVPLEX when I met Everstone and his fiancée in person. They're both toxic, and I tossed my chips on the table that night, knowing I was throwing away my chances at the award," Kate said. "I've taken pictures of this event's before and after, and I'll upload those to my website. I don't need an EVPLEX to showcase my versatility."

"It's stunning in here," Imani said, tactfully avoiding comment on the EVPLEX vanishing from Kate's future. "Where did you get the idea for this whole black-and-white theme?"

Kate nodded at one of the guests entering the house—already with a pair of the required blue surgical booties over his feet to protect the hardwood floors—and looked around objectively.

It was pretty perfect.

Lit by crystal chandeliers, and draped with gauzy, dark-gray material, the entire mansion was filled with black and white pumpkins that she and Imani had spray-painted in the backyard on some tarps and set up this morning after they'd finally dried. In the main foyer, as well as in the backyard, stood inflatable movie screens where a silent, black-and-white version of *Dracula* was projected onto the background, paying homage to the rich horror traditions of the past.

"I got it from a book I read recently," Kate said, not wanting to admit she'd gotten the monochromatic idea, complete with featuring a silent vintage film, from Drake's historical romance draft—the one she'd stupidly left behind at the café. The one whose pages had been found by a fan and then shared on a blog, which quickly went viral. Although all the social media coverage after the impromptu press conference seemed positive, she still hadn't heard from Drake since that last terrible conversation.

She'd called him a few times, but after he refused to answer, or open her texts and instant messages, anger overtook her sorrow. His last comment gutted her.

It was a mistake. All of it. Trusting you, having you help me research, introducing you to my family, sleeping with you, for God's sake—all of it was a mistake. Drake's words rang through her mind whenever she slowed down enough to let in outside thoughts; hence, she'd done her best not to slow her breakneck pace.

Imani's phone buzzed, interrupting Kate's grim thoughts.

"Drake's here." Imani patted Kate's arm. "Chin up, Katie. You crafted an amazing scarily-ever-after to be proud of, and nobody can deny that this launch is a win for *Halloween Hacker*. And for Drake Matthews. You mastered the chaos and turned out a spectacular event."

Kate bit her lip as her best friend walked away.

That's what Drake had once said to her—that chaos followed her around like a lapdog, but she'd mastered it. Too little, too late, it seemed, for their relationship.

It stung, thinking of what could have been. She'd thought Drake had gotten to know her—the real person, not the event planner—and it hurt that he'd believe she'd be so selfish as to pull a stunt like "misplace" his manuscript to win a stupid award.

Kate shook off her sorrow, tapping her earpiece to activate it.

"The guest of honor has arrived. Is everyone in position? All the guests are seated?"

"We're set, Kate. Waiting for the command, and we'll make it rain," came Carl's voice.

Her trusted assistant and friend had helped rescue his boss from a potential catastrophe, pivoting with the new plan without a whisper of annoyance.

Kate felt absurdly grateful for Carl and the rest of the Wellsville crew she'd hired for the event. At least her business, and her reputation of being on time and on budget, was still intact. She'd fulfilled her side of the bargain, not that she'd ever entertained walking away, despite Drake's threat. She would never abandon a client, no matter how irascible they were.

Kate took a deep breath. This was it.

She closed the pocket doors to the front parlor, where guests weren't allowed, and she slipped another doggie treat into Sasha's crate.

"It'll all be over soon, Sasha," she cooed to the sweet shih tzu, who sat down contentedly to snack, her tail wagging against the side of the crate. "For better or for worse."

Kate walked toward the kitchen and into the

backyard where the tables and chairs were set up under rented white tents lit by fairy lights with miniature skulls she'd pushed over each individual bulb—five thousand of them in all—giving her a blister on the side of each thumb, covered now in twin bandages. She'd made sure the place was filled with skulls, all right.

Drake would soon arrive to his *Halloween Hacker* book launch. She had replanned the night to be fun, honest, and good-hearted—like Drake. Hopefully, he would at least see beyond his anger for a second to recognize she'd meant well. At the very least, she wanted him to know how much he meant to her—how much these weeks had meant in her life.

Kate's heart was in her throat as the door from the kitchen opened and Drake's tall shadow appeared. With a shaking hand, she activated the microphone for Carl, giving him the last command of the night.

"Let the hatchets fly."

CHAPTER 22

If it weren't for his brothers, Drake didn't think he'd have had the courage to face the book launch. This was harder than that time he'd tandem parachuted out of an airplane with his brothers, back before Ryker was injured. In fact, it was the middle Matthews sibling who'd jumped out of the plane first, whooping and giving a thumbs-up for the helmet-cam footage. Like that day, it was Ryker who'd been the one to leap first into the fray.

He'd always been the one to step up, when others stepped back.

"Mom's freaking out that you're embarrassed and going to skip out on the launch tonight," Ryker had said when he'd called this morning, waking Drake up from a deep hangover sleep at the Manhattan hotel. "She said to remind you that the whole universe is turning out for this thing, and that she's made your favorite cupcakes. Three hundred of them. I've been elected by the family to ensure you show up, so when's John 'coptering you in?"

Drake groaned, clapping his hands over his eyes to block out the sunlight coming through the two inches where the curtains didn't meet over the hotel's massive, room-length windows.

"I think I caught a bug. Or something," he'd croaked into the phone, feeling his stomach roil.

Last night, after all of his interviews with the late-night hosts had wrapped up, he'd returned to the hotel, adrenaline still coursing through his body. He hadn't been able to turn off his mind from his last conversation with Kate—hadn't been able to get that note of hurt in her voice out of his head; the sound of tears, barely suppressed, were renting space in his mind, making it impossible to do any writing, any relaxing, any sleeping. He'd thought it might help to sample some of the alcohol in the mini-fridge.

Drake didn't stop until every miniature bottle was empty, along with the chips, candy bars, and the package of stale trail mix. The drinks had done their magic for a while, and he'd lain there on the white sheets of the hotel bed, alternately staring up at the fake crystals of the chandelier and watching an old black-and-white television episode of *The Munsters* he'd found while flipping through the channels.

It was the episode where Herman Munster, the guy who looked like Frankenstein, had gotten a night job so he could afford to buy his wife, Lily, a nice gift for their hundredth anniversary. He'd wanted to buy her something so exquisite, she'd really know how much he loved her. Meanwhile, Lily had done the same thing, and they were both running to their clandestine jobs, each trying to keep the secret from the other, which caused them, in turn, to question their partner's feelings. He recognized the play on the classic short story *The Gift of the Magi,* and he'd fallen asleep before the final reveal, where they both were bound to realize they'd been working hard to surprise each other, while meanwhile sacrificing what was most important: their time together. In spite of everything going on, his creative mind clamored for resolution to the characters' conflict, and he couldn't put it out of his head.

On the other end of the phone, Ryker snorted.

"I know that bug. It's called too much Jack Daniel's, and the cure is getting your ass out of bed and into the shower right after you call room service for coffee, breakfast, and ibuprofen. Quit your bitching. You're not missing your book launch."

At the mention of breakfast, Drake's stomach gurgled in a lethargically hopeful way. He sat up, waiting for the room to spin or for the contents of his belly to make a dramatic reappearance. When neither happened, he got to his feet, shuffling into the bathroom.

"You obviously haven't watched the news," Drake whispered, pawing through his toiletries bag for pain reliever. Palming the caplets, he washed them down by bending down to the bathroom sink and scooping water into his mouth with his hand. "I'm not going to miss much at this launch. All anyone wants to do is give me grief about the historical romance. C'mon, Ryker. I know you want to say shit about it, so go ahead. Heap it on. Everyone else is."

His younger brother was silent for so long, Drake squinted at the phone to see if he'd hung up.

But then he spoke, his normal, jovial tone subdued.

"What do you think I'm going to say? You're my big brother. Always there for us, supporting us financially

and otherwise. I'm not the smartest Matthews brother—
I'm a grease monkey. I understand gears and engines,
and how to fix things. Maybe even make old things
useful again. I could never do what you do—write
things from your imagination that are so good, people
would rather read your books than live their own lives.
Whether you're creating horror or romance, you're
going to take a minute to celebrate with those who
love you and love your writing, because what you do is
impressive. And I'm so damned proud of you, bro. I'm
just so damned proud..."

Ryker's voice choked off, and Drake found himself
blinking back unexpected moisture from his own eyes.
After taking a deep breath, he answered.

"Okay. You're right. I'll go. I'll be there." Drake
peered at his reflection in the mirror. His unshaven face
and the bags under his eyes made him look haggard,
like a pathetic caricature of a man who had given up
on happiness.

"One more thing," Ryker said, his voice steady
again. "About Kate. I've seen her. Twice. She's been
working her ass off over at the old house. She hasn't
said anything to me except 'hi' and 'see you later,' and
although she's always got a smile pasted on her face,
underneath that she looks...pretty broken up. I don't
know what went down with the two of you, but I do
know one thing."

"What's that?" Drake asked, when it became clear
Ryker wasn't going to offer it on his own.

"Love is probably the only thing on this planet
worth fighting for. Worth losing everything for. You're
a fool if you let pride stand in your way."

Last night's rerun episode from *The Munsters* came

back to Drake, and its lack of resolution. All Herman Munster had to do was to tell Lily his feelings—that's all that was required to resolve the conflict. Easy-peasy, and the author in him recognized that it was a scene that could be told in less than four pages. Was it as simple in real life? Was the answer dropping his other plans, and his pride, and telling the woman he'd fallen for what was in his heart?

One last task he'd scheduled for his trip to the city registered in his brain, reigniting a spark in the blood-shot eyes staring back at him from the mirror.

"I hear you," he told Ryker. "I've got one errand to run before I leave the city, but don't worry. I'll get John to fire up the chopper, and I'll be there tonight."

Ryker had to borrow Drake's truck from the airport parking lot to help his mother with the cupcake delivery and display setup, so it was Zander who picked Drake up at the airport.

"You look good, all things considered" was Zander's greeting when Drake hopped in the Prius. He'd worn the same suit he'd brought for his publicity interviews, with a fresh shirt and the black paisley tie Kate had picked out what seemed like a lifetime ago. His brother nodded to the Gatorade and protein bar nestled in the car's cup holder. "Brought you the ultimate recovery drink, and some sustenance. Nobody wants to see the Knight of Nightmares yak because he overindulged in self-pity. Bottoms up."

Drake snorted, but uncapped the drink, guzzling down half the contents before unwrapping the snack.

"Thanks, man." He chewed, and reached over to crack the window open, letting the cool October air blow on his face as they exited the airport, turning on the hilly country road back into town. He took off his glasses, massaging the bridge of his nose as he mentally tried to ready himself. "I feel like I'm gearing up to run the Crucible."

His brother, of course, immediately got the reference to the ultimate challenge at the end of Marine boot camp.

"You're my brother. I'm always there for you, giving you what you need even when you don't know you need it." Zander flipped on his turn signal. "Just like Sasha."

Drake paused, mid-chew.

"What?" He worked the words around the protein bar.

Zander gave him a "duh" expression. "You really didn't think some rando fan put a shih tzu puppy, already house-trained and complete with shot records, bag of food, and crate, in your front yard, did you?"

Drake swallowed, gobsmacked.

"But—the scrawled name on the front. I thought it was some kid's dog."

Zander rolled his eyes. "I wrote it with my left hand. We all knew how low you were when you moved back from California and that train wreck of a book from your ex came out. Ryker did his thing to boost your ego, gifting you a bitching ride. My gift was more of a soul-boosting furball. I thought you'd guessed a long time ago."

Drake was silent, letting the truth soak into his skin.

"Thanks, Zan. I don't even know what to say."

They rode the rest of the way in companionable

silence, Drake wondering how he was going to apologize to Kate.

When they got into the village, the car slowed to a crawl to avoid the hundreds of kids in costume zipping around Main Street, trick-or-treating at the local businesses.

"Damn!" Drake slapped his forehead. "I forgot to buy candy for the kids. We always get so many trick-or-treaters—"

"Kate's got it under control." Zander pointed out a couple dressed in vampire costumes, waving and giving out handfuls of candy to kids as they approached the Matthews house from the side street, away from the adults standing in long lines on his sidewalk. "See? She's got someone out there by the far side of the gates with bins of candy. Don't worry, dude. The woman thought of everything."

Of course she had. Drake's heart wrenched a little sideways in his chest, but his voice was normal when he spoke.

"Why aren't we parking in the back in the driveway?"

"Because your truck, the caterer's van, Mom's car, and Kate's and Imani's vehicles are all parked in there. No room. Besides, Kate gave explicit directions she wants you coming in from the front door, not the back."

His brother expertly maneuvered the Prius to a spot in front of his house that had been blocked off by orange cones and black caution tape with white print that read *Horror Zone.*

"Let's go. Kate will string me up if you're late." Zander jumped out.

Drake did the same, then froze, taking in the

entire scene. There weren't a few dozen people, but *hundreds* of them, queued up behind velvet rope that wound, doubling back on itself, on the sidewalk outside his gates, and then into his front yard, where a more elaborate maze-like system awaited his fans.

When they saw him, they frantically waved, holding up signs that ran the gamut from *Drake Matthews's Books ROCK* to the more original. One girl, wearing a vintage dress with makeup on that made her face appear as if it were made of cracked porcelain, clutched a sign that read *Let Me Be Your Dark Doll* and a big, pot-bellied guy with a trucker hat held one that said *You are the Knight of my Nightmares.*

Then, he spotted one brave fan who held up a folded cardboard sign saying *You had me at "Drake Matthews Romance!"* and Drake's face was as hot as if he'd stepped in front of a blazing fire.

He scanned the crowd for the hate signs—there was always one. Someone advocating censorship in the name of Matthew, Mark, Luke, or John. Yet he saw nothing but support.

"We love you, Drake!" came the scream from some woman in the crowd, and then everyone started to yell.

"Wave, dude," Zander said, coming around to nudge him in the side. "They're your fans. They are here to celebrate with you. Wave!"

Drake did as he was told, and his insides thawed enough for him to approach the crowd, summoning a smile as he entered the batwing gates to his house. A murmur snaked up the line of people ahead of him, so that they all turned to watch as he walked by them. He realized this line of people waiting patiently in single file were all there either to tour his house or to take a picture on the porch in front of his house.

All because of what he wrote.

"You're acting like a kook," Zander said in a low voice, stopping him with a hand on his arm. "Say something, for Pete's sake!"

"Uh, thank you all for coming." Drake cleared his throat, filling his lungs to pitch his voice toward the very back of the queue. "I hope you enjoy the tour...and that you all live to tell the tale!"

The fans cheered, and Drake's smile came more easily.

"Happy Halloween, horror fans! See you on the other side."

He waved, and Zander tugged his elbow, motioning him to move. Drake gazed around in awe at the number of readers who had turned out for this. As Kate predicted, they were all there to see if what they'd imagined was his reality, and it wouldn't matter what they found inside. Somehow, it would all fit within their perception of him, be it positive or negative.

Kate.

The thought of facing her again after saying such rotten things to her made his steps falter. Zander nudged him from behind, and he continued walking to his front door.

He knew he had to go inside. A Marine didn't walk away from a conflict. They walked toward danger, even if danger was a petite, red-haired event planner who wore killer heels and wielded binders of spreadsheets. The picture of Kate in those stilettos, hair unbound, face blurry with pleasure, hit Drake's confidence then, like a pack of hungry piranhas, tearing off bits and chunks until he was raw and bloody inside.

Kate had planned for the queue to end at the bottom of the porch, where, originally, the spider dropped down, giving the guests one last scare before heading inside. Now, the entryway was draped in dark-gray fabric, with pumpkins painted black or white scattered in artful arrangements here and there. Perfect for a fan photo opp.

It was simple and tasteful, yet still evocative enough that people's eyes were popping as they took in his house, the filled-in fountain out front, the turret-like attic where a single candle-shaped light flickered in the window.

It wasn't a circus. It was actually pretty cool.

The two Matthews brothers bypassed the line, where a crew of people was helping the visitors put on blue, surgical-type booties over their shoes. Even women in heels were reluctantly sliding on booties, looking a little ridiculous as they waited for a chance to walk in his house.

Drake and Zander refused the blue booties, and the volunteers laughed, recognizing and congratulating him as he and his brother maneuvered around the queue to enter the house, moving into the front parlor where the crowd hadn't been allowed.

"Dude, is that a thesaurus in your pocket, or are you just happy to see me?" Zander asked once they'd closed the door behind them, gesturing to Drake's black dress pants.

Drake adjusted the long box bulging unattractively in his front pocket and finally cursed, pulling it out to put it in his inside suit jacket pocket.

"It's for Kate. It's my apology."

Zander gave a dubious look at the odd rectangular bulge at Drake's side. "It's none of my business, but that box is too big to be a ring and too small to be fifty dozen roses. If you're not proposing, and you're not groveling with flowers, what are you doing? Because I hate to tell you, big brother, but you screwed up royally. Girls like Kate don't come along every day. You need to bring your A game."

"This is it. Let's pray it works."

About a week ago, after another Cobb salad lunch with Kate where he'd delighted in listening to an embarrassing story she told about why she'd had to quit taking dance classes with Imani as a girl, Drake had sat at his computer, still grinning from ear to ear as he often did after spending time with his event planner. He'd had the idea then to get Kate a gift as a thank-you for working so hard on his launch, and maybe even a pre-congratulatory gift for being considered for her EVPLEX. He'd thought about flowers or candy, and quickly discarded them as too impersonal. The idea of buying her a new crystal pen crossed his mind, but she seemed pretty attached to her pink one.

Stumped, he'd been absently flipping through his yellow legal pad when he spotted the perfect gift, and he'd made a few calls, sent over his specifications, and paid a hefty sum to rush the jeweler to create this piece in time. All he'd had to do was pick it up in Manhattan after his publicity tour, which he'd done after Ryker had convinced him to attend his book launch and be man enough to tell Kate what he felt.

Tonight, his master plan was simple: apologize to

Kate, give her this box, tell her his feelings... and hope for the best.

As far as plans go, it was a pretty flimsy one, but it was the best he could do once he'd realized what an ass he'd been to her. He'd let his past with Rachel color how he'd viewed Kate's actions.

"Oh, there you are!" The bright, cheery voice made both brothers start. It was Imani, clad in a chic black dress, her deep mahogany hair loose and curled down her back. She beckoned the two men toward the other pocket doors that led from the parlor into the dining room and then to the kitchen, where she pointed to the door to the backyard.

"Drake, stand in front of the door, and don't open it until I give you the word. And you..." Imani paused, clearly searching for his brother's name.

"Zander. Zander Matthews, the best Matthews brother, at your service." His youngest brother gave her his megawatt grin, trying to look cool and flexing at the same time.

Drake stifled a laugh. The guy never could resist a pretty woman in charge.

Imani raised one eyebrow, but did not crack a smile. "The best Matthews brother? That seems pretty subjective."

Zander's smile dimmed.

Then Imani winked. "I'm kidding. Okay, best Matthews brother, you stay right here with me, and we're going to wait until the guest of honor enters before we go in." Imani toggled her earpiece. "He's entering in three. Two. One."

With that, Drake was shoved out the back door of his kitchen into what appeared to be a massive white tent, lit entirely by skull-shaped twinkle lights strung along every edge and corner of the canvas. Tables, covered in black cloths, held tiny black and white pumpkins, tiny tea lights and...was that? Yes. She'd covered the tops of the table with silver glitter.

The corner of Drake's mouth canted up in a half smile.

Kate. You could take the girl out of her glittery events, but you couldn't take the glitter out of the girl. No matter how dark, Kate always found a way to reflect and refract light.

He scanned the crowd, but before he'd stepped onto his back porch, a man's voice filled the night air.

"Here he is," came a deep, unseen voice from a disguised sound system. "The Knight of Nightmares himself, Drrrrraaaakkke Matthewwwwwssss." The announcer stretched his name out, like he was entering a boxing ring instead of his backyard.

And if he'd misjudged the strength of his apology to Kate, it might be.

As his guests cheered, papers floated down on the entire assembly from the tent's top. Gazing up, Drake spied white sheets that had been attached to the ceiling, which had a thin rope at one end. Black-clad helpers had tugged the rope down, releasing what appeared to be a waterfall of cascading book pages.

His guests cheered louder, snatching at papers around them in delight. A piece of paper fluttered onto his head. He plucked it off, and then grinned.

It was a cunningly designed, hatchet-shaped bookmark for *Halloween Hacker,* complete with a blurb, written so that the text carried on over the entire thing, as if it were a page ripped from a book.

Drake knew. It was the "Aww!" moment Kate promised, but with a horror twist. Perfect for his launch.

He glanced up, scanning the crowd for his event planner. Where was she?

He spotted his mom and Ryker toward the back, where hundreds of cupcakes were set up in a display around an old Mac computer, keyboard, and mouse, being operated by... yes! That was the skeleton from his mother's front porch in front of the Mac, with one hand holding up his new release, and the other on the keyboard, as if he were manipulating it to play a silent version of his "book trailer" promotional video.

Super clever.

Above the posed skeleton and the mass of cupcakes were what he sincerely hoped were plastic hatchets hung from invisible fishing line from the tent top. They swayed in the air currents inside the tent, dramatic and spooky, but oddly classy at the same time.

Where was Kate?

He smiled and waved at the crowd, his gaze raking every face. He recognized neighbors, friends, other writers, amid a vast, nameless sea of VIPs and readers sitting at the pumpkin-carving stations, clustered around the snack table, or grabbing a drink at the bar next to a large, inflatable movie screen. Drake stared at the screen, playing the original *Dracula* in black-and-white, the silent movie and dramatic subtitles giving the whole thing a low-key, Gothic effect.

Suddenly, he was hit with a wave of remorse.

He'd heard about the permit issue, which nixed the maze and the massive mechanical spider from the plan, but he'd figured there'd be another circus stunt taking their place. Now, to find this? How had she cobbled together such a perfect event in such a short amount of time?

Drake wanted to give himself a forehead smack for being such a jackass.

He ignored the microphone being thrust into his hands by another assistant, as he spotted a woman dressed in a white suit half-hidden behind the inflatable movie screen. Her auburn hair was slicked back in an updo, but it was the black stilettos—those hot ones with the silver tips—that were a dead giveaway, as was the clipboard she held to her chest as if a million dollars, instead of a spreadsheet, were clipped to it.

His heart leaped.

Kate.

Drake threaded his way through the crowd, pulse racing. He had the impression she was avoiding him, but then a small woman behind Kate grabbed her elbow, and to Drake's astonishment, the woman wagged her index finger in Kate's face, as if dressing her down.

Drake frowned. Who was that? One of the town council, maybe? A guest, bitching because there wasn't a gluten-free alternative to the cupcakes?

Jaw clenched, Drake shoved through well-wishers toward Kate when, suddenly, a man stepped in front of him, sticking his hand out to shake. Drake almost barreled through the guy, except his green eyes looked familiar.

Then, the man spoke.

"You must be Drake Matthews." The thin, balding man gave his hand a hard shake, his mouth unsmiling as he motioned for the woman holding tight to Kate's elbow to come this way. "I'm Kevin Sweet, Katherine's father, and I've got a real problem with you."

CHAPTER 23

Kate thought she'd found the perfect hiding spot—standing behind the silent movie screen she'd rented—where she'd remain concealed until Drake had been introduced and made his speech. That way, she could lurk and do her job, armed with her spreadsheets and earpiece, but avoid having to explain to anyone why her skin was blotchy and her eyes were bloodshot.

Even Imani, bless her heart, had offered her friend some eye drops for those "allergies," playing along as if she didn't guess that Kate had been crying this morning before the workers arrived.

Well, she only had to suck it up for another few minutes. Then she could disappear into one of the off-limits rooms until this was all over. If luck was in her corner, she'd never have to speak with Drake Matthews again.

"Uh, Kate, we have a problem," came Carl's voice in her earpiece.

Kate peeped out from behind the movie screen. The hatchet bookmarks were still floating around, and the guests were joyfully scooping them up, pocketing several each, as Kate had planned. She'd coordinated this promo bit with Imani, who'd gotten it okayed and printed by Cerulean Books on the side and shipped directly to Drake's mom, to be sure it stayed a surprise for Drake.

At first, it had appeared that her idea had hit its mark. Drake's face had that thoughtful, bemused look she'd come to know was a precursor to that slow, sweet smile of his, but she'd ducked her head back down to avoid that extra arrow to her heart.

"What's wrong?" Kate shot back, frowning.

"Mr. Matthews is refusing the microphone. He's… uh, he looks like he's leaving."

Kate groaned, rolling her eyes. "Someone give me the microphone, and I'll kick off the party then. Sooner we get things started, the sooner it's over."

Annoyed, she strode around the inflatable movie screen to check out the scene.

And ran directly into her mother.

"Katherine, I'm so mad, I could shake you!" Then Kasey Sweet did just that, snagging the arm that wasn't holding Kate's clipboard and giving it a squeeze-shake. Her mom was dressed in a chocolate-brown sheath dress Kate had never seen before, and she'd actually styled her short brown hair, putting in more effort than she did before heading to work. "Why didn't you tell me you were working for Drake Matthews? Here I thought you were just flitzing around. How could you have kept this to yourself?"

"Wh-what are you doing here?" Kate allowed herself to be dragged along behind her mother out into the crowd of Drake's fans as if she were a recalcitrant child. Then she spotted her father.

Standing right next to Drake Matthews.

Her heart fell to the very soles of her sore feet. She'd been sure nothing could make her feel worse tonight...and then chaos said, *Hold my beer*, and bam!

Her parents were here.

Kate dislodged her arm from her mother's pincer grasp as they approached her dad and Drake. She felt the heat rise from her chest to her neck and face like a crimson tide of anger and embarrassment.

"Who invited you?" Kate asked her parents, deciding that question trumped all others.

Before they could answer, a skinny arm was tossed across Kate's shoulders, and she felt herself dragged into a hug where her nose was mashed against the shoulder of a much taller woman dressed in a black pantsuit.

"I did," said her sister, Kiersten, grinning down at her in her usual impish manner. Then, with a toss of her deep auburn pixie cut, she nodded toward Drake. "Well, actually, he did, but I relayed the message. He wanted to surprise you."

"That was the call I took on your cell in the attic that day," Drake said, clearing his throat. "I invited them before everything—"

Kate held up a hand, not wanting him to lay out all that had happened at her family's feet.

"Yeah. We don't need to go there."

"Well, it's a good thing he did invite us, otherwise we'd never have spoken to you," Kate's mom said, indignant. "You've been ducking our calls for a month, and you missed out on a golden opportunity! Did you know that your father called in a personal favor to get you into the last spot for the MCAT prep class offered in person at—"

"Give it a rest, Mom," Kiersten said, talking over her mother's diatribe, rolling her eyes. She gave Kate a wink. "Can't you see we're having a 'Take Your Family to Work Day' with Kate? About time. And this is all great, by the way. Thanks for inviting us, Mr. Matthews. Don't you think it's great, Dad?"

Her father, whose nose had been deep in a glass of wine, swallowed. His green eyes scanned the crowd, and Kate saw the moment when he'd recognized several A-listers from not only the Lloyd Harbor area, but the national scene.

"It's a wonderful event, Katherine. Clearly, top-notch. I can see now why you didn't want to do our grand opening." Her dad gave her a nod, as if acknowledging a good move on the chess board. "I suppose we're pretty small peanuts in comparison to this."

"Well," her mother said, smoothing down her sheath dress, "you can't blame us for asking. I mean, we are your parents."

"Wait. What? You wanted me to help with the grand opening as . . . your event planner?" Kate asked. "Not to work at the surgery center?"

"Of course! Something you'd know if you'd return our calls," her mom said. Then her eyes got that crafty look again. "Plus, maybe if you see what we're doing there, you might just find you have it in you to finish up those twelve credits."

"Mom!" Kiersten gritted her teeth in a smile as she elbowed her mother in the ribs. "Give it a rest."

Her mom's face softened, and to Kate's surprise, she found herself wrapped in a brief hug.

"Kiersten's right. We'll have plenty of time to talk about that later, and this is a fantastic book launch you did for Mr. Matthews. I had no idea..." Her mother waved her hands to encompass the decorations, the food, and the beaming guests, and then Drake himself, her eyes wide with what Kate swore was admiration. "...that *this* was the level of things you did."

"And after Kiersten told us the job you were working on, we worried that the reason you weren't answering our calls was that this guy," her dad said, jerking his thumb in Drake's direction, "was working you to death. Or worse."

Drake's eyebrows rose, and not in a politely interested way. "Worse? Worse how, exactly?"

Kate struggled with who to focus on first—her parents, who'd just given her the validation she'd been striving for since college, or Drake, who looked angry enough to spit nails at her father's tacit insult. Finally, she blew out a breath, shaking her head.

"I don't have time for any of this right now. I'm working," she said, pivoting on her heels...and spinning directly into Imani and the three drinks she was balancing in her hands.

"Oh, Katie!" Imani gasped in dismay as red wine sloshed out of the glasses and onto Kate's white suit. "I'm so sorry! I was bringing drinks for your folks. I-I didn't expect you to turn!"

Kate held out her dripping clipboard, her eyes widening at the cold, wet shock of the liquid hitting her skin.

"Oh, shit," came Carl's whisper in her earpiece.

Dreading what she'd see, Kate looked down at

herself. The wine transformed her into a woman who'd apparently just survived a gruesome stabbing.

"Perfect." Kate shook wine from her plans. "Just fantastic. Now I look like a character from *Halloween Hacker*. I'll just wander over to the cupcake table and stand behind there and blend right in. Like a damned prop."

Imani set the empty glasses down on a nearby table. Snagging the wet papers on the clipboard with two fingers, she shook off the excess wine. "I'll take it from here and introduce Drake to do the welcome speech. You've got lots of time. Go inside and find another shirt."

"Imani, we're so happy to see you, sweetheart," Kate's mom gushed, giving Imani a bigger hug than she'd just given her own daughter. "It's been so long. Do you know, the other day I was looking through some old boxes, and I found some photos of when you lived with us after your mom passed. I thought you might want—"

Kate stalked away, trying not to let this wardrobe snafu, coupled with her parents' arrival, be the factor that drove her over the cliff into a full-on flip out. She was Kate Freaking Sweet. She was a boss. No. She was *the* boss. She . . .

Was attracting a crowd.

Everyone in the backyard had quieted as she strode past them, some with half-expectant grins, like she was part of the scare team, or paid entertainment, representing some dead character from a past Matthews book. Ignoring the stares from guests, she wove through the rest of the people, retreating into the Victorian's back door and into the fifties-era kitchen—an area blocked off from anyone but family. And staff, like her.

"Kate, wait!" Drake's voice sounded behind her. "Take the back staircase and I'll get you a shirt from my room."

"I don't need your damn shirt," Kate spat, but raced up the back staircase, thinking to at least use the larger bathroom to sop up the stain with a towel. "In fact, I don't need anything from you, Mr. Matthews."

She shoved the antique door at the top, and when it wouldn't give, she used her hip against it just as Drake came up behind her, pushing with his forearm.

The door gave way with a loud creak, spilling them into the upstairs hallway, both grappling for balance and using each other to avoid toppling over. A line of fans extending from the middle of the hallway to the stairs that led to the attic all turned to gawk at them, as did the posted security guard.

One man in a black concert T-shirt that said *Disturbed* slowly raised his cell phone. "Is that...? Hey, that's Drake Matthews!"

It was creepy how fast the orderly line of people devolved into a berserk mob of reaching hands, flashing cell phones, and shouting. The security guard was knocked down in the melee, and fans stumbled over his body to race down the hall toward them.

Kate stood there, gaping in disbelief, until Drake grabbed her around the waist from behind.

"Get in here!" Drake lifted her, hauling her backward into the closed door that led to the guest room. Fumbling with a key from his pocket, he held her in one arm against his hip, away from the crowd, high enough so that her feet only skimmed the floor.

Finally, he had the door open, dragged her inside, and the door slammed before a fan could reach a hand or foot to stop them. He jammed the door closed with his shoulder against the wood, as he worked an old bronze skeleton key into the keyhole, managing to get the tumblers to turn and lock it. People knocked and then pounded on the other side.

"It's like a zombie movie," she gasped.

Drake set her down in the dark room. "Thank God Zander gave me the key, or we'd have been crushed outside the spare bedroom."

Kate heard him cross the floor and then turn on a vintage green glass lamp, lighting the small bedroom and probably, she knew, her blotchy skin and blood-shot eyes. She turned away, staying silent.

"Kate. I'm so sorry," Drake said behind her, his voice low and intense, compared to the fans outside still knocking, shouting, and creating a ruckus that drowned out the security guard's shouted orders for them to get back in line. Drake was silent for a heart-beat, and then admitted, "I've been a total jackass."

"Which time?" Kate crossed her arms over her stained suit coat, then grimaced as the cold, wet fabric hit her skin. She unbuttoned the jacket, shrugging out of it and folding it so the stain was on the inside before setting it on the hardwood floor. She was glad she'd worn a black shell underneath. While it was wet, it didn't show the stain. "You mean when you talked to Kiersten and invited her and my parents to the launch without consulting me, or when you accused me of selling you out for my own gain?"

"Both. Although I'd meant the invite to be a good surprise. You'd said your parents had never seen your work, and I wanted them here to see you hit your goal," Drake said, and as Kate spun to face him, he shrugged.

"I knew whatever you planned tonight would be perfect and EVPLEX-worthy."

"Well, you got that wrong on both scores." Most of the steam had evaporated from her anger, leaving only exhaustion.

"No." Drake closed the distance between them but didn't reach for her. "You may not get an award for tonight, but nobody can deny the perfection you created."

"Mr. Matthews!" shouted a man's voice outside the door. "Can you please sign this?"

A pen came shooting into the room via the crack under the door, followed by a piece of wrinkled notebook paper.

"Oh, this is ridiculous!" Kate tapped the earpiece still in her ear, activating it. "Carl? Can you please send security up to the second floor of the Matthews mansion?"

"Uh, sure, boss," came Carl's voice. "You're not thinking of bouncing the guest of honor, are you? Because I don't think that's wise. Cooler heads need to prevail, Kate."

"No, the security isn't for Drake. Yet." Kate gave Drake a sour look. "We've got a mob of readers who overpowered the upstairs guard and have me and Drake barricaded in the guest bedroom at the end of the hall."

"The bedroom? How terribly inconvenient for you both." Carl snickered.

"Just send the security guys," Kate snapped. "I'll have Drake down as soon as possible."

Before Carl could say anything else suggestive, Kate tugged the earpiece out, tossing it on her suit coat.

When she stood, Drake was a foot from her. As she opened her mouth to tell him off, he held up a hand, a pleading look on his face.

"Please, Kate," he said, pushing up his glasses, then running a hand through his hair. "Give me a chance to apologize. Then we'll all go down and fake smile, and I'll sign books. You can leave, and your crew will clean up, and we can all go our separate ways, if that's what you want. Before that, I need to apologize to you, sincerely, for being such a fool."

Kate crossed her arms, willing herself to be hardened steel. She would not cry in front of this man!

"Go ahead."

"I'm a writer. My job is all about living in my head, using my imagination to invent subplots where none exist—usually with characters who have the worst motives possible. When those pages were leaked, my knee-jerk reaction was to assume you'd purposely done it, like Rachel, for your own gain." Drake gave her a crooked smile. "After drowning myself in booze and pity, my family reminded me of something: fiction isn't reality. And you'll never be the villain, Kate. That's not who you are."

Kate's chin wobbled, and her eyes filled. She blinked rapidly, sniffing.

"I can't believe I left those pages behind, Drake. It was unforgivable." Her throat constricted with unshed tears. "And the resulting hoopla was all my fault. I totally ruined your book launch!"

The pool of tears in her eyes had gotten so deep, Drake's face doubled and blurred in her vision until they finally cascaded down her cheeks like a fast-moving waterfall of misery.

"Don't cry." Drake groaned, closing the remaining distance between them and enveloping her in a fierce embrace. "You ruined nothing. After the council shut down your permits, you still pulled off an unbelievable event in a little over two days. And it's not a circus."

Kate clung to him a moment more, then made herself unwrap her arms from around his neck. She came off her tiptoes, swiping at her eyes, grateful for the waterproof mascara she'd thought to wear this morning.

"A-are you just saying that?" Kate gazed into his warm, amber eyes. "Do you like everything?"

Drake's hand cupped her face, his thumbs wiping the remaining moisture from her cheeks. Instead of answering, he slowly lowered his mouth to hers, his gaze questioning as he gave her ample time to dodge.

Dodging his kiss was the last thing Kate wanted to do, and she tilted her chin up, meeting him halfway. His lips met hers in a soft caress, and then he eased his tongue into her mouth. She moaned, sinking into him, and Drake deepened the kiss, sending off sparklers of desire through her body.

She crushed against him, wanting to eliminate any space between them, and something jabbed her chest.

"Ow!" She backed away, cupping her breast. "Something's stabbing me."

"I forgot." Drake unbuttoned his suit jacket and reached inside, pulling out a long, white rectangular box. He handed it to her, and then looked around the bedroom, sighing. "This isn't where I'd hoped to give this to you—in my guest bedroom, with the zombie horde pounding on my door. I wanted to give you this gift as a thank-you for putting up with me these weeks."

A gift? Kate knew she was flushing—she couldn't remember the last time she'd gotten a gift from a guy. Curious, she lifted the lid and gasped.

"Oh my gosh! This is exquisite!"

Kate pulled a silver necklace from the box, holding it to eye level to appreciate the design. It was an intricate glasswork of yellow and orange ovals embracing a blue, shield-like shape in the middle, all surrounded with thin black leading.

It was an exact miniature of the stained-glass window pendant she'd drawn him while they were in the mausoleum, on their first "research" trip together.

"This is my apology to you for being a jackass, and it's also a promise," Drake said. "You can plan as many of my book launches as it takes you to win that EVPLEX. I promise to give you carte blanche for whatever outrageous, crazy extravaganza your mind dreams up, and I'll strong-arm my neighbor next time into okaying every, last, insane permit idea too."

Kate laughed. "That's sweet, but someone once reminded me that there's more to life than winning some award. Besides, with Everstone involved, I'm not sure I want to be associated with it."

Drake wrapped his arms about her waist, holding her from behind so they could both stare at the prisms of light coming through the tiny glass window replica.

"Do you recognize it?"

"Of course I do," Kate said, her voice soft as she recalled the day in the cemetery.

"When we stood there, under that old, dusty, stained-glass window, and you described how you'd have your imaginary groom give it to his bride, I saw it then, Kate."

"Saw what?" Kate asked, twisting in his arms to see his face.

"I pictured the scene—me giving the necklace to you. And telling you how much you meant to me and explaining why I'd chosen to have your necklace idea from that morning brought into reality." Drake's finger came up to play with a wisp of hair next to her face, winding it around as he spoke. "It's because when you stood under that window, sharing your vision of that fictional bride and groom moment, I realized I'd started to fall in love with you."

Kate gulped. "And...now? How do you feel now?"

Drake leaned forward, placing a reverent kiss on her forehead.

"Now, I'm in so deep, I'd do anything to get you to stick around. Our story began with a crazy, fortunate collision in my front yard. Then, after a series of happily chaotic, sometimes awkward scenes later, we have our hero and heroine potentially together." Drake hesitated, his gaze uncertain behind his glasses. "I love you, Kate Sweet. And I want to see what our next chapter brings."

Kate released the breath she'd been holding. She stood on her tiptoes, planting a kiss on his lips.

"I love you too, Drake Matthews," Kate said, mimicking his formality. "And I can already tell you that answer."

Drake's eyes held a hopeful light. "You can?"

"There can be only one logical plan." Kate curled her fingers into the hair at the back of his neck, tugging him back to her lips. "I am the Queen of Happily Ever Afters, after all."

EPILOGUE

Kate glanced at the *New York Times* Imani handed to her, snorting in amusement at the headline: "Famous Hollywood Producer Indicted."

Gazing into the mirror in the makeshift dressing room, Kate applied one last coat of waterproof mascara to her lashes. The mirror only showed about a foot's worth of her reflection, so it was impossible to gauge the overall effect of her look, but she trusted her best friend's hair and dressing skills.

"It's hard to believe I used to covet recognition from Evan Everstone," Kate said, shaking her head to be sure her vintage hairclip with white netting, a borrowed piece from Drake's grandmother, was securely fastened. Then she touched her stained-glass pendant around her neck for the same reassurance, having worn it every single day since last Halloween. "You know, as they say, all things happen for a reason. Lucky for me, it all fell apart, and I wasn't eligible for an EVPLEX."

"No doubt." Imani snorted, putting a hand out to the tiny room's walls to steady herself as the boat rocked to the left. "Honestly, though, I'd have never thought Everstone and Drake's ex, Rachel, would be so bold as to embezzle two million from the award committee. Pretty wild stuff."

"Speaking of wild," Kate said, gesturing to the part she'd ripped from the center of the *Times* earlier. "Did you see that *Memory's Lane* is already breaking pre-order records, even though the release is still three months out?"

Imani grinned. "Well, with me as your fiancé's publicity guru, and you handling the launch event at Arlington Cemetery, how could it not be?"

"It's not a book launch, it's a wreath ceremony to honor our fallen," Kate corrected, smoothing her dress and spinning to her friend, exhaling in an attempt to quell the jitters. "Well, this is as good as it gets. How do I look?"

"Like a woman about to discover how sweet it is to marry the man of her dreams."

A knock came at the metal door.

"Katherine, may I come in?" her mother's voice sounded from outside the white, riveted door.

When Imani let her mom in, Kate was surprised to see the normally stony Dr. Kasey Sweet tear up.

"Oh, you are stunning in that dress! I'm so honored you chose it for your something old. Even if it does get soaking wet out there, it's been my dream to have one of you girls wear my dress. You sure you still want to go with this, honey? I mean, with your...career, it might be expected you'd opt for something more...traditional."

Imani squeezed out of the way so that Kate's mom could give Kate a one-armed hug.

"Drake and I are both in agreement. This is exactly what we wanted, a day to enjoy family and each other in the most awe-inspiring place we know. I wouldn't change a thing," Kate reassured her mother with a smile, kissing her cheek in silent thanks for her finally realizing there would be only one Sweet daughter joining the family business. But Kate had agreed to plan every major Sweet Surgery event, in perpetuity. "Now go out and make sure Kiersten's got Dad and he's not off puking somewhere. He's got to walk me down the railing, after all."

Her mom bustled around, spraying more hair spray on Kate's already shellacked updo, and then finally allowed herself to be ushered out.

"Okay, are you ready to start your new life as Mrs. Sweet-Matthews?" Imani asked, her cherry-red tinted lips perfectly matching the maid of honor's dress she'd chosen for herself.

Kate inhaled, and then exhaled, slowly, nodding. "I think I'm ready."

"One last thing." Imani took her black tote from against the wall and dug to the bottom, pulling out two blue plastic packages, handing her the one with white and pink writing on the back. "Okay, your dress is something old, your shoes are your something new, your hair clip is your something borrowed, so we're only missing one thing to ensure your marital bliss!"

"What in the world?" Kate asked, unrolling the blue plastic, finally holding it up. It was a rain slicker with beautiful, scrolled letters that said *Starting Our Happily Ever After* on the back.

"Drake's got one too, so you match. I thought the Queen of Happily Ever Afters deserved an 'Aww!'

moment," Imani said, her eyes filling along with Kate's as she hugged her best friend. "Now stop blubbering, or you're going to ruin my makeup! I gotta look good—I'm hitting up Drake's brother Zander later. See if that big hunk of a man can dance as well as he sweet-talks."

Kate's eyebrows rose. "All right! Go get you a Matthews man. I promise he's worth the trouble."

Kate followed her best friend out of the tiny captain's quarters onto the slick wooden deck of the *Maid of the Mist VII* where her sister stood, clutching her father's arm as the boat rocked back and forth in the waves.

"I'm so happy for you," Kiersten said, handing Kate the simple arrangement of red roses and sniffing and dabbing at her eyeliner to check it wasn't running. "Here are your flowers. You've gotta keep Dad moving or he's going to barf. Let's get you hitched!"

Her dad, who'd been leaning against the nearby wall, straightened and beamed, in spite of the slightly greenish cast to his face.

"You are a vision." Her dad kissed her cheek and then adjusted her white vintage veil so that it covered her face. "The groom is waiting for you, and if I'm not mistaken, he hasn't been made in the crowd yet. You're two beautiful young people getting married in the Honeymoon Capital of the World—just the way you'd planned it. I'm so happy for you, sweetheart."

Kate squeezed his hand. "Thanks, Dad. Now let's pray I don't do anything embarrassing, like fall overboard."

The boat was approaching Rainbow Falls, and true to its name, the sun gleamed down through the clouds of mist, creating rainbows in three different places.

Although the crowd around them hadn't figured out who was aboard, they guessed why. Even with the raincoat, it was hard to miss her white dress and veil, and people clapped and cheered as Kate carefully stepped in her flat white ballet slippers toward the bow of the boat, where a man in a look-alike blue slicker over a tuxedo stood, his hands clasped in front of him. It reminded her of the time he stood like that with his silver Tin Man's suit on, and despite the nervous flip of her stomach, she laughed.

Drake, who'd been chatting with his brothers, spotted her then, walking between a rapidly parting crowd of mist-soaked tourists, and that serious frown he had when she knew he was really concentrating evaporated. A huge, joyous smile lit up his face, making Kate's heart skip in her chest.

This guy.

The one with the dark hair, the glowing golden eyes behind mist-spotted glasses. He was the reason she'd decided to become a bride today—to give him the ceremony he wanted, and the happily ever after they both deserved.

Kate joined Drake by the rail's edge, the roaring waters of the falls providing a dramatic white-and-rainbow backdrop as their tiny group of family and friends gathered around them in a tight-knit half-circle.

The ordained minister they'd hired began the simple, quick ceremony, straining to be heard over the din. Drake and Kate laughed as they shouted their vows to each other, feet splayed on the slippery, mist-soaked deck as they carefully shoved rings on each other's fingers.

"By the powers vested in me by the state of New

York, and in the presence of God, your family, and friends, it is my greatest joy and privilege to declare you husband and wife!" The minister stuffed the paper into his poncho, gripped the railing next to him, and finished, shouting, "You may now kiss the bride!"

The boat sloshed over a wave, and Kate clung to Drake, her lips pressed to his in a wet, laughter-filled kiss. It seemed like everyone on board cheered, but Kate could hardly hear anything over the rushing water and the giddy beat of her own heart.

"Congratulations, Mrs. Sweet-Matthews!" Drake yelled in her ear, his arms around her waist, holding her safe and still in his embrace.

Kate pressed her mouth next to Drake's ear. "Now that we're married, tell me, world-famous romance author. What's next for our love story?"

Drake pulled Kate's blue rain slicker hood over her head, tucking a loose curl around her ear before he answered.

"The best part about our romance is that it's not plotted out. I never know what the next chapter will bring with you." Drake kissed the tip of her wet nose. "But if it's anything like the rest of our story, I have a feeling we'll be together until 'The End.'"

Kate lifted herself onto her tiptoes, knocking off his hood and her own as she brought him in for a kiss, and the mist rained down, casting rainbows all around.

KEEP READING
FOR A SNEAK PEEK
AT DYLAN'S NEXT BOOK!

CHAPTER 1

It's only vomit. It'll come out," Imani Lewis said with far more confidence than she felt. She dabbed regurgitated kiwi from her vintage Hermès white silk shirt with the last of her emergency wet wipes, waving away the distraught mother's apology. "What with the bumpy landing and watching dance recitals on my phone, Jasmine got motion sick—used to happen to me all the time as a child."

Jasmine's mom—whose name Imani hadn't caught in the chaos of entertaining her daughter during the flight from JFK to Buffalo—grimaced as they deplaned.

"You're so prepared," she said, as Imani deposited the vile pile of used wet wipes into a plastic bag she pulled from the left zippered pocket of her purse. "And you've been so tolerant with my little bundle of energy."

The culprit, a three-year-old who had escaped her own *Exorcist*-like projectile vomiting without a drop staining her daisy-printed shirt, smiled. She skipped ahead of them on the ramp leading to the airport terminal. Her Princess Tiana backpack acted like a bumper, pinballing her off other passengers.

"Watch me! I can twirl like those ballerinas, Ms. Imani." The elfin toddler's yellow-and-white beaded braids flew out like rays of sunshine as she whipped around in a joyful string of full-body-flinging pirouettes. Whatever she lacked in grace she made up for in vigorous enthusiasm, and Imani's heart squeezed as it did every time she watched young dancers. Her Tuesday/Thursday volunteer gig at the Bronx Barre Belles was the highlight of her week and probably the only thing she'd miss during this unpaid leave of absence.

Well, that and the paycheck from her publicist job.

Her cell phone buzzed like an angry nest of wasps in her purse. She'd turned it back on as they were taxiing, but before the device had synched up, she'd gotten a chestful of vomit. She pulled out her phone and peeked at the display, stumbling in her only pair of Louboutin heels.

She'd racked up twenty texts during her forty-five-minute flight.

A glance revealed fifteen were from her number one romance author about some snafu with the book-signing itinerary, four were from her contact at the Florida bookstore asking where their scheduled author was, and one was from the man filling in for her during her leave...wondering where she kept the stapler.

Then she saw she'd received a voicemail from her boss at Cerulean Books.

Crap. Trisha never called unless things were seriously off the rails.

Imani sucked in a breath through her teeth. Dread coiled like a serpent in her guts, constricting her in a way that had become hideously familiar these past few months. Her mind skittered into action, crafting a checklist:

☐ Call star romance author. Take ownership of any problem, including acts of God.

☐ Resolve itinerary issue.

☐ Call bookstore manager. Grovel until everything is back on track.

☐ Call assistant publicist to see why he isn't assisting. Tell him where to find stapler. (Note to self: Breathe. Resist urge to tell him where to shove said stapler.)

☐ Craft email re-explaining itinerary, highlighting how EASY it is to follow because it's color coded, for heaven's sake!

☐ Delete the snark. Then send email.

☐ Call Trisha to reassure her the issue is resolved. Fend off questions about the promotion to publicity manager she's offered you. Remind her Wellsville has poor reception. Find polite way to make boss understand that, for a few weeks, communication will be spotty at best. (Note to self: Maybe compare Wellsville to the Bermuda Triangle in terms of cell reception?)

☐ Hang up before boss hears your voice go up at the end like it always does when you stretch the truth.

☐ Call Katie and relax for the summer. (Yay!)

Her inner list maker was interrupted as the toddler grabbed the edge of Imani's overstuffed purse. Her eyes sparkled and she grinned in expectation.

"Did you see my good twirling?"

"Jasmine, she doesn't have time now," the mom said, catching hold of her daughter's hand. "She's going to visit her grandmother, like we are."

Imani blinked at the mention of her grandmother. Her Gigi.

Releasing her death grip on her phone, Imani dropped it back into her purse. She fixed her face, smiling at the tiny, frenetic ballerina and shoving back the exhaustion from last night's sleepless, pillow-flipping extravaganza.

"You are so talented, Jasmine!" Imani bent down to clasp the girl's hands, still so small you could see tiny dimples instead of knuckles. She formed the girl's arms into a round hoop in front of her daisy-shirted chest. "Now, pretend like you're hugging a giant, fluffy panda bear who is so big your fingers can barely touch! Then we have to imagine a string holding you up nice and tall, and then we raise up on our tiptoes and twirl with nice round arms, like this!"

She spun Jasmine in a pirouette, clapping as the child held the form for three in a row.

"You've got a natural here, Mom," Imani said to the mother, who gave her a thankful smile as she gathered up her still-spinning daughter and headed toward baggage claim.

Peeling off to the bathroom, Imani hauled her phone out again. She rapidly scanned the texts and surmised the problem: Leann Bellamy's limo hadn't arrived at the Sarasota location to take her to the Tampa signing, forcing the popular romance author to take a cab. That wasn't typically an emergency; however, the cabbie decided to take the Skyway bridge en route from Sarasota to Tampa, unaware that Leann Bellamy had gephyrophobia—a raging fear of bridges.

Her star romance writer was currently sitting on the side of some road that led to the Skyway, hopefully still inside the cab. But maybe not.

Knowing this conversation was going to take a hot minute, she mentally rearranged her to-do list, opting for the most enjoyable task first: calling her best friend.

Shutting herself in the handicapped stall so she could use the sink in privacy, she hit Kate Sweet's face in her Favorites menu, then began working on her shirt's stain.

"Well, finally! I was beginning to wonder if Gigi decided not to get her knee surgery, or if she'd some-how talked you out of coming. That woman has mad persuasion skills." Kate's rapid-fire patter was like a sliver of sunshine in this crap-tastic morning. "But then Drake told me he'd had a call from your boss letting him know you were on your way to go over his book signing and movie cameo trip next week. I knew you'd never dare to ditch both Gigi and my husband!"

"You know I'd never keep anyone waiting, regard-less of their infamous reputation. So sorry, Katie. The flight got delayed with the rain." Imani dabbed at the splotch of green yuck with a wad of toilet paper and water, grimacing as it did little to fade the stain on her vintage white blouse. Neither did a fierce scrubbing with her emergency Tide pen. Instead, it made the whole section below the pattern of keys printed along the neckline practically transparent over her left nipple. Blowing out a breath, she abandoned the effort, the urgency of her next bunch of calls squeezing her chest. "I'm heading to baggage claim in a sec. I got barfed on during the flight, and then I deplaned in time for a major work crisis, so I'm doing some cleanup. Literally and figuratively."

"Oh no!" Kate's voice wavered between a laugh and a cry of dismay. "Well, take your time, and let me know if I can help. We're unstoppable when we team up, and although it's been a while since I broke out the Roy G Biv gel pens, you know I've got your list-making back. I'm so glad you're here, Imani—I can't wait to catch up and tell you the plans for the gender-reveal-slash-baby-shower tomorrow."

Imani smiled at her friend's enthusiasm. She'd never imagined her busy, event-planning best friend to be the one married and expecting so soon, but Drake Matthews's charms had evidently proven too hard for Kate to resist.

"I'm honored you chose me as the baby's god-mother. I saved the reveal envelope with the sonogram results, still closed like you sent it to me. I'll open it at the party, and we'll both be surprised on the same day. It's right in my purse."

"Where else would it be but in the Mary Poppins bag?" Kate joked. "And that's sweet. I'm so happy you're going to be here for Baby Matthews as Auntie Imani."

A warmth spread in Imani's chest at the name.

"Aw, really? The baby can call me Auntie?"

"Well, we've lived together on and off for years, so we're sisters in every way but genetics," Kate said with the easy, breezy way that only someone who already had siblings could manage. Then Kate gasped. "Oh, I forgot to tell you! The venue I reserved had a plumbing issue, so we're having the shower at Zander's studio. He's got this ceramic thing we can smash after you fill it with the appropriately colored starch for the reveal. I was freaking out when my original place canceled, but this is so much better! You remember Zander, right?"

At the mention of Drake's youngest brother, Imani felt her face tingle with pricks of heat, and the cleansing breaths halted in her chest.

Zander Matthews.

Yep, she remembered him, all right. He was her first and only one-night stand. Well, technically, it was two nights, two mornings, and one long, glorious afternoon, nine months and twenty-five days ago. But who was counting?

Kate must've assumed her memory had sinkhole-sized gaps, as she quickly supplied details. "He's the taller, beefier Matthews brother who has the smoldering Jason Momoa vibe that's broken hearts all over this county. Oh, remember? He's the guy you did that fun dance with at my wedding—what was it called again?"

"Bachata." Imani felt the tension in her guts move up into her chest, constricting the breath there. No. Not so soon! She'd thought she'd at least have a week to tell Kate about her hookup with Zander and, more importantly, explain why she'd kept this secret from her best friend whom she'd confided everything to since elementary school. And Zander—she thought she'd have more time to figure out how to explain why she'd never answered his texts and calls, how the intensity of that weekend had sounded every alarm bell in her heart...

But she was facing him tomorrow. At his studio. In his element.

Inhaling, Imani figured she might as well just plunge in. "Yes, I remember him. Listen, I've been wanting to tell you something but haven't known how to—"

"You can tell me about it in the car," Kate interrupted, "because I've got to pee again. I swear, these next six weeks can't go by fast enough. I need to meet this child who is making a punching bag out of my bladder! I'll see you when you get done with baggage claim."

"Wait, I need to—" Imani realized Kate had already disconnected. "Damn."

She winced, anticipating the confession to come, gazing into the airport bathroom mirror. Before locking up her tiny Bronx apartment this morning, she'd tied her long brown hair back in a low ponytail and taken care with her makeup, going heavy on the concealer. But the dark smudges under her bloodshot brown eyes were like a billboard screaming *Insomniac!* Her normally olive complexion—a credit to her half-Hungarian heritage—looked pale and washed out, and coupled with the sheer, almost nipple-revealing wet spot on her boob...well, suffice it to say she wouldn't be 'gramming this look.

She snagged her favorite red lipstick from her purse and applied it generously. She'd read once that people perceived you as "put together" as long as you had on lipstick.

She was about to challenge that perception.

Her best friend was a stickler for details, so she'd

notice Imani's fatigue and maybe go easy on her for keeping such a secret from her for this long. Anyway, it wasn't like Imani would be spending a lot of time with her two-night flame. They'd see each other for maybe a couple hours? Although Wellsville was a small town, it was big enough to avoid the youngest Matthews brother, if she tried.

Besides, Zander was all about the casual lifestyle. Her discreet inquiries to Kate after her weekend fling revealed that while he'd dated dozens of women in the past, he was still friends with them post-breakup. She figured he'd moved on from their weekend long ago, which was for the best.

Imani shrugged off the worry. This trip wasn't about her. It was about her best friend's baby shower first, followed by Gigi's double knee replacement. Then she could relax! Something she hadn't done in...she couldn't remember how long.

She smiled, imagining her leisurely summer. It was worth taking the unpaid leave from work, worth the hit to her pocketbook, and worth putting a bookmark in her career, as long as she got to chill out for a while. She'd bask in the cooler, Western New York summer temps, enjoy the food that was tied to happy memories, sit on Gigi's front porch, and figure things out.

Like her life.

Imani replaced the lipstick and stain-removal pen in her tote, zipping it with finality. Soon she would no longer be worried about puke stains, authors stuck on the roadside, massive career decisions, or wondering if her red lipstick was distracting enough to hide the widening cracks in her armor. She'd be with her best friend in a town from her past, spending all summer with her grandmother—the woman who was the closest genetic relative to the mother she'd lost more than a decade ago.

It was going to be amazing.

As she rode the escalator down to baggage claim, Imani multitasked, calling the bookstore to let them know Leann Bellamy was stuck in traffic. Then she dialed Leann's number as she searched for Kate in the crush of people surrounding the revolving luggage carousel, maneuvering to the front so she could spot her bright-turquoise suitcases. The number for the romance author's cell rang busy, and Imani juggled with her phone to hang up, just as she spotted her luggage trundling toward her.

Suddenly, a tall white man whose broad shoulders strained at his fitted T-shirt stepped in front of her, snatching her big bag, along with the smaller matching one, off the belt.

"Excuse me! Those are mine," Imani said to the back of the six-foot-five guy.

Something in the way he moved gave away his identity before he turned to flash her with his sparkling, devil-may-care grin.

Her jaw dropped.

It was Zander.

Zander freaking Matthews.

He of the hot bachata moves, and the hotter under-the-covers moves, stood in front of her at the Buffalo airport. Kate had been right—if you darkened his dirty blond, surfer-like curls, the guy could be a stand-in for Jason Momoa in *Aquaman*, as they had the same broad shoulders, bulging biceps, and legs like tree trunks.

"It's you," she breathed.

"It's me." His low voice and sexy smile hit her square in the libido. "The car is parked outside, and Kate's waiting for you there. You set?"

Her mind noted with dismay that he was just as scrumptious as he'd been that weekend. It hadn't been her imagination embellishing his solid frame, the thick, corded muscles that said he did more physical labor than throwing clay in his studio.

"I—I've got everything," she squeaked, dazed. For two hours, she'd be stuck in a car with the guy she'd slept with and then practically ghosted, plus her best friend who knew nothing about it? Could this be any more awkward?

Imani followed as Zander hefted her luggage and carried both of her bags on his back, refusing to roll them for some reason known only to him. He stopped shy of the exit's revolving doors, gesturing to the restrooms.

"We've got time if you need to towel off." Zander aimed a pointed look at her chest, his expression amused. "So . . . did you win?"

Imani blinked. "Did I win?"

"The wet T-shirt contest. I'm guessing you were a shoo-in for your flight. The other passengers didn't stand a chance against that lacy bra."

Imani scowled, refusing to laugh. "A gentleman would have politely averted his gaze."

Zander shrugged, leading the way through the revolving door.

Was that all he had to say to her? Not "Hi" or "Nice to see you again" but some crack about her wet blouse? Imani's eyes narrowed as she spoke to his back.

"A gentleman would have said how nice I looked, even if I'd been puked on by a kid who'd just eaten a sliced kiwi. A gentleman would not—"

"Let me guess." Zander's smile became razor sharp. "A gentleman wouldn't call out the woman whose only reply to his texts and voicemails following their amazing weekend together was 'Yeah, that was fun.' He wouldn't ask why she'd blocked him from her life without a *single* conversation. No gentleman would put the woman who'd practically broken his heart in that awkward position. Would he?"

"Broken your h—" Before Imani could finish, a car beeped behind them. She spun, and her anger was replaced by a spasm of embarrassment as she recognized the driver.

It was Drake Matthews. Bestselling horror writer and her number one client.

Next to him, hanging out of the window, waving like a goon, was Kate, his wife and Imani's best friend.

Imani forced a smile. "H-hi, Kate. And Drake. It's good to see you. I didn't think you'd have the time to pick me up, with your book's deadline. And you *all* came. I feel so...special."

"I always have time for my publicist." Drake peered out Kate's open window, pushing his dark glasses up his nose to give her a warm smile as he gestured to the Prius. "Sorry about the tight squeeze, but Kate's car is in the shop and my truck doesn't have a back seat. My brother offered his car as long as I agreed to drive and take him with us to get some wings. Hop in! My wife is dying to talk sex with you and Zander."

Imani sucked in a breath.

Zander chuckled. "That's my favorite kind of talk.

Although I have to say, you're a little late. Dad had that talk with me twenty-some years ago. But I appreciate the thought."

Kate rolled her eyes.

"Drake, why do you purposely set Zander up like that? No, I want to talk to you about the sex of the *baby*. I think I've changed my mind. I want you two to tell me tonight. But not now—over dinner." Kate's green eyes lit up. Her auburn hair had grown longer and more luxurious, and she glowed with pregnant happiness. "I'm dying for some Buffalo wings, and trust me, this restaurant's homemade blue cheese is Lactaid-worthy."

Imani crossed to the car, her face aflame. Apparently, Zander hadn't told Kate and Drake about their hookup. Yet. Maybe this was karma warning her to come clean to her best friend?

Kate's face went from shining to dim, reading something in Imani's body language.

"What's wrong? And why are you soaking wet?"

Imani's forehead felt as though it had its own sprinkler system. Brushing away sweat with her free hand, she opened her mouth, unsure of what she was going to say but determined that if her best friend and her famous client were going to hear of her sleeping with Zander, they were going to hear it from her.

Suddenly, Zander spoke in her ear. "You're lucky I'm a gentleman."

Imani felt Zander's arm around her shoulder, but before she could say more, he was talking to Kate and opening the back passenger door.

"Aww, she's just mad because I pulled her out of the wet T-shirt contest before she could show skin to win."

Zander shoved her bigger bag in, then swept his hand as if sending her into a throne room instead of the squished back seat of his car.

"I don't think my suitcases will fit." She ducked inside, holding her tote on her lap like the little old ladies did on the subway.

"My car's like your purse. It holds more than people give it credit for." Zander tossed her smaller turquoise bag into the trunk and piled in next to her, somehow closing the door. "Told you we'd fit! Let's get the momma-to-be some wings!"

Without warning, Zander reached across Imani, tugging the seat belt out from under the suitcase and hooking it over her. He clicked it home, his thick fingers grazing her hips, perilously close to her ass. Zander's body filled the back seat, and she found herself bending toward him, like a sunflower to the sun. His smell— Irish Spring soap and a hint of something warm and spicy—enveloped her. Despite everything, she breathed in deep, sucking him into her lungs.

Damn. How did he always smell so freaking good?

His blue eyes met hers as he fastened his own seat belt. He grinned, as if sensing his effect on her.

"Buckle up," he said in a low voice. "It's going to be a bumpy ride."

ACKNOWLEDGMENTS

I wrote the first draft of this book in Florida and edited it in a Victorian parlor in Wellsville, New York—my hometown and the inspiration for the novel's setting. Yet without the hard work, research, and encouragement by so many, this book would not exist.

First, a loud cheer for agent extraordinaire Cori Deyoe at 3 Seas Literary, who has been in my corner, championing my writing, for years. You rock! I am also blessed to work with the talented Leah Hultenschmidt at Hachette's Forever books. The fact that Leah thought a horror writer hero was as perfect as I did is as amazing as her ability to make manuscripts sparkle. My thanks also to Sabrina Flemming, Estelle Hallick, Stacey Reid, Becky Maines, and the rest of the Forever team.

I'd like to thank the following Marines for their service to our country and for sharing with me their Corps knowledge, experience, and grit for this story, and the series: Sergeant Jonathan da Cruz, Sergeant Michael MacHose, Corporal Jamey Clovis, and Infantryman

Josh Langston White. They were invaluable resources, and any mistakes are entirely mine.

Much love for my beta readers, Rhonda Kauffman and Annette Miller. You ladies are pure gold! Thank you to the book cheerleaders in Newton's Neighborhood Facebook group, as well as Eric Head, John O'Brien, Thomas and Thomasine Kennedy, Faith Powers, Lakisha Garcia, Sherri Feltz, Caro Carson, Robin Cumbie, Jodi Bailey, Vicki Turner, Lauri Drake, Molly Call, and others who helped influence this book. I am so blessed to call you my friends.

A puffy-hearted thanks to Devon and Ava for their plot point help. You two are my favorites. And to Mike, who inspires me daily—I love you and your Mike-ness so much!

ABOUT THE AUTHOR

Dylan Newton was born and raised in a small town where the library was her favorite hangout. After more than a decade working in corporate America, Dylan quit to pursue her passion: writing books. When she isn't writing, Dylan is pursuing her own happily ever after with her high school sweetheart as they split time between Florida and Upstate New York with their two much cooler daughters and a tone-deaf cockatiel.

Check her out at:
    DylanNewton.com
    Facebook.com/DylanNewtonAuthor
    Instagram @AuthorDylanNewton

Fall in love with these small-town romances full of tight-knit communities and heartwarming charm!

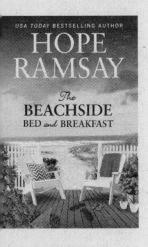

THE BEACHSIDE BED AND BREAKFAST
by Hope Ramsay

Ashley Howland Scott has no time for romance while grieving for her husband, caring for her son, and running Magnolia Harbor's only bed and breakfast. But slowly, Rev. Micah St. Pierre has become a friend...and maybe something more. Micah cannot date a member of his congregation, so there's no point in sharing his feelings with Ashley, no matter how much he yearns to. But the more time they spend together, the more Micah wonders whether Ashley is his match made in heaven.

THE SUMMER SISTERS
by Sara Richardson

The Buchanan sisters share everything—even ownership of their beloved Juniper Inn. As children, they spent every holiday there, until a feud between their mother, Lillian, and Aunt Sassy kept them away. When the grand reopening of the inn coincides with Sassy's seventieth birthday, Rose, the youngest sister, decides it's time for a family reunion. Only she'll need help from a certain handsome hardware-store owner to pull off the celebration...

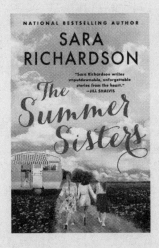

SOMETHING BLUE
by Heather McGovern

Wedding planner Beth Shipley has seen it all: bridezillas, monster-in-laws, and last-minute jitters at the altar. But this wedding is different—and the stakes are much, *much* higher. Not only is her best friend the bride, but bookings at her family's inn have been in free fall. Beth knows she can save her family's business—as long as she doesn't let best man Sawyer Silva's good looks and overprotective, overbearing, older-brother act distract her. Includes a bonus story by Annie Rains!

HOW SWEET IT IS
by Dylan Newton

Event planner Kate Sweet is famous for creating happily-ever-after moments for dream weddings. So how is it that her best friend has roped her into planning a best-selling horror writer's book launch extravaganza in a small town? The second Kate meets the drop-dead-hot Knight of Nightmares, Drake Matthews, her well-ordered life quickly transforms into an absolute nightmare. But neither are prepared for the sweet sting of attraction they feel for each other. Will the queen of romance fall for the king of horror?

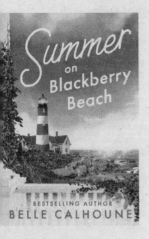

SUMMER ON BLACKBERRY BEACH
by Belle Calhoune

Navy SEAL Luke Keegan is back in his hometown for the summer, and the rumor mill can't stop whispering about him and teacher Stella Marshall. He never thought he'd propose a fake relationship, but it's the only way to stop the runaway speculation about their love lives. Pretending to date a woman as stunning as Stella is easy. Not falling for her is the hard part, especially with the real attraction buzzing between them. Could their faux summer romance lead to true love?

FALLING FOR YOU
by Barb Curtis

Just when recently evicted yoga instructor Faith Rotolo thinks her luck has run out, she inherits a historic mansion in quaint Sapphire Springs. But her new home needs fixing up and the handsome local contractor, Rob Milan, is spoiling her daydreams with the realities of the project... and his grouchy personality. While they work together, their spirited clashes wind up sparking a powerful attraction. As work nears completion, will she and Rob realize that they deserve a fresh start too?

HER AMISH SPRINGTIME MIRACLE
by Winnie Griggs

Amish baker Hannah Eicher has always wanted a *familye* of her own, so finding sweet baby Grace in her barn seems like an answer to her prayers. Until *Englischer* paramedic Mike Colder shows up in Hope's Haven, hoping to find his late sister's baby. As Hannah and Mike contemplate what's best for Grace, they spend more and more time together while enjoying the warm community and simple life. Despite their wildly different worlds, will Mike and Hannah find the true meaning of "family"?

THE AMISH FARMER'S PROPOSAL
by Barbara Cameron

When Amish dairy farmer Abe Stoltzfus tumbles from his roof, he's lucky his longtime friend Lavinia Fisher is there to help. He secretly hoped to propose to her, but now, with his injuries, his dairy farm in danger, and his harvest at stake, Abe worries he'll only be a burden. Yet, as he heals with Lavinia's gentle support and unflagging optimism, the two grow even closer. But will she be able to convince him that real love doesn't need perfect timing?

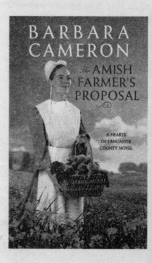